MICHELLE SAGARA

CAST IN SILENCE

LUNA™

www.LUNA-Books.com

LUNA™

Recycling programs for this product may not exist in your area.

First trade printing August 2009

CAST IN SILENCE

ISBN-13: 978-0-373-80300-2

Copyright © 2009 by Michelle Sagara

Author photo © by John Chew

www.LUNA-Books.com

Printed in U.S.A.

AUTHOR NOTE

One of the best things—for me—about writing fantasy is that a writer can enlarge issues that people face on a daily basis by making the stakes higher; it's not often that you can cause the end of the world in real life because of choices you've made. But the end-of-the-world feeling is a very real dread day to day. The consequences are always bigger, but the emotional response is rooted in a writer's experience, and our experiences don't actually include dark gods, primal chaos and perfect immortals. Except maybe when we're sleeping.

Kaylin Neya started life on the page as a Private in the arm of law enforcement know as The Hawks—her city's version of a cop. But, as is so often the case, her known life started before that, and what there was of it was buried in the organizational nightmare I often refer to as my notes. Some of that past came to light in her first outing, *Cast in Shadow,* because a lot of her story makes no sense without it.

She doesn't live in the past, although she will always be affected by it, and she's managed to keep a lid on it—until now. *Cast in Silence* is about the missing six months of her life, between her life in the fief of Nightshade and her life as a Hawk. To say she's ambivalent about those six months would be a bit of an understatement.

But to me, it echoes a lot of ambivalence about choices we made for various reasons when we were younger or less experienced. Or at least choices I made. If you're returning to Kaylin and Elantra, I hope you enjoy reading the book as much as I did writing it.

This is for Ayami, the sister-in-law
who makes having a brother a blessing.

ACKNOWLEDGMENTS

Living with a writer is not easy. My children are probably used to it because it's all they've ever known, but my husband, Thomas, had a sane and reasonable upbringing, and still manages to create the space in which I do write, day in and day out. He and Terry Pearson form my alpha reader team, and are brave enough to argue with me when reading raw first draft (and I mean raw).

If living with a writer is not easy, it's my suspicion that working with a writer is often just as fraught, so I am deeply grateful to Mary-Theresa Hussey, who has been the very model of patience and understanding, and who continues to provide a home for Elantra. And to Kathleen Oudit and the art staff for the fabulous job they continue to do when creating covers for these books. If writing a novel is a solitary endeavor, *publishing* a novel is teamwork, and I have been blessed with a great team.

CHAPTER 1

"It's eight o'clock in the morning. Please remember to fill out your reports and hand in your paperwork." Had the cheerful and musical voice belonged to a person who could be easily strangled, it would have stopped in midsentence.

Sadly, it was the melodious voice of the streetside window which interrupted the bustling and vastly less perky office in which the branch of Law known as the Hawks was based. That window, which had been installed complete with a magical, time-telling voice in some misguided attempt at humor, had been adjusted in the past couple of weeks by Acting Sergeant Mallory, and no one who had to work where they could hear it—and were prevented by office regulations from destroying it—considered the adjustments to be an improvement.

Sergeant Marcus Kassan, the large and currently bristling Leontine behind the central desk in the Hawks' Office raised his fist and flexed his fingers. Long claws, gleaming in the sun's light, appeared from beneath his golden fur. He had not yet shattered the window—and given it was installed with the guidance of

Imperial Mages, that would have been damn hard—but he looked like he was on the edge of finally doing it in. The betting pool had not yet been won, but at least three people were out money, Private Kaylin Neya being one. The office had discovered, however, that the windows couldn't be scratched, and Kaylin had argued vociferously that this should have counted as a victory condition. She'd lost.

Then again, Leontines were generally all about the clawing, biting, rending, and ripping out of throats; they weren't as good with smashing things.

Kaylin's personal favorite was the new end-of-day message, wherein the cheerful voice of the window told the departing staff that they were to be in the office at 7:00 a.m., and they were to be shaved, where shaving was appropriate, and otherwise clean. She was less keen on the last bit, in which the Hawks were reminded to check the duty roster for last-minute adjustments.

"Why doesn't he just have the mages shut it down?" she asked Caitlin, as Marcus drove new furrows into his desk.

"I think he considers it a reminder of the differences between Sergeant Mallory's temporary tenure and his more permanent record," Caitlin replied. The reply, like the question that engendered it, was very, very quiet. This didn't guarantee that it couldn't be overheard, but unless Marcus had it in for you, he was capable of a bit of selective deafness. If he hadn't been, his office would be half manned for at least an entire duty cycle, and the half that was left alive would be too busy cleaning up to cause trouble.

"Neya!" Given Marcus's current mood, the fact that there had been no bloodshed was pushing the goodwill of whatever gods watched over underslept and underpaid police. "You're due out on beat in five minutes. Stop bothering Caitlin and hit the street."

Kaylin's beat was Elani Street and its surroundings, and her partner was—as it so frequently was, these days—Corporal Severn Handred. He was already kitted out and ready to go when she careened down the hall to the locker room. He raised an eyebrow, one bisected by a slender scar, while he watched her use the wall as a brake.

"What? I'm not late yet."

"Not yet. It's hard to be late when the window is nagging."

She grimaced. "Marcus took his claws to it yesterday."

"Don't start."

"I think that should count."

"Is the window still in one piece? Then it doesn't count." Severn was at the top of the betting pool at the moment, and looked to be secure in his position, but they'd both grown up on some pretty mean streets, and "secure" meant something different to them.

This was probably why they got along so well with the Barrani Hawks. The Barrani were noted for their love of the political. Political, in the context of their race, usually involved assassination, both literally and figuratively, and smallish wars. They understood that anything they owned had to be held against all comers. Those who held less were perfectly willing to test the definition of "secure," often to the breaking point.

Of course, unless one of those assassination attempts was lucky, the Barrani weren't about to expire of old age; they didn't. Age, that is. They had long memories, and they could easily hold a grudge for longer than Kaylin's whole life; at least two of them did. On the other hand, they made immortality look like one long gripe fest, admittedly with killer clothing, so it was hard to begrudge them their eternity of suffering. Or of making everyone else they knew suffer. Kaylin, as a human, would eventually clock out, which would in theory earn her some peace.

She dressed quickly, straightening out the cloth and underpadding that had managed to crumple in the wrong places the way it always did, and then rearranged her hair so it was pulled tight and off her face. It wasn't immortality that she envied the Barrani; it was their damn hair. It never got in the way of anything.

She made it out of the locker room with seconds to spare; Severn caught her by the shoulder and adjusted the stick that held her hair tightly in place so that it actually did the job.

★ ★ ★

Elani Street was, of course, Charlatan Central. It was also, unfortunately, where real magic could be found if you didn't have access to the Imperial Mages, or worse, the mages of the Arcanum, which access pretty much described ninety-nine percent of the city of Elantra. Kaylin had never understood how it was that people capable of genuine enchantments were willing to hunker down with total frauds.

The end result, however, of some fraud was ire, and the end result of ire, if not checked, was directly the purview of the Hawks. It was more colloquially called murder. It didn't happen in Elani often, because even if you were *almost* certain the so-called magic you'd purchased was a lump of rock, you couldn't be as easily certain that the person who'd sold it to you was incapable of something more substantial.

There were, however, no murders on the books today. Or at least not murders that Kaylin knew about, and therefore not murders that she would be called in to investigate. She'd wanted a few weeks of quiet, and she'd had them. For some reason, it hadn't improved her mood.

Severn noticed. Then again, it was hard not to notice. While he frequently walked streetside, Kaylin's accidental mishaps with merchant boards now numbered four.

"Kaylin." He stepped to her left, and took up patrol position merchant-side.

She couldn't bring herself to say it was accidental, although she did try. But the boards that promised to find you your One True Love were a particular sore spot for Kaylin, in part because it was impossible to walk past the damn things at *any* time of day, and not see people waiting in the storefront, behind glass. Some had the brains to look ill-at-ease, but if they had the brains, they clearly lacked self-control; some just looked desperate and flaky.

All of them would be disappointed.

"You know they piss me off," she muttered.

"On the wrong day, sunlight pisses you off."

"Only in the morning."

"Noon is not considered morning by most people. Tell me," he added. "Because if you keep this up, Margot is going to file an incident report, and you'll be in the hot seat."

Margot was the name of the proprietor of this particular haven for the hopeless. She was a tall, statuesque redhead, with amber eyes that Kaylin would have bet an entire paycheck were magically augmented. Her voice, absent the *actual* drivel she used when speaking, was throaty, deep, and almost sinful just to *hear.*

Kaylin was certain that half of the people who offered Margot their custom secretly hoped that she would be their One True Love. Sadly, she was certain that Margot was also aware of this, and they'd exchanged heated words about the subject of her lovelorn customers in the past. Petty jealousy being what it was, however, Kaylin was liked by enough of the *other* merchants, mostly the less successful ones, that Margot's attempt to have her summarily scheduled out of existence—or the existence of Elani Street—had so far failed to take.

"If I knew what was bothering me," she finally admitted, "I would have warned you this morning."

"Warned me?"

"That I'm in a foul mood."

"Kaylin, the only person who might not notice that is Roshan, Marrin's newest orphan. And I have my doubts."

"I have no idea what's wrong," she continued, steadfastly ignoring that particular comment. "The foundling hall is running so smoothly right now you'd think someone rich had died and willed the foundlings all their money. Rennick's play was a success, and the Swords have been cut to a tenth their previous riot-watch numbers. I'm not on report. Mallory is no longer our *acting* sergeant. Caitlin is finally back in the office after her leave.

"But—" she exhaled heavily "—there's just…something. I have no idea what the problem *is*. And if you *even suggest* that it has something to do with the time of month, you'll be picking up splinters of your teeth well into next year."

He touched her, gently and briefly, on the shoulder. "You'll let me know when you figure it out?"

"You'll probably be the first person to know. Unless Marcus radically alters the duty roster."

The day did not get better when their patrol took them to Evanton's shop. Kaylin didn't stop there when she was on duty, because rifling his kitchen took time, and sitting and drinking the scalding hot tea he prepared when she did visit took more of the same.

Like most merchants, Evanton's shop had a sandwich board outside. The paint was faded, the wood slightly warped. His sign, however, did not offend her; she barely noticed it. She certainly didn't trip over it in a way that would snap its hinges shut.

But she did notice the young man who came barreling out of the door toward her. Grethan. Once Tha'alani. Hell, still Tha'alani. But crippled, shut off from the gifts that made the Tha'alani possibly the most feared race in the city. He couldn't read minds. The characteristic racial stalks of the Tha'alani, suspended at the height of his forehead, just beneath his dark, flat hair, still weaved frantically in the air in a little I'm-upset-help-me dance, and most people—most humans, she corrected herself—wouldn't know he was incapable of actually putting them to use to invade their thoughts.

"Kaylin!" he said, speaking too loudly in a street that was sparsely populated.

The people that were in it looked up immediately. You could always count on curiosity to dim common sense, *especially* in Elani Street. Evanton was known to be one of the street's genuine enchanters; he would have to be, given that he was also one of the few who still had a storefront and never offered love-potions or fortunes. Had he visible size or obvious power, he would probably have terrified most of the residents. He didn't.

She spoke in a much lower voice. It was her way of giving a subtle hint; the less subtle hints usually got her a reprimand, and Grethan looked wide-eyed and wild enough that she didn't think he deserved them. Yet. "Grethan? Has something happened to Evanton?"

He took a deep breath. "No. He told me you'd be coming, and he set me to watch."

Had it been anyone other than Evanton, Kaylin would have asked how he'd known. Evanton, however, was not a man who casually explained little details like that to an apprentice, and if Grethan was valued because he was Evanton's first promising apprentice in more years than Kaylin had been alive, he was still on the lower rungs of the ladder.

He was also, she thought, too damn smart to ask.

"You're not busy, are you?" Grethan asked, hesitating at the door.

"Not too busy to speak with Evanton if he has something he needs to say," she replied.

Severn, damn him, added, "She's busy plotting the downfall of Margot."

Grethan snorted. "You're probably going to have to stand in line for that," he told her, his stalks slowing their frantic dance. "But Evanton's in a bit of a mood today, so you might not want to mention her by name."

"I never want to mention her by name. You'll note that it wasn't me who did," she replied, giving Severn a very distinct look.

"Evanton is also not the only one who's in, as you put it, a bit of a mood," Severn told Grethan. "Maybe the two of us should wait outside somewhere safe. Like, say, the docks."

Evanton, contrary to Grethan's report, was seated by the long bar he called a counter. It was a bar; some old tavern had sold it to Evanton years before Kaylin had met him. If you could see one square inch of its actual surface, it was a tidy day. Given that Evanton was working with beads, needles, leather patches and some herbs and powders, Kaylin didn't immediately recognize it, it wasn't a day for surface area.

He looked up as she approached, his lips compressed around a thin line of needles. Or pins. She couldn't see the heads, and couldn't, at this distance, tell the difference. He looked more bent and aged than usual—which, given he was the oldest living person she'd ever met if you didn't count Barrani or Dragons, said something. Age never showed with Barrani or Dragons, anyway.

"Grethan said you wanted to see me," she said, carefully removing a pile of books from a stool a little ways into the shop. Books were the safest bet; you couldn't break most of them if the precarious pile chose to topple, and you couldn't crush them—much—by accidentally stepping on them.

He began to carefully poke pins into the top of his wrinkled apron. When he'd pushed the last of them home, he looked like a very bad version of a sympathetic magic doll, handled by someone who didn't realize they were supposed to stick the pins in point first. "*Wanted* is not the right word," he said curtly.

Kaylin, accustomed to his moods, shrugged. "I'm here anyway."

"Why?"

"Because Grethan said—"

"I mean, why were you sent to Elani today?"

She frowned. "We weren't *sent*. This is our beat, this rotation. For some reason, we're expected to be able to handle the petty fraud and swindling that passes for business-as-normal in Charlatan Central."

"*We* would be you and your Corporal?"

"He's not *my* Corporal, and yes."

Evanton nodded. He set aside the cloth in his lap, and put beads into about fifty different jars. He did all of this *slowly*. Kaylin, whose middle name was not exactly patience on the best of working days, sat and tried not to grind her teeth. She knew damn well he could talk and work at the same time; it was what he usually did.

"This does not strictly concern the Hawks," he finally told her, as he rose. "Can I make you tea?" Evanton did not actually *like* tea; he did, however, seem to find comfort in the social custom of being old enough to make it and offer it.

"I'm on duty, Evanton."

"Just answer the question, Private Neya."

She sighed. "Yes," she told him. "If you'll talk while you're doing it, you can make me tea. I don't suppose you've found cups that have handles?"

The answer to the question was either no, or she'd annoyed him enough by asking that he'd failed to find them. He made tea, and she waited, seated at the side of a kitchen table that was—yes—cluttered with small piles of daily debris. Still, none of the debris moved or crawled, so it was more or less safe.

"Evanton's brows gathered and his forehead furrowed as he sat across from her. This only deepened the lines that time had etched there. "Very well. This does not, as I mentioned, concern the Hawks. It does not, entirely, concern me yet."

"But you told Grethan to watch for me if I happened to pass by."

"I may have. He was hovering, and I dislike that when I'm working."

Had he been in less of a mood, she would have pointed out that he usually disliked the *absence* of hoverers when he was working, because he liked to have people fetch and carry; not even his guests were exempt from those duties. She bit her tongue, however. It was slightly better than burning it.

"I was in the elemental garden this morning," he added.

She stilled. When he didn't elucidate, she said, "Isn't that where you do some of your work?"

"I work there when I am not at all interested in interruption," he replied. "That was not, however, the case this morning."

All of Kaylin's many growing questions shriveled and died. She even put her hands around the sides of the cup, because she felt a momentary chill.

Evanton sighed. He rose, and pulled the key ring from his left arm. It was a key ring only in the loose sense of the word, being larger around than any part of that arm. "Private," he said gravely.

"I'm not sure I ever want to set foot in your garden again," she told him, but she pushed herself away from her teacup.

"I'm sure you don't," was the terse reply. "Especially not to-day. But I'm tired. If you see it for yourself, you'll spare me the effort of coming up with words."

Because he was Evanton, and his home was a mess, the halls they now walked were narrow and cramped. Shelves butted against the walls, in mismatched colors and heights. "Is this one new?" Kaylin asked, in a tone of voice that clearly said, *how could you cram another bookshelf into this space?*

"I have an apprentice now," Evanton replied. "And I'm not about to move *my* work so that he has someplace to shelve his."

She winced. She'd had issues with Grethan in the past, but at the moment she felt sorry for him; having to deal with Evanton in *this* mood should have been enough to send him screaming for cover.

Then again, he *was* out somewhere with Severn.

Evanton reached the unremarkable door at the hall's end. It looked, to Kaylin's eye, more rickety and warped than the last time she'd seen it. He slid the key into the lock, but before he opened the door, he turned to Kaylin and said, "Don't be surprised to find the garden somewhat changed since you last visited."

Having offered warning, he pushed the door open.

It opened, as always, into a space that was larger in all ways than the building that girded it; it had, for one, no obvious ceiling, and no clearly visible walls. This garden, as Evanton called it, was older by far than the city of Elantra; it was older than the Dragons or the Barrani. According to Sanabalis, it had always been here in one guise or another, and while the world existed, it always would.

Evanton was its Keeper.

As jobs went, it certainly promised job security. Sadly, a bad mistake on the job also promised to end the world, or come so close what was left wouldn't be in any shape to complain or fire him.

Kaylin blinked at the harshness of this particular daylight, and she followed Evanton in through the door—and into the gale.

On the first occasion Kaylin had come here, led by Evanton, it had been breezy, warm and quiet. He had assured her at that time that that state was the norm for his garden. Looking at his back, she saw his grubby working tunic had been replaced entirely by deep blue robes—and that these robes were now the new homes of trailing rivulets of water. The wind picked at his sodden hem and strands of his hair. Clearly the garden wasn't giving him much respect.

Kaylin's hair flew free as the stick Severn had carefully adjusted was yanked out by the wind; this lasted for at most half a minute before the strands were too heavy. They now clung to her face.

"Evanton!"

He didn't turn at the sound of his name, and Kaylin shouted it again, putting more force behind it. When he still didn't turn, she took a step toward him, and saw that the grass—or what had once been grass—was actually a few inches of mud. Her boots sank into it.

If the small and separate shrines that had been dedicated in corners of this place were still standing, the visibility was poor enough that she couldn't see them.

She almost shouted his name again, but he turned just as she reached his back. "Follow," he told her, cupping his hands around his mouth and shouting to be heard.

CHAPTER 2

The garden's size was, and had always been, somewhat elastic. Kaylin, who had previously walked a few yards to pay her respects at the elemental shrine of Water, with its deep, dark and utterly still pool, had *also* walked for miles and hours to reach the same damn shrine. She did not, therefore, react with any obvious surprise when Evanton's trek through the gale took an hour. It might have taken less time if not for the mud, the wind and the driving rain.

But when Evanton called a halt to this grueling trek, it was obvious why: he had reached a door. Not an entire building, of which a door would be a part. That would have been too simple. No, it was a standing door, absent frame or wall. It did not, however, possess a doorward; Kaylin was spared the brief and magical discomfort of placing her palm against it before she was granted entry.

She was not, however, spared the effort of forcing the door open; the wind seemed to push from the other side, and it required all of her weight, shoulder against cold, wet surface, to move the damn thing—which didn't even *have* hinges.

But when the door was open, the howl of the wind suddenly stopped, and Kaylin saw a glimpse of crackling fire in an old, stone hearth before Evanton unceremoniously shoved her out of the way. The door shut, and on *this* side, she could see both its hinges and its frame.

They seemed to be standing in a squat cottage of some type. Or they would have been, if cottages had been made of solid stone.

"Sorry," Evanton said, pulling the hood of his dripping robe from his face. "But I can't even hear myself think in all that noise."

As his robes were still recognizably the same dark blue, Kaylin assumed they were still within the space he referred to as the garden. She pushed her hair out of her face; she would have to wait to pin it back, because the wind hadn't returned the stick it had yanked out.

"We'll try the tea again," Evanton told her, peeling his sleeves off his arms. "This time, I *might* even condescend to drink some of it."

When they were seated around a small—and miraculously un-cluttered—table, two solid mugs between them, Kaylin said, "Water, earth and air."

Evanton raised a white brow, and then nodded. "Yes. The elements of this particular storm." He added, after a pause, "It's good to know you're still observant."

"That's generally considered my job."

"Yes. Well. It's generally considered the *job* of most of the residents of Elani Street to find true love, define fate and tell the future."

Kaylin almost choked on her tea, and Evanton graced her with a wry, and somewhat bitter smile. "They do, however, construct elaborate fantasies for people with more money than brains, which takes some creativity."

"You were eavesdropping," she said, when she found her voice again.

"If you don't *want* people to hear you, speak quietly, Private."

"Yes, Evanton." She shoved hair out of her eyes again, and he handed her a towel. It was the same color as his robe, and while she was curious about how it—and the mugs and the kettle—had arrived in this place, she didn't ask. Had he been in a better mood, she would have. The towel, she accepted with gratitude; wiping her wet hands on anything she was currently wearing was just moving water around. She knew this because she'd tried a few times.

"How's Grethan doing?"

Evanton raised a brow, but the severe lines of his face relaxed a bit. Which didn't really change the multitude of wrinkles; it just rearranged them. "He's doing well. Better than I'd expected, and I will thank you not to repeat that."

"Well enough?"

"Well enough that I won't let him get lost in the garden, if that's your concern."

She knew that he'd taken other apprentices, and she knew that they hadn't worked out; he'd said as much. What she'd never explicitly asked was what happened to the ones that didn't. Knowledge about this space was very hard to come by. Not even the Eternal Emperor could force his way in.

Which he probably hated.

She hesitated, and then nodded. The truth was, she liked this old man and always had. She trusted him. She didn't enjoy today's mood, but only an idiot would; she also expected it to pass. "So…what's happened in the garden?"

"What do you think has happened?"

Grimacing, she said, "I recognize this. I have a Dragon as a teacher. You, however, aren't responsible to the Eternal Emperor for my marks and comprehension, so you don't get to play that game with me."

He chuckled then, and to her surprise, he did take a sip of the tea. He didn't appear to enjoy it, so stability of a kind was preserved in the universe. "It wasn't that kind of question. Although to be fair, Grethan would now be cowering behind you if I'd asked him the same thing."

Kaylin, who *did* enjoy the tea, relaxed a bit. Since her life didn't depend on her answer, and since she'd been thinking of nothing else since she'd stepped through the damn door—with the single exception of the *dammit* reserved for loss of her hair stick—she said, "The elements here are alive. I'd say that at least three of them are upset. I can't tell if it's anger or panic," she added. "Because I can't really hear their voices."

Evanton nodded.

"But the fire's not there."

"No. Fire has always been a bit unusual in that regard. The fire," he added, pointing to the hearth, "is *here,* and a damn good thing, too. You might tell it a story or two—that seemed to work well the last time."

"Evanton, did I mention I'm on duty?"

"At least once. Possibly twice. I admit I was slightly distracted, and I may not have been paying enough attention."

"And if I believe that, you've got a love potion to sell me."

"At a very, very good price, I might add." He brought his mug to his mouth, and then lowered it again without taking a sip.

"Does this happen often?"

"No."

"But it's happened before."

"Yes."

When Evanton was monosyllabic, it was not a good sign. "Can I ask when?"

"You can ask."

"Evanton—"

"You know far more about this garden than anyone who isn't a Keeper, or who isn't trying to learn how to be one, has a right to know."

"And you're not about to add to that."

"Actually, I would very dearly love not to add to that, but I am, in fact, about to do just that. What you actually *understand* about the garden is not my problem. That you understand that this is significant, however, is."

"Why me?"

"That would be the question," he replied.

"I haven't done anything recently. Honest."

"No. You probably haven't. But something is happening in the city, and the elements feel it. They're not," he added, "very happy about it, either."

"No kidding. Why do you think it has anything to do with me?"

"Because," he replied, lifting his hands, "if you take the time to observe some of the visual phenomena, it's not entirely random. The elements are *trying* to talk."

Given the lack of any obvious visibility in the driving sheets of rain, Kaylin thought this comment unfair. Given Evanton's mood, Kaylin chose not to point this out. While she was struggling to stop herself from doing so, Evanton's hands began to glow.

Out of the light that surrounded them, a single complicated image coalesced on the tabletop, between their cups. It was golden in color, and it wasn't a picture. It was a word.

An old word. Kaylin's eyes widened as she looked at it.

"Yes," he said, as her glance strayed to her sleeves, or rather, to her arms. "It's written in the same language as the marks you bear."

Those marks ran the length of her arms, her inner thighs and most of her back; they now also trailed up her spine and into her hair. She had toyed with the idea of shaving her head to see exactly how far up they went, but she'd never gotten around to it. Her hair was her one vanity. Or at least, she thought ruefully, her one *acknowledged* vanity.

Something about the lines of the word were familiar, although Kaylin was pretty certain she'd never seen it before. She wasn't in the office, and she had no mirror; she couldn't exactly call up records to check.

"You know what this means," Evanton said, anyway.

She shook her head. "No, actually, I—" And then she stopped, as the niggling sense of familiarity coalesced. "Ravellon."

He closed his eyes.

The silence lasted a few minutes, broken by the sound people made—or Kaylin did, at any rate—when drinking liquid that was just shy of scalding. Eventually, she set the cup down. "You recognize the name."

"Yes. I would not have recognized it, however, from this rune."

"You can read them?"

"I have never made them my study; I am old, yes, but not *that* old."

She lifted her cup, watching him, and after a moment, he snorted. "I can, as you must know, read some of the Old Tongue. This, however, was not familiar to me."

"You don't know the history of Elantra?"

"I know the history of the city very well," he replied. His voice was the type of curt that could make you bleed.

Since Kaylin had lived for most of her twenty-odd years in ignorance of this history, she shrugged.

"I know what once stood at the heart of the fiefs." He lifted a veined and wrinkled hand in her direction. "And before you ask, no, I don't have any idea what's there now. It's slightly farther afield than I'm generally prepared to go at my age. But yes, I know it was once called Ravellon by the Barrani."

"And the Dragons," Kaylin pointed out.

"At the moment, my interactions with the Eternal Emperor's Court are exactly none. The one exception to my very firm rule, you already know, and no exception would have been made had I not been indisposed."

While she technically served the Emperor's law, the law was a distinct entity. That the Emperor held himself above those laws was a given; he didn't, however, require Kaylin to do the same. Of course, if he contravened those laws and she spoke up, she'd be a pile of ash.

Evanton contravened those laws by simply existing, as far as Kaylin could tell. For practical reasons, reducing Evanton to a pile of smoldering ash was not in the Emperor's cards, and if she'd had to bet, she'd bet that the Emperor wasn't entirely happy about it, either. The elemental garden, with Evanton as its Keeper, was literally a different world—with unfortunate placement: it demonstrably existed within the boundaries of the Empire, and the Dragon Emperor claimed *everything* in the Empire as his personal hoard, the single exception being the fiefs.

Dragons were very, very precise about their hoards. Kaylin didn't understand all the nuances of what, to her mind, boiled down to *mine, mine, mine,* but she was assured that they existed. By, of course, other Dragons.

The store, however, could not be moved. And if it ceased to exist, the elemental wilderness contained behind one rickety door at the end of a dim and incredibly cluttered hall, would break free and return to the world from which it had been extracted. Which would pretty much end most of the lives that Kaylin cared about, although to be fair, it would probably end the other ones, as well.

The Emperor, therefore, overlooked this thumbing-of-nose at his ownership and his authority.

Evanton's reluctance to talk with Dragons made sense. Their reluctance to speak with him, she understood less well.

He opened his mouth, and snapped it shut again. He still had all his teeth. "*Ravellon,*" he said, after a long pause, "is a Barrani word."

"I don't think so," she began.

"It's *not* the Old Tongue, then. Can we agree on that?"

Since he probably knew more than she did, she nodded.

"But you recognized the rune *as* Ravellon. Why?"

"I don't know. Don't look at me like that, Evanton. I honestly don't. I'm not even your student—why would I try to make *your* life more difficult?"

"Good point. I should apologize for my temper. I won't, but I should. It has been a very, very trying day."

"Why is it only the three elements? Why not all four?"

"Fire in the natural world is contained, for the most part. If we were living over a volcano, and the elements felt this kind of flux, fire would be in the mix, as well. We're not, thank the gods." He paused, and then said, "I don't have to tell you that none of this should leave this garden, do I?"

"It probably doesn't hurt." Pause. "Can I tell Severn?"

"You may tell your Corporal, yes. He's as quiet as the dead. Well, the dead with the decency to stay buried, at any rate." He looked, now, at his hands. "Ravellon." He shook his head, and then stared across the table at her.

"Don't even think it," she replied.

He did not, however, snap back. Instead, in a much quieter voice, he said, "The fief of Ravellon—if it's even a fief at all— is impassible."

She nodded.

"But, Kaylin—something is stirring in the fiefs. Something is twisting in the heart of the city."

"Evanton—"

"Be prepared, girl. What you see in that rune is not the word itself, not as spoken. But it disturbs me. Ravellon, like Elantra, was meant to be a geographical marker, not a true name."

"It's not. A true name."

"As you say."

Severn took one look at Kaylin's very wet and bedraggled face, and turned away.

"If you're laughing, you're dead," she told him. The passage back through the garden had been about as much fun as the passage to the small stone building; her boots were in her hands. Evanton was willing to put up with the rivulets dripping from every square inch of her body; he was not, however, willing to put up with the mud she would have otherwise tracked down the hall.

"It pains me to agree with anyone today," Evanton added, "but even so, I concur." Crossing the threshold of the door had returned dry clothing to Evanton, but his hair and his beard were plastered to his face. "And now, you both have your patrol. I have work. Where did Grethan disappear to?" he added, in a tone of voice that made Kaylin cringe on behalf of the unfortunately absent apprentice.

"Billington decided to pay a visit to Margot," Severn replied, in as neutral a voice as he ever used. "Grethan saw him pass by and decided to investigate." He glanced at Kaylin, who glanced at her boots and her very wet surcoat.

"Figures," she said, heading for the door. "Did he take his goons with him, or was it just the usual courtesy call?"

"Until there's actually an incident," Severn told her, following in her wake, "we can leave out the name-calling." He nodded in Evanton's direction.

"What? Evanton's called them far worse."

"I," Evanton told her, "have no professional interest in Billington."

"Hopefully, neither do we today," she replied with a grimace. She pushed his door open, sat heavily on his steps and worked wet feet into equally wet boots. She could swear she heard squelching.

It was not as loud, however, as the sound of shattering glass. She swore under her breath, tying laces with speed that should have rubbed her fingers raw. Thank gods for calluses.

Severn was already down the street. So was half the neighborhood. They weren't actually pressed around the broken shards of glass; they weren't *that* stupid. But they were between Kaylin and Margot's.

What Kaylin did not need on a day that included a testy Evanton and an insane elemental garden was the responsibility of protecting Margot, a woman she despised. What Kaylin needed didn't seem to make much difference.

And if it came right down to it, Kaylin wasn't exactly Billington's biggest fan, either. He was a cut above Margot when it came to business on Elani, but that wasn't saying much; he didn't have her face, her figure or her sheer magnetism. And to date, he'd been unable to buy or hire it, although the constant stream of young women who worked for a week or two in his storefront always caused speculation when things were slow on the beat.

He charted stars, read palms, tea leaves and hands; he also specialized in reading bumps on the head that were conveniently hidden by hair in most cases. His biggest seller, ironically enough, was a cure for baldness, if you didn't count aphrodisiacs. Kaylin was not a tax collector, and she'd therefore never had call to examine the books of either merchant, but she was willing to bet that Margot's love potions outsold anything Billington tried to push.

Billington was a man who was keenly aware that there were only so many people to fleece, so his envy often got the better of him. Usually this happened when he'd been drinking, and at this time in the morning, most of the bars and taverns were closed for business.

Kaylin glanced at Severn, and froze. His hand had dropped, not to his clubs, which were regulation gear, but to his waist, around which his weapons of choice lay twined. He was closer to the store than she was, and even if he hadn't been, he was taller than most of the milling crowd, and could see above their heads.

Kaylin, who'd never been, and would never be, as tall, made do. She tapped two people on the shoulder and told them, tersely, to get the hell out of the way. Her hands were around the haft of her beat stick; nothing she had seen had made her draw daggers. And drawing those daggers on a crowded street was an invitation to a hell of a lot of paperwork; her instinctive dread of reports usually kept her in line in all but real emergencies.

The people started to argue, took one look at her surcoat and her face and backed away. They backed into one or two other people, who started to speak, and then did the same. If this was the effect of being soaking wet in Elani Street, Kaylin thought buckets of water might actually come in useful for something other than dishes.

As they cleared, she saw that Billington had, indeed, brought goons. The window hadn't shattered by accident, and in the back of the shop, well away from the shards of broken glass, she could see the dim outline of Margot's clientele. Margot, however, was not cowering with them. She had turned a particular shade of red-purple that clashed in every way with her hair, but somehow suited it anyway.

That, and she wasn't a fool; she had seen Kaylin trip over her sign, and she had seen Severn right it. She knew they were walking the beat, and she knew that Kaylin's intense dislike of her business would mean at least someone was watching her like a proverbial Hawk.

Either that or, Kaylin thought grudgingly, she wasn't a craven coward. It's funny how hard it was to see anything good in someone you disliked so intensely.

But in this case, it was impossible to miss. Billington was there, and Kaylin couldn't actually see his face, but she could count the backs of his goons. They were standing along a half circle behind him, and they were armed. None of this seemed to make a dent in Margot's operatic, if genuine, rage.

Kaylin snorted and started to walk toward them; Severn's hand caught her shoulder. She glanced back at him and frowned.

"Something's up," he said, his voice pitched low enough that she had to strain to hear it. "They broke the window. But Billington hasn't raised his voice. He's not drunk."

She turned to look at the display of backs again; Billington's was the broadest, and also, by about three inches, the shortest. Severn, however, was right. Margot's voice could be heard clearly. It always could. But no one else seemed to be talking much, and that was unusual. They seemed, in fact, to be waiting.

Broken window—that would get attention. The possibility of unrest in Elani would get attention. Whose?

Theirs. The Hawks.

She tightened her grip on her stick; Severn, however, unwound his chain. The blades at either end, he now took in each hand. He did not, however, start the chain spinning. She wondered, not for the first time, and no doubt not for the last, what he had been like as a hunting Wolf. Who he had killed? Why?

But this was not the time to ask, if there ever was one.

She took a deep breath and waded through the last of the sparse crowd until she was three yards from the closest of the backs. Lifting one hand—and her voice, because no normal speaking voice would cut through Margot's outrage—she said, "What seems to be the problem here?"

The man standing closest to Billington's back turned.

The world shifted. It wasn't a man. It was a stocky woman, with a scar across her upper lip, and a pierced left eyebrow. Her jaw was square, her hair cropped very short—but Kaylin recognized her anyway. The others turned, as well; Kaylin was aware of both their movement and Margot's sudden silence.

One of the men said something to Billington and handed him a small bag. He also handed a similar one to Margot, whose hands grasped it reflexively. Even at this distance the sound of coins was distinct and clear.

"Apologies for the misunderstanding," the woman said to Margot. It was a dismissal. Margot's lovely eyes narrowed; Kaylin saw that much before the woman turned to her.

"Hello, Eli."

Words deserted Kaylin. She shifted her stance slightly, and her knuckles whitened.

"You don't recognize me? No hello for an old friend?"

"Hello, Morse," Kaylin said.

Morse. Here.

"So," she said, as she met Kaylin's widened eyes, "it's true. You're a Hawk. You got out." Her smile was thin, and ugly. The scar didn't help.

Kaylin nodded slowly. "Yeah. I got out."

"Well, I didn't."

"You're not in Barren now."

"No. But I'm running a bit of a mission for the fief lord. You want to try to arrest me?" She laughed. The laughter, like the smile, was ugly and sharply edged.

Kaylin's hands shifted on the stick she carried. But she put it up. "No." Drawing a deep breath—which was hard, because her throat and her chest seemed suddenly tight and immobile—she added, "Unless Margot wishes to press vandalism charges."

Margot, however, had opened the bag that had been placed in her hands.

Morse shrugged and turned, almost bored, to look at Margot. "That should cover the cost of the window, and the inconvenience to your customers. Do you want to cause trouble for us?" The words shaded into threat, even blandly delivered.

"I will if you ever break another one of my windows," was the curt reply.

"Fair enough," Morse said, and turned back to Kaylin. "Well, *Officer?*"

Kaylin walked up to Margot, trying to remember her intense dislike of the woman. It was gone; it had crumbled. Margot wouldn't cause trouble for Morse. No one with half a brain would. "Margot?"

"It was probably a misunderstanding of some sort," the exotic charlatan replied. She took a second to cast a venomous glare at Billington who, with his lack of finesse and class, was standing in the street, openly counting his new money.

Kaylin was certain word of his ill-gotten gains would be spreading down the street and the bars and taverns would be opening conveniently early to take advantage of him. Couldn't happen to a nicer man.

"Well, then," Morse said cheerfully. "We'll just be going."

Kaylin said nothing for a long moment. Then she turned. "Morse."

"I always wondered what had happened to you," Morse told her. "I couldn't pass up the opportunity to confirm the rumors." Her eyes narrowed slightly as she looked at Kaylin's face.

It took Kaylin a moment to realize what Morse was looking at: her mark. Nightshade's mark. It was so much a part of her by this point she could forget it was there. But Morse had never seen it.

"You haven't changed much," Morse told her, her expression replacing the harsh edges with growing distance. "Except for your cheek, you almost look the same."

"Why did you come here, Morse?"

The woman shrugged. "I told you, I'm running an errand."

"Is it legal?"

"I live in Barren. You haven't been gone so long that you don't remember the definition of law, there."

"You're not there now," Kaylin said, shading the words differently this time.

Morse hesitated, the way she sometimes did when she was about to say something serious. "I am. In any way that counts. You're not." She looked as if she would say more, but one of the men with her approached them, and the moment, which was so thin it might cut, broke. "Yeah, legal. Unless running messages breaks Imperial Law these days."

"Depends on what's in the message."

"Judge for yourself, Eli." Morse shoved a hand into her shirt, and came up with a flattened, squished piece of paper. Or two. "It's for you. Obb," she added, "get your butt out of the damn glass. We're heading back. We're late."

Kaylin took the letter and stared at it. Then she glanced at Severn, whose hands were still on his blades. She flinched at his expression, but she didn't—quite—look away. She managed a shrug.

"I'll come by later for the reply," Morse told her.

Don't bother, Kaylin almost said. But she couldn't force the words out of her mouth. What came out, instead, was "Later."

Morse nodded, and walked away; the others trailed after her like a badly behaved shadow. Only when they'd turned a corner a few blocks down the street did Severn relax enough to approach her.

"Kaylin?"

She looked at him, and then shook her head. Bent down to pick up a small slab of glass.

"Leave it," he told her, catching her wrist. "Margot can clean it up. She's got the money for it at the moment, and it'll employ someone for a few hours. If she fails to clean it up, you can charge her with littering."

She nodded, stood and looked down the street. Morse. Here.

"I knew her," she told Severn, without once looking up at his face, "when I lived in Barren."

He was silent. He didn't ask her when that was; he wasn't an idiot, he could figure it out. What he said, instead, was "Did you meet the fief lord of Barren while you were there?"

She nodded, almost numb.

CHAPTER 3

For the rest of the day—admittedly one shortened by two hours in the elemental garden—Kaylin didn't bump into another offensive sandwich board. Severn assumed the street-side stretch of their patrol. He didn't speak, and as Kaylin didn't have much she wanted to say, the rest of their round was pretty damn quiet. By the end of it, she was mostly dry.

So was the letter she was carrying. She wanted to read it. At the same time, she wanted to burn it or toss it into the nearest garbage heap. Elani was fairly tidy, on the other hand, so the garbage heaps were not that close to their patrol route.

Morse, she thought. She glanced once at Severn, and remembered walking different streets, with an entirely different goal, beside Morse. Morse who could talk you deaf or cut you without blinking. She hadn't been so scarred, back then. She hadn't looked as old.

But she'd always looked as dangerous.

"Dinner?" Severn asked, as they headed back to the Halls.

"Will it come as much of a surprise if I say I'm not hungry?"

"Actually, it would."

She grimaced, dredging a small smile out of somewhere. Where, given her mood, she honestly couldn't say.

"Did you figure out what was bothering you?"

"Probably not. On the other hand, whatever it was couldn't be as bad as what's bothering me *now*." She hesitated. Glanced at him as they reached the steps that lead into the building. "Severn—"

"We can talk over dinner. We can not talk over dinner, as well. You did a pretty good job of that on patrol." His smile was slight, and it was shadowed, but he offered it anyway. "I told you, the past is the past. I don't care to know what you don't care to tell me."

She nodded. She knew he meant it. But he didn't know what she knew. She'd tried to tell him, but only once. Now, she had no desire to even try. Telling him about the past was one thing; telling him about the past when it had crept, unwelcome and unexpected, into the present was another.

What had she expected?

When she'd crossed the bridge over the Ablayne, when she'd stepped foot on the cobbled and patrolled streets of the Emperor's city, she had never truly expected to stay here. She hadn't come to escape.

"Kaylin?"

"Sorry, did you say something?"

He grimaced. "Not much. Lockers. We can file a nonreport in the morning."

She nodded and fell into step beside him; they'd managed to make it to the Aerie without any conscious awareness, on her part, of passing through the doors. She remembered the first time she'd come in through the front doors. She remembered the first time she'd arrived at the Halls of Law. They weren't the same.

For a moment, the Halls of Law looked so insubstantial she could almost see the street through the stonework. But the streets she saw weren't the streets of Nightshade; they weren't the streets of the city whose laws she had vowed to give her life enforcing.

They were darker, grayer, devoid of even the hope she'd felt in Nightshade at Severn's side.

Barren.

"Okay," Severn told her. "Stay here a minute."

She shook her head and dredged up what she hoped was a smile. Judging from his grimace, it was a pretty pathetic one. "I'll go get changed," she told his retreating back.

She walked into the locker room, found her locker and leaned her forehead against its door for a minute.

"Hey."

She jumped back from the locker door, wondering whether or not she'd fallen asleep standing up. Having done it on one or two occasions, she didn't wonder if it were possible, but it was never anything like good sleep, and it usually ended abruptly with the unpleasant sensation of falling, and the even less pleasant sensation of landing.

"Teela?"

Teela grinned. Barrani didn't smile or laugh much as a general rule, and when they did, it was usually at someone else's expense. "You look like crap," she told Kaylin. "Come on, get changed. We're not going out if you're dressed like that. Iron Jaw would have our hides pinned to the dartboard by morning. If he waited that long."

Kaylin's body started to obey; she stripped off her tabard and her armor, taking care to set Morse's letter on the inside of her locker. But her brain caught up, and she stopped, tunic halfway over her upper body. "What do you mean, we're going out?"

"Severn seems to think you need a drink."

"I'm not going to get a drink if I go out with you!"

Teela's shrug was lazy. "Tain's been bored all day."

"Oh, no, you don't. I am *not* going out drinking with Tain. Not when he's bored."

Teela, stripping off her own gear, laughed. "We're not going to cause too much trouble. Your Corporal is going with us."

"You've gone drinking with officers and you've managed to wreck half a tavern!"

She shrugged, her lazy smile spreading across her full lips. "They weren't conscious for most of it."

"Teela—"

"And I'm guessing your Corporal can hold his drinks a tad better. Which, all things considered, would be a pity."

"Teela, don't even think it."

"Last I heard, thinking wasn't illegal. Come on, Kaylin. I've never gone drinking with Severn."

"Obviously not, if this was his idea. I'm going to kill him."

"Can you kill him after I'm finished?"

"No."

Teela laughed as someone started hammering on the door. That would be Tain, Kaylin thought. "You get it," she told Teela, as she belted her tunic. "I've had a bad enough day already."

It had been several months since Kaylin had gone drinking with Teela and Tain. Several months, in fact, since she had appeared at work, slightly gray-faced, with dark circles under her eyes and a headache that she was certain at the time not even beheading would cure.

Teela had shrugged her way out of her regulation gear. Since Teela was tall and almost preternaturally beautiful—a characteristic she shared with all of her race—she would look stunning in sack-cloth; the change of clothing did not actually make that much of a difference. The same could be said of Tain, although Tain had a chipped tooth. That single flaw had made him the first of the Barrani that Kaylin could easily distinguish; they all looked very similar when she had first joined the Hawks.

Severn, however, wore black and gray, and he looked very different. He had set aside his obvious weapons, although he still wore his chains; they were wrapped around his waist like a fashion statement. It was not exactly cold in Elantra at this time of year, but Kaylin wore the usual long-sleeved shirt. The marks on her arms made her self-conscious, and she could live more easily with sweat.

They approached the front doors. Clint was on guard duty. When he saw Kaylin beside Teela, he grimaced. "Teela—"

"We're off-duty," she told him cheerfully.

He rolled his eyes. Kaylin privately thought he'd lost his mind if he expected responsibility from that quarter.

Severn, however, smiled at Clint. "I'll stop them from trashing the tavern."

Clint grimaced. "You've clearly never gone drinking with Teela and Tain."

Severn's idea of drinking was not Teela's idea of drinking; he led them to the Spotted Pig. Kaylin glanced at Teela; she was betting they had about fifteen minutes before Teela decided to go somewhere else. Only on a very lucky day would her "go someplace else" not involve dragging Kaylin with her when she stormed out.

Barrani clientele was always a mixed blessing, because about a quarter of the time, something ugly happened. The definition of *ugly* was a real-life lesson in cultural paradigms, because nothing had ever happened that Teela did not find amusing.

The fact that neither Teela nor Tain said a word when they entered the quiet and rather unpretentious environs of the Spotted Pig was a bit suspicious. Given they were Barrani, suspicion was only natural; Kaylin took a seat—at a table—beside Severn. Teela and Tain occupied the bench across from them. They seldom ate much when they went anywhere; human food was not generally to their taste, although Kaylin, having eaten with the Barrani in no less a place than the High Court, didn't really see why.

They ordered food and wine; the wine arrived before the food, and it arrived in mugs that were better suited to ale.

Kaylin looked at Severn.

"What exactly is going on here?"

"We're having a bite to eat, and something to drink. Maybe," Tain added, glancing around the quiet room. "I can't imagine—"

Teela stepped on his foot. Kaylin couldn't actually see this, of course, but she could hear it, and frankly, very little else would cut Tain off.

"Severn."

"Oh, leave him alone, kitling."

Kaylin's eyes narrowed. It had been years—with a few exceptions—since anyone but Marcus had called her by that name. And most of those years had gone into living down the rank of Office Mascot. She stared at Teela, who smiled her slow, lazy, catlike grin. "What's this about, Teela?"

"You tell me. Severn said you met an old acquaintance on your rounds in Elani."

"No one you'd know."

Tain, who had been mostly silent, started to drink. "This isn't terrible," he told Teela, mock surprise in every word.

She cuffed the side of his head, although her fingers trailed sensuously through the length of his hair afterward, which ruined the gesture, in Kaylin's opinion. "Kitling," she said, resting her elbows on the scarred, old wood, "we were told not to ask you many questions."

"And you listened about as well as you normally do."

Teela shrugged. "It's habit. When you first wandered into the office, Marcus made clear to everyone there—particularly the Barrani—that you were not to be too heavily discouraged. Or damaged," she added.

"Too bad he didn't make that clearer to the drillmaster."

"If you'd blocked the way you said you could, he wouldn't have broken your arm. And you didn't, that I recall, lie about your abilities again after that. Don't make that face. It healed quickly enough," Teela pointed out. "You came to the Hawks as a fledgling. You've made this job your life."

Kaylin tensed slightly, waiting for the rest. But she was surprised at where the conversation now went. She shouldn't have been; she'd seen Teela drive, after all, and she knew what Teela's steering was like. Unpredictable was probably the kindest thing she could call it.

"I came to the Hawks from the High Halls. It wasn't considered upward mobility," she added with a grimace, "and it wasn't exactly peaceful."

"You didn't break any laws before you joined."

"How would you know? You spent a couple of days in the High Halls, under the watchful eye of the Lord of the West March. I spent my life there. I underwent the test of Name. I lived in the Court." She lifted her mug and drank wine as if it were water—and she was parched. "The Caste Laws apply in the High Court."

"Teela—"

"Hush. Hear me out."

"Why are you telling me this?"

Teela glanced at Severn. Kaylin, who had always been curious about Teela's life—about all of the Barrani Hawks, if it came to that—didn't. But it took effort.

"Caste Law applies in the High Court," Tain said. He waved at the barkeep, his mug empty. "Fief Law applies in the fiefs. The two are not entirely dissimilar."

"They're completely different."

"No, they're not."

"You've never lived in the fiefs."

"And you," he said pointedly, "have never lived in the High Halls without the title Lord."

She considered this quietly. Teela nudged her drink, and Kaylin said, "I'm not going to finish it, if you want it." This earned her a brief grimace and a kick under the table.

"You've met my cousin," Teela said, picking up the reins of the conversation again.

"As far as I can tell, half the High Court is related to you."

"Not half."

"Which cousin?" Kaylin asked. She wasn't being disingenuous; she honestly had no idea.

"Evarrim."

"Ugh." Evarrim was an Arcanist. Arcanists, as far as Kaylin was concerned, were slightly lower on the decency scale than drug dealers. She didn't understand why the Emperor tolerated them; he had his own mages, after all, and at least half of the Wolves' hunts had been former Arcanists.

Tain waved the bartender over again.

"His mother was blessed with five children over the course of her marriage. Evarrim is the last one left standing. It was noted, of course."

"What—he killed the others?" Kaylin grimaced. She'd meant it as a joke, but it had fallen flat even before Teela nodded.

"Teela—"

"If Evarrim hadn't been the sole survivor, one of the others would have. He was canny enough, and powerful enough, to beat them at their own game. I played Court games," she said quietly. "I also survived. Do you understand?"

After a moment of silence, Kaylin nodded.

"But even survival can become boring after a while."

"You joined the Hawks because you were *bored?*"

Tain said, "No."

"Then—then *why?*"

"Because she did not trust me," he replied, "not to dare the Tower and take the test of Name."

Kaylin stared at them both, and then turned to Severn. "If this is your idea of cheering me up, you need better ideas."

He shrugged, but did grimace. "With the Barrani, you take whatever they offer."

"No, with the Barrani, you *don't ask.*" But she took a swig of the wine, and glanced at Tain.

"What she was trying to say," he told Kaylin, "is that it doesn't matter. What she did in pursuit of survival would probably give you ulcers, and she isn't about to recount it all—it would take two months."

"Three," Teela drawled.

Tain rolled his very attractive eyes. Although he was serious—

which seldom happened—those eyes were a shade of deep green; what he said was fact, not dirty secret. "What we did in the High Courts, we don't do in the Imperial City. We uphold the Emperor's law. We generally find it amusing," he added, with a nod in Teela's direction. "It's certainly less formal; it's usually less dangerous." He said the last with a tinge of regret. "The laws that defined our lives there, and that define Teela's life when she is called to Court, aren't the same.

"Although we have better drink," he added.

It was true. Kaylin looked up as food joined drink on the pocked table. It was some sort of cubed chicken with rice, potatoes and—ugh—little peas.

"I do not understand your people's obsession with potatoes," Teela said, her nose wrinkling in mild—for Teela—distaste. It wasn't the first time she'd said it, and no doubt it wouldn't be the last, but it was oddly comforting.

"The High Court is no longer my home. And the fiefs," she added pointedly, "are no longer yours. Understood?"

"You think I'd go back there? Do I look stupid?"

"Generally," Tain said helpfully. "Look, if they try to blackmail you, ignore it." At Kaylin's sudden tightening of expression, he rolled his eyes. "It's completely obvious that's what you're afraid of. You can read it in your face a mile off. And you're probably right," he added with a shrug. "They'll try, if they know where you are."

They did, and that fact had bothered Kaylin almost as much as seeing Morse again. They *had known* where she would be, and with enough notice that they could find Billington, pay him to stir up a bit of trouble, break a window and time both things so that they'd catch her attention. If someone in the office was feeding information to the fief lord of Barren, it was more than simple trouble. If someone *wasn't* feeding information to Barren, it was worse: it meant Barren had some way of looking into the Halls of Law that no one had yet noticed. Neither of these things were good.

But she hadn't gone back to the office to talk with Marcus; she hadn't even tried to point it out. It was what she damn well *should* have done. But had she, she'd have to answer questions. She wasn't quite up to that, tonight.

"You can laugh in their face if it helps. I generally find breaking things attached to them more helpful, but you've been known to be squeamish, on occasion. On the other hand—"

"Shut up, Tain."

"—you've also been known to—"

Teela elbowed him, hard. He did stop talking, but he turned a blue-eyed and murderous glare on his partner; her own eyes had shaded dark, but she was smiling.

"All right," Severn whispered. "You win. This was ill-advised."

And *that* did make Kaylin feel a bit better.

They did not, as it turned out, end up dead drunk. An attempt to insult the barkeeper fell so totally flat Kaylin wondered if he was deaf. On the other hand, neither Teela nor Tain had worked themselves into that dangerous state the Barrani called boredom. They were, Kaylin realized, genuinely worried about her.

And given that they were Barrani, they might continue to do so when they knew what she'd done. If they ever knew.

"I was in Barren for six months," she told them. She hadn't intended to say it; it had just fallen out of her mouth. She set her cup aside.

"You were in Nightshade," Teela pointed out, "for thirteen years."

"Barren was different," she said quietly.

"Why?"

"It was—it was just different."

"Find out what they want, Kaylin," Tain told her quietly. "Or we will." He nodded in Teela's direction.

"You can't just walk into Barren and demand answers."

"We can try. I've never been into the fiefs," he added, "but Teela used to head there when she was bored."

"She went to Barren when she was bored?" Kaylin could have sounded more appalled if she'd really worked at it—but not by much.

"Not just Barren," Teela added, grinning broadly. The grin faded. "But the fiefs aren't what they were when I was young. Find out what they want. Do *not* do anything stupid."

Kaylin hesitated, and then reached into the folds of her tunic. When she withdrew her hand, it held the letter that Morse had given her. Funny, how it didn't burn; it should have. "I wanted to keep this to myself," she told them all: Severn, who hadn't spoken a word, Teela, Tain. She especially did not want to talk to Marcus or Caitlin. She didn't want to hear a word that someone out of department, like, say, Mallory, had to say. She just didn't want to see the looks on their faces.

Teela shrugged. "Yes, that was obvious. And clearly your Corporal is willing to let you do that—but we're not."

Kaylin set the letter on the table, and picked up her mug. "You didn't leave Tain behind," she said.

"Pardon?"

"You came to the Hawks—you brought him with you. You didn't leave him behind in the High Courts."

Teela was silent for a moment, and the silence wasn't punctuated by her slow grin. It was almost human. "No," Teela said at last, "I didn't. This person you met in Elani was a friend?"

"Maybe. A lot can change in seven years."

"Remember that."

Kaylin nodded, swallowing wine and something more bitter as she did. She picked up the letter, unfolded the paper and cringed before she'd read the first word. It was Barren's handwriting. Maybe some things never changed.

Elianne,

I've been following your progress as I can—I admit it's surprised me. You didn't fall from the Tower, although the Hawklord's still in it. You landed on your feet; he probably has no idea why you made your way out of the fiefs in the first place.

I know you didn't like working for me; no one does.

Doesn't matter. You like working for the Hawklord, and I'm fine with that—everyone has to eat. But you probably want to keep on working across the river.

Working for the Law has its drawbacks. I don't care what you are or what you've done—but the Law does. You know that.

The way I look at it, girl, you owe your life to me. You wouldn't be where you are if I hadn't sent you. And you probably can't stay where you are, if they know why. I've got the information, and I can make your life very, very difficult without ever crossing a bridge.

But I'm not a malicious man. I'm a fief lord, and I aim to stay that way.

You're going to help me, if the rumors are true. I'll be generous. You've got three days before a small packet crosses the bridge in the hands of one of your old friends. In three days time, you can head it off at the bridge; if she sees you, she'll bring you home, and the package will travel with you.

—Barren

She lifted the mug, drained it, choked enough to bring tears to her eyes. Then she handed the letter to Severn, in silence. Her hands were shaking.

He took it and set it down without reading it. "Kaylin—"

She picked it up again, and shoved it into his hands. This time, she met and held his gaze. "I tried to tell you," she whispered.

"Yes. And I told you I didn't care."

"Care now. Just read the gods-cursed thing."

A brief pause. Severn's brief pause, in which she could imagine almost any thought, any concern and any anger. He ended it with a nod, and he turned his attention to the letter—but she felt it anyway. It didn't take him long to read it, and when he'd finished, he set it down in the exact same place on the table.

"He was clever enough not to say anything at all."

"Three days," she replied.

"Are you two going to share that?" Teela asked, holding a hand out across the table.

"No." Kaylin picked up the letter and folded it. "Teela, Tain—I'm almost grateful for tonight. But I don't want you involved with Barren."

The silence that followed this statement was exactly the wrong type of silence, coming as it did from Teela. When she broke it, her tone could have frozen water. Or blood. "And we're somehow at more risk than a human Corporal?"

Severn's brow rose, but he was smart enough not to answer.

"Severn trusts me enough that he'll let me do what I feel I have to do," was Kaylin's very—*very*—careful reply. "You both think of me as if I'm still a thirteen-year-old mascot, trailing around under Marcus's claws."

"And that's inaccurate how?"

"My point. You don't trust me."

"I trusted you," Teela pointed out, each word sharp and staccato, "with the life of the Lord of the West March."

"Yes—but he was as good as dead. You had nothing to lose."

Severn caught Kaylin's wrist. She met his stare dead-on, and after a moment, she grimaced. Without another word, she handed the letter to Teela, whose hand had conveniently not moved an inch.

"Honestly, Kaylin," Teela said, taking it, "you make the biggest fuss about the littlest things. It's such a human trait."

"We don't consider them little."

"Because you've only got a handful of years in which to attempt to truly screw things up. Try living a millennia or more. It'll give you perspective."

"I bet when you were young, you had to personally dig your own wells just to get water, too," Kaylin said, under her breath.

Teela, who appeared to be reading the letter, said, "I heard that." She looked up, handed the letter to Tain, and said, "So, why exactly did Barren send you out of his fief?"

She looked across the table; she could not look at Severn. But even not looking at him, she felt his presence as strongly as she had ever felt his absence. "He sent me," she said quietly, "to kill the Hawklord."

CHAPTER 4

Teela's brows rose; the rest of her face seemed frozen. "He sent a thirteen-year-old human child to assassinate the Hawklord?"

Kaylin nodded. She felt curiously numb, now that the words had left her mouth. She didn't even feel the panicky need to claw them back, to make a joke of them. What did it matter, in the end? She could do whatever Barren wanted her to do, but if she did, she'd lose the Hawk anyway. If she didn't?

She'd lose it, as well.

"Why?"

"Why?"

Teela frowned. "Pay attention, kitling. *Why* did he send a child to kill the Hawklord?"

"I don't know. I think he was trying to make a point."

Teela shrugged. She didn't seem disappointed in Kaylin at all—but then again, she was Barrani. It wasn't the good opinion or the approval of the Barrani Kaylin was afraid of losing. Hells, given the Barrani she might even rise a notch or two in their estimation. "This is what you're afraid of? He sends in so-called proof of that, people will be laughing for months."

Kaylin, however, did not seem to find this as vastly humorous as Teela. Or Tain, judging by his smirk.

Severn covered the back of one of her hands with his. He asked no questions, and he made no comment; he didn't even seem particularly surprised.

"Since you obviously failed to follow his orders—"

"I didn't."

"The Hawklord, last I saw, was still breathing."

"I didn't fail to follow his orders," was the quiet reply. "I just failed to succeed."

Tain chuckled. It was the only sound at the table. Even Teela, not normally the most sensitive of the Hawks—which, given she was Barrani, was an understatement—was somber. "You tried to kill the Hawklord."

Kaylin nodded. The lines of her face felt too frozen for expression; she wasn't even sure what she looked like.

"If the Hawklord already knows—and I can't imagine he doesn't, unless you were truly, truly terrible—you've little enough to fear."

Kaylin shook her head. "What I did in the fiefs, he won't or can't touch. What I did in the Tower? It *counts*. Marcus doesn't know." She lowered her face into her palms. Took a deep breath before she raised it. "I don't want him to know," she told them both.

Teela glanced at Tain.

"Don't even think it."

"Think what?" Tain asked. Barrani did a *horrible* mimicry of innocent.

"Barren's a fief lord."

"He's human, isn't he?" Teela asked, with her usual disdain for enemies who were merely mortal.

"I'm not sure that counts in the fiefs. Not when you're the fief lord."

Severn touched her shoulder, and she turned to look at him. "How much different is Barren from Nightshade?"

"The fief or the Lord?"

"Either."

"The fief is—" Kaylin hesitated. "I'm not sure we would have noted the differences when we were kids. The people still live a really miserable life, the ferals still hunt. Barren doesn't have public cages or hangings—he doesn't need 'em. If you piss him off, he throws you to the ferals."

"The ferals aren't that dependable."

Kaylin grimaced. "No. I don't know if he knows when they're coming or not. He'll wait it out with his victim until he hears the howls. He cuts them," she added, staring at the tabletop as she spoke. "And then he makes them run.

"If they can survive until morning, they're more or less free to go."

"Happen often?"

"Pretty much never." She started to rise, to shed the bench and its confinement, and his hand tightened.

"Severn—I don't want to talk about Barren. I'll talk about anything—and I mean *anything*—else."

He met her gaze and held it, and she found it hard to look away. After a moment, she sat, heavily. He hadn't forced her back down; her legs had given way. They waited in silence.

Kaylin surrendered. "There's a bit more foot-traffic coming over from the right side of the bridge. Barren's got storehouses and brothels on the riverside. But his own place? It's not at the heart of the fief. He lives near the edge."

"Which edge, Kaylin?"

She shook her head. "Inner."

"You've been there." It wasn't a question.

She looked away again. "Yeah. I've been there. It's not like Nightshade's Castle."

"It's an old building, though?"

"I don't know if it's any older than the rest of the buildings there. There *is* a building that's kind of like the Castle, but it's older and more decrepit. I don't think anyone lives there." She paused, and then added, "I don't think anyone who tries survives."

"But Barren doesn't."

"No."

"You're going to meet him."

"No. I'm probably going to meet Morse. I don't know where she'll take me, or what she'll tell me to do." She looked across the table at Teela and Tain. She wanted to either drink a lot more, or have drunk a lot less. "I don't want Marcus to know," she whispered. "He thinks I'm a kit. He thinks I was a—a child—when the Hawklord dumped me on his division."

"Kitling," Teela said, almost gently, "you were."

"He thinks I was a *good* child, turned thief because I had no *other* way of living in the streets of Nightshade."

"But you know better?"

"Don't patronize me."

"I'm not. I'm treating you like a self-absorbed and ignorant human. Patronizing is different." Teela lifted her mug. "Look. What humans do when they're desperate is just an expression of fear. What they do when they feel safe is a better indication of whether or not you can trust them."

"I thought the Barrani were allergic to trust."

Teela shrugged. "It's a figure of speech. What you've done, feeling safe? Volunteer with the midwives. The foundling hall. You've been, in Marcus's estimation, a better officer than most of his Barrani. You've got nothing to be ashamed of. You did what you did—"

Kaylin let her talk. It did not, however, make her feel any better; the words felt hollow, built on a foundation that was shaky at best. Not as she remembered Elianne, who'd fled Nightshade after the deaths of Steffi and Jade. Fled Nightshade and ended up…elsewhere.

"Kaylin?"

Severn's voice pulled her back from the sharp bite of memory: her first night in Barren. She tried to school her expression, to force it into casual, neutral lines. It would change nothing. He knew what she was thinking.

She had taken a name for herself, not once, but twice: when she had first met the Hawklord, and when she had seen the Barrani pool of life. The one had been a lie that had slowly enfolded her, becoming a truth she desperately wanted to own; the other?

She had given it to Severn.

He *knew* what she was thinking. But as he could, he now gave her room.

It never went away. The regret. The guilt. Sometimes it ebbed for long enough that she could believe she was beyond it, but that was wishful thinking, another way of lying to herself. She didn't want to share this with Teela and Tain. Sharing bar brawls and near-death, yes. But this?

"Come on," Severn told her quietly. "Let me take you home."

"I can find home on my own."

He waited.

Teela snorted and rose. "This," she said coolly, "is as much fun as the High Court."

"Less," Tain added. "No danger."

"Pardon me for boring you both," she snapped.

"We might. I have a question for you," Teela said, as she rose. "You left Nightshade, and you entered Barren, yes?"

Kaylin nodded. It was brusque, and invited no further questions— but that was too subtle for Teela when she was determined.

"Did you notice nothing at all about the transition?"

"Transition?"

"You left Nightshade."

"I enter Nightshade and leave it now. I don't notice it either way."

"Now, you're not *of* Nightshade." Teela glanced at Tain, who shrugged.

"It was a straight run along the border nearest the river," Kaylin told them both. "I wasn't close to the—the other border."

"No. If you'd run in that direction, you'd never have met the Hawklord. And," Teela added, "our lives would generally be less interesting for the lack." She nodded to Severn. "Tain and I have a little drinking to do. See that she gets home."

He didn't even bridle at the casual order.

★ ★ ★

"I'm not angry anymore," Kaylin told Severn as they walked along the river's side. Her gaze traveled across its banks, and into the shallows of night. Night in the fiefs was death unless you were armed and trained. She could walk there now without much fear, and that was something she'd never even dreamed of as a child.

Severn said nothing.

"I know why you did—what you did."

He nodded. "But?"

She frowned. "It's Barren," she said quietly.

"The fief or the Lord?"

"I'm not sure you can ever separate a fief from its fief lord. But…the fief. The first night. The first day. I don't think about it much anymore." She kicked a loose stone with her right foot, and found that it wasn't as loose as it had looked. The pain was almost a relief, it was so mundane.

"But then?"

"I wanted to kill you." She stopped walking and turned to face him. What he saw in her expression made him look away. "I wanted to *be able* to kill you. I thought, if I did, it would end the nightmares. It would somehow let Steffi and Jade rest in peace."

In the muted streetlights, she could see his face; it was shadowed, and it was stiff. She searched around for another stone to kick, because it was better than looking at what was—and wasn't—there. "It was the only thing I could think about, when I could think at all." She lifted her hands, found they were almost fists, and lowered them again.

He watched her. He said nothing.

But he didn't turn, didn't walk away. She would have. She knew she would have. "I'm sorry," she whispered.

"Don't," he said, his first word. He lifted a hand, palm out. "Don't apologize to me. What you did, what *we* did, is in the past. Leave it there, Kaylin."

"I did. I thought I did," she added bitterly. She lifted Barren's missive and waved it in the air. "But it's *here*. Again."

"Ignore it. Walk away. Don't walk back."

She knew, then, that's what Severn would do.

And what could she say that wasn't pathetic? *I don't want Marcus to know.*

"Marcus will understand, Kaylin. Trust him to do that much. Given a choice, he would never, ever have you walk back into Barren."

"I do trust him," she said quietly. "I want him to *keep on* trusting *me*."

He nodded, as if he'd never really expected her to say anything else. Maybe he hadn't. "Take me with you."

"No."

"He didn't tell you to go alone. Take me with you."

"No. Because—" she stopped. Looked at his face, at the lines that had hardened in his expression. Closed her own. "Severn— I don't want you to know, either."

And then, before he could answer, she did what she had often done—she turned and she ran.

There was no light in her apartment that wasn't supplied by moon; it was cheap, and all she did here at night was sleep, anyway. She checked the mirror, but it was dull and silent. No messages. No *other* emergencies. Tonight, for a change, one would almost have been welcome.

Her hair fell as she pulled out the new stick that bound it; she struggled out of her tunic and dumped it on the chair that served as a closet. *It's not your fault,* she told him in bitter silence, because he couldn't hear her. *I didn't know why. I didn't stay to find out.* She believed it, now; those deaths weren't his fault. But she had run to Barren, numb and terrified, and when the terror had finally lapsed, the guilt had almost destroyed her.

It was a slow, slow destruction, and she ached from it, from the memories of it; they were almost physical. What she'd told him was true: she had only wanted one thing. To kill him. To be able to kill him. She'd been thirteen; it wasn't hard to be focused, to let desire consume everything, overshadowing all but the need to eat, and the need to sleep.

She grimaced. It wasn't hard to be that focused *now*. But she no longer wanted to kill him. The years with the Hawks, with the foundling hall, and eventually, with the midwives, had given her other things to want, other things to live for. The first time she'd set eyes on Severn in the Hawklord's tower had been the first time she'd thought about killing him in months. Maybe a year.

And what had she done then?

Cringing her way out of her leggings, and struggling with laces in the dark, she closed her eyes. She'd tried, of course. In front of the Hawklord, in his Tower, as if all the intervening years had never happened. She'd managed to pull back, but it wasn't the last time she'd tried, and the last time?

In front of the *foundlings*. In front of Marrin.

Lying back in bed, she reached for her sheet and the blankets that were too hot for this time of year. She hated to leave any part of her body exposed when she slept, even though it made her sweat. It was stupid, but a small corner of her mind still believed that they would protect her from the shadowy, childhood monsters that lurked at the foot of the bed, waiting their opportunity.

It was *stupid*.

She could honestly say she loved Severn. She could say, as well, that she trusted him with her life. She could almost say that she would trust him—now—with the lives that meant at least as much to her, although that one was touch and go.

But Jade and Steffi still haunted her. And waiting just behind them now, Barren. The one truth couldn't obliterate the other, no matter how much she believed it already had.

Lord Sanabalis of the Dragon Court was familiar enough with Private Neya—who might, one day, rise in the ranks if she could manage to be consistently on time—that he did not schedule his lessons at the beginning of a normal day. The beginning of Kaylin's day was, to be polite, staggered.

It was with some suspicion, then, that he noted the door to the West Room had been palm-keyed. Private Neya stood in the door's frame as it opened, looking as if she had failed to sleep or eat. She was, however, on time.

She walked to the large, conference table and took the seat closest to Lord Sanabalis; she didn't even grimace at the candle that he had placed in its usual position, which in Kaylin's case, would be just out of range of her fists.

He waited for her to speak.

Normally, speech was not an issue; getting her to stop, especially if she felt aggrieved by the exercises, was. She remained, however, silent; she did not appear to notice that the candle was awaiting her attention.

He began the lesson by reminding her of the import of the candle flame. She was, of course, to light it, and that simple task had so far eluded her, although she had once managed to melt the entire thing.

She offered none of the usual resistance; she even nodded in the right places. But he had some suspicion that this was rote, and when he inserted a word or two that was, strictly speaking, out of place, she failed to notice.

She didn't, however, fail to notice the fire that singed the stray strands of her hair, and she cursed—loudly, and in Leontine—and fell back over her chair, rolling to her feet near the door. "What the *hell* was that for?"

"I wanted to see just how much attention you were paying."

"To what?"

"Exactly. Private, my time is of significant value, at least according to the bureaucrats who charge the Hawks for these lessons. I expect, when you are in class—which would be anywhere that I happen to be delivering a lesson—you will be *awake* and *aware*. Is that clear?"

She got to her feet. "You've spent too much time around

Marcus," she told him, rubbing her elbows where they'd hit carpet a little too hard.

"I've spent too much time around students," he replied. His eyes were mostly gold; he wasn't actually on the edge of angry. "At my age, I should be living in graceful retirement."

She took her chair again, after righting it, and sat down.

He hit the table with the flat of both his palms. The table was hardwood, and even axes had problems denting it. But the whole damn thing moved about three inches.

"Sanabalis—"

"I had hoped that on our first day back in class we would at least be able to pick up where we left off. It appears that I was, as is often the case with students, wildly optimistic. What, exactly, is troubling you?"

"Nothing," she said, sharply and a little too quickly. *That* brought the orange highlights to his draconian eyes. She swallowed, trying to decide whether getting out of the chair would annoy him more than staying put.

"You are making Lord Tiamaris look like a model student," he told her, in a clipped and slightly chilly tone of voice.

That was a new one. Tiamaris was the youngest member of the Dragon Court, and as far as Kaylin could tell, he was about as stiff, formal, and tradition-bound as its older members. A flicker of curiosity wedged itself into the grim worry that had been the start of the day. "He was this frustrating?"

For some reason, the question lessened the intensity of the orange streaks in Dragon irises. Dragons were never going to be something Kaylin understood.

"He was possibly—just possibly—worse." But Sanabalis's shoulders slid into their normal curved bend. "He seldom came to my rooms this distracted."

"Sorry."

He raised a white brow. "I had *hoped* to have this session well underway before I interrupted it with matters that might prove even more of a distraction. I see I was entirely too hopeful. Yesterday, during your normal rounds, you visited Evanton on Elani Street."

She nodded. She didn't ask why he asked because she had a very strong suspicion she didn't actually want the answer. Some days, the universe gave you everything you didn't want.

"Apparently you were called into the...store."

Kaylin nodded again. She knew, now, where this was going. "Yes," she said quietly. "Evanton wanted to speak to me for a bit."

"For well in excess of an hour."

She grimaced. "I wasn't exactly counting minutes, Sanabalis."

"No. I imagine that's not one of your accomplishments. I will, however, point out that you were on duty at that time."

"And?"

"And you failed to file a report."

Honestly, the day could hardly get any worse.

"Sanabalis—"

He raised a hand. "A report, however, is not entirely necessary. I was making an attempt to be humorous," he added gravely. "But your presence, and the length of your visit, was noted.

"As," he added, in a softer tone, "was the state of your clothing when you left the premises—carrying your boots."

"They were wet."

"And, apparently, muddy." His eyes were a clear gold, which was made brighter when he lowered his inner membranes. "Kaylin, what happened? It is seldom that someone the Keeper apparently considers safe enough to allow into his domain emerges in that condition. I was personally asked by the Emperor, in case you think this is idle curiosity, to inquire."

Which was his way of saying she couldn't weasel out of an answer.

"The elements are, apparently, upset," she finally said. "Which is where the water and the mud came from. The wind helped," she added. "For a value of help that made me look like a sodden cat."

He became very still, and she wished—not for the first time—that she had locks on her mouth, and that someone who *had* more wisdom kept the keys. "Sanabalis, please. I am not *supposed* to talk about this."

"I highly doubt," the Dragon Lord replied, "that Evanton expects you to keep silent in the face of Imperial dictate."

"You clearly don't know Evanton." She glanced at the table, and then at the Dragon sitting behind it. "You should," she told him, surrendering. "I think you'd get along just fine. If you didn't kill each other on sight on a bad day." She rose. "The elemental garden wasn't much of a garden; it was a storm, but worse.

"But Evanton said—and I do not argue with him when he's in a mood—that the elements do this when they're trying to communicate."

Sanabalis raised a brow. She actually liked that expression on most days. Today was not one of them. "You're not going to like it," she told him, in a quieter voice.

"I'd guessed that."

"And I *was* going to tell you."

The brow rose farther; it hadn't actually come down.

"Well, before other things came up."

"I'm sure they were vitally important," he said, in a very dry tone. Since he could breathe fire, that type of dry usually showed up when he was just on the edge of annoyance. She'd never, thank the gods, seen him angry.

"Something is happening somewhere close by." She hesitated again. "The elements were trying to write a—a word. Evanton showed me what it was. I couldn't see a damn thing in the storm. I could barely see my own feet."

"You recognized the word." It wasn't a question.

"I didn't—" She glanced at the slightly copper tint to his eyes. "It's not as simple as that. I didn't recognize it because I'd seen it before, if that's what you mean. I— It felt familiar."

"Was it in a living language?"

He was such a smart old bastard. "No."

"Was it similar, in style, to the marks on your arms?"

"Not—" she glanced at her sleeves "—not exactly."

"Kaylin, do not force me to strangle you."

"I'm trying to answer the question—"

"You are trying to answer the question without actually saying all of what you know. If you are going to do that, *learn from your Corporal*. It is actively painful to watch you flail, and the attempt is—I assume unintentionally—insulting. Because you are young and demonstrably ignorant, I am exercising patience, but my patience, while vast, does have limits."

She tried not to grind her teeth. "It's not a rune I recognize. I don't think it's written on *me*, but I admit I haven't actually looked at the back of my neck in records recently. But it felt familiar anyway." He said nothing. He didn't move a muscle. Not even the corner of his mouth twitched.

"It felt like…Ravellon."

Sometimes, he pretended to be old. It was only very, very rarely that he actually *looked* it. He did, now.

"The Keeper was aware of this?"

"No. And he looked about as happy at the mention of the word as you do now."

The Dragon Lord rose. "I believe," he told her quietly, "that we have now concluded the lessons for the day. I believe that I understand why you were so distracted."

He didn't. She had no intention of enlightening him.

"I will have to speak with your Sergeant, and with the Hawk-lord, before I leave. You will not speak to anyone else about this without Imperial permission."

"The Hawklord?"

"I have just said that *I* will speak with the Hawklord." He walked to the door, opened it, and then turned back, his robes swirling like liquid at his feet. "But I believe you should check your duty roster carefully in the next few days."

"Sanabalis—"

"And it is just possible that I may be able to barter for a delay in your etiquette lessons, although the time is coming when they will be sorely needed."

CHAPTER 5

The lesson had ended early.

It was too much to hope that this meant an hour and a half of downtime, but Kaylin sat, slightly slumped in one of the heavy but uncomfortable chairs by the table, staring at an unlit candle anyway. One of the advantages of this particular set of classes was that she got paid for attending them. Well, that and she got to live. She folded her elbows across the table and stared at her blurry reflection.

Ravellon.

She had never really thought much about what lay at the heart of the fiefs. Growing up in Nightshade, there had been Nightshade and the rest of the world, and only one part of the world had captured her thought and attention: the city across the bridge. Of course, in her daydreams, she'd been somehow rich and pretty and free from fear or insecurity because she knew she *belonged* on the right side of the river boundary.

That kind of transformation had, no surprise, failed to happen. But the transformation that had happened, over seven long years, had the advantage of being—until yesterday—*real.*

Idiot. Think.

What, in the heart of the fiefs, could upset the elements? She knew what upset the Dragons, of course: the only living Outcaste Dragon Lord. Kaylin had faced him twice; the first time, he had retreated; the second time? He had broken her arm. She hadn't seen what had happened after she'd fallen.

But if he were dead, she thought the word *Ravellon* would have no power to disturb Sanabalis. Given how often Kaylin had tried—admittedly when she'd reached the edge of screaming frustration, and was trying very hard not to pick up one of the heavy-duty chairs and crush the damn candle that *would not light*—the fact that he was disturbed was contagious. It unsettled her.

She stared at the candle.

When the door opened at her back, she straightened her shoulders slightly, but didn't lift her head off her hands to see who was standing in it. If they wanted her, they'd let her know.

Marcus growled, and she vacated her chair so quickly it was a wonder her feet didn't leave the ground. "Sanabalis left—" she began. He growled again, and she shut up, quickly.

"*What* have you been doing *this time?*"

"Not lighting a candle?" And pushing her luck. His eyes were almost the same orange Sanabalis's had been, although Kaylin was certain it wasn't because of anything she'd done. Yet.

"Kitling."

She grimaced. "Evanton told me something when we dropped by his place yesterday."

"And you told Sanabalis." No honorific for him from Marcus today. Apparently bad moods spread like plagues.

"You know the Emperor has Evanton's shop under constant surveillance," she continued, in her own defense. "Someone probably reported it to the Emperor, or the Imperial Service, and the Emperor told Sanabalis to ask me." Seeing his expression she added, "I'm not an idiot. I am *not* standing between Evanton and the Emperor. What the Emperor wants, he gets." Besides which, technically, the Emperor paid her.

Marcus covered his eyes, briefly, with his hands. His claws, Kaylin noted, were extended; she wondered how much damage he'd done to his desk. "Sanabalis said something to you?"

"Yes."

She winced; that would be a lot of damage. A tone that cold could freeze blood. She wanted it to be someone else's. "W-what did he say?"

"I am not at liberty to discuss it."

This was code for "Ask Caitlin." Kaylin nodded. "Is he still here?"

"Speaking with the Hawklord."

"Oh." She waited, and after a moment, he growled again.

"They're waiting for you in the Hawklord's tower. I was sent to find you." She nodded and headed for the door. Which he was still standing in. "Kitling, *try* to stay out of trouble."

"I always try."

"Try harder."

The office was not dead silent, which meant that Marcus hadn't gone fur ball while speaking with Sanabalis. But it wasn't exactly a bustle of conversation and gossip, either, and Kaylin felt every eye—with the exception of Joey and Timar's, because they were engaged in a heated debate about something that was probably more interesting when you couldn't actually hear the words—follow her as she made her way to the stairs.

She was a little bit tired of winning money for other people, and that wasn't about to change anytime soon; she could practically hear bets being placed behind her back. Ignoring this was hard; it was almost like ignoring decent food. But not even Kaylin kept the Hawklord waiting because of office betting, which he generally overlooked or ignored if it wasn't shoved under his nose by a weasel like Mallory.

She mounted the stairs slowly, remembering the first time she'd come to the Tower.

She had watched it for days. She'd timed the opening and closing of the dome, and the infrequent aerial activities of the

Aerian officers. It was easy to see the Hawklord leaving the Halls of Law; he didn't use the halls or the front stairs. The dome opened. He flew. But he didn't seem to fly on schedule.

That was why she watched. She told herself that. She even believed it. The part of her that saw the Aerians and thought them—yes—beautiful? It stayed silent. But it had been there. It was still there now—but not even the Aerians tried to fly up these stairs. They couldn't fully extend their wings here. When they came to the Tower by ground, they climbed like the rest of the wingless, gravity-bound Hawks.

She remembered, as she climbed, the way she'd watched the Aerians in flight. The way they seemed to rise above life and its ugly concerns, and soar on thermals, weapons gleaming sharply and sporadically as they caught sunlight. There were, as far as she knew, no Aerians in Nightshade or Barren. If there had been, their wings would have been clipped adornments, no more; nothing but small birds flew in that sky.

Small birds, she thought, remembering the Outcaste Dragon Lord, and Dragons. Of the two, she had a strong preference for the birds. But her preference in Nightshade mattered about as much as it always had. And in Barren?

She hadn't cared. Not about birds. Not about Dragons. Not about anything, really. Strange that it was Barren, in the end, that had brought her here. Here, where the stairs were familiar, and the routine, familiar, as well. Where she had enough to eat—on most days—and a roof over her head. She had a family in the Hawks, and in their fanged Sergeant. She had a job that she could actually take pride in.

She'd had no stairs, the first time. And no invitation, either, if you could consider Marcus's curt and growly command an invitation. But then again, if you timed things right, the *dome* had no hand-wards to pass through, and no hand-wards to set off an alarm.

Today, however, she was out of luck. The doors were closed. Gritting her teeth, she lifted her palm and placed it firmly against the magical ward. She felt the usual brief explosion beneath her hand; it left no mark, but it was very, very unpleasant. The Hawks had told her, in her early days here, that most people didn't even notice the magical effect of the doorwards. It had taken her two weeks to believe that they weren't having a good laugh at her expense.

The doors rolled open.

The Hawklord and Lord Sanabalis stood in the center of the chamber; they were both watching the doors. Sanabalis's eyes were an unfortunate shade of bronze. She couldn't quite see the color of the Hawklord's.

"Private Neya," the Hawklord said, inclining his head. His wings, she noted, were *mostly* folded at his back. Which probably meant they were an ounce of irritation from spreading. This was an indication that good behavior was required.

She saluted sharply, and then stood at attention. For some reason, this seemed to irk Sanabalis; the Hawklord, however, accepted it as his due.

"Lord Sanabalis has voiced some concerns over an incident that occurred during your patrol yesterday."

"Sir," she replied.

"I would like to know if you feel his concern is unfounded."

She always hated the trick questions. Which would be any question which clearly had a right answer—one that wasn't immediately obvious to her. On the other hand, not answering was not an option. She glanced at Sanabalis, which was helpful only in the sense that it was clear that her answer was bound to annoy one of them.

"No, sir."

He held her gaze for a few seconds too long. "Unfortunate," he finally said. This was said in the tone of voice that was generally followed with a dismissal. He did not, however, dismiss her. Instead, as if she weren't in the room, he turned back to Sanabalis.

"Your point is taken," the Hawklord said. "However, at present, Private Neya is not the ideal candidate for your investigation. I would suggest," he added, in a tone of voice that made clear to

Kaylin that this was not the first time in their discussion he had done so, "that you approach the Wolflord."

"If you feel that it is wise to partner Private Neya with a Wolf," Sanabalis replied.

Kaylin, standing at attention, wanted to turn and crawl out of the doors.

"Out of the question."

Or the windows. It would probably be less painful, in the end.

Forty minutes—and a lot of verbal fencing—later, Sanabalis left. Dragons were heavy, and as Sanabalis was not perhaps entirely satisfied with the conclusion of the discussion, he didn't bother to pick up his feet; she could feel his passage across the floor. She was not, however, dismissed; the Hawklord stood in perfect silence until the Tower doors closed—loudly—on the retreating Dragon Lord.

Only then did Lord Grammayre relax. If that was the right word for it.

"He wants me to go to the fiefs, doesn't he?" Since that much was obvious, the Hawklord failed to reply. The question would be filed under "wasting his time," which was never the smartest thing to do.

In spite of herself, Kaylin continued. "It wouldn't be the first time I've been sent to the fiefs." But she remembered the first time, because it was also the first time she'd laid eyes on Severn in seven years. In this Tower, in the presence of this man.

His wings now did unfold, until they were at half height, but full extension.

"For the moment, I would prefer that you do not enter the fiefs." His gaze grazed her cheek and Nightshade's mark.

She frowned. "Why?"

And he raised a pale, graying brow. "I spoke, briefly, with Corporal Handred this morning. He seemed to suspect that a request of this nature would be forthcoming, and he seemed to feel it exceptionally unwise."

She didn't ask him why. But she understood now why the conversation with Sanabalis had gone the way it had. She was torn between anger at Severn and a bitter gratitude and, as usual, couldn't decide on the spot which to choose. But she had nothing, in the end, to hide from the Hawklord.

He seemed to expect her to say something.

"Marcus looked pissed off," was what she managed.

"I imagine that *Sergeant Kassan* is not greatly pleased." He walked over to the long, oval mirror that stood a few feet from the wall. As mirrors went, it was definitely more cramped than the mirrors in the rooms the Hawks used for real work, but it was taller and wider than any reflective surface in the office downstairs. He lifted a hand and touched its surface.

Records could generally be called up by voice; hand activation was rare, and only partly because it left fingerprints which some poor sod then had to clean up.

But Kaylin had some idea of why he used touch, here. Some of the records were keyed not to voice, which was relatively easy to mimic, but to physical artifacts and aura, which were not. The reflective surface stirred and rippled, distorting the view it held of the domed Tower and the man who ruled the Hawks in the Emperor's name.

When the image reformed, it was still the same view of the Tower, but it contained, instead of the reflection of the Hawklord, a reflection of Kaylin Neya.

Kaylin at thirteen.

She wore dark clothing, a wide strip of cloth across her forehead and another across her lower jaw; her arms carried yards of thin, strong chain links, looped as if they were rope. Metal pitons dangled from the ends; she could hear them hit one another so clearly she might still have been wearing them.

"What do you see?" he asked her softly. "When you look at this girl?"

She stopped herself from cringing, which was hard, and from squinting, which was easy; the latter could be accomplished by simply stepping toward the mirror itself. "Someone stupid enough to climb the Tower walls," she finally said, making the effort to keep her voice even. This close to the mirror, she examined the girl as if she were a stranger. "You've never showed me this before."

"No."

She wasn't much taller now than she'd been then. She wasn't as scrawny. But what struck her, looking at herself, were the eyes. "She—she doesn't look like she has a lot to live for."

He nodded quietly.

"You never told me why," Kaylin said, as the Hawklord touched the mirror again, and the image broke and vanished, her younger self trapped in permanent, private records, and hidden from all external view.

The Hawklord said nothing. But it was a quiet nothing, and it radiated no irritation or disapproval.

"Why didn't you send me—send me away?"

"One day, Kaylin, if the answer is not obvious, I will tell you. But not today. Lord Sanabalis has offered to attempt—and *attempt* is the correct word—to delay your etiquette lessons. I am not entirely certain however that he will succeed."

She grimaced.

"And I do not feel that a delay of any kind is in your best interests."

She felt her brows rise, and tried to pull them down.

"The Emperor is aware of you," he continued, "as you well know. It is only a matter of time before you are called to Council. The matter of time," he added softly, "is unfortunately not dependent on those lessons; it is coming. Ravellon." He shook his head, and his wings did rise. "What you did in Nightshade was necessary. What you did for the Leontines saved Sergeant Kassan, and possibly his wife.

"But what you saw there means that I will not be able to keep you from Court, and if the Keeper is correct, you will be needed. Sanabalis has spoken on your behalf in Court before, but you are progressing beyond his understanding—and the Arkon does not leave the palace. Sooner or later—and I think sooner likely—you will be asked to report to the Dragon Court's council.

"Without those lessons, it will not, I feel, go well. Even with Lord Sanabalis's intervention."

"Will you be able to keep me out of the fiefs?"

After a long pause, the Hawklord said, "Dismissed."

She met Marcus, who was on the way up, when she was on the way down. His eyes had not lost their orange tint, but he didn't ask her what had been discussed; instead he told her to go wait downstairs—quietly, if she even understood what that meant—and he headed up past her.

When she reached the office, she was surprised to see Sanabalis seated to one side of Marcus's desk. She was not surprised, on the other hand, to see that Marcus was a few weeks closer to needing a new desk. As buying a new desk for Marcus generally meant she was allowed to haggle as fiercely as she wanted, she didn't mind the latter so much.

But Sanabalis inclined his head toward the second, empty, chair. She stood beside it. His eyes were almost the exact same shade Marcus's had been. "Lord Grammayre feels that, for some reason, it is inadvisable for you to enter the fiefs at this time."

Since that had been about forty minutes' worth of their discussion, he wasn't telling Kaylin anything she hadn't already heard. He did, on the other hand, say it more quietly.

"Is it true?"

She hesitated. She knew that the Emperor knew about her past. She would not be surprised if Sanabalis did. But the rest of the office *didn't* know, and she didn't particularly feel like sharing. Ever. She met the eyes of her teacher.

"I don't know."

This didn't appear to irritate him. On the other hand, his eyes didn't shift color.

"Very well," he said instead. "It appears that I will have to fall back somewhat on contingencies."

★ ★ ★

The afternoon was spent patrolling with Severn. Marcus, in a foul mood, played switch-the-shifts-around; it was a game that was *bound* to give him someone to growl at. It was also a great unifier on the force: everyone complained. Everyone hated it. Marcus tended to spread a foul mood as far as it would go; he'd had a lot of practice, so it was pretty damn far.

The switch in shifts put Kaylin squarely in the market district, where trouble—if it came—would be in the form of petty thieves and annoyed merchants. It was about as far away from magic as she could geographically get in the city, although the market, like Elani, had its share of fraud.

She'd taken the time to check the schedule, and she knew that Teela and Tain were out on the streets, as well; it would keep them out of trouble. In particular, it would keep them out of *her* trouble. She tried not to dwell on Morse and Barren.

She mostly succeeded because she was hungry, and because Severn didn't ask her any questions. He didn't speak much at all.

But when they arrived back at the Halls at the end of the day, Kaylin ran into Sanabalis's contingency plan. Almost literally.

Lord Tiamaris of the Dragon Court was standing just around the corner, near Caitlin's desk. He was wearing the Hawks' tunic.

He nodded to Severn; Severn had taken the corner at a slow walk. "Private," he added, turning to Kaylin.

She said nothing for a long minute, looking across Caitlin's desk. Caitlin winced. "Lord Tiamaris was sent," Caitlin told her quietly, "by the Eternal Emperor." Which meant no help would be forthcoming from any quarter.

Tiamaris nodded; he did not look terribly pleased about it, either.

"Why are you here?" Kaylin asked, coming to the immediate point.

"I think you'll find, if you check your duty roster, that I am to accompany you on your patrols for the next several days."

Severn stiffened, but said nothing.

She glanced across the office at Marcus, who was not looking at her.

"I don't suppose those patrols are bordering the fiefs?"

"Not bordering, no."

She cursed Sanabalis roundly in all of the languages in which it was possible. Tiamaris made no comment, which for Tiamaris meant about the same thing.

Morning, never Kaylin's friend, landed through the window in her face. She rose, started to reflexively close the shutters, and then groaned and opened them wider instead. This hurt her eyes, but her eyes could just suffer; she had a winning streak of on-time days she didn't want to break. Money was, of course, riding on it. Although the betting did concern her, she'd been allowed in. It had taken some whining. But whining about money was beginning to come naturally.

Tiamaris was waiting for her when she reached the office. He was seated primly in one of Marcus's chairs. Marcus was seated, far less primly, across from him, his increasingly untidy desk the bastion between them. The Hawks' Sergeant was never going to be friendly to Tiamaris. Tiamaris, himself not Mr. Personality, seemed to take this in stride.

Kaylin understood *why* Marcus was so frosty; Tiamaris had voted, in Court Council, to have her killed outright. But that had been *years* ago, and it had occurred well before Tiamaris had actually met her; if *she* was willing to let bygones be bygones, Marcus should be able to do the same. She was not, however, foolhardy enough to tell Marcus this. Not today.

She approached his desk as if she were a timid tax collector who had the misfortune to leave her burly guards outside. He glanced at her as if she were the same thing. "Reporting for duty," she told him.

He grimaced, gritted his teeth, and waited for the window's mellifluous hourly phrase. She could hear his claws grinding desktop as the window told the office what the hour was, and demanded that they be polite, friendly, and collegial at the start of this busy, busy day.

Tiamaris raised a dark brow. "That," he told them both, "could be irritating."

"Enraging," Kaylin replied quietly.

"I assume it's magically protected?"

She nodded.

He shook his head. "You must have angered someone, Private Neya."

"It's a long list."

"Don't," Marcus told her curtly, "add me to it, Private."

She stood at attention.

"Given what happened the last time you went into the fiefs," he told her grimly, "I am on record as opposing this investigation."

"Sir."

He said nothing for a long moment. Then he stood, scraping his chair across the floorboards loudly enough to break most conversations. "Your partner for the duration of this investigation will be Lord Tiamaris of the Dragon Court."

She nodded.

"You will investigate the borders of Nightshade, with special attention to the interior." He *was* in a mood. His Elantran was strained enough that his words had a distinctly—and angrily— Leontine cast to them. "If anything is out of the ordinary—" he also spit this word out in outrage "—you are to take note and report it immediately. The report will come to *this* office."

"Sir."

"Dismissed."

She glanced at Tiamaris, who hadn't moved.

On cue, Marcus looked at him. "Off the record," he told the Dragon Lord, although it was highly unlikely to remain that way, "I will hold you personally responsible if Private Neya is returned to the infirmary on a stretcher again. I understand the concerns of the Dragon Caste Court, but whatever else she might be, she is *not* a Dragon, and the Caste Court's laws and concerns, unless specifically made public, are *not* the concerns of the Halls of Law. Do I make myself clear?"

"As clear as good glass," Tiamaris replied. He did rise, then.

Severn was waiting by the office doors. He held out one hand as she passed him, and she frowned.

"What?"

"Bracer," he said quietly.

She glanced at her wrist, and shook her head. "If I remove it here," she told him quietly, "Marcus will rip out someone's throat. Or try. It always comes back to you; if I need to remove it, I'll remove it by the Ablayne and toss it in." The bracer was not an optional piece of equipment; it was mandatory. It confined Kaylin's magic. She even did most of her lessons with Sanabalis wearing it, although when he was frustrated, he had her remove it and lay it on the table beside the offending, and unlit, candle.

Severn laughed, then. It was one of Kaylin's favorite things to do with the bracer, when she was in a mood. Because it was ancient and because no one understood how it functioned—or at least that was the official story—no one knew why it chose a Keeper; it had chosen, not Kaylin, but Severn. When she tossed it in the river, it appeared—sometimes dripping—in Severn's home. He told her it was making the carpets moldy.

"I don't think we're going to run into any trouble. Not in Nightshade."

He said nothing, and she lifted her hand to the mark on her cheek. He glanced away, then turned and caught her wrist. "Stay in Nightshade, Kaylin."

The only way she now lied to Severn was by omission. She said nothing until he let her wrist go. But when he did, she leaned forward and kissed his cheek. "I'll be careful," she told him. "Please don't threaten Tiamaris."

He raised a brow.

"Oh, please, do if it will amuse you," the slightly irritated Dragon Lord added. "I'm collecting threats today." He paused. "But for the sake of variety, attempt to be either more dire—or more original—than one Dragon Lord, one Leontine, and one Aerian."

Kaylin winced. "I'm not a child," she told Tiamaris stiffly. "I don't know why—"

"I do," was his grim reply. "And while I would like to discuss the relative states of our respective maturity, I would like to do it from the safety of the other side of the Ablayne."

"Safety?" Kaylin muttered as she lengthened her stride as far as it would go and still failed to match Tiamaris's headlong walk.

"The Halls of Law have no purchase in the fiefs," was his reply. "There, they only have an Outcaste Barrani, an Outcaste Dragon, and a handful of overly ambitious ferals."

The sun had completely cleared the horizon when Tiamaris and Kaylin reached the bridge that crossed the Ablayne into Nightshade. Kaylin had never quite understood *why* the Emperor allowed the bridge, which was clearly in decent repair, to remain standing. While it was true that people did cross it, it was also true that some of those people went in the wrong direction, just as Kaylin and Tiamaris were now doing.

This was not the only bridge across the river, of course; it was not even the only bridge out of the fiefs that Kaylin had ever crossed. But it had defined many of her early dreams in the fief of Nightshade, and she always approached it as if it were a doorway between the present and the past. She did so now, but she was aware that Tiamaris, who had slowed enough to allow her forced jog to keep up, had had no such dreams.

"What are we looking for?" she asked Tiamaris.

He glanced at her, and then slowed to a walk, as if the weight of the bridge's symbolism had finally reached his feet. "Borders," he told her quietly. "I know that Evanton is known to you as something other than the Keeper, but his words—if you relayed them with any accuracy—are significant to the Eternal Emperor. They would be significant, as well, to any of the fief lords."

"You want to talk to Nightshade." She turned and after a pause, rested her elbows on the rails. Strands of dark hair curled gently around her cheeks as she bent over the river itself. It was never still; it reflected nothing.

He surprised her. "I want nothing from Nightshade, fief or Lord. I admit that I find the fief lord slightly…irritating. But he is not my Outcaste; he is Barrani."

"You just don't like his sword."

One glance at Tiamaris told her that she'd failed to annoy him; his eyes were still a lambent gold. The lower membranes were, however, raised. "I don't, as you quaintly put it, care for his sword, no. But he *is* Nightshade. And if the heart of the fiefs is contained at all, it is contained by the fiefs as they stand. What lies in Ravellon will not determine the shape—or strength—of Nightshade's border while Lord Nightshade rules.

"And nothing you say, or do here, will change that fact. I am not here, nor was I sent here, to speak with Lord Nightshade."

"Then what—"

"The Keeper's message was, in its entirety, yours. I am here," he told her, "to act as your guard should the need arise. That is my only function at the present time. If you feel it is wise or germane, you will travel to Lord Nightshade's castle, and you will speak with him; if you feel it is neither, you will not. I will go where you go."

"Yes," she told him, after a long pause. "Nightshade. If for no other reason than that we'll be nosing around his fief on the edge of a border neither of us particularly wants to see again." She glanced at him, and then headed down the slope of the bridge. "You know he'd send word if the Outcaste Dragon came anywhere near Nightshade."

"He has not historically proven himself to be entirely aware of the Outcaste," was the slightly cool reply.

"He doesn't have to be. It's in his interests to have the two of you fight; it saves him both time and the effort of finding new men."

When he glanced at her pointedly, she shrugged. "Well," she said, kicking a small stone, "it makes sense to me."

CHAPTER 6

Lord Nightshade was waiting for them.

This surprised neither Kaylin nor Tiamaris. The small mark on Kaylin's cheek, which was regularly mistaken as a tattoo by anyone who wasn't Barrani or hadn't been racially warring with them for way too many years, was in fact his mark. Kaylin was still hazy on the details of what, exactly, it signified, but she understood two things about it: removing it would generally involve removing her head, and it acted as a conduit, in some ways, between Kaylin and the Lord of the fief of Nightshade.

She generally went out of her way not to think about the rest.

Lord Nightshade was not, of course, considerate enough to wait *outside* Castle Nightshade. This meant that both Kaylin and Tiamaris—the latter with somewhat chilly, if respectful, permission from the Barrani guards—were forced to enter the castle through its nefarious and much-cursed portal. The portal looked very much like a lowered portcullis. It wasn't. It was a magical gate that led directly into the front foyer of the Castle, in which Nightshade greeted his guests.

Unfortunately for Kaylin, her sensitivity to magic made the passage extremely disorienting and difficult, and she usually ended up on the other side on her hands and knees, trying very hard not to throw up. Today was, sadly, no exception.

Tiamaris never seemed remotely fazed by the transition—but he was a Dragon; you could probably cut off one of his arms with a nail file and he wouldn't do more than grimace. He was, however, accustomed to Kaylin's vastly less-dignified entrance, and bent to offer her a hand when she at last lifted her head. She only did this when the room had stopped spinning.

Lord Nightshade was waiting at a polite distance. He nodded as she gained her feet. "Kaylin," he said, inclining his head. "Lord Tiamaris."

"Lord Nightshade." The Dragon Lord extended the fief lord a precise bow. He didn't hold it long, but it was in tone and texture a very correct one.

"I was expecting you," Lord Nightshade told Kaylin softly, "a day ago."

She grimaced. She certainly hadn't expected to end up here, but her life was like that.

After a pause, Lord Nightshade turned and indicated, with the gesture of a hand, that they were to follow. Her knees still slightly wobbling, she did; it didn't pay to lag behind Nightshade in this castle. The halls had a tendency to change direction—and orientation—for anyone who wasn't their Lord. She glanced at Tiamaris. Their Lord, she added to herself, or a very stubborn Dragon.

It always surprised Kaylin that the Lord of Nightshade could value the quiet and graceful austerity of simple flowers, but they rested in tall, slender vases in small alcoves along the hall; light touched them, some of it glancing from windows recessed in the ceiling. While the outside of the Castle resembled some ancient keep, with arrow slits instead of windows, and manned walls instead of galleries, the inside was another story. A long, complicated one.

She expected Nightshade to lead them into one of the rooms

in which he chose to entertain visitors; he often had food and wine waiting.

Today, however, he led them to a different room. She recognized it. She didn't recognize the halls that led to it, but she'd long since given up expecting to be able to do so; this was Castle Nightshade, and all the observation in the world wouldn't make it mundane enough to become familiar.

The room was adorned with mirrors.

Mirrors, in the Empire, were the heart of its communication system. Oh, they were also used for more mundane purposes of vanity, or at least personal grooming, but the lesser use was not significant here. Then again, it was probably never significant to the Barrani, who seemed to ooze grace and elegance no matter what they were wearing.

Teela had once tried on some of Kaylin's clothing; it had been entirely disheartening. For one, it shouldn't have fit. And it didn't. But even shortened as it was by Teela's much taller frame, it had looked instantly spectacular. Kaylin tried to imagine Nightshade standing in front of a mirror and straightening the fall of his robes, tunic or cloak. She gave up.

Tiamaris, however, used the reflective surfaces of the mirrors to raise a brow in Kaylin's direction. She grimaced, and replied with a very slight shrug.

"You are aware that there is some difficulty in the fiefs," Lord Nightshade said quietly.

They both looked at his reflection, meeting his gaze that way.

"We were aware," Kaylin replied quietly, "that there was the possibility of difficulty." When he raised a brow in her direction, she added, "We're not living here. We don't know."

"But you are here," he told her softly.

She nodded. "It was either come here or attempt to cross the borders into a different fief." Drawing breath, she added, "Ravellon."

His hand fell reflexively to the hilt of his sword and rested there. "Why do you speak that name?"

"It was spoken to me. Well, written."

His expression didn't change at all, but something about him stiffened; she felt something that was not exactly fear, but close. Seeing the lines of his face, she knew that Tiamaris wouldn't notice it; it wasn't obvious to anyone who did not, in the end, hold his name.

No, he told her softly. *But from you, I can hide little if you choose to notice. You seldom so choose.*

"Has there been trouble in Nightshade?" she asked, avoiding any answer to the hidden, the intimate, voice.

He hesitated. This hesitation, even Tiamaris could mark. "There have been no unusual occurrences in the fief," he replied. "No increase in the number of ferals, and no…other…encroachments."

Something about his answer was wrong.

"No deaths?"

"There have been," he told her, with deliberate coolness, "the usual number of deaths. They are not zero, but they are not worthy of remark or note."

For just a moment, her jaw clenched. So did her fists. On a day over seven years ago, two of those deaths had driven her from Nightshade. It was hard not to speak, but she swallowed the words, almost choking on them. Rage, when it blind-sided her, did that.

She almost missed the cold curve of his lips. He was smiling. It was a very Barrani smile. The rage drained from her, then. What was left was cold.

We are what we are, he told her.

It was true. She endeavored to be a professional. "What, exactly, have you noticed?"

"The difficulty is not within my fief," he replied.

"You don't exactly pay social calls to the other fiefs." So much for professional.

He raised one brow. Tiamaris was silent, but it was the silence of sudden watchfulness. "Indeed," Lord Nightshade finally said. The Dragon, on the other hand, didn't relax much. "But Nightshade is bordered by three fiefs. Or perhaps more; we count the interior as one, and that may be erroneous."

He lifted one hand and the images in the mirror—admittedly somewhat mundane for the Castle, given that two of them were Hawks—rippled and vanished in a moving silver swirl. When that swirl stilled, the surface of the mirrors no longer offered reflections. Instead, laid out like a very intricate map, she saw the boundaries of the fief of Nightshade.

It didn't even feel like home.

To the south, the city in which Kaylin served the Dragon Emperor lay across the narrow bridge; the Ablayne ran along the whole of that boundary, and beyond. That much, she recognized. She waited for him to speak.

"To the east," he said quietly, "Liatt." He hesitated, and glanced at Tiamaris. She felt the way Nightshade considered hoarding words, hoarding information, but in the end, he chose to speak. He always chose his words with care; the decision was merely between those words and silence. "Liatt is ruled by a woman; in seeming she is as human as...Corporal Handred. She holds the Tower of Liatt, and it is from that Tower that she rules. To the west—"

"Wait." Kaylin lifted a hand. "You've met her?"

"Oh, yes," he said softly. "But as you say, the fief lords do not pay social visits."

"When you say human in seeming—"

"She is mortal."

Kaylin nodded, and apologized for the interruption, which caused Nightshade to raise a brow. This time, the smile that turned the corners of his lips up was not so cold, and not so cutting; it held no satisfaction. It did not, however, appreciably change the lines of his face.

"To the west," he said softly, watching her face, "is Barren."

She was silent for a full beat. "And Barren is ruled by?" she asked.

"Barren is purported to be ruled by a human male."

"Purported? You've never met him?"

"I may, indeed, have had that privilege."

"But you're not certain?"

"No."

"How can you be certain that you've met Liatt?"

"Liatt *is* Liatt," he replied softly. "Just as I am Nightshade."

Tiamaris cleared his throat. Dragons had a way of clearing the throat that made earthquakes seem mild; it wasn't a roar, but it implied that a roar might follow severe inattentiveness. What followed a roar was generally considered death, even by the optimistic.

On the other hand, the Barrani and the Dragons had had centuries—at the very least—in which to thumb their figurative noses at each other's subtle threats. Nightshade turned.

"Are you implying that the fief lord of Barren does not hold the fief?" the Dragon asked.

"He rules it," was the quiet reply. "But it has long been my suspicion that he is merely clever, canny, and adept."

"Merely?"

"He understands how to hold the territory he has claimed as his own. But it is a claim with no substance." He turned to Kaylin, lifted a hand, and trailed the tips of his fingers down her cheek. The mark glowed faintly as he touched it. "I knew Liatt," he told her softly, "because the fief knew Liatt. Barren's name had no such resonance." He let his hand fall away. "But my experience with the fief of either Liatt or Barren is small. Yours, however, might be more germane."

Words deserted her for a moment. She glanced at Tiamaris; she couldn't help it. If he was surprised by Nightshade's words, the surprise didn't show. She wondered if he was, or if he knew. He was part of the Dragon Court.

The mirrors rescued her; Nightshade gestured, and the view zoomed in, losing the boundaries of Liatt and Elantra.

"Lord Tiamaris understands," Nightshade said softly.

Kaylin, frustrated, tried not to grind her teeth. Tiamaris had a head start of possibly a few centuries of experience and knowledge—but she resented being the person who had no clue.

Then learn, Nightshade told her.

"Hold that image," Tiamaris said, above the quiet, private words.

The image froze.

"Kaylin, did Barren have more of a problem with ferals than Nightshade? Do you recall?"

She hesitated for a moment, and then nodded. "The fief had more of a problem with both ferals and the occasional other creature. It was why most of Barren's men were stationed near the border. The interior border," she added.

"You saw this?"

"No. I was told. I didn't visit the fief lord at night. None of us did." She drew a sharp, cutting breath. "I was thirteen, Tiamaris. It was for six months. I wasn't—in any way—capable of becoming one of his lieutenants. Not then. What I have is rumor, and a bit of experience. It's not a lot to judge a fief by."

"But the ferals, at least?"

She nodded, thoughtful now. "Have you met the other fief-lords?" she asked Nightshade.

"No. I have met only those whose borders touch mine. There is some blurring, although it is not extreme." His smile was cool. "Why?"

"You said Liatt ruled from the Tower. *The* Tower?"

He nodded. "As I rule from the Castle."

Tiamaris failed to hear the exchange. He had walked up to the mirror, and he now examined the image in some detail. "How long?" he asked Nightshade.

Nightshade did not pretend to misunderstand him. "The current fief lord of Barren has ruled for ten years. Perhaps nine. They are mortal years, in the reckoning of Elantra."

"How?"

"I am not privy to even rumor. But the former fief lord—Illien—was not human. The fief lost its name along the border. I do not hear it."

"But you hear Liatt?" Kaylin asked.

"When I touch the boundaries of my realm, I hear Liatt."

"Would I?"

"You, perhaps. Lord Tiamaris would not."

She didn't ask him why, but she touched the mark upon her cheek almost reflexively.

"Was Illien alive?"

Nightshade said nothing.

"Ten years," Tiamaris said softly. "I would have said that was impossible. Ten years of rule without—" He shook his head, drawing the words back before they were spoken. Kaylin successfully fought the urge to slap him. "The borders here—can you magnify them? They are not clear."

"No, Lord Tiamaris, they are not. As I said—and as I imagine you suspect—the boundaries between fiefs are somewhat unstable. What the mirrors show you now is what *I* see. Do you understand?"

The Dragon Lord offered the fieflord a very graceful nod. "You honor us."

"It is expedient for me to do so at this time. It is also," Nightshade added, "no risk to me. What I see, you cannot see without my aid, and could you, you could do nothing with it while I lived." His smile was slight and cool.

"But here—"

"Yes. I see more and less clearly than I would otherwise see if Barren was stable. But what you see along the blurred edge is accurate. The shadows of the interior have changed shape over even the past decade. They have been on the move—slowly—into the fief of Barren."

Kaylin frowned.

"You've had word from the fieflord of Barren, have you not?" Nightshade asked her softly.

She glanced at Tiamaris, who didn't seem to be surprised, and gave up. "Yes. But I didn't understand why. And I still don't understand why *now*." The words sank into the silence that followed them. "It's gotten worse," she said, voice flat. "Recently."

Lord Nightshade said, "It has, as you guess, recently become much more unstable."

"Do you know why?"

"No. The interior is completely invisible to both my magic and my information network."

"Do you *think* it has something to do with the Outcaste Dragon?"

"He was injured, when he retreated from our previous encounter," Nightshade replied, his voice completely neutral. "The injuries he sustained were not insignificant, and unless he were capable of healing them quickly—" his tone made clear that he thought it highly unlikely "—it is doubtful, to me."

She slid her hands to her hips, and then let them fall back to her side. "Nightshade, please—"

"When the tainted Leontines ran into the heart of the fiefs," he told her softly, "it is just possible that their need and their voices woke something that should *not* have been woken. This is conjecture, on my part, no more, and for that reason I am hesitant to offer it."

She swallowed. "I–it can't be them." The shakiness of her words failed to convince even Kaylin, and she'd *said* them. She looked at Tiamaris.

The Dragon Lord said, quietly, "The Eternal Emperor and the Dragon Court have decreed that the child of the tainted is not to be killed. They will not destroy him when they receive word of Lord Nightshade's conjecture, Kaylin. That much, your service has bought the infant."

That much, Kaylin thought. She tried to ignore her fear, but fear was hard that way. Swallowing it, she turned back to the mirror. Wondering what might wake in the shadows and the darkness of something that had looked, at first glance, like the rest of the city.

"Tiamaris, what happens if Barren somehow falls?"

"Falls?"

"If the shadows—if the heart of the fief—somehow expands to fill it?"

"You've lived in Nightshade," was his quiet reply. "Your life was informed, in some ways, by the presence of those shadows, whether you knew it or not. The Emperor will hold the city," he continued, after a pause.

Lord Nightshade raised a brow, but did not comment.

"But it will know ferals, and possibly worse. The Imperial Palace is not what Castle Nightshade is."

"The High Halls—"

"The *Barrani* High Halls," Tiamaris said.

She winced.

"You see the difficulty."

She did. But she plowed on, regardless. "Could the High Halls hold out against the—the shadows?"

"Almost certainly, given the change in rulership. But it *will not* happen while the Eternal Emperor still breathes. He will not surrender an inch of his established domain to the Barrani."

Lord Nightshade nodded. "I can enter Barren," he told her quietly. "But it is not, then, safe for Nightshade. Not now; there is already too much instability and too much weakness."

She had lived most of her life under Nightshade's rule. In no way could she call it either just or fair. But the shadows—in the fiefs, and under the High Halls—would be far, far worse, and she accepted this. Because, she thought bitterly, she lived on the *outside,* where his law and his casual cruelty had no purchase. For just a moment, the bitterness of that hypocrisy caused her throat to thicken. She swallowed it, anyway. Time to move on.

"What borders Barren on the other side?"

"Understand that what I tell you is not fact in the way that Liatt is fact; the fief does not border *me.* But if information gathered in the fiefs in the usual way can be trusted, Candallar."

"Will Candallar hold?"

Nightshade said nothing. It was not helpful.

Tiamaris bowed to Nightshade. "I must leave," he told the fief lord.

Nor did the fief lord appear surprised by the abrupt announcement. "Will you allow the Private to remain for a few moments?"

"I cannot leave without her; the orders I were given were quite…explicit."

This, too, did not appear to surprise Nightshade. Kaylin felt his amusement, but also his annoyance; they were almost perfectly balanced. His eyes, however, were the emerald green of Barrani calm, with perhaps a hint of blue to deepen the color. "Then escort her," he told Tiamaris. "She will return." He offered the briefest of bows to the Dragon Lord. "The information I can surrender in safety, I will. If anything changes along the borders, I will inform Private Neya; she may then inform the Emperor."

Tiamaris nodded and turned to leave the room, but Lord Nightshade had not quite finished. "Kaylin."

"Yes?"

"I will not surrender you to Barren."

Tiamaris did not run back to the bridge. Dragon dignity was good for something. He did, however, walk *quickly,* and the difference in their relative strides meant that Kaylin's dignity had to suffer; she had to jog to keep up. Only when they had crossed the bridge itself—with a distant crowd of witnesses who were too curious to clear the streets and too damn smart to approach—did he turn.

"We go to the palace," he told her.

She nodded; she'd expected that much.

"You are not yet relieved of your duty for the day. Accompany me."

She nodded again, not that he noticed. "Tiamaris—" she began, as he stepped into the street.

He failed to hear her, which was probably deliberate. Dragons didn't flag a carriage down; they simply stood in the way and waited for it to stop. This was, in Kaylin's experience, a risky proposition, but on the other hand, Dragons were built in such a way that if the risk played out poorly it didn't exactly kill them.

"Tiamaris," Kaylin said, as she climbed into the cab, "if you're going to make a habit of this, station an Imperial carriage by the bridge."

He ignored her advice.

"I mean it. We have enough trouble with the Swords as is—I

don't need to file a counterreport to explain a small riot or a large panic if we don't luck out with a decent driver."

When they reached the palace gates, guards met the cab. They didn't lead it into the courtyard, but they did clear the path as Tiamaris emerged. His eyes were a shade of orange that looked a little too deep, and none of the Imperial guards could fail to understand what that meant, but just in case, he lowered his inner membranes, so the color was much more pronounced. If they noticed his tabard—or Kaylin's—they failed to be offended by it.

She followed Tiamaris into the Great Hall, and then stopped as he lifted a hand. "Wait here," he told her quietly. "I go in haste to the Emperor, but even in haste, your poor understanding of Court etiquette would not be excused."

She started to argue because it was automatic, and snapped her jaw shut before the words left her mouth, settling in to wait. Waiting in *these* halls, with the stray glances of guards who were no doubt paid triple what she earned was a bit intimidating, but she didn't have to wait there long; Sanabalis emerged from the doors at the far end.

"Private," he said as he approached her, making clear what the tone—at least in front of the guards—would be, "please follow me."

She hesitated, aware that any other guard here wouldn't have.

"No," he added, when he noticed she wasn't immediately dogging his footsteps, "I am not leading you to either an execution or a meeting of the Imperial Court."

Since they would probably amount to the same thing, Kaylin relaxed and trailed behind the Dragon who was, truth be told, her favorite teacher, not that this said much. He led her to the rooms he used to meet with individuals, and she paused by the large, leaded windows that looked out at the Halls of Law. They seemed distant and remote to her, and she didn't like it.

"Lord Tiamaris has made a preliminary report," Sanabalis told her, as he sat heavily in an armchair designed to take the weight of a Dragon. "Some research is now being done by the Arkon, which may give you the luxury of a small break. I suggest," he added, gesturing at the food that had been laid out on the small round table in front of him, "that you use it."

The Arkon was the palace's version of a librarian. He was also the oldest Dragon at Court, and technically not called Lord, and his hoard *was* the library. Kaylin's understanding of the Dragon term *hoard* wasn't exact, but time had made clear that it meant "touch any of my stuff and die horribly."

She nodded and took the chair opposite Sanabalis. She even picked up the large sandwiches that had been made for her. Sanabalis never seemed to eat, and he deflected most of her questions about Dragon cuisine. Then again, he deflected most of her questions about Dragons, period, which was annoying because he was one, and could in theory be authoritative.

"Do you understand the significance of what Lord Nightshade revealed?" he asked her, coming to the point while she chewed. His tone of voice made clear that he expected the answer to be no.

She grimaced, wiping crumbs from the corners of her lips. "There's some strong connection between a fief and its Lord," she finally said.

He nodded.

"Liatt, a fief lord, rules the way Nightshade does. Barren doesn't."

"Do you understand why?"

"No. I'm not a fief lord. It's never been one of my life ambitions, even when I thought I'd live there forever." Seeing the stiffening lines of his face, which weren't all that significant, and the slight darkening of the gold of his eyes, which was, she added, "I can infer that there is a building in each fief that is similar to Castle Nightshade."

The color didn't exactly recede, but it didn't darken to orange. Sanabalis was not, by any stretch of the definition, in a good mood.

"If there's a building like that in Barren, Barren doesn't own it. He's not its Lord or its master."

"Did you know this?"

"Sanabalis—I was *thirteen*." She spread her hands, one of which was full of sandwich, in a gesture of self-defense. "I'd never been inside the Castle—how the hell was I supposed to know it was significant? It was where Nightshade lived; the only chance I was ever going to see it involved death by cage. In public."

"And in Barren?"

"More of the same," she said.

He said nothing for a long moment, and it was Kaylin who looked away. "Not the same," she said, and the food turned to ash in her mouth. "But I didn't know that Barren wasn't like Nightshade. I didn't know—" She stopped. Swallowed. "What I knew doesn't matter."

Sanabalis nodded, conceding the point. "Do you understand what alarmed Lord Tiamaris?"

She nodded. She did. "Barren is unstable," she said quietly. "And whatever lies at the heart of the fiefs isn't contained anymore. If we can't stabilize Barren—somehow—that will spill across the Ablayne."

"And into the Emperor's city, yes."

"But Barren's held it—"

"For ten years. Much longer," Sanabalis added softly, "than we would have suspected was possible. We don't know what's changed," he added, a note of warning in the words, "but something has."

"What are you going to do about it?"

He spread his hands across the knobs at the end of his armrests. "What am I going to do? At the moment, very little."

She snorted. "Fine. What am I going to do?"

"A more salient question. You are going to accompany Lord Tiamaris to the fiefs to investigate the difficulty. Think of how you're going to approach this," he added, as he rose. "If you require entry into Barren—"

Kaylin lifted a hand. "I know how I'll get in," she told him curtly. Then, trying to smooth the edge out of her voice, she added, "I have no idea how to do it with Tiamaris tagging along."

"Tiamaris," Sanabalis replied, "is not optional."

★ ★ ★

Sanabalis left her abruptly, but his departure wasn't the usual mystery; a Dragon roared, the palace shook, and when the tremors had died down, he was already out the door. She thought the voice sounded familiar, but it was hard to tell; the roar had momentarily deafened Kaylin.

She ate in silence, although she did so from the ledge of the window, watching the flags atop the Halls of Law. If she had sneered at those Halls as a child—and she must have, being a fiefling, although she honestly didn't remember it—she felt no similar disdain now; the Halls served a purpose. One only had to cross the Ablayne to see the effects of the districts beyond their reach. Yes, the law wasn't perfect; yes, its officers and representatives made mistakes.

But the alternative was so much worse. She'd lived it; she knew.

She had avoided the fiefs for over seven years now, approaching them solely at the request of her superiors in one Hall or another. It wasn't simply cowardice or distaste; it wasn't a desire to separate herself from her roots or her past. She was afraid of what the fiefs contained.

But if she let that fear govern her, unspoken and unacknowledged as it so often was, the fiefs would come to her. They would eat away at Barren, and if Barren himself deserved it, the people who eked out a miserable living in his fief probably didn't; they did—as Kaylin had done in Nightshade—what they needed to, to survive.

She couldn't judge them; didn't even want to. That wasn't her job.

The door opened, and she turned slowly to see Tiamaris—and the Arkon. Sanabalis, slightly shorter, stood behind them.

The Arkon lifted a slender, wrinkled hand. "Private Neya," he said.

She slid off the ledge, and offered him a full bow. If it wasn't a good bow, he didn't appear to notice. Neither did Sanabalis, but she could see that in his case, it took effort.

"I am prepared," the Arkon told her, as he entered the room, surveyed the chairs, and took the one Sanabalis habitually occupied, "to discuss Ravellon."

CHAPTER 7

Kaylin had once been warned not to ask the Arkon about Ravellon if she valued her life, or at least having all her limbs attached. She reminded herself that she hadn't asked as she took the nearest chair that would support her weight. Given the room was a hospitality suite for a Dragon Lord, that would be any of them.

"Lord Tiamaris, if you will be seated?" the Arkon said, in a tone of voice that made Marcus's commands seem polite and obsequious.

Tiamaris, in this, was Kaylin's superior; he apologized instantly for his inattentiveness, and he took his seat in perfect silence.

"Private Neya, it has come to my attention that you spent some time in Barren recently."

She opened her mouth. Tiamaris stepped lightly—for a Dragon—on her foot. "By *recently*, of course," Tiamaris told her, "the Arkon refers to anything that happened during the course of my lifetime."

"Oh."

The Arkon raised a white brow. "Understand that our knowledge of the fiefs is…incomplete. What understanding we have is not entirely reliable. The fiefs are not hospitable to those who are not their masters."

She nodded.

"Was our information accurate?"

"Yes. I was in Barren seven years ago." She spoke quietly, and without her usual confidence. "I don't know much about the fief that anyone who lives there every day wouldn't know." This was not entirely the truth, but it was enough of the truth, if you narrowed the definition of *everyone* slightly.

The Arkon didn't appear unduly suspicious. "Did you ever have cause to meet with the fief lord there?"

Her silence was more pronounced. But Dragons lived forever, absent things that were actively hostile; time meant less to them. "Yes. Yes, I met Barren."

"Good. What can you tell me about this fief lord?"

"What do you want to know?"

"Is he human?"

She nodded. "As human as I—as—"

His lips curved in a smile. "As human as most of the citizens of Elantra?"

"As that, yes. He was older than I was. He's probably forty now, maybe a little older. Possibly a little younger. The fiefs tend to age people."

"Where did he come from?"

"Come from?"

The Arkon glanced at Sanabalis. "I believe I asked the correct question?"

"Yes, Arkon."

"I—I don't know. He was the fief lord. I didn't exactly ask."

The Arkon frowned. "And he did not choose to enlighten you?" Even the Arkon could read the silence that followed his question. "Very well. The fief of Barren—as do all fiefs— border the heart of the fiefs themselves. We cannot pierce the shadows there," he added. "By any means save entering them.

The Aerians can fly over the edges, but in the center, flight falters."

"How do you know?"

"How do you think we know?"

She swallowed and thought of Clint. But she didn't ask more, mostly because she was afraid the answer would enrage her; she'd always loved the Aerian Hawks. "Why do you think they can't fly over the heart of the fiefs?" It was a safer question, as comment seemed expected.

His brows rippled slightly, but he didn't seem annoyed. "One of two possibilities exist. The first: that the heart is magically protected in some fashion, and in a way that defies the expedience of simple geography. It is not the explanation I favor," he added. "The second is slightly more complex. How far did you proceed in your studies on magical theory?"

When she failed to produce an answer, the brows rose again, but this time, the expression he offered was less benign. "You *have* studied magical theory? Sanabalis?" Clearly, the shock of her second nonanswer caused him to forget the nicety of something as simple as a title.

"Her studies in magical theory were not considered mandatory for a member of the groundhawks."

"It is hardly possible to have a conversation with someone who has no grounding in the basics. I might as well speak in my native tongue for all the good it will do."

"Indeed," Sanabalis replied.

"Alleviate the difficulty. You *are* teaching her, are you not?"

"Yes, Arkon."

Kaylin wilted visibly. She'd long since realized that there were whole days that did not reward getting out of bed; she thought it a bit unfair that whole weeks could also be like that. "Pretend I'm ignorant," she began.

"It hardly requires pretense," the Arkon replied stiffly.

Reminding herself that she liked her limbs attached, she swallowed. "Explain it anyway?"

He was very slow to relent, but did. "I am not responsible for your inability to understand," he told her. "And I therefore am not responsible for any questions that arise from your incomplete comprehension. Tiamaris may answer them in my absence."

"Arkon," Tiamaris replied.

"Very well. You have heard the world theory, yes?"

Sanabalis raised a brow. "I think it completely irrelevant to the Hawks and the Imperial Law. It is unlikely that she has been forced to study something considered that esoteric."

"Very well. There is, in theory, more than one world."

"More than one?"

The Arkon nodded.

"How many?"

Sanabalis winced. Clearly, this was not the right question.

"More than one. Right."

"Each world has a magical potential."

She nodded.

"And each world has a magical field, if you will, a level of power that permeates the whole. If our own studies are anything to go by, that level of power can fluctuate from place to place. Do you understand the concept of power lines or power grids?"

She wanted to nod, but she didn't. She could guess how amused the Arkon would be by a simple fib. She could also see that her silence had caused his eyes to shade into a dark bronze. Sometimes ignorance had its appeal.

"Sanabalis, I am entirely unamused."

"Arkon."

"Very well, Private Neya. Magical potential seems to form along lines; we are not certain why. Those lines can cross, and in some areas, they will form a grid, in some a knot. Those knots are areas in which magic, when it can be used at all, will be at its most potent. It will often also be at its most wild."

"Wild?"

"Sanabalis can explain that later. My time is valuable."

Hers, on the other hand, wasn't, at least if you went by pay scale. But she absorbed the words, made as much sense as she could of them, and then braved a question. "The buildings in the fiefs—like the Castle—are they on those knots?"

He raised a brow. "Very good. This may be less painful than I anticipated. Yes. They are, as you put it, on potential knots. The magic that defines the boundaries of a fief seem to follow lines that extend from the central knot, and out. But there is some blurring of boundary, as has been discussed elsewhere.

"In the heart of the fiefs, in what was once called Ravellon by the Barrani, we believe potential exists such as exists nowhere else in our world."

"What does this have to do with other worlds?"

Clearly, this was a bad question. "Nothing. But you bring me to my previous point. Our world has a very high magical potential. It is why we believe the Aerians are capable of flight. It is why they exist at all."

"But—"

He raised a brow. She closed her mouth.

"In a different magical environment, the Aerians would, in theory, be incapable of sustaining their own weight in flight. They might have wings, but the wings would serve no function, except perhaps in a cultural way. There are sages who have made this study their life's work. Perhaps you can find one of them to question."

Kaylin bit her lip. She did not dislike the Arkon in the way she disliked the pretentious and snobby nobles who occasionally crossed her path—but even so, she didn't like being all but called a moron. Instead of concentrating on her injured dignity, she concentrated on his words. Her eyes widened.

"You think that Ravellon is—"

He raised a brow.

"You think it exists in more than one world."

"Why do you say that?"

"You didn't think the first explanation was true, although it would make sense, you believe the second explanation. And the theoretical existence of other worlds ties into that explanation.

You think that, near the heart of the fiefs, there is some other world that's touching ours that wouldn't support Aerian life."

He raised both brows. "Sanabalis," he told her tutor, "she shows serious potential as a student. Why has this not been explored?"

"For a human, she is much like Lord Tiamaris was in his youth."

This clearly meant more to the Arkon than it did to Kaylin; the Arkon actually grimaced. "Very well. They are both rather young." He spoke as if youth was a failing. "Yes, Private Neya. That is what I believe."

"It is also," Sanabalis finally said, "not relevant at the moment."

"Do you think the shadows come from somewhere else? I mean, some world that isn't ours?"

"No. The shadows, as you call them, are at the heart of our world. They are the scions of the Old Ones."

"But the Old Ones are gone—" She stopped. Glanced at her arms, the marks covered as they always were by layers of cloth.

"It is possible that the magic that once sustained the Old Ones exists only in a very few places now. We do not understand what happened to them, and why they retreated—but no life as we know it would exist had they not."

"But they created—"

"Yes?"

"The Barrani. The Dragons. Even the Leontines." Although admittedly that was less widely known. "They created everything."

"Not everything. But even if they did, it does not refute my argument. What the world is now, and what it would have been, is not the same. Do not look for a return of the Old Ones, for if they returned, it would not only be the forefathers of our races, but also the forefathers of the ferals, and the darker creatures which have no name."

She was silent for a full minute before she trusted herself to speak again. "Ravellon," she began.

He raised a brow, but nodded.

"It was supposed to be the heart of a city. There was supposed to be a library there that was bigger on the inside than—" her eyes widened slightly "—the outside. You think—"

"Yes?"

"That the library did exist. And that it existed in a space between worlds somehow."

He said nothing.

"It was supposed to contain all of the knowledge about *anything* that had ever, or would ever, exist."

"Yes. That was the legend." He glanced out the window. "And for the sake of that legend, many have died."

She nodded. "Knowledge is power," she said softly, quoting someone, although she couldn't remember who. Probably an Arcanist.

"Yes. But power is not entirely unaligned," he replied. He rose. "And what once lay at the heart of Ravellon—and Ravellon is not a traditional fief name—may or may not now exist. What exists around it, however, in layers we cannot pierce magically or by mundane means, is shadow. We do not know if the shadows came searching for what we sought. We know only that they are now rooted there, and we cannot unseat them by any means we currently have in our possession."

"You've seen ferals, no doubt."

She nodded.

"You've seen, by all accounts, worse."

She nodded again, glancing at Sanabalis.

"It is for that reason, Private Neya, that we are prepared to allow you to investigate. You have experience with what you might find along those borders—or within Barren as it now stands—and you have, better yet, survived. You do not seem, to my admittedly inexperienced eye, to be insane. Nor, if your last involvement with the Courts was an indication, have you developed a love of power, and the casual indifference that comes with it.

"Therefore it is felt that you might approach—*approach, mind*—the borders." He reached into his robes and pulled out a crystal. She grimaced. "You recognize this, no doubt. You are expected to carry it with you wherever you go in the fiefs. It will record what you see."

"But I—"

"There is some magic involved, yes. I have heard that you have some sensitivity to magic, and it may cause you some discomfort. You will live with it. Come here."

She cringed, but rose and held out her palm.

He placed the crystal firmly into that palm, and then caught her wrist. He spoke three words—three loud, thunderous, Dragon words—and all of her hair stood on end. She barely felt the stinging pain of the crystal's edge against her palm, her ears hurt so much.

By the time the ringing had cleared, the Arkon was seated again, his hands folded in his lap; the crystal, with its sharp and unpleasant edges, was gone. "I am expected at the library," he told her almost curtly. "And I will endeavor, for that reason, to be brief.

"What we know with any certainty about the fiefs is due to the investigations that Tiamaris, in part, undertook some time ago. He was not always the most careful or fastidious of investigators, no doubt a deficiency in either his teaching or his aptitude."

Sanabalis and Tiamaris now exchanged a silent glance. The Arkon did not appear to notice that he had casually insulted them both. "However, what we were told," and this time he did pause to give Tiamaris a pointed glance, "was that the fiefs pass from one ruler to another when a new ruler takes over the central building. If this was, indeed, the case, then the fief of Illien would never have become the fief of Barren. Yet it did.

"You are tasked with finding out why." He paused, and then added, "Anything of use you can discover about the nature of the fiefs will also prove valuable at this time." He rose. "I must return to the library. I have left instructions, should I be unavailable, that you are to be granted entry—with or without Lord Tiamaris— should the need arise.

"Familiarize yourself with the rules of my library," he added gravely. "At the moment, breach of those rules would have unfortunate consequences."

Great. On the other hand, what she recalled was pretty straight-forward: touch or break any of his stuff, and die horribly. Not much leeway there for accidental errors.

He walked to the door, and then paused there again. "There was some discussion about your role in this investigation, Private Neya. I spoke in favor of it, but I have misgivings. I am not," he added, as she opened her mouth, "about to explain them again. The explanation would probably deafen you, because I am now old enough that I find certain complications difficult to discuss in anything but my native tongue—a tongue which, by Imperial decree, is to be used sparingly in public places."

"Wait!"

He froze there, and she was reminded, by his glacial expression, that there were forms she was expected to observe. "Arkon," she said quickly, bowing. This did not, judging by his expression, mollify him much. "What did the Outcaste find? He said he found—"

The Arkon frowned at about the same time Tiamaris stepped on her foot.

"He found shadow. Possibly the last resting place of the Old Ones. If the library existed at all, it was no longer his concern. Do not be arrogant, Private. Your marks—your existence—might afford you some protection, although what that entails, and what its boundaries are, none of us can say. But what *he* could not do in safety, you cannot do. Do you understand?"

She swallowed, remembering the great, black Dragon, his name so large and so intricate that she could not even begin to *say* it, although she could see it clearly. "Yes."

"Good. Tiamaris, Sanabalis." He nodded curtly, and this time, she didn't call him back.

"Lord Sanabalis or Lord Tiamaris, however, may feel free to enlighten you." He glanced at both of them. "I assume at least one of them was paying attention."

Tiamaris's grimace waited until the door had closed; Sanabalis's expression, however, did not change.

"I think I like him," Kaylin told them both, as she settled back into her chair. "What were his misgivings about me?"

The two remaining Dragons exchanged a glance. "The Outcaste," Sanabalis said quietly, "went to Ravellon. What he found there changed him. He was not without power. He is not without power now." They both hesitated. Kaylin marked it.

"Why did he want you two to talk about this? He could—"

"He dislikes caution in speech." It was Tiamaris who replied. "And he dislikes politics. His definition of politics involves anything of consequence that occurs outside the boundaries of his library."

"Oh."

"There are matters that the Eternal Emperor does not consider suitable for public consumption. Public, in this particular instance, involves anyone who lives or breathes that is not Dragon and does not serve him."

"Meaning me."

"Meaning, indeed, you."

"So…there's something they're worried about, and whatever it is, he can't tell me because I'm not a Dragon."

"No. There are many things that are discussed. A few of them have bearing—at least at this juncture—on our duties in the fiefs. But sorting out which of those things can be touched upon and which can't requires the type of conversational care that the Arkon finds taxing. Left to his own devices, he would not emerge from his library at all, and his concerns would lead him to discuss certain historical issues which the canny—and you are that, at least—would then dissect."

Kaylin made a face. "Just tell me what I need to know."

Sanabalis chuckled. "It's a pity you're human. I believe you would find some sympathy in the Arkon, otherwise." Fingers playing through his slender conceit of a white beard, he watched her in silence. After a moment, he said, "Tiamaris."

She recognized the tone of voice; she might as well have been locked in the West Room with an unlit candle in front of her face. Tiamaris grimaced.

"He was always like this?" she asked him.

"Always," the Dragon Hawk replied. "Understand that the Arkon and the Outcaste were, in as much as any two beings can be, friends. It is hard to surrender an ancient friendship, no matter how dire the circumstance. Even the Arkon is not immune to some trace of sentiment."

Clearly the Dragon word *sentiment* didn't really intersect the human one in any significant way. Kaylin managed to keep this thought to herself.

"It was the Arkon who noted the change in the Outcaste upon his return from the heart of the fiefs. He did not immediately make his concern clear." There was another hesitation, and it was longer and more profound. "In the end, however, it was the Arkon who was left to confront the Outcaste, because it was the Arkon who possessed the only certain knowledge we, as a race, held."

Kaylin frowned. "I'm not sure I understand."

"I'm sure you don't," Sanabalis replied quietly. "And after a brief pause for comprehension, you will once again resume all appearance of ignorance. This will not, one assumes, be difficult."

She grimaced.

"The Arkon," Tiamaris continued, as if Sanabalis hadn't spoken, "has never said this explicitly, even when pressed. The Emperor has never commanded him to speak," Tiamaris added. "Not even the respect the Arkon commands could stand in the face of his defiance of a direct order, and the Emperor does respect him greatly." He glanced at their mutual teacher once more. Sanabalis nodded evenly.

"But we believe that they were brothers in all but blood, the Outcaste and the Arkon. We believe," he added, lowering his voice, "that the Arkon knew the Outcaste's name."

Given the way the Barrani guarded theirs, and given the significance of the name itself, Kaylin understood why the Arkon had been loath to speak. If Dragons or Barrani had souls—and Kaylin had her doubts—they were entwined in the name; knowledge of the name was so profoundly intimate no human experience approached it.

But she frowned. "If—" And then she stopped.

The silence went on for a long time.

"Yes," Sanabalis said heavily. "He attempted to use the name, to bespeak the Outcaste."

This time, it was her silence that weighted the room. It passed for thought, but she didn't need much time to think; she only needed the time to choose her words. Normally, she didn't bother, but she had a strong feeling that was about to change, and like it or not, she would live with that.

"He didn't answer," she finally said. As word choices went, it wasn't impressive.

But Sanabalis nodded anyway. "No."

"Sanabalis—"

He waited, as if this were a test. Or as if all conversation from this moment on would be one. She really, really hated this type of lesson; it was all about failing, and interesting failure often didn't count for part marks. She glanced at Tiamaris, and saw no help coming from that quarter, but he was as tense as she was. And why? It was only conversation.

"His name," she said quietly.

"Yes?"

"His true name."

Sanabalis nodded again.

"It was different."

The Dragon Lord closed his eyes. "Yes," he finally said. "We believe that something in the heart of the fiefs changed the very nature of his true name."

"And when the Arkon spoke it—"

"He did not, and could not, hear it. Not as we hear the truth of our names when they're spoken."

She was silent, then, absorbing the words and letting them sink roots. "I don't understand," she finally said.

"No. No more do we."

Hesitating, she glanced at the carpet. It was safest. "When I went to the Barrani High Court—"

"Speak carefully, Kaylin."

"I'm trying." And so much for the effort. "When I went to the High Court, I saw—I learned—how Barrani are named."

"Yes."

She glanced at him. Rock was more expressive.

"Look, Sanabalis—I was born mortal. I was born the usual way. We don't *have* true names. We don't even understand them."

"No. You are not bound by them, either."

"But—the Barrani don't *wake* until they're named."

"No."

"Do the Dragons?"

He failed, deliberately, to answer.

"From what I understand, the name *is* what they are, somehow. What *you* are."

"That is also our understanding."

"If his name changed, would he be—"

"He is not what he was, Kaylin."

"Yes—but he remembered everything. He lied, based on that knowledge. He tried—"

"Yes." Sanabalis lifted a hand. "He did those things."

"So you can lose your name and still remember your whole life?"

Tiamaris cleared his throat. "Had you a true name," he told her quietly, "the Arkon would not have been swayed."

But she did. She *had* a name. She had no idea what it *meant* to have one, but she had taken one burning, glowing rune for herself from the waters of Life beneath the Barrani High Halls, and she still bore it. Severn knew it. Severn could call her.

But…he had never tried to *use* the name against her. She wondered if he even could.

"Wait."

"Yes?"

"You *have* a name." She spoke to Tiamaris.

"Indeed, Kaylin."

"But—"

"If I am not accompanied by you, I am not to enter Barren," he replied.

Her eyes narrowed. "You know something you're not telling me."

"It does not affect our mission."

"And your mission," Sanabalis said quietly, "starts now. Private," he added, rising, "understand that you are now seconded—as a Hawk—to the Imperial Court. What we have discussed in these rooms is not to be discussed with anyone save a member of that Court. If your Sergeant chooses to demand a report, the report you file must first go through the Court. Lord Grammayre may ask about your progress. You will take Lord Tiamaris to these meetings, and you will *let him do the talking*. Is that clear?"

"As glass."

"Good." He didn't smile. "Your life depends on it. You have not yet met the Emperor, but that will not save you if you cross the lines he has drawn. Understand this," he told her quietly. "Because if you do, nothing I can do or say will affect his decision.

"You may, however, question Tiamaris at your leisure, as he is part of the Court and privy to Court matters. If you have any leisure time." He gestured and the door opened. So much for economical use of power. "You have been given permission to remove your bracer. I suggest you wait until you've crossed the Ablayne."

"Oh, I will," she told him. Because that was where she usually threw the damn thing.

Tiamaris escorted her out of the Imperial Palace. They'd spent most of the day there, one way or the other, and Kaylin, glancing at the Halls of Law in the distance, grimaced. "Barren."

"You don't want to return."

"No. Never." She could afford to be that honest with Tiamaris.

"Kaylin—"

"But it just so happens we're in luck." She used irony here as if it were a blunt weapon. Against the force of Dragon humor, it pretty much had to be. "I met an old friend of mine on the way from Evanton's shop."

He raised a dark brow. "An old friend?"

She nodded. "She expected to see me. I sure as hells didn't expect to see her. But she had a message for me. How much can we stall?"

"Stall?"

"How long can we hold off our investigation? A day? Two?"

"If there's reason for it, but—"

"It had better be a damn good reason?"

Tiamaris nodded.

"We can probably go there now," she told him quietly. "It depends on how desperate we want Barren to think I am."

"Desperate?"

"He's sending a messenger with a letter for the Hawklord," she told him, voice flat. "I can either fail to show or intercept the message before it crosses the bridge. If we go now, I have no doubt at all that we'll be taken to Barren—but if I go *now,* he'll know he has the upper hand.

"If I wait, he'll be pretty damn certain he has it anyway—that's Barren all over."

"Does he?"

She swallowed. Glanced at the river that had been the dividing line of her life. "I don't know," she finally said.

"Then decide, Kaylin. You have the advantage of personal experience. I don't."

She nodded, grateful to him for at least that. If Barren thought he had the upper hand, he wasn't likely to be careless; that level of laziness would never have kept the fiefs in his hands.

Finally, she exhaled. "We'll take the risk. I'm not sure how I'm going to explain *you,* though. I don't suppose you'd care to wait?"

"I would be *delighted* to wait," he replied, in a tone of voice that was clearly the effect of serving, however briefly, with the Hawks. "I would not, however, survive it should it come to light."

"Figures." She shrugged and began to walk. "Let's see what we're up against."

A Dragon brow rose over bronze eyes. "Please tell me," he said, as he fell in step beside her, shortening his stride so he didn't leave her behind, "that that is not the extent of your ability to plan."

"I don't generally make plans when I have no information."

"Or at all?"

She shrugged. "I don't see the point of planning everything when things could change in an eye blink. Let's see what Barren's got. We can plan then."

"It is a small wonder to me," Tiamaris replied, although he didn't stop moving, "that you've survived to be the insignificant age you currently are."

"Stand in line."

CHAPTER 8

The Ablayne moved through the city in what was almost a circle. Kaylin, who had never been outside of the city, thought nothing of it; Tiamaris, who had, explained why. She tried to listen. But as she passed the bridge that connected her to Nightshade, and the part of her past that she *wasn't* ashamed of, his words joined the buzz of the street's crowds.

Although the merchant market was not located on the banks of the Ablayne, enterprising independents—who were often forced to move damn quickly, by tolls, Swords, and legitimate merchants—often set up small stalls near the river. Why, she never quite understood, but there was traffic.

She didn't walk quickly and Tiamaris, while a Dragon Lord, wasn't stupid. He stopped at the midpoint between the two bridges.

"Kaylin."

She glanced at him.

"The Imperial Court knows what the Emperor knows," he told her quietly.

She nodded.

"There is nothing to hide, not from me."

"It's not about hiding," she told him, although she wasn't certain she wasn't lying. "Barren," she said, swallowing, "is different. Look, it doesn't matter. We're going." She started to walk, and she walked quickly. This wasn't her beat; she didn't have to fall into the steady, quiet walk that could take hours.

"What concerns you, now?"

She almost said *nothing*. But he was going where she was going; he had some right to know. "I don't know what he wants from me. I don't know what he knows about me. He implied he knows a lot, but that was always what he did. Imply knowledge, let people assume you know everything, and then pick up what you didn't know from what they let slip." She paused and then added, "He knows why I went to the Hawklord's tower. He knows I'm not dead. He doesn't know what happened.

"But there are only two conclusions he can draw. The first, that I tried to carry out his orders. The second, that I turned on him immediately."

"The latter is the concern."

"Let's just say he's a fief lord. You don't get to keep your title—if it's even that—if people can turn on you without consequences."

"And you're afraid of him?" Tiamaris's brows rose. Both of them. He placed one hand on her shoulder. "You were thirteen years old when you left Barren. By the reckoning of your kind, you were barely out of childhood. You are not that child, now." He glanced at her wrist, and she grimaced.

"Sorry," she muttered. "I almost forgot." Opening the bracer and tossing it into the nearest trash heap or stretch of moving water was one of life's little luxuries; today, it just didn't seem to matter. She pressed the gems along the inside of the wrist in sequence, and waited for the familiar click of freedom. When it came, she pulled the bracer free, exposing, for just a moment, the blue-black lines, swirls, and dots of the marks that encompassed over half her body.

"I had these marks, then," she told him softly, pulling her arm back and tossing the bracer in a wide, glinting arc that ended with an audible splash. "I thought they would kill me."

"They may, yet," was his reply. From his expression, she thought it was meant to be comforting. Dragons had pretty damn strange ideas of what passed for comfort. He began to walk; it was clear he knew the way to Barren.

"How many other fiefs did you visit?" Kaylin asked him.

"Pardon?"

"You entered Castle Nightshade, before you met me."

"Ah."

"Did you go to Barren?"

"No. I went, however, to Illien in its time. The borders are largely the same. Or," he added, "they were."

"And the others?"

"Some of the others."

"Why?"

This particular nothing stretched out for a while. Which meant he wasn't going to answer. She obligingly changed topics as the bridge across the Ablayne came into view. It was a narrower bridge than the one that crossed from Nightshade.

Standing on the other side of the narrow bridge, lounging against the rails, was a figure she recognized.

Morse.

Morse smiled. The scar that marred the line of her upper lip stretched as she did, whitening. Morse's smile could scare a much larger man into silence. Kaylin had seen it happen. "You're tricked out," she said, nodding at the surcoat.

"You're not."

"Not more than usual." Morse ran her fingers through the short brush of her dark hair. The ring that pierced her left eyebrow glinted in the sun, which was near its height. "Had some word that you might be by," she added, still lounging.

Kaylin shrugged. "I bet. I'm here."

"And not that happy about it?" Morse rose, then. "Happens. Who's your friend?"

"A Hawk," Kaylin replied. It was always touch and go, with Morse, unless the seven years had changed her a lot.

"No kidding." The smile deserted her face. "We don't need groundhawks on this side of the border, if you take my meaning."

"Fine. Tell Barren that." Kaylin folded her arms across her chest.

Morse was silent for a long moment, and Kaylin watched the ring that pierced her brow. It was—it had been—a decent indicator of Morse's moods, which could turn on a half-copper without warning. If it dipped or it rose too rapidly, you were on shaky ground. If it stayed steady, regardless of the words or the threat, you probably had a few more guaranteed minutes of life.

It was steady, now.

Kaylin? Not so much.

And if Kaylin had learned to read Morse seven years ago, Morse had also learned to read Kaylin. "Eli," she said quietly, the word completely neutral. "He should never have sent you across the river."

Kaylin said nothing. Nothing much to say. But she didn't correct Morse's use of her name, because to Morse, she was Elianne. Not more, not less.

"Why did he?" Kaylin heard herself ask. She almost bit off her own tongue, because she realized it was the only thing she could do that would stop it from flapping.

Morse shrugged, and turned her glance toward the sluggishly moving waters of the Ablayne; it had been a dry season, so far. "Ask him," she finally said.

"I don't care what he thinks," Kaylin replied. The part of her that was shouting shut up was seven years too old. "I want to know why you let him." The part of her that was seven years too old didn't matter.

"*Let* him? Have you forgotten who's the fief lord and who's the grunt here?"

That should have shut Kaylin up. It *should* have. But an anger that she hadn't felt in years was burning her mouth, and the only way not to be consumed by it was to open that damn mouth and let it out.

"I was thirteen, Morse. I was stupid." How old had she been before she finally realized that it was just a setup, just a way of killing her at a distance? Fourteen? Fifteen? Twenty?

"You were one of his best, even then."

"Doesn't say much about the rest of his recruits, does it?" Kaylin spit to the left. It was the Barren equivalent of Leontine cursing. She did not, however, aim at Morse; that was the Barren equivalent of telling the Emperor to shove off. "*I wasn't good enough* to do what he ordered me to do. I could've spent another decade, and I would never be *that* good. He couldn't have expected me to succeed." Her voice rose in the stillness. She tried to throttle it back. But her hands were shaking.

You thought you didn't care, she told herself in bitter fury. *You thought it was all in the past. It was done. You could walk away.* And she had. She'd walked. Now she was walking back. Funny, how the fires you didn't put out the first time were there to burn your sorry butt when you returned.

"You thought you could." Neutral. The ring hadn't budged.

Kaylin, however, was past caring. Stung, she said, "Yes, *I* thought I could. You told me I could, and I believed it."

"You wanted to believe it," Morse said, and for the first time, the brow ring did shift—it went down. "You always did. You always wanted some damn thing to believe in. 'Am I good enough, yet? Am I ready? Will I ever be ready?'" The mimicry was harsh.

And it was deserved. Kaylin, white, stood on the rise of the narrow bridge, looking down at Morse and trying to remember how to breathe.

"If he wanted me dead," she said, when she'd remembered as much as she was going to be capable of, "why didn't he just tell you to kill me?"

Morse was utterly silent.

It was the wrong type of silence. "Morse?"

The world was shifting beneath Kaylin's feet. It wasn't just the boundaries of Barren, it wasn't the shadows of the past. The past never truly died, anyway; you just boxed it up and put it in storage, hoping it wouldn't come back to bite you later. But it did, and sometimes you bled.

"You weren't the only one who was young and stupid," Morse finally said. "Seven years, Eli. A lot can change in seven years." She shoved her hands into pockets, and away from the hilts of her very prominent daggers, as if that was all that kept her from drawing them. "You coming, or what?" She turned and stepped off the bridge. Morse hadn't been big on symbolism; a dagger was a dagger, a fist was a fist and a corpse was a corpse, although admittedly she took some joy in creating them in the right situation.

But Kaylin? At thirteen, Morse's harsh words notwithstanding, she had looked for signs and portents. She cringed at the memory. "Yeah. Coming. But not without my friend."

"Suit yourself." Morse shrugged.

"You expected me to come alone?"

"I didn't expect you to come at all," Morse snapped. "I thought you'd gotten smarter in seven fucking years." She did turn, then. Apparently, they were both being burned by the same damn fire. "I watched you, Eli. I watched you in these damn streets for weeks.

"I saw you with your new friends. I saw your shiny uniform. I saw you at work. Only you could find a fucking Lord whose idea of a reward for an assassination attempt was a fucking *job*."

It was Kaylin's turn to pause. Other people's anger often had the effect of dampening hers; there was only so much fuel for fire, after all. And put that way, her whole life seemed so damn improbable. She swallowed. Offered Morse a very familiar shrug. "Yeah," she finally said.

"I knew you, then. He thinks you turned, you must have turned." Morse folded arms across her chest. "But I know you. You tried."

It shouldn't have been a comfort, to hear that admission. Shouldn't, but it was. "Yeah. I tried."

"And if you tried, Barren's got *nothing* on you. Nothing. What the *fuck* are you doing here, Eli?" Morse vented her spleen on a stone. It travelled a long damn distance before it struck a wall.

"My job," Kaylin replied.

"The Law doesn't come into the fiefs." She pointed at the Hawk emblazoned across Kaylin's chest.

Kaylin nodded.

"We don't need you, here."

"You probably never did."

At that, Morse grinned. It wasn't pleasant. "You got that right. Come on. Barren's expecting you."

Kaylin cringed. "I hope I'm not costing you anything."

"It was a small bet," Morse replied, shrugging. "Barren's been...tense. No one's been up for a big one." She turned and began to walk down the streets.

Barren didn't employ Barrani guards. No surprise, there. Barrani power structure generally demanded that the most obviously powerful person be in charge, and in the Barrani view of power, the most old and decrepit of their number—and how they decided who this was, given that none of the damn Barrani ever aged, Kaylin didn't know—was easily a match for a human, no matter how deadly he was.

It wasn't always true, but it was true enough. If there were Barrani working in Barren, they'd be working from the top, not *for* it.

However, in Kaylin's memory of Barren, the lack of Barrani enforcers didn't make that much difference to the people who eked out a living in the streets of the fiefs; she might as well have been in Nightshade. Morse was one of Barren's lieutenants; people knew it, somehow. They saw her, and they moved to one side of the street or the other, falling silent and getting out of the way as quickly and efficiently as possible.

They did, however, stare—but Kaylin knew they weren't staring at Morse; they were staring at her. And at Tiamaris. She glanced at the Dragon Lord and grimaced; he walked as if he owned the street. Then again, it was a street full of humans, most of them in mismatched or poorly fitted clothing; they had no weapons besides the simple knives almost anyone wore, and those weren't about to be drawn anytime soon.

She knew these streets. Not as well as she knew Nightshade, but then again, she hadn't seen as much of Barren. She hadn't been born to it, and she hadn't grown up in the shadow of its Castle, because it didn't *have* one. But…this *could* have been Nightshade.

She hadn't seen it, when she'd lived here, walking by Morse's side, as she did now.

"Tomorrow," she told Tiamaris under her breath, "we ditch the uniforms."

"As you say."

Three blocks into Barren, Morse met up with a patrol. It was a patrol only in the fief sense of the word; to Kaylin's eye it was a lounging group of men in armor, wearing obvious swords. They looked about as friendly as Morse did, but where Morse was laconic and disturbing, they looked nervous.

Seeing Tiamaris didn't help, although Kaylin thought only one of the four men recognized him for what he was. She didn't ask, and as she had no intention of speaking to them, she didn't feel the need to point it out.

"Barren got the message," the man in the lead said. "We're here to help out, if you need it." He grinned at Kaylin; he was missing one of his lower teeth. "Fief's a big place," he told her. "We wouldn't want you wandering off and getting lost."

"Lost," she told him curtly, "is what you can get."

He whistled, and followed it up with a chuckle that was condescending enough Kaylin's hands curled into fists. "That tone don't work on this side of the bridge," he told her. "Here, *we're* the law."

"Oh? I thought Barren was."

"We work for Barren," the man replied, losing the smile.

"What, everyone competent got eaten?"

"Eli," Morse said sharply.

Kaylin ignored her. "Or maybe anyone competent crossed the bridge." She shifted stance, and waited.

She didn't have to wait long. He smiled, shrugged, and turned away as if to walk; it was a feint. She knew it because she'd used it.

When he turned back, it was sudden; the smile hadn't left his lips but it had frozen there, as if he'd forgotten he'd left it behind. He swung in with his left arm, but he swung high, and she shifted her head, avoiding his hand easily while she waited for the second swing. It came in low, toward her stomach; she slid to the side, grabbed his wrist, and used his momentum to toss him to the side.

"Carl, stuff it. We don't have time," Morse said.

Carl listened about as well as Kaylin did. He stumbled, but he didn't lose his bearing—not until Kaylin snapped out with a foot and kicked him hard in the butt. His knees hit the dirt, followed quickly by his hands. Kaylin backed up and waited for him to regain his footing.

Carl—a man she didn't recognize—rose. This time, he *was* carrying a weapon. A short knife. Serrated edges. That must have cost him enough to justify the money he hadn't spent on clothing.

Morse swore. Kaylin bent her knees, but she didn't draw a dagger in response. She waited. Carl bent into his knees, as well, throwing the dagger from one hand to the other. Kaylin said, and did, nothing. She understood that he was attempting to intimidate her, but as he was the one who'd just picked his sorry self off the street, she wasn't impressed.

When he lunged, it wasn't even a surprise. He was good at keeping expression off his face, she'd give him that; she couldn't read movements from the subtle changes there. But she could read them from the rest of his body language; from the slight shift in shoulder, the minute differences as he shifted weight. It was a decision.

She didn't see what the result of that decision was, however.

Morse, looking bored, kicked him in the side of the head. He reeled back, but he was now being careful enough that he didn't fall; he used momentum to get the hell out of her way. Smarter man than Kaylin had initially given him credit for.

The Hawk? It didn't scare him at all. Kaylin was, in his eyes, the *law,* and that had only one meaning in Barren: she was hampered, prissy, correct.

Morse was none of those things. If Carl worked for Barren, Morse helped Barren run the fief, and the death of someone stupid enough to attack her wouldn't cause Barren to blink twice. Or once, really.

Carl showed some sign of intelligence. He sheathed the dagger and raised both of his hands. He lowered them quickly and leapt back as Morse kicked out again.

"Morse!" he shouted. "I'm done! I'm done!"

"Almost," she snapped, spitting to the side. "Listen, you sorry piece of shit. You're not insulting *her.* You're insulting *me.* You just told them both that I need your help to escort them through Barren."

Carl paled.

"Stop using your brains as fucking seat warmers." She looked at Carl, but it was clear she was speaking to all of them. And all of them had a pretty clear idea of just how stupid it was to insult Morse in any way. "You can all back the fuck off," she added. "Unless you want to—"

"We're off, we're off," Carl said, nodding to the men who had, Kaylin noted, already started to retreat toward the wall of the nearest building. Morse shrugged, shoved hands into pockets and began to walk away. Kaylin, ignoring them, followed.

Tiamaris had not lifted a hand.

When they were four blocks past the patrol, Morse laughed. She'd never had a girlish laugh, and she hadn't, in seven years, developed one. Her voice was deep, rich, and clearly amused; it was also tinged with contempt and easy malice.

Kaylin froze and had just enough time to duck, which meant Morse's fist connected with air. Morse did not, however, lose balance; her hand just stopped about an inch past the back of where Kaylin's head had been.

But the laughter had been real; it wasn't a feint. It was one of the things that made Morse so unpredictable. "I'd've let you dust him off," Morse said, as if the jab were a shake of the hand and meant in a friendly way, "but that'd make you look too good and the rest of us look too incompetent. Can't have the Law looking tougher than the rest of us."

"Yeah, sorry. I should've ignored him, but you know how much I hate—"

Morse raised a hand. "You've changed," she told Kaylin. "But not that much. Yeah, I could see that coming once he'd opened his stupid mouth."

"We'll lose the Hawk tomorrow. If we're back tomorrow."

"You mean, if you leave?"

"That, too." Kaylin shrugged. "You have any idea what Barren wants?"

"Some."

"And you're not sharing."

Morse shook her head. "I could knife that idiot and leave him bleeding in the street and Barren? He'd laugh. But not this."

Kaylin nodded again. She glanced at the streets, and the rundown buildings, at the faded stalls, peopled by men and women who still managed to shout to attract their custom. They did not, she noted, shout at Morse.

The fief of Barren was very like the fief of Nightshade in this regard; the streets were grungier, and the buildings weren't kept up well. But the people? They still filled the streets—in any space that Morse wasn't moving through.

They met two more patrols, but these, Morse headed off. Kaylin, on the other hand, managed to keep her twitching hands by her sides in deference to Morse; she understood that the first pat had been a test. Whether she'd passed or failed, she didn't know. Shouldn't have cared.

But dammit, she almost did.

She had no illusion about the length of the walk; it wasn't going to be a short one. Morse took her down streets that were tantalizingly familiar. This wasn't Nightshade, it was never going to *be*

Nightshade, but Kaylin had lived here for six months, and those months had left their mark.

More than their mark.

"Hey, Eli?"

"Hmm?"

"Where'd you get the tattoo?"

Kaylin's hand rose to her cheek. With a grimace, she forced her hand to fall. "It was a gift," she said, lips twisting, "from Nightshade."

Morse stared at her. "His mark?"

"You've heard something." It wasn't a question.

"Yeah. Well. I hear a lot."

Kaylin didn't ask her what she'd heard, although she wanted to know. Morse wouldn't give her anything, and it would make Kaylin look weak. Weak and Morse were not a very good combination on most days.

"Look, my companion—"

"Dragon." No question at all in Morse's voice. "Not bad looking, either."

"Is a Dragon Lord. He's a Hawk, but he's part of the Emperor's Court."

Morse shrugged. "Here, that means diddly."

"True. But he can—" Tiamaris caught her arm, and pressed his fingers into it. Kaylin thought they would leave a bruise, but she took his meaning and shut up.

Morse, watching them, assessed their relative power. It was what she did, and she did it before she remembered to do almost anything else in a day. Like, say, breathe. But she frowned as Tiamaris lowered his hand. "You any good in a fight?" she asked Tiamaris.

"I have been trained," he replied at length. Clearly, talking to the streetlife of Barren was designated a Kaylin job.

"Good. Because we're about to cross Old Holdstock."

Kaylin frowned as the street name conjured up a hazy image of the Barren geography she knew. "So?"

"Things have changed in seven years," Morse told her. "I heard you were good. You'd better be."

★ ★ ★

The first thing Kaylin noticed was the sudden change in population density in the streets. Without thinking, she glanced at the position of the sun; it was still high. High enough that the streets shouldn't have been this empty. But they were, for the fief; there were one or two people who, scurrying between buildings, glanced furtively over their shoulders, but there were few others.

No children, for one. No one playing in the street. No one glancing longingly at the relative finery of the Imperial uniform and daydreaming about mugging a Hawk, rifling their pockets, and stealing their weapons and armor.

Kaylin glanced at Morse, as if to confirm what she saw. Morse had gone from bored, which was her resting state, to watchful. She didn't look scared, but Morse would die laughing, grinning or screaming in rage; Morse didn't have a register left for something as pathetic as fear.

Kaylin did. She hated it, but she did. She could feel her shoulders tense, her hands curve round the hilt of her daggers. She glanced over her shoulder, and instead of Severn, saw Tiamaris. But he still wore the Hawk, and he was still a comfort, regardless.

The road continued, bending slightly to the right, toward the boundary of the fief itself. Barren didn't live on the edge—almost no one did—but he lived as close as a man could, in safety. It was one of his boasts, and one of the things that made him so feared. It also made him damn hard to reach.

But at least at the moment she didn't have to turn a blind eye to what was happening on the streets; nothing was. She could see faces in open windows, and through the turned slats of warped shutters; that was it. Here, in the heart of Barren, there was very little in the way of glass. It made the winters cold.

Cold.

She stopped walking as the shadows at her feet suddenly sharpened and lengthened. Turning, she looked up to see the tower.

"Eli?"

And down, to see the broken, slanting fence, rust eating through metal, and grass, taller than her waist, hiding stones. Hiding children, she thought, remembering her first night in Barren.

"It was here, wasn't it?" she asked Morse.

Tiamaris spoke her rank. But she was in Barren, now; rank didn't matter. It wasn't a name.

Morse turned to glance at the tower. She frowned; the frown was slow to clear. "Yeah," she finally said. "I think you're right."

"About what?" Tiamaris asked, looking at them both oddly.

"This," Kaylin told him softly, "is where Morse first found me."

Tiamaris looked at the tower, and then he looked back at Kaylin. "She found you here?"

"I ran. From Nightshade."

"Across the border."

She nodded.

"You didn't feel the transition."

"It wasn't the—the internal border. It was just a street."

Tiamaris said nothing for a long moment. "You ran from Nightshade to here. Why did you stop?"

She pointed at the tall grass. If the fief had changed in seven years, the grass apparently hadn't. "I needed a place to sleep," she told him evenly, her gaze falling on things that existed only in memory. "I needed a place to hide. There weren't many open doors, not for me, and even if there had been, I wouldn't have taken them.

"I was tired. I was—" She shook her head, trying to clear it. "The grass was tall, then. Just as tall. The fence was just as broken. I stepped through the opening there, and I burrowed into the grass."

He frowned. "Which opening, Private?"

So much the Dragon, Tiamaris was. Cautious, as well. He didn't use her name—which he used at any other time—in Morse's hearing. *We don't have true names,* she thought. She wanted to tell him that. *We just have tags that people use to get our attention.*

"There."

Tiamaris frowned. Kaylin frowned, as well, but it wasn't the same expression. She snorted, mumbled a brief apology to Morse, and then headed toward the break in the fence, where the iron tines had fallen away and the grass—she could still *see* it—had grown through.

"Here." She tried not to use his name, but she was human.

Tiamaris glanced at Morse. "You found her here?" he asked, in entirely the wrong tone of voice. It wasn't that he was angry or threatening; he wasn't. But the question implied knowledge. In fact, it implied a shared knowledge—between him and Morse.

Morse shrugged. "She was on the other side of the fence," she finally told the Dragon Lord. "Huddling over there in the grass."

"How did you see her?"

"In my line of work?" Morse laughed. It was bitter and sharp; it was also short. "You don't notice something as simple as someone huddling in grass where they shouldn't be, you're generally called a corpse."

"Did Morse come in to fetch you?" Tiamaris asked Kaylin.

"No."

"You came out to her."

"Yes. Look, Tiamaris, what the hell is going on here?"

"If I am correct, *Private,* neither Morse nor I can see the opening at which you are pointing."

She started to tell him that Morse had, in fact, seen something once, but bit the words back. They weren't relevant here.

CHAPTER 9

Kaylin walked over to the gap in the fence. She didn't push her way past either Morse or Tiamaris, but it was a near thing. She had always hated being the odd man out, especially when it came to information or secrets. Yes, this was unreasonable. She'd just have to live with it.

She passed through the fence, stood in the grass. Heard the wind through it; felt the heat of the sun. It wasn't high summer, but without enough of a sea breeze it was damn hot when she was kitted out. Another thing she'd learned to live with. The days when she could just shuck her clothing and run mostly naked through the streets had died even before her mother had.

She was tired. She hadn't slept well, but she never did when she was worried. The midwives hadn't called, and there were no emergencies at the foundling hall. In all, she couldn't complain. She wanted to, mind. Barren was a threat. But…he was a threat she could almost understand.

The worst he could do was remind people she knew of who

she really was. Or who, she thought, almost dispassionately, she had once been. Had she changed? Had she *really* changed?

Standing here, the answer had to be no.

She remembered this place so clearly. And she remembered, as she turned, seeing Morse that first time.

Barren: Elianne

She woke, damp with dew, chilled by it. Small burrs clung to her hair. Steffi liked to brush them out, so she didn't mind them too much.

Steffi.

She sat up, gagging, her empty stomach all that prevented her from throwing up in the long grass. Sunlight slanted between buildings, between crooked, leaning fence posts. It was morning. She wasn't certain where she was but she knew one thing: she was alive. The ferals whose voices were always a distant chill had hunted elsewhere.

She could see sunlight, but she wasn't in it, and she listened carefully before she began to move out of the long shadows cast by the building at her back. That building was tall—taller than Castle Nightshade—but it seemed in poor repair; there were obvious cracks in the stone and what looked like loose mortar. Mortar. Severn had taught her that.

Her hands became fists, and she tore up grass before she realized she was doing it. He was gone. He wasn't dead, not yet. But he would be.

Pulling her sleeves down to cover the marks on her arms, Elianne glanced over her shoulder and froze.

Someone was standing in the opening she'd slipped through, watching her. It was not immediately clear to her whether or not that someone was male or female; the hair was cropped so short you could see skull through it in the morning light, the face was square, the jaws wide. But beneath a leather tunic, she thought she saw the slight swell of breasts; it was either that or fat, and while the figure seemed large to her, none of that girth suggested fat.

In the fiefs, people seldom grew fat.

"Strange place to hide." Woman's voice.

Elianne found herself relaxing, but only slightly. She stood, parting grass. "It was here," she said quietly, "or the streets."

The woman raised a brow; a scar bisected the left side. A scar also adorned her upper lip, in a puckered, obvious white. "Family toss you out? Or did you pull a runner?"

Elianne shrugged. "Ran," she said. *Not that it's any of your business.* She kept those words to herself. The woman didn't *look* unfriendly. But given the scars on her face, she didn't exactly look safe, either, even though Elianne knew many people who had scars. Scars, she'd been told, just meant you'd survived. Or that you could.

"I'm Morse," the woman said. "You?"

"Elianne." *Don't tell them your real name.* Severn's voice. She hated it. Hating it, she disobeyed. What difference would it make, anyway?

"Where do you live?"

"Over by the Four Corners."

Morse frowned; the movement flattened the scar. "What's the fief?" she finally asked.

It was Elianne's turn to frown. "Nightshade."

Morse whistled. "You're not in Nightshade now," she said, casually.

"Not…in Nightshade."

"You're in Barren."

"Barren."

Hearing what Elianne didn't say, Morse shrugged. "You pulled a runner, and you crossed the border. You going to stay in there all damn day? I got things to do." It was almost an invitation. She waited.

"Here's as good as anywhere."

"Suit yourself." Morse turned. Walked a few feet. Stopped. She didn't turn back, but her voice drifted over her shoulder. "You got no family here. No friends. You might want to make some."

"What are you offering?" Elianne asked quietly. She asked it of the woman's back; the woman still hadn't turned.

"What do you want?"

"I want to be able to kill a man."

Morse laughed. Still laughing, she did turn. "Kid," she said, when the laughter had eased enough that she could speak, "you came to the right place."

"Private?"

Kaylin shook herself. The memory had been so clear she could almost step into it. *I want to be able to kill a man.*

She could have asked for food or shelter. Those would have been a better, saner, place to start. Of course, she thought with a grimace, they wouldn't have done much for Morse. "Sorry. I was just—I was thinking."

Tiamaris snorted. "Do you mind thinking on this side of the fence?"

"Why?"

He glanced at Morse. Morse shrugged.

"Because short of removing the fence itself—"

"Don't try," Morse told him. Something in her voice had shifted from dead bored to serious.

Tiamaris raised a brow.

"I don't fancy scraping bits of you off the street."

He snorted again. "I'm not certain how you'd be able to distinguish them from the rest of the detritus."

"I am." Morse folded her arms. This was not generally considered a fighting stance in most people.

"Tiamaris," Kaylin said, more sharply than she'd intended. "Don't."

He raised one dark brow, and then offered her a shrug in place of action. "I believe," he told her quietly, "that the attempt will have to be made sooner or later."

"Make it later."

"As you say. Will you join us?"

She nodded. But she turned to look at the tower before she left the tall grass behind. At thirteen, it had been just another run-down building in a very strange place, and given what she'd just experienced, a building didn't matter.

Now? She thought it old, and given the look and patina of age, she was surprised that it was still standing. It was wide at base—wider than a solid fief house—and it narrowed very little as it stretched toward sky. The stones that had gone into its construction were half Kaylin's height, and twice that in width, at least at the upper foundation.

If it had windows, the shutters concealed them. Kaylin suspected that it didn't. Glass—and a building like this must have had it—was usually the first casualty of a vacancy. She frowned.

"Tiamaris," she said, in an entirely different tone of voice. "This tower—you've seen it before."

He nodded gravely.

"Does it have a gatehouse on the other side?"

"Not now."

"Did it, when you saw it?"

He was silent. She took that as a no.

"If the two of you are finished?" Morse asked.

Kaylin nodded absently. "Morse, has Barren ever been here?"

Morse didn't answer.

Kaylin emerged from the long grass, just as she had done seven years ago. She had a burr attached to her tabard, and some of the seed that the grass was shedding; given the state of most of Barren's men, she didn't bother to remove them. When she'd reached the street again, she turned to look at the tower, and at the fence.

Shaking her head, she frowned. "I can see it," she finally said. "Tiamaris?"

"No."

"I don't like it," she told him.

Morse laughed.

"What's funny?"

"Nothing." But the laughter faded into a grim chuckle before it deserted Morse's voice. "Remember what I told you, back then."

Kaylin frowned. "You told me not to mention where you'd found me."

"Still applies."

"But—"

Morse raised a brow.

Kaylin fell silent. "Why'd you take me in?"

Morse shrugged. "You wanted to be able to kill a man," she said. "I thought you were a girl after my own heart."

Tiamaris raised a brow, but didn't offer further comment; he glanced at the tower.

Please, Kaylin thought suddenly, *don't tell me that this Tower is the Tower of Illien.* Maybe he heard her somehow. He didn't say another word.

They walked down streets that were familiar to Kaylin. She recognized the faded signs, the faded facades of wooden buildings; she recognized, as well, the turn of the badly cobbled streets. Almost subconsciously, she fell in beside Morse.

"You got my back?" Morse asked her.

"Always," she replied, before thought could catch up with words.

Morse grimaced. "You don't think much these days, do you?"

"Not more than strictly necessary," Kaylin replied. "But then again—"

"You never did. I got that." She stopped walking just a second after Kaylin did. Something like a high, soft growl had been carried by breeze through the nearly empty streets. It was hard to tell which direction it had come from, for if it wasn't loud, it seemed to permeate the air.

"Tiamaris?" Kaylin said, voice quiet.

"I heard it," he said softly.

Kaylin turned to Morse. "That wasn't a feral."

"No. But that," Morse replied, raising her voice slightly, "was a scream." She glanced at Kaylin, and her smile was all edge. "Let's see what you're good for."

★ ★ ★

They ran. If the first sound had been hard to track, the second, a very human scream, had not. It didn't last, and Kaylin had no hope; they weren't running to the rescue, here. But if they got there in time, there would be no *other* screams.

As always, when she ran, the streets grew long and narrow, like a tunnel without any necessary light to show its end. She reached for her daggers, drawing them without breaking stride. Remembered—and why now?—her mother's sharp admonition about running while carrying sharp things.

But when they cleared the last street, when they rounded the bend, they froze. Even Morse stood motionless for a second, her mouth slightly open—Morse's equivalent of dropping her jaw in shock.

What stood in the street was in no way a feral—Kaylin had been right about that. Ferals looked as if they *might* be alive. This creature suffered under no such limitations. It had a body, a short, squat body with six legs, reminiscent of a spider's. But even that was the wrong word: the legs were solid and muscular, and they ended in long, sharp claws. From where she stood Kaylin could see that they'd dislodged and broken stones.

It had a head, of sorts; the head was half the size of the body beneath it. It should have overbalanced the creature when it swiveled, because it swiveled so damn fast. It didn't, of course. The creature's mouth was an angry, livid slash of red against an obsidian background; the creature's skin gleamed like chitin.

But it was the eyes that were the worst: it had not two, but several, and they seemed to ring its head, at varying chaotic levels, as if they sought to form a crown.

Kaylin muttered a Leontine imprecation.

Tiamaris joined her.

"You recognize it?" Kaylin asked him, not taking her eyes off the creature's feet.

"Not as such," the Dragon replied.

"How bad is it?"

"We'll...see." He hadn't shrugged himself out of his armor. She waited for a moment, to see if he would start the transformation that would have him unfold in full Dragon glory in the middle of Barren's streets.

The creature snarled.

Tiamaris opened his mouth, his very human mouth, and *roared*. The inner membranes of his eyes went up, but even muted, those eyes glowed crimson. Kaylin stepped back, keeping Tiamaris close.

The creature paused, and then its mouth, its much larger, lipless hole of a mouth, turned up in what might have been a smile. Which was bad.

Worse, though, was its voice. "Well met," it said and, bunching its massive legs beneath it, it leapt.

Tiamaris was not there to meet it when it landed; he threw himself clear of both claws and body, and *just* managed to miss the beam of light that suddenly shot out from an eye on the side of the creature's head. Kaylin, already in motion, had done the same.

Morse, not immediately a target, was slower.

"Morse!" Kaylin shouted, adding Leontine invective for emphasis, forgetting for a moment who she was with, and where.

Morse didn't answer; she rolled to her feet.

"Watch its eyes! Tiamaris has most of its attention! We just need to—" The street two inches short of Kaylin's feet exploded. She swallowed dust, threw herself clear of the beam that was continuing to dig a runnel in the road, and rolled instantly to her feet.

Morse shouted her name. It was the wrong name. "Over here!" She threw an arm out, pointed at a door. It was closed, but that generally didn't mean much in the fiefs. Kaylin hesitated, turned to look over her shoulder. Caught a glimpse of Tiamaris, a glimpse of the creature, a billowing spray of something that wasn't light, but that glittered anyway.

"In!" Morse kicked the door open, threw herself through it.

Kaylin heard Tiamaris roar again. The street broke as the creature leapt and landed; Tiamaris was, once again, well out of the way of its feet. But he pulled something free of his belt—not a sword. She couldn't, at the moment, remember him ever using one.

What he held, she couldn't see; it was small enough that it might have been a dagger. Or, she realized, a focus. It was a focus. A reminder, for Kaylin, of the fact that Lord Tiamaris had spent some time under the tutelage of the Imperial Order of Mages.

Morse grabbed her arm and dragged her around the door's frame as the wood just beside Kaylin's head blossomed into splinters.

"You get that kind of thing here all the time?" Kaylin asked.

"Not that one, no." Morse, still serious, added, "I'm alive, after all."

"You and how many others?" She regretted the words almost the instant they left her mouth.

But Morse wasn't like most people; she shrugged. "Not enough," she conceded.

"How long?"

"How long what?"

"How damn long have things like—like that—been wandering the streets here?"

"Not long. Won't be that long, either," Morse added, as something shook the building. She grimaced. "Look, I've never seen one of those before, all right? Can he stop it?"

Kaylin shrugged. "Maybe." She shook herself free of Morse's restraining hand. "He'll do a whole lot better with some help."

Morse laughed; it was terse, and it was higher than usual. "Have anything in mind?"

"Yeah. In the future? Carry crossbows." She looked at the daggers in her hands, and grimaced. "I'm going to be eating gruel in the brig for weeks if I lose these."

"Worry about being alive to eat gruel."

"You've never met the quartermaster," Kaylin replied. She didn't ask Morse if Morse could throw a knife. Morse had taught her.

And in a pinch, Morse never played the idiot. "You want us to take out the eyes." No question in the statement.

"If it's even possible. I'm not sure the blades will travel through whatever it is it's shooting out of them. Tiamaris has got the body, the claws, and the fangs; we just need to keep moving."

Morse stared at her for a minute, and then shook her head. "I am out of my fucking mind," she muttered.

"Oh, it's real."

"That's not what I meant. What I meant," Morse added, crouching well below eye-level and peering into the very loud street, "is that I should be running about now."

"To where?"

"Anywhere that doesn't have *that* in it."

"Good point." Kaylin sucked in air, and crouching, added, "If he goes down, we're dead anyway. I don't think we have much of a chance at outrunning the creature."

"I'd be willing to give it a shot."

"Be my guest."

Morse shook her head. "There's nowhere for me but here," she said grimly. "There's no Hawk waiting for me at the end of the bridge."

The way she said *bridge*? It was the way the outer Elantrans might use the word *rainbow*. Kaylin knew; she'd been a fief ling for most of her life. She wanted to argue, but now was *so* not the time.

And truthfully? Morse killed people. It's what she did. How much of that could she leave behind? How much of that did she *want* to?

"Ready," Morse said, rising and backing away from the door.

"Back entrance?"

Morse nodded. They retreated from the frame of the door where a watchful eye—one at any rate—was probably waiting.

The door opened into dirt and something that would, on a non-rainy day, pass for an alley. They slid out that door. The building itself might as well have been deserted for all the attention anyone paid them; no doors opened; no curious faces peered around them. Even the window shutters were closed.

The building was narrow; the passage between it and the next was one stout person wide, no more. Kaylin started forward, bumped into Morse and stopped. So much about Barren made her feel young again, but some of her training, some of the life she'd lived since she'd left it on Barren's mission, held.

Morse raised the broken brow, and then nodded. She had no dignity in a fight like this; let someone else take the lead. She shadowed Kaylin as they walked down the alley, moving quickly and quietly.

Tiamaris was alive. He was not in melee with the creature, and he was not in full Dragon form. She wondered why; had she the ability, she would have been. But if he wasn't scaled and huge, his hands were glowing; he held ground by force of the magic she had never really seen him use.

There was no way to sneak up on the creature's eyes; she approached, instead, at a run. Halfway to Tiamaris, she leapt out of the way of a beam that grazed dirt, kicking up a cloud. She didn't wait for it to clear; instead, she rolled up on her feet and kept moving.

When she was in range, she let one of her daggers fly. The eyes weren't human eyes; they were as large as fists. The dagger glinted as it flew, and it flew true. The eye itself shot out one beam; Kaylin didn't wait to see what had happened to the dagger, because she was in its way. She jumped clear, holding her second knife.

She heard the creature's growl. High-pitched, it reminded her more of keening or wailing than aggression.

"Got it!" Morse shouted. She wasn't certain whether or not Morse was speaking of herself or of Kaylin, and it didn't matter. She ran at that eye again, pausing just long enough to throw first the dagger and then herself. Over her head, a beam passed, green and gray; she heard wall splinter in the distance.

Ducking back into the alley, she drew two more knives. They weren't as good as the ones she'd just let fly; they were for emergency use, and it showed. But they were the right shape, and they held an edge. Drawing these, unaware of where Morse was, she crouched low, rolled up to one side, and then began to run.

It was harder, now; the creature was tossing that head from side to side in wild fury. But the eyes were still open, and presumably still searching for a target. She had to pause to take aim. It almost killed her. She threw herself clear, lost hold of the dagger, and stumbled back, landing heavily on her hands.

Rolling, she was hit by a spray of dirt and loose rock; she could hear stone ding against her armor, as if she were a badly padded bell. She managed to get her knees under her, to raise herself up and fold her feet so that she landed on them.

Purple beam, bad. The dirt left in its wake was sizzling. One dagger left, she thought. That, and *keep moving*.

It was hard to both run and wait. The creature's gaze shredded street, staving in a wall or two when Kaylin got too close. She didn't have much choice; the streets weren't wide enough for decent running maneuvers. But the wood, like pipe leaves under fire, curled and blackened. The buildings would follow, she thought, and when they did, people would either run into the streets, into the alleys—or die.

Given the shuttered windows, she was pretty certain which of the three it would be. She chanced stillness, raising her dagger hand, and as she searched for a target, she saw Morse.

Morse wasn't running, not the way Kaylin had run; she wasn't leaping to avoid the strafing beams of those eyes. She'd—damn her anyway—found a moment to run *in*. Kaylin could see her moving at speed, a long knife in either hand. She didn't leap to the side to avoid the one beam that turned on her; she rolled forward, head tucked in, knees to chest, and came to her feet under the angle of the beam.

Smart, sort of. She'd brought herself into range of claws, range of ragged jaw. But the beams wouldn't get her, not unless the creature wanted to lower its head, exposing the back of its neck— if it even had one—to Kaylin. To Kaylin or Tiamaris. Morse drove both knives into the underside of that head, and then threw herself clear, rolling away from the forepaws that broke ground in their attempt to skewer her.

While she did, Kaylin threw her knife, and it flew in a fast arc toward its target; the point pierced open eye, and the dagger's un-adorned hilt jutted from iris. One lid tried to close over that eye, as if to protect what remained of it. Fire flew from Tiamaris—hand or mouth, Kaylin couldn't see—distorting air as it struck another eye.

The beams were fewer now; the creature's head turned slowly. It was easier—thank the gods—to avoid them.

From the underside of the creature's massive, misshapen head, shadow trailed in wisps, like dark blood made of smoke. Smoke that moved against the breeze, not that there was much of it, as if it were seeking something. West, toward the city, it stretched, thinning, and east, toward the heart of the fiefs.

She cried out a warning to Tiamaris, who stiffened. But stiff, he was not still; his arms rose, and he threw back his head and roared. Dragon words. Dragon voice, even contained by his human throat. The ground shook with the force of it and the air *shook,* as well, tearing at the shadow that stretched in either direction.

And then he lowered his head again and he breathed.

The creature was thrown back by the force of that breath, driven ten feet, its legs digging trenches in the earth. Smoke of a different kind began to leave the moving body.

She had no weapons now but a long knife, and this she drew; she couldn't throw it worth a damn, and she wasn't about to close with the flames. But she'd seen enough fights; this one was over. All that was left was the paperwork.

"Get them out!" Tiamaris shouted.

"Out's death!" Morse shouted over him.

But Kaylin nodded. At who, she wasn't certain. She turned toward the buildings that had started to burn, and she kicked one door open and headed in.

Morse managed to keep most of her disgust to herself when the street was finally full of people. Many of those people were either too young or too old to run; they were certainly not in any position to defend themselves, and given what they'd just seen in the streets, it wouldn't have mattered much if they had been. Kaylin knew she and Morse would have died had Tiamaris not been with them, and she silently thanked Sanabalis for his presence.

Kaylin, who had had some training in dealing with frightened crowds, raised her voice and ordered people to follow her. Morse looked as if she might argue, but she shrugged instead; her clothing was torn, and her armor looked as if it had absorbed at least one claw-strike—and at that, not well.

"Follow her," she said to the stragglers, who were indulging in their fascination with fire and the buildings it was slowly consuming. That, and the horror of it; it wasn't by the look of it much of a home, but it probably contained most of what they could call their own.

Except their lives, Kaylin thought grimly. She took them to the border street, and when Morse nodded, she asked them to find friends, family or deserted buildings and wait. She didn't tell them the fire would be put out, because she had no idea at all whether or not it would; it would depend on the fief lord's response.

After they'd gone, or at least, after Kaylin had left them somewhere that was theoretically safe, she turned back to Morse. "That was clever," she said quietly.

Morse shrugged. "You might remember I don't like running much."

Kaylin nodded.

"But you look like you could have kept that up for hours."

"Maybe hour. You've fought one of those before?"

"Hell no. Do I look like I'm dead?" She glanced at Tiamaris. But Morse generally didn't offer thanks to anyone, so she didn't actually speak to him. "You're lucky we're not on a tight schedule," she finally said.

"Oh?"

"If we were, we'd be late. Barren's always been big on punctuality."

"Big word," Kaylin said, falling in step beside Morse as Morse began to walk.

"Learn something, you hang around important men like Barren," Morse replied.

Kaylin nodded. She certainly had. "Anything worth learning?"

Morse chuckled. It was not a happy sound. "Same as always." She walked another two blocks before she stopped, wincing.

"Ribs?" Kaylin asked quietly.

"All there. Might not all be in one piece. Look, Eli, you've seen what we're facing."

"You said you hadn't seen—"

"I haven't. But then again, the big ones? They don't often come in exactly the same shape or size. They don't make the same noises. Some talk. Some don't. They can be killed," she added, "but it gets harder and harder with time. That was something special." She spit to one side to underline the last word. "Doesn't matter. You've seen it, you understand what it means.

"You still want to talk to Barren?"

"I never wanted to talk to Barren," Kaylin replied. "Not then. Not now."

"Go home."

"Can't."

Morse shrugged. "Your life, Eli. No one has to know you came this way."

Four people already did. She started to mention this, remembered who she was talking to, and stopped. Morse could kill them without blinking or breaking a sweat, and they both knew it. She was offering to do that now.

Kaylin owed them nothing. Less than nothing, really. But she shook her head. "You're not going to like this much," she told Morse, "but Barren is our last line of defense. We don't stop whatever is causing this problem, and those creatures are going to be eating their way through the rest of the city. The rest of the city," she added, touching the Hawk on her chest, "hasn't had years of ferals and nighttime curfews to get them ready for this kind of thing."

Morse grinned. "I know. It's the only thing that makes facing my own death bearable."

CHAPTER 10

Elianne had been with Morse for six weeks before Morse took her to see Barren the first time. Six weeks of training, albeit not the variety of training she'd see later with the Hawks. She'd learned how to hold a knife, and how to use it a little, in the years she'd lived with Severn, but Severn had never intended her to fight.

He'd never intended her to kill.

Morse was not Severn. Not to look at and not to live with. She'd given Elianne her first throwing daggers, and she'd taught her how to use them. She'd said nothing about self-defense; she only cared about Elianne's aim. And her arm strength. "Scrawny arms like that, and it doesn't matter how well you throw; dagger's going to go an inch through flesh, and it won't scratch shit out of armor."

Morse had occupied a large flat in a run-down building by Buckler. Her neighbors were quiet and well behaved, at least around Morse. Morse had taken the time to introduce them all to Elianne; she hadn't bothered to introduce Elianne to them. Their names, Morse reasoned, weren't important—they were nobody.

"I work for Barren," Morse told her, "and they all know it. You work for *me,* and they now know that, too. They give you any trouble, it's the last thing they'll do."

Elianne had nodded, and Morse grinned. "You want at least one of them to step out of line, though."

"Why?"

"Practice."

Morse had asked her, "Who was he?" at the start of their third week of training. Elianne, who had come in from a run in Barren, and now sagged against the wall completely winded, had taken her time replying. She'd known enough then to emphasize her lack of breath; Morse wasn't patient, and if angered, she'd let fly with either harsh words or the back of her hand.

"Who?"

"The guy. The one you want to kill."

"I thought he was a friend," Elianne had replied.

"A friend?"

"I can't remember when I didn't know him. He was there before my mom died."

Morse shrugged. "How old were you?"

"Five, I think."

"How old was he?"

"Ten."

"But he took care of you."

Elianne had nodded. "Yeah. He took care of me. Taught me how to look pathetic and cute, if it would help; taught me how to steal, when it wouldn't. Even taught me how to know the difference." She rose and began to walk; the first two days Morse had taken them out on a run, her legs had cramped horribly after they'd finally stopped moving. "I trusted him," she told Morse.

"Yeah," Morse said. "We're all stupid once. If we're lucky, we survive it. If we're good, they don't. What'd he do to you?"

Elianne closed her eyes.

"Eli?"

And opened them to the streets of Barren, seven years later. "Sorry. Thinking."

"Didn't look like thought."

Kaylin shrugged. "What passes for thought, these days. I remember the first time you took me to see Barren."

Morse didn't bat an eyelash.

"You got any more weapons?"

Kaylin, suddenly hit with an image of the quartermaster, winced. "There wasn't much left of the blades. I should have kept them anyway."

Morse shrugged. "Why?"

Explaining the quartermaster to Morse was not high on the list of priorities for the day. Any day. Tiamaris, however, handed her two knives. They weren't regulation wear, but they had their own sheaths. "For now," he told her. "And I will make the quartermaster seem like a lamb if you lose them."

She glanced over her shoulder.

"Casualties of battle are not the same as a loss."

"If you ever get tired of Court," she told him with a grimace, "you've got a career as a quartermaster ahead of you."

The streets were empty. Even empty, they became familiar as Kaylin walked them. Maybe it was because she walked them with Morse; she couldn't quite say. She hadn't lived here long enough to know them as well as she knew Nightshade's—but Nightshade had been her childhood home, and until the last day of her life in it, she had managed to find ways to be happy living there.

There was no happiness in Barren. Barren, she thought, had lived up to its name, although her rage and her guilt hadn't let her be that ironic at the time. What would she say to her younger self, if she met her in these streets?

And what would that younger self say to her, if she knew that Severn was not only still alive, but her partner? *I want to be able to kill a man.* She'd tried. But she wasn't *still* trying. Some days she woke from the nightmares of Steffi and Jade's deaths. But they vanished into the past; they no longer withstood sunlight by chilling her until she could feel nothing else at all.

Barren's memory, however, was not theirs.

Morse raised a brow. On her face, it looked like a twist, but everything about Morse seemed twisted. "You worried?"

Kaylin shook her head.

Morse snorted. "You were always crap at lying."

"And you," Kaylin shot back, "were always good at asking questions you already knew the answers to. If you know, why bother?"

"Maybe it's a test."

"I suck at those. Trust me."

"Only the small ones. You suck at the big ones, you'd already be dead."

Kaylin shrugged. Coming from Morse, that was almost embarrassingly glowing praise. "I'm not afraid of him now," she said, voice low.

Morse stopped for a moment. "You're not thirteen anymore."

"No."

"He won't touch you, much. You're marked," she added. "He can't afford to piss off Nightshade. Not now."

As if, Kaylin thought, Morse could see right through her. She frowned. "Morse?"

"What?" Morse started to walk.

"How old were you when Barren found you?"

"Older than you."

"Than I was?"

"Yeah. Older, smarter. But he was new, then," she added. "He had a lot to prove, but he had to prove it in a way that didn't deplete his ranks."

Kaylin frowned. "Morse?"

"What?"

"Do you remember Illien?"

Morse froze, then. Just froze. "Where'd you hear that name?"

"Nightshade told me. Lord Nightshade," Kaylin added with a shrug. When Morse raised a brow, she said, "He's the fief lord. He's *also* Barrani. They like their titles."

"Yeah," Morse replied after a pause. "I remember Illien."

"You met him?"

"No. You weren't born here," Morse added quietly, "or you'd know the answer to the question. You wouldn't need to ask. I never met him. I'm still alive."

She nodded. That had been how she'd felt about Nightshade, growing up in the streets of his fief. But she'd met him, and she was still alive. How much of Morse's response was that primal, certain fear, and how much of it was fact? "Was Illien human?"

"With a name like that?"

That would be no.

"How did Barren kill him?"

Morse stopped walking again, and then she laughed. "Since you're so fond of questions, why don't you ask Barren?"

Which meant, Kaylin thought sourly, that it was exactly the wrong thing to ask Barren—unless she wanted to enrage him. She glanced at Tiamaris. Tiamaris did not do her the favor of returning it. He was watching Morse closely, although he wasn't openly staring. "Perhaps," he said at length, "I will spare the Private the embarrassment of asking such an obvious question. By asking it," he added, "myself."

Having seen Tiamaris fight, Morse had nothing to say to that; she shrugged. "I should warn you," she told the Dragon Lord, "that Barren may be human, but he's got power."

Tiamaris did not condescend to reply; his silence had Dragon arrogance written all over it. Kaylin didn't speak because some treacherous part of herself wanted to see him square off against Barren.

Barren didn't live in the heart of the fief. He lived—he had always lived—near its edge. She'd wondered about that, when Morse had first brought her here. But then, at thirteen, she hadn't known about the heart of the fiefs, and she hadn't seen what could emerge from them; it hadn't occurred to her that ferals weren't actually alive.

But if he didn't live in the fief's heart, he didn't live in a hovel, either—not that any of the buildings in Barren could be said to be grand or ostentatious. There was, on these streets, some evidence that previous generations of Elantrans—with money, even—had chosen to build homes here. Most of those buildings were in disrepair; one of them was not.

It was to that familiar building that Morse now led them. And she did lead; at some point—Kaylin wasn't certain when—she had fallen behind in her step. But Barren's White Towers, which was what he called his residence, now loomed in the distance a few blocks away. There were flags flying atop the two, squat ends of the building; they weren't, in any real sense, Towers. But they were three stories tall, and given that anything *else* that tall had probably crumbled or fallen into a state of shoddy neglect, they stood out.

The building was fenced, and the fence—unlike the fence that had opened so fortuitously on the night that Kaylin had run here—was in solid, even shining repair; there was a functional guardhouse which was probably not more than nine years old. Someone—she wasn't sure who—had even sheared the grass, and if there were no flower beds, there were standing trees that didn't look too badly in need of pruning.

But the guards, rather than looking like the official adornments that often accompanied a gatehouse, looked as if they'd seen action; their armor was scuffed, and it was entirely practical. They didn't have tabards—but in Barren, they wouldn't—but they had that undershaven, underslept look that Kaylin associated with stakeouts and trouble. There were also more of them than Kaylin remembered.

Tiamaris nodded toward the building. "This is where Barren lives?"

Kaylin nodded. "It hasn't changed much," she added quietly. "And at least it doesn't have cages and a gallows."

"Lord Nightshade always did have a penchant for the melodramatic," was the Dragon Lord's reply. "It is not entirely necessary, however."

"No," she replied. "Morse?"

"Waiting for the two of you to finish jabbering. Barren never likes the sound of any voice that isn't his."

True enough. Kaylin took a breath and stopped talking. Morse didn't ask her if she was ready; she was here. It was too late to change that. But she did walk up to the gatehouse. The guards—none of whom Kaylin recognized—nodded at Morse. They gave Kaylin the once-over, sneered openly at the Hawk, and then glanced at Tiamaris. Give them this much, she thought, they don't look bored.

From their reaction, only one of them recognized Tiamaris for what he was. The other three? They assumed he was, like Kaylin, a Hawk. The Law wasn't much feared in any of the fiefs, but it wasn't generally subject to this kind of open contempt.

She seriously hoped they'd keep their mouths shut. She could take it—more or less, and when she felt like it—but Dragon dignity was a finicky and unpredictable thing. Morse said nothing at all, but they must have seen something in her nonexpression, because they finally nodded and let them all through.

They didn't all stay at the gatehouse; they sent a runner.

The runner moved far more quickly than Kaylin, Morse or Tiamaris, even though the distance from the fence to the house wasn't that long. The doors opened just as they reached them. A bristling row of guards—two abreast, and three deep—greeted them.

"We'll take over from here," one of them told Morse.

Morse shrugged.

"And you," he added, pointing to Tiamaris, "are to wait outside."

Morse grinned. "Good luck with that," she told the guard. "I'll just step back and see how it works out for you."

Even the most dense or stupid of men wouldn't have misinterpreted Morse's amused malice; this guard was neither. He turned to Kaylin and said, "Ask him to wait outside."

Kaylin now shrugged, mimicking Morse. "I can't," she told him blandly. "He's an officer." She glanced at Tiamaris.

His eyes had shaded to orange, and he lowered his membranes

to make this difference clear. The man who was speaking, and who Kaylin therefore assumed was in charge, took a step back. He stopped before he hit the man behind him, and turned and whispered something quickly.

The man then pushed his way through the rest of the guards and headed up the stairs. They were set well back, and there was enough room in this entrance for a real fight, swords and all; the ceiling here ran the full three stories of the building. But no one drew a sword; no one drew even as much as a dagger.

When the man clanked his way back down the stairs, he spoke to the guard.

"All right," the man told Tiamaris. "You've got permission to enter."

Tiamaris said nothing at all, but his eyes did not shade back to their familiar gold. He did, however, raise his inner membranes, muting the clearest sign of Dragon temper. The guards spread out, losing their look of uniformity, and with it, any suggestion of real training. They took front and back when they reached the stairs, and Kaylin and Tiamaris formed up in the middle.

Together they were escorted up the staircase and down the long and impressive hall that led to Barren's office. The doors were closed, and Kaylin saw with a grimace that they were warded—something new, and something she didn't see much of at all in the fiefs. But it wasn't her palm that was going to do the stinging; a guard reached out and touched it.

The doors rolled open, and seated behind a large and completely clear desk, sat Barren, Lord of the fief.

Almost seven years had passed since she'd last seen him behind that desk. Seven years, most of them spent tagging along underfoot of one Hawk or another. She wasn't scrawny in the same way she'd been then, and she wasn't a child. She tried to see Barren from that perspective, while her hands curled in loose fists and her mouth went dry.

He was, seated, not a tall man; when he rose—and he would,

she thought—he was slightly taller than Tiamaris. He wasn't fat, and he wasn't old; he was older, and he had one new scar that ran the length of his cheek. It hadn't faded to white, but it didn't make him look any worse. His hair, which had always been a shade of pale gold, hadn't obviously grayed; his skin was dark, but he'd just passed through summer.

His eyes were still blue, and at that, the gray-blue that always seemed so unfriendly. And his hands were still that square, callused set of hands; he held a dagger in one as if it were just a piece of jewelry. He was not, however, ostentatiously dressed in any way; that wasn't his style. He also didn't wear armor, at least not in the Towers. When he went out in the streets, he usually did.

"Welcome back, Elianne," he said, and at that point, he did unfold. "You're looking well."

She said nothing, and he frowned.

"Did you miss Barren?"

"No."

He shrugged slightly. Smiled. It was, as far as smiles went, much a match for Morse's. "I hear that the Hawklord is still alive."

"There's always a Hawklord," she replied, keeping her voice even.

"But it's the man who's ruled the Hawks for the past—how many?—several years."

She shrugged. It was a fief gesture. She kept her expression as even and neutral as possible as he came out from behind his desk. When he didn't speak, she said, "You wanted to speak to me."

"I did. I had hoped the conversation might be private." He glanced at Tiamaris as he said this. Kaylin didn't. And she didn't take her eyes from the dagger in his hands, either.

He noted this, and his eyes narrowed slightly.

Before he could speak, Kaylin did. "If you're about to remind me who the boss here is, I need to remind you that I don't work for you, anymore."

"I spent a few months training you, girl."

She shrugged. "They spent a few years."

"And they pay you as well as I did?"

She exhaled. "Better, in most ways."

He spit to the side. "I know what you're paid."

"And where I work, apparently."

He lifted the dagger, and she smiled. It was not, to her surprise, a forced smile. "I've had a long week," she told him softly. "And I've got a Dragon as a partner." She closed her mouth on the rest of the words; they would have been a threat. And, she thought, they would have gone on for days, and once they'd started, she'd never be free of them. "I owe you nothing," she continued. "You sent me to hang just to deliver a cheap thug's message."

His brows rose, and then he laughed. "When did you figure that out?"

She didn't answer.

"I didn't think you had it in you, to be honest," he replied, still chuckling. "I should have paid more attention to you, Eli. I never cared much for stupid girls."

And that, Kaylin thought, with a burning bitterness, was exactly what she'd been. Stupid. Terrified. Angry. Desperate to prove herself. And to whom? To *what?* This man. A fief lord who had— No.

I was thirteen, she reminded herself, forcing her hands not to curl into fists. She turned to Tiamaris. "I think we're done here," she told him curtly.

Tiamaris nodded. He didn't shrug, but the nod was almost the equivalent, it was so careless.

"We're not finished yet," Barren said.

Tiamaris lowered the inner membranes of his eyes. "If you don't wish to be finished," he told Barren, speaking for the first time, "I'd suggest you make clear what your *request* is."

"It's not a *request.*"

"It is," Kaylin told him. "I came here for my own reasons, but in the end? I don't give a shit if you send a wagonload of personal letters across the bridge. Send them to the Hawklord. Send them to the Emperor."

Barren grinned. "You're bluffing."

"Maybe. But you're desperate. We've both got our cards on

the table, and we can both see most of them. You want to play your hand now?"

The grin deserted his face. What was left in its wake passed for thoughtful, with Barren. Thought and Barren usually meant trouble for the poor sod he was thinking *at*. "You've gotten better at this game." His eyes flickered, so briefly it might have been a trick of the light, to Tiamaris and back. She thought, if the Dragon Lord hadn't been present, the game—as Barren called it— would have taken a turn for the deeply personal.

"No," she told him quietly. "I stopped playing it years ago. That's why I don't live on this side of the bridge, in *any* fief."

"No?"

"No."

"Pretty mark, that." He gazed at the nightshade that adorned her cheek. In this context, it was clear what he was inferring. And implying.

Don't let him know that it hurts, Morse said, over the distance of years, the words so clear they might have been spoken yesterday. *If he knows how to hurt you, he's got you; he'll never stop.*

What about anger?

Same difference, Morse said. *It's all the same thing, in the end. Play it cool, Eli. Play it as cool as you can.*

It was a very bad day when memories of Morse could somehow come to your rescue. "It is. It's not generally my style, but I've grown into it."

"I bet you have."

Her hands did clench, then.

"You know," he added, deliberately turning his back on her as he moved toward his desk, "at least I never felt the need to mark you to prove anything."

She wanted, for just that moment, to kill him. To flay his skin off his body, while keeping the rest of him alive; to make him suffer and to make damn certain that he knew *why*. It was a blinding rage, a sudden, visceral desire.

"Private," Tiamaris said.

Her rank cut through the worst of the rage. His fingers on her wrist—nothing more than a momentary, gentle pressure, cut through most of the rest.

What was left? What was left was ugly, but she could work with it. Barren turned, his lips twisted in a self-satisfied smirk.

"No," she told him. "You had way bigger things to prove, didn't you, Barren? It's probably hard to be fief lord in name only."

She had the pleasure—and it was, and it was dark and bitter and glorious—of watching him flinch, and of watching that flinch transform itself into an echo of the anger that had, seconds ago, immobilized her. He wanted to kill her.

And he couldn't.

And he considered trying anyway.

But he recovered. Not as well as she had—but then again, a small voice inside her head told her, she'd had help. "I'm fief lord," he told her grimly, "until I'm dead. After that, I don't give a shit."

"That's the way the fiefs work," she replied. She paused, pulled back the words, the desire to twist the knife in the unexpected wound she'd made. "What do you want, Barren?"

"There was a Dragon in the fiefs, near the interior border," he told her.

She nodded. "There were two."

"I only care about one of them." He glanced at Tiamaris, and the gaze added, *for now.*

"You don't ask people to fight Dragons unless you want to feed the Dragons lunch," Kaylin replied. "And I've already been served as lunch once; not even I'm stupid enough to play that role again. You're hedging. You tell me what you want, and I'll tell you what I've got."

But Barren had also managed—barely—to retreat from his rage. "Your friend," he said, for he hadn't addressed Tiamaris directly at all, "was he the other Dragon?"

Kaylin's lips compressed in a tight line.

But if she had no intention of answering, Tiamaris felt no such constraint. And why would he? In the end, he was a Dragon; he had nothing to fear from Barren. "I was," he replied.

"And you're here with her now."

"Obviously."

Barren glanced at the guards who were now lining one side of the room. "You, and you," he told two of them, "go drag Morse's sorry ass up here."

Tiamaris let them go. "Before you make plans based on my continuing presence, fief lord," he told Barren, "I have a few questions to ask you."

Morse appeared as the doors opened. Contrary to Barren's stated demand, she had clearly not been dragged from the foyer to the office; she walked flanked by guards, but she walked slightly ahead of them, and they kept a respectful distance. As respectful a distance, Kaylin thought, as they would have kept had they been escorting the fief lord. She wondered if they were aware of it; she could tell that Barren was.

There was no strict etiquette that governed Barren's guards. They did not salute the way Nightshade's did; they did not bow formally and they did not offer other formalized gestures of respect. Morse met Barren's gaze and nodded. She didn't look away and she didn't simper. Then again, she didn't shrug and she didn't speak, either. She stood in front of his desk, her hands loose by her sides, waiting.

"Your kitten's grown claws," he finally said.

Morse did shrug, then. "That's what happens if you don't drown them at birth. Fact of life."

He smiled. It was a typical Barren smile. "I did try."

Morse said nothing. Kaylin also said nothing, but this was harder.

Barren seldom attempted to bait Morse. Not never, but Kaylin couldn't recall a single time it had worked in the past. Morse, looking bored, waited. Barren might have let it drag on, but Kaylin—and more important, Tiamaris—were waiting. And listening.

"Did you have any trouble on the way here?"

Given the condition of Morse's clothing, it didn't take a brilliant or perceptive mind to notice. "Some."

Barren's expression shifted, his eyes narrowing. Morse gave real meaning to the word *laconic,* which Kaylin had acquired on the other side of the bridge. Then again, Barren seemed to know her well enough to understand what she meant, and Kaylin felt a mild twinge of envy at the brevity of the report. If she tried that with Marcus, she'd be writing out a detailed report for four days—a report he'd leave unread in prominent sight on top of one of the ever-shifting piles on his desk. She knew this from bitter experience.

"How bad?"

"It was a one-off."

He spit to one side of the desk. "Where?"

At this, Morse did hesitate. He could read the hesitation; knew, before she answered, that he wasn't going to like it. That much was clear to Kaylin. "Capstone."

He swore. It was brief. "These two?" he asked, not bothering to look at the two Hawks who stood to one side of his desk.

"They're alive," Morse replied.

"Anyone die?"

"No one else was with us."

"I told Carl—"

Morse shrugged. "Didn't tell me. You'd've lost him," she added, as if Carl were as significant as a hairpin.

Barren shrugged. It was like fencing, but without the weapons. He didn't argue; no point. Kaylin had seen Carl fight. It wouldn't have broken her heart to see him dead; she agreed with Morse's evaluation. So, clearly, did Barren.

"One-off," he said. "How bad?"

"Eyes."

"Fuck. Any other damage?"

"One building'll probably burn down. The roads there are pure shit anyway. Nothing happened to them that could make 'em any worse." Morse didn't mention the fact that the people inside that building had escaped the flames. Barren, on the other hand, didn't ask. Kaylin didn't need a reminder of why she hated the fiefs, but it was there anyway.

"Were these two any good?"

"They're alive," Morse repeated.

"Would they still be alive if it hadn't been broad daylight?"

Morse thought about it for a minute. Kaylin wasn't sure if she did this to irritate Barren or not. She had never understood the way they interacted. *Yes, idiot, but you were thirteen. Pay attention now.*

"Good chance of it," Morse finally told him.

Barren actually whistled. He turned to Tiamaris, as if he hadn't been ignoring him until now. "What are your questions?"

"A moment." Tiamaris now turned to Morse. "Is it unusual to get these creatures in broad daylight?"

"It's unusual," Morse replied, putting sarcasm into the second word, "to get them materializing way the hell up on Capstone. We've got an early alert system set up." She frowned, and then turned to two of the guards. "Tell Seeley to check the two west posts."

The guard nodded, and glanced at Barren. Barren nodded, as well. *Careful, Morse.*

"Unusual for daylight, or at all?" Tiamaris asked, as if he had not noticed the brief exchange.

"Daylight."

"I assume you have ferals during daylight now."

"We've got 'em all the time." The shrug she offered made clear just how much of a danger she thought they were. "But they don't range farther than Old Holdstock. At least they haven't, yet."

"You think it's going to get worse."

Morse shrugged. Which meant yes.

"Thank you." Tiamaris turned back to Barren. "My questions," he replied with deliberate care, "all involve the previous fief lord."

Everyone in the room tensed; Kaylin did, as well, but hers was an instinctive response to their reaction. It didn't matter; she waited just as if she were still working for Barren and someone had been stupid enough to insult him.

Tiamaris was the only living thing in the room that seemed not to care. He waited without apparent concern; Kaylin was certain that the cockroaches and the mice which were so ubiquitous in the fiefs were about to expire from lack of oxygen, because they were probably also holding their breaths.

Barren didn't shrug. But after a moment, he nodded grimly. "Morse," he said, without looking at her, "clear the room."

None of his guards were stupid enough to argue. Morse didn't even have to tell them to leave; they were already heading toward the door. They did manage to scrape together a few shreds of dignity; they walked at a normal pace and they didn't collide with each other in their hurry to get the hell out of the way before Barren said anything. Kaylin didn't blame them; if Barren felt it was necessary to answer Tiamaris, he would; he was a pragmatic man.

He was also, however, ferociously proud. If he was going to answer questions he didn't like, and anyone who *wasn't* necessary happened to be around as witnesses, they'd have a lifespan, in days, that Kaylin could measure on one hand. If they were lucky.

When the door closed, Morse was still in the room. Barren did not appear to notice, and Morse—unlike the rest of his men—appeared to be in no hurry to leave.

"Ask," Barren said to Tiamaris.

CHAPTER

11

"Before I begin," Tiamaris said quietly, "I wish to make one thing clear. I owe allegiance to the Emperor, and only the Emperor."

"Emperor doesn't rule the fiefs," Barren said. But he said it quietly; the words had no patina of boast wrapped around them.

"No. He is therefore unconcerned with the particulars of any single fief." Tiamaris frowned. "Which means," he continued, "that he doesn't particularly care which fief is ruled by which Lord. He is unconcerned with the significance of the name of any one fief.

"The only thing that concerns him at all is that the fiefs *be* ruled. I am therefore free to participate—as I deem wise—in any defense of any fief. At the moment, I am in Barren. Where your concerns do not clash with my Lord's, I am free—again, at my discretion—to aid you.

"You are not, however, my Lord."

Barren nodded. He had never been stupid; he didn't ask what the Emperor offered Tiamaris, and he made no attempt to better whatever it might be.

"This is not the first time that I've traveled these streets," Tiamaris continued. "But it is the first time I have traveled through Barren. When last I came, the fief was Illien, and the fieflord, as well. I had no cause to meet him," he added softly, "and I dared the Tower only twice. I survived."

"You—you attempted to breach the Tower?"

Tiamaris nodded. He watched Barren carefully. After a moment, he said, "Did you not do the same?" His first real question.

Barren shrugged. As far as answers went, it was pure fief. Tiamaris was strictly an outsider; it wasn't going to fly with him. But instead of repeating the question, Tiamaris asked a different one. "How well do you understand the fiefs?"

"I understand Barren," he replied.

Fair enough, Kaylin thought.

"Barren does not exist in isolation—as you are no doubt now well aware. How well do you understand the fiefs?"

"I know what the Tower was," Barren replied. It was half an answer.

"This is not a game," Tiamaris told him. "I am not a rival. I have no interest in being chained to the fief. You call yourself fieflord," he continued, "and the people in the streets of this fief accept that title as truth."

"I am fieflord."

"You have held the fief for ten years. I am willing to grant some truth to your claim; were there not some element of truth to it, Barren would have already ceased to exist." He paused. "Your name."

Barren's eyes widened slightly. Only slightly. But for Barren it was an open admission of surprise. "Morse," he said curtly. "Get out."

Morse shrugged.

"Take Eli with you."

"I'm afraid," Tiamaris said quietly, "that that will not be possible. She is under my protection—where she goes, I follow."

Had Kaylin been in a betting mood—and she wasn't, which was rare—she would have bet that that was the end of the conversation. She would have lost.

"Morse," Barren said again.

Morse turned and left the room. She glanced once at Kaylin just before the doors closed.

"What about my name?" Barren looked once at Kaylin. Every threat he had ever spoken existed in the silence of that gaze.

"The fief takes the name of its Lord. Or so lore implies. But there are very few men who are named Barren."

Barren shrugged. "It's a name," he said.

"Was it yours, before you came here?"

The silence was tense and stretched. "No."

Kaylin was almost shocked. Tiamaris, however, nodded. Damn the Dragon Court anyway.

"It was the fief's name," Barren said.

"It was," Tiamaris replied, "the fief's name. In a fashion. When did you attempt the Tower?"

Again, the silence was marked. Barren turned away. "Ten years ago," he answered.

"How many times?"

Barren laughed. It was quiet and bitter. "Once was enough."

"How much of it did you see?"

"I saw enough," Barren replied. Evasion. "I learned enough to hold the fief."

"To hold it," Tiamaris replied, "for nine years." He folded his arms across the breadth of his chest, obscuring the Hawk. "The Tower didn't kill you. You have some strength." He paused, and then said, "Did you meet Illien?"

Barren stiffened. "If Illien were alive, the fief would have had a name."

"In theory, yes. That was not, however, an answer."

"It was," Barren replied. He turned to face Tiamaris again.

This time, it was Tiamaris who evinced surprise; it was as subtle a physical expression as Barren's had been. "He was not dead."

"No."

Kaylin said, "He had no name."

They both turned to look at her.

★ ★ ★

Kaylin cleared her throat. Had she the choice, she would be outside in the hall with Morse. "Tiamaris," she said quietly, "ask him how he found the Tower."

Tiamaris frowned.

"He said—when you asked—that the fief's name was Barren. The fief's name *wasn't* Barren ten years ago. We know that," she added. "He wasn't born here. He didn't come up through the streets."

"Careful, Eli," Barren said.

"Why is it significant? I found the Tower," Tiamaris told her.

"You found the Tower when Illien ruled from it."

He frowned.

"Barren found the Tower when it was, in theory, empty."

Barren was watching her. She realized, then, that he had *always* watched her. His attention, profoundly unwelcome, had always made her uncomfortable; it had never occurred to her, not at thirteen, that the entire point of that watchfulness wasn't her discomfort or her revulsion.

Careful, Kaylin. Careful. Now is not the time to go there.

"You found the Tower," Kaylin said, forcing herself to remain in the present. "But you were *looking* for it. Was Barren?"

Tiamaris frowned again. "Were you?" he asked.

"No more than *she* was," he replied. Kaylin knew that if the fate of his fief wasn't hanging in the balance she wouldn't have left the room alive. He wouldn't have taken his time, either; she would just be dead.

"She has answered all relevant questions," Tiamaris replied, as if the momentary venom of Barren's answer was beneath concern.

"She hasn't answered mine."

"Ah. I believe I am misunderstanding what must be a human interaction," Tiamaris replied.

Barren raised a brow.

"You are asking for aid. We are in a position to offer it. We are not applying for a job or a position on your staff. Your questions would seem, to me, to be irrelevant. Private?"

Kaylin shrugged. "I'd say you understand the interaction fairly well."

Barren was silent for a long moment. "I was on the run," he finally said. "It was the outer gates, the port, or the fiefs—and I didn't have much time to make a decision. Only a madman runs into the fiefs," he added. Pride and bitterness were braided through those words. "I didn't have much time to pack. I didn't expect to remain here. But it was driving rain, and I wanted shelter. I wanted shelter," he added, "that wouldn't immediately be tracked. If that had been less of a concern, I would have kicked a door in."

"You were worried about witnesses in the *fiefs?*" Kaylin said. Tiamaris gave her a look.

"I wasn't familiar with the fiefs at the time," Barren replied. His tone and his language had shifted in subtle ways as he spoke. "I knew the stories," he added, "and I knew the legends."

"Legends?"

"I don't expect someone who was born in the fiefs to know them."

Kaylin shrugged.

"You refer," Tiamaris said, "to the heart of the fiefs."

Barren said nothing. After a long pause, he continued. "I saw the Tower. It didn't look occupied."

Tiamaris frowned. "It was in the same state of disrepair it is currently in?"

"Yes. I climbed the fence."

"In the rain," Kaylin said.

"Private."

"He didn't climb—"

"It doesn't matter," Barren snapped. "I went over the damn fence. The wall isn't solid. Some of the rocks near the foundation have crumbled. I found a way in through those." He looked across at Tiamaris. "The inside was not what I expected."

Tiamaris nodded. Even Kaylin was not surprised.

"You didn't enter the Tower?" Barren asked her.

This wasn't a conversation; it was an interrogation. Kaylin knew this, but in spite of that, she answered. "No. It wasn't raining. It was dark. There were ferals somewhere nearby—I could hear them. I went to ground behind the fence, in the grass."

"Grass doesn't usually stop ferals."

"Fences do. Sometimes."

He shrugged. "You're not as smart as you think you are."

"No one ever is."

Tiamaris nodded as if he approved of the reply, which was good—it wasn't the first one that had come to mind, and she'd had to struggle to offer it.

"I am not entirely interested in what the Tower looked like," Tiamaris told Barren. "I am interested only in its occupants. You said that you met Illien."

Barren's nod was slight.

"You invaded his Tower. He could not have been pleased to see you."

"Oh, he was pleased," Barren replied. He smiled, and the smile was a thin, sharp edge of an expression. "At least he was at first."

"What did he want from you?" Kaylin asked.

"I imagine he wanted the same thing from me that he wanted from you."

She gritted her teeth. "And that would be?"

"Power."

"He wanted you to serve him?"

"No. In fief terms, he wanted to eat me."

"Barren—"

Tiamaris lifted a hand. "Private," he said. At least that's what she thought he said; the two syllables felt an awful lot like "shut up." He faced the fieflord. "You were an Arcanist," he said. It wasn't a question.

Barren's brow rose. After a moment, he nodded.

"Fief Law and Imperial Law are not the same."

"Tell the Wolves that."

"The Wolves are not here. And even if they were, I think it unlikely they would look for their quarry in the fief lord."

Kaylin looked back and forth between the Dragon Lord and the fief lord. Barren had been hunted by Wolves. And he had come here. She should have been surprised, but she wasn't. She didn't even wonder what he had done to merit the peculiar death sentence of a hunting Wolf. Or Wolves. She'd spent almost five months under his tutelage; she had no trouble imagining that he deserved it.

But…she had never seen Barren use magic. It's true that he might have chosen the more subtle, and less visible, spells—but she'd never felt the uncomfortable and painful prickly feeling that magic almost always caused.

"Tiamaris," she said quietly. This time he nodded. "I spent months in Barren, and I spent some time in his company. He didn't use magic."

Tiamaris nodded, as if this were not a surprise.

"You don't know Barren," Kaylin continued. "If he were an Arcanist of any note, if he were dangerous enough that they could send the Shadow Wolves after him, he *would* have used magic. He's not a subtle man. He's always been all about the power."

Tiamaris nodded again. And then, as if he were Sanabalis, he said, "What does this tell you, Private?"

"That he didn't have any."

"Not of note, no."

She'd had a long damn day. It took her a moment to understand what he was implying. But when she did, she looked at Barren. "Illien," she whispered.

He said nothing for a long moment, and then he nodded.

"Now," Tiamaris told the fief lord, "I understand why the fief did not fall immediately. Whatever power protected its borders, and however weakly—it wasn't Illien's. It was yours. You should have contested his control of the Tower."

"With *what?*"

The Dragon Lord did not reply. Instead he turned to Kaylin. "Private," he told her quietly, "we are done here for now." He paused, and then he offered Barren a bow. "We will return on the morrow. We can discuss the nature of the fief, and the defense of the fief, then."

Barren nodded. He almost spoke, but chose to withhold the words. The door opened on Tiamaris's sentence.

"Good," Morse told them both. "Because we've lost two sentry towers."

Barren looked up as if slapped.

"I sent Seeley," Morse continued. "He's cleaning up now."

The fieflord turned to the Dragon Lord.

Kaylin, however, turned to Morse. "Cleaning up?"

Morse nodded grimly.

Kaylin glanced, briefly, out the window. "It's barely late afternoon," she told Tiamaris. "We're not due back to report for hours, yet."

"The information that we've received is not information I fully understand," Tiamaris replied. "And it is crucial, if we are to participate in the defense of the fief, that we speak to those who might."

Morse shrugged. "Go," she told Kaylin. "We'll still be here in the morning."

"Hell with that," Kaylin snapped. She turned to Tiamaris. This time the Dragon Lord nodded.

"Go, Morse," Kaylin told her. "We've got your back."

Morse looked as if she would speak, but she glanced at Barren instead, and shrugged. "Boss?" she said.

"Take them."

Kaylin noted that the fieflord did not leave the room.

"What the fuck is an Arcanist?" Morse asked as she jogged down the walk and toward the guardhouse. Morse had been listening in, then. No surprise.

"Mage," Kaylin replied, just as tersely. Morse was pissed, but Kaylin wasn't much happier. "We'll still be here in the morning?"

"What the fuck was I supposed to say?" Morse could spit words as easily as she could throw daggers. "You want sniveling and groveling, go kick a door down."

"You could have—"

"I didn't want you back in the first place. I don't want you here now."

"Why?"

"You *don't get it,* do you? You know what an Arcanist is. You understood most of what Barren said—and you still don't get it. I don't have all that fancy education—and I do."

"What I *got,*" Kaylin replied, as the guards in the guardhouse got the hell out of their way, "was that you're not certain you won't die here." They headed out into the street. The streets looked pretty much the same as they always had, this close to the White Towers: they were lined with buildings that seemed dingy, but here at least, they stood alone; whoever had built them once, in a bygone age, hadn't packed them cheek by jowl. They were also empty.

The shutters in the buildings that faced the Towers were closed. Kaylin wondered if anyone lived in them, now. No one with anywhere else to go would—but if you lived in the fiefs, you probably didn't have many other options.

But the buildings were standing; they hadn't burned down, and they hadn't been riddled with holes; if creatures like the one she had faced on Capstone were as common as Tiamaris feared—and he did fear it, even if he kept that fear to himself—she thought the streets would have been a standing wreck.

"I'm never certain I'm not going to die," Morse said. "Hey! We're not going that way. West and Southwest watches."

Kaylin shook herself. "Sorry. Old habits." She reversed direction, and once again kept pace with Morse.

"You and your damn old habits." Morse slowed for a moment, dragging her hands through the short brush of her hair. "Tell me you at least killed him."

"Who?"

"Whoever you wanted to kill so badly you came to work for me."

Kaylin, no longer thirteen, looked at Morse. "No."

Morse swore. She began to jog again, but this time, Kaylin had a much clearer idea of where they were going: she could see smoke rising in the distance.

"Did you?" Kaylin said, keeping as much of a safe distance as an attempt to combine running and conversation allowed.

"Did I what?"

"Kill the man you wanted to kill so badly?"

It could have gone either way. But Morse chose to grimace, and she chose to keep up her steady jog. "No. But I'm not done yet. You?"

Kaylin shook her head. "I'm done," she told Morse quietly.

"You ever kill anyone outside of Barren?"

Kaylin flinched and looked away. "Yeah."

"Good."

She almost smiled. It was Morse, after all; Morse never regretted any death she caused. "Good?"

"Hate to see my time go to waste," Morse told her. She slowed as they turned a corner.

Kaylin froze.

"Welcome," Morse said, with a grin that was pure black, "to Barren."

What Kaylin had assumed was smoke at a distance was not, in fact, smoke. It rose and it twisted in the air in thin, amorphous streams, and it was dark enough—at a distance—that it should have been smoke. But there was no fire beneath it.

She stared, her head falling backward as she craned her neck up. "Tiamaris," she whispered. "What do you see?"

She couldn't tell if he looked at her at all; for a moment all she could see was the azure of sky paling into insignificance before the tendrils that reached into its heart.

"I don't see what you see."

She swallowed. "There's shadow here." It was an understatement. Shadow enfolded the wooden legs of what might have been a tall, freestanding structure. A watchpost, Morse had called it. It climbed up those legs, blackening wood as if it was trying to consume it.

"Yes. That much, I *can* see."

She closed her eyes. "Morse, what are we going to find there?"

"If you're lucky, corpses," Morse replied, in a tone of voice that made clear just how unlucky Morse thought they would be.

"Kaylin," Tiamaris said, touching her shoulder. She turned to look at him. "What do you see?"

"I thought it was smoke," she told him.

"Now?"

"It's— I think it's a sigil."

"What the fuck is a sigil?" Morse said. Her voice was not as faint as Kaylin's and it was a good deal less friendly.

"It's a mage thing," Kaylin replied. "The reason we can track mages—and, you know, kill them if we need to—is that they leave a...a signature when they work a spell."

"A signature?"

"Not on purpose. It's just an artifact of the magic. Every mage alive works slightly differently. There's some theory that says—"

Morse spit.

Fair enough. Kaylin had rolled her eyes—like a spoiled, wayward child—the first time she'd heard this, seated in the confines of a classroom that had never felt so far away. "Never mind. We can tell who cast a spell if we've seen that mage's work before."

"And you see that here?" Morse said sharply. "'Cause I see squat. Besides the shadow."

"I see a sigil. A sigil," Kaylin added softly, because she was almost afraid of the words, "that's taller than the tower itself."

Tiamaris swore. In Leontine.

Morse looked at Kaylin. "What did he just say?"

"It wasn't in Elantran."

"Got that. Dragon?"

Kaylin shook her head. "Leontine. Leontine has a huge number of words that are useful at times like this."

"So you have been learning something useful." Morse grinned. It was a gallows grin, but Kaylin had responded in kind before she could stop herself.

"Yeah. I'll teach you the good ones. There are a few Aerian phrases, as well. Dragons and Barrani don't need 'em; they just tend to rip out your throat or cut off your head if they're pissed off."

"Which your friend isn't."

"He's surprised," Kaylin told her. "Which is usually a bad thing." She swallowed and let the grin fade from her face. The sigil still hovered. "What does it mean, Tiamaris?"

"What do you think it means?" Anyone else had said those words, they would have been laced with sarcasm; the Dragon's voice held none.

"My skin's itchy, if that helps."

"Not perhaps as much as I would like," Tiamaris replied. His eyes were a shade of bronze that was verging, slowly, toward copper. His inner membranes were high; his hands were fists. He grimaced, loosened those fists, and began to gesture; the gestures were both familiar and strange.

She had known for a while that Tiamaris had been one of Sanabalis's students. His second last. She'd seen him use magic precisely once—but the way the hair on the back of her neck was suddenly prickling, she thought she was about to see a second incident. She couldn't say why, but Tiamaris actually *using* magic seemed wrong, to her.

Maybe it was the Hawk.

But whatever magic he now invoked was subtle. No fire erupted; no light fled his hands; nothing appeared before him in the air. He simply stood there, staring at the sky. He frowned once or twice, and he repeated his gestures, but the repetitions were shorter, sharper. He finally said another curt, Leontine word, and turned back to Kaylin.

"I cannot see it," he told her.

"See what?"

"The sigil."

"Try again," she told him. "But expand the field of vision. Pretend you're looking at a spell that's affecting something the size of our port."

"For someone who has yet to master the simple act of lighting a candle," he said, through slightly gritted teeth, "you seem comfortable giving advice." He actually *sounded* irritated.

She shrugged. "Sanabalis didn't try to teach me the one I think you're doing."

"He hasn't tried to teach you anything."

"Well, he said he was working on teaching me patience."

Tiamaris snorted. "I imagine," he told her, his brows bunching together, "that he is continuing to work on *mine*. If he weren't, he would have sent any *other* Hawk." His gestures changed only slightly. His expression changed a whole lot more.

"It's not a sigil," he told her, voice flat.

"What is it?"

"It's a storm." He glanced at the buildings that girded the street. "Stay out of it. Stay out of its reach."

"Tiamaris—"

"What?"

"I think you're wrong. If it's a storm, it's directed. It looks like a huge version of the shadow-sigil I saw in the Leontine quarter."

"It may well be both," he told her. "Kaylin, I cannot go into that shadow. Not now. We must avoid it."

But Morse said, "Can't."

"Why?" The word was a rumble that reminded Kaylin of the thunder that sounds almost immediately after lightning has flashed.

"Because if we avoid it, there's not much cleanup done. We can run," Morse added.

"Your one-offs come out of that shadow?" he asked her.

"I'd guess that's exactly where the one we fought today came from."

"You're expecting more?"

Morse's expression was unexpectedly grim. "Not like that," she finally said. "I hear swords up ahead." She took a sharp breath and then drew a long knife in either hand. She glanced at Kaylin, who had daggers equipped, and nodded before she headed directly for the base of what had once been a watchtower. "You'll see."

Kaylin glanced at Tiamaris.

Tiamaris shook his head. "You and your friend—and her compatriots—may well be able to weather what lies at the heart of that shadow. I, my kin, and the Barrani, would not necessarily do as well. I will wait for you," he added. "I will not prevent you from following. What you see, remember."

It was a reminder. Her hand ached briefly as she remembered the memory crystal the Arkon had placed into her palm. She nodded.

But he hadn't quite finished. Glancing at the sky, seeing whatever it was his spell allowed him to see, he said, "This is what we feared."

Morse said, "So there are things even a Dragon is afraid of."

"Looks like."

"What about you? What are you afraid of?"

"You know me," Kaylin said with a grimace.

"Too damn stupid to be afraid." Morse grinned. It was an ugly expression, but it held no anger; it held what some strange alchemy of emotion made anger from. Pain, maybe. "You'll need the throwing knives here," she told Kaylin, forcing that glimpse of the abyss from her face. "And you'll need to be able to move.

"Don't let them touch you. If it comes to that, kill them first."

Kaylin nodded.

"Eli."

"What?"

"I *mean* it. No stupid shit here. Whatever you see, whatever the hell you think you see—it doesn't matter. It's all shadow, it's all a mind-fuck. What comes out of that shadow, whatever it is that comes for you—kill it."

"If it's a mind—"

Morse slapped her. Kaylin raised a hand and a knife glinted in the sunlight; it was inches from Morse's throat, but Morse didn't raise a long-knife to block it; she stood there as if she were made of stone and the worst Kaylin could do with the damn knife was blunt it.

"Welcome to the shadows," Morse snarled. "What you see *can* be killed. Whatever you see, kill it if it won't keep its distance."

"Morse—"

"Because if you don't, I'll have to kill you."

The shadow that had seemed so dense and confined grew amorphous as they jogged down the street. If Kaylin had wondered where Morse was leading them, she had her answer: there were men at the end of the street, in the more natural shadows cast by the overhang of taller buildings. These men, in workaday armor, with weapons that would never have passed inspection in the Halls, looked up as Morse slowed.

"Morse," one said, "get your ass out of the street!"

"Good to see you, too, Killian. Where's Seeley?"

The man, older than Morse by a good five years, lifted a hand and slid it across his throat. Morse swore.

"We were late," Killian said grimly.

"How many we lose?"

"Those buildings," he replied, pointing. There were two, facing each other, the watchtower—or what was left of it—in between them. There was nothing remarkable about either building; each was tall, and it was separated from its neighbors by dead grass and weeds.

"Many people in 'em?"

"It's the watch border. Not many. No one smart."

"What about the men on the tower?" Kaylin broke in.

Killian glanced at her, and then back at Morse. "She's new," he said. No question.

"Hasn't been in these parts for a while, at any rate." Morse added, to Kaylin, "They were dead before the shadow started to take hold. Trust me."

"How many?" Kaylin asked.

"Four per tower. We can't spare more. If they're paying attention instead of playing dice, they've got a good chance to get out with their lives." She shrugged. "Killian, word from the Southwest Tower?"

"Not yet, but that's looking good. Compared to this."

"Yeah, well. So is hell."

Killian snorted; it was his version of a brief laugh. "When we get there," he told Morse, "they're going to have to come up with something good, 'cause compared to this, they got nothing."

"Only if you listen to priests," Morse snapped. She didn't.

But Kaylin wasn't done yet, and she wasn't—quite—content to be a passive observer. "How do you fight it?" she asked them both, gesturing at the mass of shadow.

"We don't. We kill anything that comes out of it, and we wait. We wait long enough," Morse added, "and either something big comes out and kills most of us, or it shrinks and goes back to hell. Something big came out, but it didn't stick around here. We're left with the waiting and the cleanup."

"But you don't just pull back."

Morse shook her head. "Cleanup's necessary. Learned that the hard way. Heads up, Eli."

Kaylin settled instinctively into a fighting stance and turned toward the shadow, the wall of the building at her back. She expected to see ferals, or something similar, coalesce out of the shadows that moved as if caught in the heart of a storm; she'd seen shadow this dense beneath the High Halls, and she'd seen what it produced.

But she was wrong.

Struggling her way out of the shadows, its tendrils wrapping themselves around her legs and arms as if they were webbing, was an old woman. Kaylin grimaced and almost sheathed her knives; Morse barked a single word that was so harsh Kaylin didn't recognize it as anything but a command to stay her ground.

It's the watch border. Not many. No one smart.

No one smart, Kaylin thought, with sudden, bitter fury, or no one mobile. No one who had somewhere else to go. Who did that leave? The elderly, certainly.

Morse darted forward, right arm raised. Right, left—with Morse, it didn't matter. You could arm her with a damn spoon and it was deadly. Kaylin, knowing this, couldn't stop herself from moving ahead of where Morse had chosen to stand. "Morse, don't—"

"There's nothing you can do," Morse snarled. "Wrap your empty outer-city head around it. There's not one fucking thing you can do."

"She's hurt—"

Morse laughed. "You have no clue," she said. But she didn't kick or strike Kaylin, who now watched the woman weave her way slowly up the center of the street. Her hands were curved in the way old hands often were, and her shoulders were hunched, as if to ward off blows. She was not screaming for help—she was in Barren, after all—but she didn't speak, either; she was keening softly in distress.

Because Morse was at her back, Kaylin didn't relax her stance; she didn't sheathe her weapon, although the weapon was hardly likely to make her look like less of a threat to a panic-stricken old woman. All of the Hawks were required, in their first year, to take riot training with the Swords; they were required to take classes—classes which Kaylin had even passed—in handling people made mindless by either fury or fear.

Barren's men—and women—certainly weren't.

Kaylin took a step forward; Morse stayed where she was. Kaylin should have known, then. She should have remembered what Morse's idea of *lesson* meant. Morse didn't have the Halls behind her; she didn't have their experience, and the laws that governed them. The only law that Morse understood, the only one that mattered, was survival.

And if you couldn't survive, you were obviously too damn stupid to learn fast enough for Morse.

The old woman moved closer, and she moved slowly; she appeared to be alone; there was no one else for her to lean on, no one else to hide behind. It wasn't suspicious, not to Kaylin—she'd seen that a lot, growing up in Nightshade. She'd almost been on the other end of the spectrum: five years old, nowhere to go, no one to ask for help.

But she'd had Severn, in the end. Severn, who had hurt her more than anyone, or anything, that she had ever faced.

She took a step forward slowly, and then another, and she sheathed one dagger; the other, she let fall to her side. Holding out a hand, she approached the old woman; she heard Morse's sharp breath, but Morse didn't speak.

Yes, she should have known.

The old woman sensed her standing there alone, and raised her pale, white-crowned head.

Her eyes were the color of black opals in the lined mask of her face.

CHAPTER 12

But it was an old woman's face that surrounded those horrible, unnatural eyes. There were no extra eyes, no stalks, no ears, no sudden tendrils of dark, roiling shadow contained in the shape of flesh. Her mouth, when it opened, contained the normal set of teeth—where normal, in the fiefs, meant a lot of extra gaps—and those teeth were the yellow, flattened teeth you could find in any underfed, old woman's mouth.

They weren't fangs, and her mouth didn't suddenly stretch and distort so it was double the length of her face. But she didn't speak; she keened. It was almost an animal sound.

It was also a sound of distress, of fear, shorn of something as sensible or intelligible as words.

Kaylin froze as the woman stumbled toward her.

Behind Kaylin—not so far behind that she was inaudible, Morse cursed. "What did I fucking tell you?" she said, her voice not nearly distant enough.

"I don't know. I wasn't listening." Kaylin was in stance now; she was set to move, if movement was necessary. But to, or away, she wasn't certain. Her dagger—Tiamaris's dagger—was cool in her palm, and her hands felt dry and cold. She wanted the Dragon, not his gift of knives, but he was gone.

The woman reached for her, and Kaylin moved, sidestepping, dancing away from both her arm and Morse's voice. She could throw the dagger, in theory. But in practice? It was hard. Her arms ached; her legs, where cloth brushed them as she shifted her feet, felt raw.

"What will she do?" Kaylin said, moving again. The old woman did *not* move quickly.

"Grab you, if she can."

"I got that."

"I should let her," Morse spit out. "It'd serve you damn right." Light flashed; Morse had raised a long knife. She moved toward the old woman with both speed and caution.

"It spreads," Morse told her. "It spreads."

"It's like a—like a disease?"

"Fuck, listen to you. No, it's not a damn disease. It's worse. It's instant. It gets you, you're not the fucking same."

"Does it leave?"

"What?"

"Does it *leave when the shadow leaves?*"

Morse, still moving out of range, managed to stare at Kaylin as if she had, in an instant, turned into a total, dribbling moron. "What the hell do you mean *leave?*"

"When it—when it goes away—" Kaylin froze for a second. It was only a second, but Morse, sliding under the restraining force of Kaylin's words, lunged suddenly in, toward the woman's throat. One stab, quick, knife pulling up and out. Blood followed in an arc, a brief flash of vivid red, and the woman suddenly staggered and fell.

Morse didn't clean her dagger, and she didn't sheathe it. But her expression was dark and, for Morse, angry. "You don't play games here," she told Kaylin evenly.

"It doesn't go, does it?" Kaylin asked quietly.

Morse said, "You're still pretty damn slow on the uptake." She turned toward the shadows that were now far more menacing to Kaylin than they had been when they had released the old woman.

Kaylin sheathed her second dagger and knelt at the side of the body. She didn't ask Morse if it was safe to touch the woman; she didn't speak to Morse at all. Instead, she caught still shoulders, and she turned the woman over.

She was already dead. Morse was good, had always been good. Kaylin could have killed easily—almost anyone could—but not with the speed, not with the efficiency, that Morse had. Morse didn't hesitate; she never really had. There was an art to this, and it was all hers.

The woman's eyes were open.

Kaylin watched as the moving opalescence slowly dimmed, fading at last into a dull, gray-black. There were no irises, no whites. Only when it was done did she reach out to close the woman's lids.

"I take it back," Morse said, as Kaylin rose. "You were never *this* stupid."

Kaylin managed to shrug, but it was costly. "Soft living," she managed to say. "Does that to a person."

Morse's laugh—and she did laugh—was black.

"How many of your own were in—were up there?"

"Should have been two," Morse said. She looked past Kaylin.

"Four," the man who had first stopped them said. Kaylin had already forgotten his name.

"How many have come out?" Morse asked, eyes once again on the velvet of shadow.

"Two."

"You've got crossbows?"

The man nodded, and then, when Morse failed to acknowledge the gesture she couldn't see, given she hadn't looked at him once, said yes.

"Get 'em out."

But he shook his head. "They're already gone," he said grimly. "Corben's gone with Walton and Messer. They're headed down the streets, setting up quarantine."

Morse swore again. She turned to Kaylin. "You've seen enough," she told her. "They'll stay."

"We're going to look at a quarantine?"

"No point. There'll just be a lot of dead people."

"But the shadow—"

"It's there. People don't go near it, they don't change. If they do, they're gone. Most are like this one—they can't speak. Some speak, and if you hear 'em, you know damn well they're not the same. They touch you, the shadow seeps into you, same as them, and you're gone. You might as well be dead."

She nodded in the direction of the base of what had been an observation tower. "Once the shadow opens up, it spits out whatever came with it, eats whatever was nearby, and then sits there. It doesn't grow and it doesn't move." She cursed again.

"Do you have any warning—any warning at all—when it's about to open up? When it's about to appear?"

Morse shrugged and glanced at her. "Us? No. But you and your fancy scaly friend might. What we're hoping for, anyway. The rest of us see it form, and we know where it's going to shed creatures and kill us. We send our cleanup crews, we kill the things that come out, and we move people back. That's it.

"We're going to have to set up a makeshift watch on one of the roofs while we build. We can't afford to be down one, and we've lost two today." She wiped her blade clean and sheathed it. "Go home. Go back across the river."

Kaylin nodded slowly.

"I'll pick you up at the bridge in the morning."

She started to tell Morse she could find the White Towers on her own, and then, remembering the creature on Capstone, thought better of it. Heading down the street, she met Tiamaris. He took one look at her face and closed his mouth.

"We're leaving," she told him grimly.

To her surprise, Severn was waiting for them at the bridge that crossed the Ablayne. It was not the usual bridge, but seeing him on the City side made it feel *almost* the same. He was leaning against one post, arms folded across his chest; he looked up as she began to cross, Tiamaris in tow.

"Bad?" he asked, as she paused in front of him. He eased his arms to his sides and glanced at the Dragon Lord.

"Bad," she agreed, understanding both halves of the single syllable question. "Barren was—Barren. But, Severn?"

He nodded.

"I think he used to be an Arcanist. Tiamaris implied as much, and further implied that he took his sorry ass to the fiefs some ten years ago to avoid being hunted down by Wolves."

Severn raised a brow, and then nodded; he made no other comment. He wasn't technically a Wolf anymore. It was just possible he wouldn't consider this his problem. Then again, in a magical world, it was also possible that he'd suddenly grow wings and fly. He wouldn't, however, say anything else about it to her, not now; she'd never been a Wolf, and even had she, she'd never been a Shadow Wolf.

"Home," he told her softly.

Tiamaris cleared his throat. "We are not yet done."

Kaylin was done. She glanced at the Dragon Lord, saw the color of his eyes, and bit back the words that would tell him just how much she was done. "What's left?"

"I believe the Arkon and Lord Sanabalis will be waiting for our report."

"I hope they're waiting with food," was her sour reply.

Severn walked with them to the carriage that was waiting. It was an Imperial carriage, to Kaylin's relief. He joined them, taking the bench beside Kaylin. She sagged against the cushioned back.

"You saw fighting."

She nodded.

"How bad?"

"Remember the cavern beneath the High Halls?"

"The one that you're *not supposed to mention* outside of the High Halls?" he asked.

She grimaced and glanced at Tiamaris. "That one."

"Kaylin—"

"I know, I know. I just wish—"

Tiamaris raised a brow.

"If people would actually just *talk,* without all the need for this stupid secrecy, it would make defending any part of this damn city a hell of a lot easier, you know?"

"It would," Tiamaris replied gravely. "On the other hand, you would probably find yourself in need of a job. Think of the difficulty as a mixed blessing."

He had a point. She tried to appreciate it as she turned back to Severn. "It was like what we faced there."

"What was?"

"The creature we met in the middle of the fief. It was wandering around on the streets like a great misshapen nightmare, trying to blast holes in things with its eye beams. It didn't do too badly with teeth and claws, either, if it comes to that."

"You met this during the day?"

She nodded. Looked out the carriage window.

"Kaylin—"

"Yeah, it's worse," she told him softly. "I don't even know what Barren wanted from *me.* I know it should matter. It probably will—but right now it doesn't." She felt one of his hands on the back of hers, and she looked up at him. "We had ferals for nightmares," she told him softly. "In Nightshade. We had ferals. They have—they have—" she shook her head. "They're going to get eaten, or worse."

He knew who she meant.

"And at this point, Severn? They're fighting a holding action, but they're losing ground day by day. I don't know if there's anything—anything at all—that they can do."

"Or that you can?"

"Or," she said, bitterly, "that I can." She held out her arms, sleeves hiding the marks upon her skin.

"You'll do what you can."

"I know. But what I can do, right now, doesn't seem like very much." She thought about the old woman, her wide and unseeing eyes an accusation.

"Kaylin," he said quietly. And then, when she failed to look up, "Elianne."

She looked, then. He stiffened for just a second at what he saw in her face, but the stiffness didn't hold him. He lifted a hand, cupped her cheek—the cheek that also bore Nightshade's mark—and left his hand, warm, callused, resting against her skin.

She stiffened, as well, but like his, hers was brief. And then she closed her eyes and leaned into the warmth of his hand.

"Stop judging your life only by the failures," he whispered.

"What should I do?" she whispered. "I'm always going to fail."

"We all do," he said softly, his voice closer now. "We *all* fail. But none of us fail all of the time."

Debriefing, as Tiamaris called it, took some time. Luckily for Kaylin, it was Tiamaris's time. They both got out of the carriage in the usual courtyard, leaving Severn behind, and they both entered the halls through the same guard posts, but they separated when they reached the interior. Tiamaris pointed her in the direction of Sanabalis's rooms and walked off.

Sanabalis was not actually *in* his rooms, but the doors were slightly ajar; she didn't have to touch the obnoxious doorwards that littered the palace doors like cheap paint. She was grateful for that, and grateful, as well, for the dinner that was set out on the small table in the sitting room. She wanted to call it a parlor, but thought it was too big for that, and she couldn't quite remember what *else* to call it.

Since it didn't matter, she grabbed the closest chair and tried to slide it across the carpet. It weighed more than she did. She grimaced and moved the small table instead, curling her legs beneath her and picking up bread rolls and a knife. Butter, beef, cheese and an assortment of fruit were also present; it wasn't a fancy meal.

But she'd missed lunch, and while she didn't feel like eating, she was hungry. She ate. That much, years of fief living had made habit. Eating in silence was less of a habit, but she'd only be talking to herself; she was quiet.

At length the quiet drove her out of her chair and toward the grand windows that the room boasted. Framed in its panels were the Halls of Law, flags flying at full mast in the breeze high above the city streets. She could see the occasional Aerian flying in that breeze, as well, and as often happened, she felt a pang of envy for the gift of flight.

When she'd first met the rest of the Hawks, she had daydreamed endlessly about waking up one day possessed of wings. She had pestered every Aerian who was on active duty and wasn't injured to take her flying, and almost every Hawk had complied, some grumbling as they did. They didn't really understand why she'd loved flight; it was like loving walking, to them.

But the streets looked so small and so quiet from the heights. The problems that plagued anyone who happened to live on the ground seemed to vanish. For whole minutes at a time, she felt as if she had shed her past, and all the crimes and failures it contained.

Landing was always hard.

This time she'd landed in Barren.

She turned away from the window, and then back, staring at the Halls. It shouldn't be like this. The Law shouldn't be confined by something as small as a river, and it shouldn't be limited by something as terrifying as shadow. It should cover the *whole damn* city. The Emperor should *care* about the people in Barren, or Nightshade, or Liatt—any of the fiefs. It wasn't as if the people who lived in them had any choice about where they were born, or how or to who. They didn't deserve to be abandoned.

They didn't deserve to die the way the old woman had died.

Her hands became fists as she stared.

"Bad?"

She glanced up at the window, and at the shadow of Lord Sanabalis's reflection. It was not yet dark enough for that reflection to be more than a shadow. She shrugged, pure fief gesture, and turned.

Tiamaris was standing just behind Sanabalis.

"The Arkon will join us in a few moments," Sanabalis told her.

Great.

"He was not greatly pleased that Lord Tiamaris failed to observe everything that occurred. Nor," Sanabalis added, "was the Emperor."

"He had his reasons."

"They were good reasons," the Dragon Lord who was also her only teacher said. "Which is why Tiamaris will continue his duties."

"Who would I have been stuck with—accompanied by, otherwise?"

"Suffice it to say that you are happy with the outcome." He glanced at the relocated table. "I'm happy to see that you ate," he added, in a tone of voice which clearly said *put things back where you found them.* It was a neat trick. She tidied while he took his customary chair.

Tiamaris seated himself as far from Sanabalis as one could, given the arrangement of the chairs, which told Kaylin as much as she wanted to know about how the debriefing had gone.

The Arkon arrived some fifteen minutes later. He entered the room and took a seat, nodding to both Tiamaris and Sanabalis; he failed to offer Kaylin a nod until she retreated from the window. She did with some speed.

"Lord Tiamaris has informed us of some of the events that occurred in the fief today," he told Kaylin when she was seated. "We would like to hear from you."

She grimaced. "Hear from, or extract a memory crystal?"

"At the moment, the words will do. The crystals are not inexpensive and they are not trivial to manufacture. This conversation is, of course, being observed and will be entered into Imperial Records. Some comparison of the information contained in your crystal and the words you speak today will of necessity be done. We are, however, aware of the ways in which human memory is fallible.

"Lord Tiamaris has said, when he became aware of the incursion of shadow—and the possibility of shadowstorm—he did not proceed into the area of the fief that was thus afflicted. You, however, did."

She nodded. And hesitated. One glance at Tiamaris's shuttered expression told her she was going to get no help from that quarter.

The Arkon however said, "Lord Tiamaris did mention that what you saw and what he saw were substantially different. You claimed that the shadow was sigiled."

"That's what it looked like to me but—"and here, she transferred her glance to Sanabalis "—I've only seen something like it once, and it was a hell of a lot smaller."

"Where?" Sanabalis asked quietly.

"In the Leontine quarter," she replied. "The magic of the tainted."

His gaze was sharp, and his eyes were an unfortunate shade of bronze, which Kaylin tried not to take personally. "The exact sigil?"

"No." She shook her head. "I don't think—I know I don't know enough about magic, but I don't think *any* two shadow sigils would be exactly the same."

Sanabalis and the Arkon exchanged a glance. It was, sadly, a significant glance, and of a type that would normally have caused Kaylin to demand an explanation in an office meeting. On the other hand, aside from Marcus, no one in the office was likely to rip her throat out or reduce her to ash for making such demands. She was pretty sure Sanabalis wouldn't; the Arkon, on the other hand? Not so much.

"You know enough," Sanabalis finally said. "But remember—what you see and what our magic shows us is not the same."

"It looked like a sigil the size of, oh, the Wolf Tower. Tiamaris couldn't see it—"

"We are aware of Tiamaris's perceptions," the Arkon said, in a brittle tone of voice. "They are not, now, our concern. His understanding is greater than yours, and any information of use on that subject has already been extracted."

"But he did something, and then he said it was a—a storm."

"As I said—"

Sanabalis lifted a hand. To the Arkon he said, "She is not of the Court, and not of our kind. It is possible that she requires more explanation than we have given."

"It should not affect her observations. They happen independent of—"

"It will affect what she observes and understands in future."

The Arkon's silence was chilly, and Sanabalis didn't break it again. But after a moment, the oldest of the Dragons present gave a very curt nod. His eyes were hard to see in this light; Kaylin wasn't certain why. She could read very little of his mood from their color.

Lord Sanabalis then turned fully to Kaylin. "Ask," he said curtly, as if aware that questions were trying to break out from between the tight line of her compressed lips.

"What is a shadowstorm?"

Sanabalis hesitated, and this time, the Arkon snorted. "Oh, no," he said, lifting a hand. "I leave the explanation, in its entirety, to you."

Tiamaris coughed.

Sanabalis grimaced.

Kaylin felt, for just a moment, as if she were thirteen years old again, and in the exotic comfort of Marcus's den, surrounded by wives who were more experienced, and far more knowledgeable, than she. They had been both terrifying and strangely attractive, and she had sat, in one corner, watching them as they rolled over and around each other, touching—always touching—unselfconsciously. They were clearly all individuals, they had different personalities, different colors, chose different words; you could even distinguish their snarls with a little practice. But they *were* a family.

They weren't what she was. They had never been what she was. They could kill—she knew that, had developed at least that much instinct in Barren—but they *didn't*. And they watched the outsider, gave her space, and left *just* enough of an opening that she could, if she wanted, find some way in.

But the way into the pridlea was a way into something that was warm, inclusive, and nurturing—if perhaps a bit bruising at times, because the cubs played rough. What the three Dragons offered was different.

She wasn't sure she wanted it, either. But they watched her, and after a moment, she said, "This has something to do with true names." She meant it as a question, but it came out flat.

They exchanged another glance, but this time, the Arkon nodded.

"The Barrani—"

"The Barrani would suffer the effect of a storm in a similar way. To you," he added, "there would be very little difference."

"Why?"

She thought no one would answer. It was, to her surprise, the Arkon who chose to do so. "It is the nature of our life, and of life as it began. We *are* our names, Kaylin. You will not and cannot see them as they are. What you see," he added, "is significant, but it is significant to you, as the bearer of those marks. The shadows and the darkness are things out of which something akin to life comes, but it is a chaos that knows and accepts no order, no governance, and no rules." He lifted a hand. "I speak not of rules of law or etiquette, but of simple biology. There are rules that govern birth, life, death, that make us in some sense what we are.

"What we are, however, is bound to the names that move us and give us life. The storms can change those."

"But—"

"The change can be either brutally obvious or subtle. It can be physical," he added, "or it can go almost—almost—undetected." He paused, and then rose. "Sanabalis and Tiamaris are both too young to remember the shadowstorms of my youth.

"But I remember them." He walked to the window and stared out. "They do not come, now. That much was won. The Old Ones do not walk at the heart of the storm, and they do not call it. The storms do not strike at random.

"But in my youth—" His voice was soft "—they did. Not when I was a child—and yes, we were all children once, even the Dragons. Then? We were the new gods."

Tiamaris's eyes rounded very, very subtly. He was surprised. Sanabalis, on the other hand, could have been carved out of rock.

"We built, Kaylin. We built cities such as you could not imagine, aeries that make the palace itself look tiny and cramped and unimposing. We had art—it was not your art, but it was ours—and magic, and we ruled from the skies."

She was certain the Barrani had something to say about that, but kept this to herself.

"But, as so many do who acquire power and the learning to wield it with greater and greater ease, we flew where we should not have flown, and we tried to acquire what we could not, in safety, hold.

"And then," he said softly, "the storms came."

Tiamaris was watching the Arkon's back as if the Arkon were the only thing in the room.

"You have, I'm informed, been told why Elantra stands where it stands. You understand the import of the High Halls, and understand why the war, at last, was laid to rest here."

She nodded. And hesitated. He marked the hesitation.

"I was told," she finally said, keeping her voice even, and more important, keeping accusation out of it, "that the City existed before that. That the heart of the fiefs was once a center of knowledge, a—a normal place."

"It was never," he said softly, "normal. Never that." He glanced at Tiamaris and Sanabalis. His eyes were lidded; the opacity of the lower membranes was almost nonexistent. "But for a time, it was a haven." He glanced out the window again, and this time she knew his gaze went, not to the Halls, but beyond it.

"We did not understand the nature of those storms at first," he said, speaking to the glass. "When the first storm struck, we did not see it as shadow. We did not understand its nature. It was not dark, not the way you perceive darkness. It was *wild*. It was the essence of chaos, unleashed." He lifted his head a moment, and she wondered if he saw this sky, or a different one.

"We did not understand why it came, and it had no immediately discernable pattern. I remember," he said, his voice deepening. "I remember flying over the plains while the storm raged."

Tiamaris drew a sharp breath, but didn't speak. Kaylin didn't, either.

"There were no cities there," he continued. "No aeries. Nothing but tall grass, and the animals that hunted or fed there. They knew," he added. "They startled, and they fled, as if from fire.

"The storm reached some who could not flee, and it changed them. It was a subtle change," he added, "but the effect was startling. Even the grass itself was slowly transformed in the wild rain. It was—beautiful, in a fashion. The animals, even changed, were not a threat to us. Nor was the grass, although it was not entirely grass as we understood or knew it. And there were flowers and trees that bloomed there, after, that were entirely new. They could not be classified, and they could not—easily—be destroyed. They were unique.

"There was magic, in the transformation," he said. "It was a magic that could inspire awe, even in Dragons. I was young, then.

"What we did not understand, until the first storm in an aerie, was what the storms *meant*."

She didn't, either. She opened her mouth to ask, and closed it again, remembering her training. Sometimes it was better to let them talk. Whoever they were.

"But they came, and when they came to the aerie, we learned. It was bitter," he added softly, "and many, many were the young who were lost to us, then. I was not among them. The eggs," he added, and this time, she saw the momentary twist of his lips reflected in the surface of glass, "we had to destroy.

"But the aerie itself was changed. Some changes were subtle. The hall of mirrors seemed unmarred, until one glanced at one's reflection. Some changes were not; the hatchery was not." His silence was longer. She wondered if he would break it.

"Some of our oldest and most powerful were sent to the hatchery to guard the eggs."

Tiamaris lifted his head.

"When they emerged from the hatchery, they were no longer, in any sense, Dragons. What they *were*," he added, "was not even a shadow, not a mimicry. They were entirely and utterly changed. They could fly, yes, and they could still breathe the heart of flame. They could speak its name as if it were their own.

"But they recognized none of us as kin. In form," he added, "they were like stone, but moving and gleaming, as if they had been reborn, and their forms were sharpened or...worse. It was not a pleasant birth." He shook his head. "They could not be unmade. But what knows life, knows change, and they were changed."

"The names?" she asked.

"Yes, but that we knew almost immediately. They were few," he continued, "or we would have perished. After we gathered, after the hatchery was destroyed, we returned to the plains and to the sites of other storms, and we studied what we could. What we discovered," he added, "was that the subtle changes in the base animals were magnified—greatly—in Dragons."

"Animals have no names."

He nodded. "Do you understand?"

She wanted to say no. Instead, she said, "The storms exist at the heart of the fiefs."

"Yes. Only there."

"But Tiamaris knew—"

"He knows what to watch for, Kaylin. All of the Dragons in the Empire do. So, too, the Barrani, although their knowledge is less expansive. It has been a very long time since a storm has escaped the heart of the fiefs."

"How far can they reach?" She looked around the room. At Sanabalis. At Tiamaris.

"Until now? No farther than the interior border of the fiefs. What was built in the fiefs was built upon the foundations of a magic not one of the living now fully apprehend. The Towers. The Castles. The High Halls is the only structure to our knowledge that retains some of that power but exists outside of the fiefs." He turned back to them, then. "We do not understand the nature of those who created us. We do not understand the nature of those who would re-create us.

"But we understand that it is our death."

After a long pause, she said, "What would a storm do to the High Halls?"

He raised a pale brow, and then nodded. "You do understand."

She frowned. "Maybe."

"Maybe?"

"I'm wondering," she finally said, "what changes the undying would suffer, if they'd suffer it at all."

"The undying."

She nodded slowly. "The undying surrender names. They attempt to live without them."

"You've seen the undying."

"Yes. It's not much of a life. But—without names—"

"They can still be affected. Or at least that is my belief. I admit that we have not experimented with the undying and the fiefs. Perhaps," he told her, "you should ask the Barrani."

She nodded. "I will."

Kaylin had no time to hit the market, and anyway, at this time of day everything would be bruised, stale or broken. There were, thankfully, no messages waiting her in the mirror when she finally made it home, other than the usual, which was offered by her reflection. She was so damn tired, she didn't even notice that Severn was sitting in her chair, having helpfully cleared it of dirty laundry, until she saw his reflection, as well. "I did give you keys?"

"More or less."

"I didn't ask for them back?"

He raised a dark brow and then chuckled. "What does tomorrow look like?"

She stretched, trying to ease the knots of tension out of the back of her neck, where they were threatening to give her a headache that would last for weeks. "Tomorrow morning I have to go to the High Halls."

He nodded slowly. He didn't even ask.

"After which, I return, with Tiamaris, to Barren." Watching his expression in the mirror, she paused. "What happened?"

"I am to accompany you when you return to Barren," he replied. "But—"

"I have been seconded, for the duration of my investigation, by the Wolves."

CHAPTER 13

To no one's surprise, Severn showed up in the morning, where morning was defined by a sky night hadn't quite finished with, and no one, of course, was Kaylin. On the other hand, he brought breakfast, and he was vastly less cranky than Kaylin herself as she crawled out of bed. The aftereffects of the fight in Capstone made themselves known as she swung her legs off the mattress.

She counted any fight a win which didn't leave her in the infirmary, and didn't require her to replace clothing. She reached, automatically, for the clothing she normally wore on duty, and then remembered where duty would take her today. That caused a spate of swearing, because duty involved two things: the High Halls and the fief of Barren. Which had precisely nothing—except for the dangers of shadow creatures and the deaths they caused—in common. And in general, someone *else* dressed you for your own funeral.

She looked at the contents of her chair, and then, grudgingly, at the contents of her small standing closet. She pulled out the dress that she had bought for use with the midwives—which seldom saw much wear—and then frowned; it was going to be next to useless in Barren. If it wasn't actively harmful.

After a few moments of indecision—none of which were silent—she finally gave up; she dressed for Barren. For, in fact, fighting in Barren. Severn said, after a pause, "Try to get a cloak of some sort."

"Why? It's not cold and they get caught in every damn thing."

"Because if it's fine enough, you can cover up the clothing that isn't."

She didn't ask Severn if he intended to accompany her to the Halls; no point. Instead, they both ate quietly, while the sky visibly paled through the one window Kaylin's apartment boasted.

When Kaylin was mostly finished, Severn said, "Review what we know about the undying."

Kaylin stretched, frowning. Records access would be useful here. Unfortunately, she didn't really have it.

"I first encountered the undying in Nightshade," she said quietly. "When Catti was kidnapped from the foundling halls. Tiamaris was with me," she added, "and he did the Dragon thing." Severn knew all of this, but didn't interrupt her. She frowned. "They didn't look classically dead. No rotting, no decay."

"You knew they weren't alive."

"They weren't—they weren't right. Yes, I sort of knew."

He nodded. "You understand why this is relevant?"

"The Barrani don't particularly *like* talking about it. And I'm going to try to talk to Barrani who aren't Hawks."

"You could try talking to Teela."

She nodded. "I could." Paused. "But if she considered it a really bad idea for me to ask anyone *else,* she'd do her damn best to make sure I couldn't go to the High Halls. I'd go—the Emperor's Court is fine with it—but if I had to get the Imperial Court to pull rank on her, she'd forgive me sometime in ten decades. If that."

He nodded. "Stop thinking about Teela," he added, because Kaylin was. "The undying."

"Their bodies are alive. In some way, they have will. They can think. They can react. But…" She frowned again. "The second time was in the streets of Nightshade."

He waited.

"We were with Lord Nightshade and his guards—his Barrani guards, not his cheap, human wannabe-Barrani. The undying met us in the streets. They attacked." She said a few Leontine words and rose. "Should we go to the office? We can access records, there."

"If you want." Which, for Severn, usually meant no.

"You think Marcus isn't going to be happy."

"That you're heading to the High Halls with no escort?"

"I'm going with you."

"I've been removed from the force for the duration of my investigation."

"That's not going to matter to Marcus—" She stopped. Cursed. Marcus took territorial to a whole new level. He'd probably forgive Severn in a decade or two. "Your point. He'd probably send Teela, if he could find her." She grimaced. "Your point again. I just ate breakfast. I am *not* getting into a carriage with Teela." Teela was the worst driver that nature had ever produced. Like bad drivers anywhere, she was under the mistaken impression that she was the *best* driver that nature had ever produced. Kaylin stood and began to pace in a tight circle.

"They looked like Barrani. They fought like them, but…slower, somehow. They didn't stop, though. They didn't stop when they lost limbs. Fire made a difference, but they fought while burning, as well."

He nodded.

"We did kill them. They did die. But—they didn't seem to care one way or the other. Look—they have to be capable of thought. They can speak. The first time, when we rescued Catti, they were about to perform some sort of ceremony. They're not mindless, they're not completely empty vessels." She hesitated, and then said, "It's something to do with their names."

He made no comment.

"The second time…" She frowned. "The second time doesn't really exist. The Lord of the Green, in the High Halls, was—almost—undying. He had attempted to divest himself of his true name."

"Which wouldn't kill him."

"No. But—the Barrani *don't wake* up without a name. As babies," she added, "they don't really…come to life…until they're given their true name." She shook her head. "I don't really understand it. I know Nightshade's true name. I can use it. But when I do, he's aware of every damn syllable. He's aware of where I am when I say it, and he probably knows *exactly* what I'm thinking at the time." She touched the mark on her cheek, and let her hand drop away; it was cool.

"If I were strong enough, if my will were even stronger than *his,* I could use that name against him. I could bend him to my will."

"But he wouldn't be undying."

"No." She grinned. "He *would,* on the other hand, be really, really pissed off." The smile faded. "The Lord of the Green attempted to give his name away, to shed it entirely, so that it could never be used against him, or his people. Given the thing that *knew* his name, and given the power behind it, it's understandable. It's a form of suicide that even I can sympathize with."

She frowned, and then got down on her hands and knees at the foot of her bed. Severn didn't ask her what she was doing; he knew. If they'd both lived on the right side of the fiefs for more than seven years, they both had old habits that would probably never leave them. She pulled up one of the narrow floorboards that started about a foot from the bed's end, and traveled, beneath the frame, toward the headboard.

She cursed when she bumped her head, but it was almost cursory; she *always* managed to bump her head when she tried to pry the damn board up. Beneath it, however, was a groove in the wood; the board was too narrow for anything like a box, and a box would have been too obvious.

She didn't own much of value; it was one of the things that

hadn't really changed between the fiefs and the outer city. But what she did own, she hid here. And one of those things was a heavy gold ring. She grabbed it in one hand, and then fumbled with the board until it was more or less pressed back into its resting place.

She crawled out again and sat back on her knees, brushing the dust out of her hair. There was an unfortunate amount of it, and catching Severn's glance, she said, "I'm never home—when am I supposed to do housework?"

He did not point out that he managed. Which was good. The ring in her hand had already started to make her skin itch, and that always made her a bit touchy. She daydreamed about running across a type of magic that didn't. "Here it is," she told Severn. The ring was still heavy, still gold, and still adorned by emerald and ivory—but this time, she could see a pattern in the intermingling of the two; the very first time she'd been given this ring, it had blurred every time she tried to study it.

"Kaylin?"

The emeralds, such as they were, were teardrop cuts that suggested the slow drift of leaves, of green. But the ivory? It lay among the emeralds like a single, slender feather. She held it up to Severn. "I thought we might need this."

"The ring given you by the Lord of the West March?"

She nodded. "It looks…different."

"You are now a Lord of the High Court," he pointed out. "Perhaps that's why."

She slid it over her finger; it was about five sizes too big—as if gold couldn't possibly be used by the Barrani in small enough quantities for a ring that would *actually* fit her fingers—but it didn't fall off. Nor would it. "I'm ready," she told Severn, and rose.

He didn't seem to notice the ring. He was frowning in that particular way that meant, for Severn, thought.

"Kaylin, when you say the Lord of the Green attempted to give his name away," Severn said quietly, "you imply that it had to go somewhere. To who, or what?"

She looked at Severn. "I don't know," she said thoughtfully. "I didn't really ask. And yes," she added, as she looked toward the door, "I should have."

"Oh, I didn't say that," he replied as he followed her. "You were dealing with the Barrani High Court, after all."

They took a normal carriage to the High Halls, or rather, to within a few blocks of the High Halls. In theory, all of the city streets were public, and could be used by any carriage that was roadworthy; in practice, suspicion and the natural fear of "outsiders" being what it was, the streets in front of the High Halls—or the very, very large grounds that eventually led to them—were for foot traffic only. The occasional bold child would wander around the gates until his parents caught up with him; the occasional foolish teenager would attempt to get through on a dare.

Other than that? Merchants, politicians, the various nobles of different castes that actually thought impressing the Barrani was important—and to be fair, they had a lot of the City's wealth in their immortal hands—were the only other people who could be seen. The Emperor was big on the entire concept of racial integration and racial harmony, but then again, the Emperor rarely left his palace.

Kaylin walked up to the gatehouse. Well, to one of the gatehouses. It was occupied by flawlessly armored Barrani guards. Gritting her teeth, she approached one—and almost had to pick up her jaw when he tendered her a Barrani bow. It was a damn good bow, even given the armor. Maybe especially given that.

"Lord Kaylin," the guard said. She had lifted her hand to expose the ring that she wore, and her hand dropped to her side.

"I'm here to see—"

He lifted a gauntlet. "I am not required," he told her quietly, "to ask permission to grant you entry to the High Halls. You are Lord of the High Court—the High Halls are your home."

She had to admire him; he said all this with a straight face. Then again, he *was* Barrani; she had seen Teela lie outrageously with a perfectly serious expression.

"Lord Severn," the guard added, offering Severn an exact duplicate of the bow he had offered Kaylin.

Severn nodded, and offered Kaylin his arm. Given that she was wearing boots and leather leggings, it felt a bit odd to actually take that arm, but she could see, by the set of his jaw, that he was going to leave it hanging there until she either walked past him and left him behind, or put her hand on it.

The Halls were as fine—and as intimidatingly tall—as Kaylin remembered. Everything in them—from the statues that adorned pillars that served as a kind of entry, to the fountains and standing vases that littered the carefully marbled floor—was calculated to imply beauty, eternity, and superiority. They made her feel out of place; she wondered if that was the point. But Severn didn't appear to notice, and she knew that if he didn't, she shouldn't. She worked on it.

She also worked on trying to remember how to get from the front of the damn building to the inner Courtyard, and gave up; she had *no idea* if that's where she would find anyone she needed to speak with, anyway. The problem, she thought, with Halls like these is that anyone who had a right to be in them—or felt they did—already *knew* how to find anything else.

And she didn't particularly enjoy looking like the idiot she was beginning to feel she was. "I need to learn how to plan," she finally told Severn, her shoulders sinking. "This is probably as stupid as showing up at the front steps of the palace expecting to find the Emperor and have a little chat."

He chuckled.

"I don't suppose I can blame you?"

"If it helps, be my guest." He put an arm around her shoulders, shedding the formal posture he'd adopted. It looked stupid with his clothing, anyway. "I'm sure they'll cover some of this in etiquette class."

She elbowed him in the stomach, and then looked around at the serene, and empty, Halls. Five minutes later, she abandoned pride and approached a lone Barrani male who seemed to be wandering the Halls as if to soak up that serenity.

"Excuse me," she said, in High Barrani.

He frowned, but turned to face her. She didn't recognize him. Then again, the Barrani looked so damn much alike most of the time, she felt she could be forgiven. He had the gleaming, long black hair and the emerald green eyes that were racial traits; he also had perfect, unscarred skin.

"I am looking for the castelord."

The man's frown deepened for just a moment, but his eyes stayed green; he didn't consider her a threat, and he didn't—yet—consider her enough of an irritation. She lifted her hand. He looked at the ring upon her finger, and the frown eased. "You are Lord Kaylin. And your companion must be Lord Severn."

She nodded.

"I am Lord Vanyor. I will not say the High Lord is expecting you," he added, "but at the moment, it is likely that he will make time to converse, if that is your desire."

She waited. So, unfortunately, did he. If he was chatty, for a Barrani Lord, he was still Barrani; he was going to make her ask for help. "Can you take us to him?"

"Ah. My apologies, Lord Kaylin. Yes, of course."

The High Lord, or the castelord, a title Kaylin vastly preferred, could be found in the gardens. *Garden,* in this case, had to be a very flexible word—the Barrani gardens were huge, and one had the sense, entering them, that the forest that surrounded them was not, in fact, bound by the walls that also surrounded them. She did not, however, have to contend with doorwards on the way there, for which she was grateful; doorwards were a bit superfluous when there were no actual doors, at least not by the route Lord Vanyor chose to take.

She walked slowly through the forest. She should have moved fast, but the trees themselves held her attention, as did the small plants and flowers that grew among them, seeking scattered beams of light. They weren't the same as they'd been the last time she'd seen them. The outer Halls were—but marble generally didn't change much in a few months.

When they broke through the artful cover of trees, she saw the High Lord, and she paused. He was deep in conversation with his consort, her pale hair a striking contrast to the rest of the Barrani present. They were elegantly, and simply, robed, and the consort was adorned with flowers that looked a bit like lilies. She paused, and she turned her head, and then she rose quickly; the High Lord followed her gaze.

He didn't rise, but he did smile as Kaylin found her feet again and began to approach. She was almost shocked when the consort walked past Vanyor and opened her arms; she *was* shocked when the consort hugged her. The Barrani were elegant and beautiful—but they were always distant.

Shock didn't stop her from returning the hug, however.

"Lord Kaylin," the consort said, when she at last let go. She took a step back and looked at what Kaylin was wearing, but even the very, very practical clothing didn't cause her to stiffen or frown. "You have been away from Court."

She hadn't been to Court since she'd left. This was the first time she'd regretted it. "I'm sorry," she said, sliding into Elantran. There was no easy way to offer an apology in High Barrani.

The consort, to her surprise, slid into Elantran, as well. "You've been busy?"

"Very."

"The midwives?"

"The midwives, the foundling hall, and my job."

"Ah. But you are not wearing the Hawk."

"No. Where I'm going today—besides here," she added quickly, "it's not really appreciated."

At this, the consort's fair skin paled slightly. It didn't make her any less beautiful, but it was a beauty it was impossible to envy or resent. "I see your Lord Severn is with you."

"He's not my Lord," Kaylin said quickly.

Severn, however, bowed. It was a Barrani bow, and it was—damn him anyway—perfect. "It is," he said, in High Barrani, "my privilege. We must beg your pardon," he added, "for our interruption."

"Then you will not be staying."

"To our great regret," he replied carefully, "no."

She nodded as if she expected no less, and turned back to the High Lord, who was now silent as he observed them. "Come," she said, looking at Kaylin over her shoulder. "He is waiting."

The bow that she'd failed to offer the consort—if for no other reason than that bows were really awkward when one was being hugged—Kaylin now offered the High Lord. There weren't a lot of Barrani present, but she was certain they'd all be watching and taking notes, and she tried her best not to embarrass him. He nodded, and she rose.

His eyes were emerald green, but they were flecked with golden light, as if they reflected the spirit of the garden over which he presided. "Lord Kaylin," he said softly. "The Lord of the West March sends his regards."

"He's not here?"

"He has returned to the lands over which he rules." He paused, and then added, with a glance at his consort, "It is likely he will return for the Festival. He has grown curious about mortals in the past months." He gestured at a low table on which food had silently and magically appeared. It wasn't actual magic—she'd've felt that—but it might as well have been, for all she'd noticed. That was the trouble with Barrani; they were distracting. At the very least.

"Sit with us," he added. "If you require privacy, the Court will grant it for the space of a simple meal."

It wasn't an order, but she obeyed anyway.

"You are not...attired...for visiting."

She glanced at him. "No," she said quietly. "I'm not Barrani—I can't effortlessly fight in anything I happen to be wearing."

"You expect to fight?"

She nodded, and then, seeing the subtle shift in his expression, quickly added, "Not here."

"May I ask where?"

"The fiefs." And then, because she was aware of her relationship to Lord Nightshade, she also added, "The fief of Barren." One day, she thought with a grimace, she would plan out entire conversations in advance.

He glanced at the consort. Although the glance was brief, even Kaylin could see it was significant. "There has been difficulty in the fief you name?"

Her gaze narrowed. She glanced around, briefly, to see who was close enough to hear her. Severn. She slid into Elantran. "I'd guess you already know the answer to that."

He raised a dark brow, but didn't bother to deny it; she took the subtle criticism of her change in language as well as could be expected.

"It was my understanding—our understanding," he added, nodding to the consort, "that you continued your employ in the Halls of Law."

"I'm still a Hawk."

He looked at the ring on her hand, and nodded. "So I see. It was also our understanding that the Imperial Laws and edicts do not—and cannot—extend into the fiefs."

Since it had been one of her pet peeves for the entire duration of her time in the Halls, she grimaced. "It's true."

"And yet you intend to travel directly to the fiefs from the High Halls."

She nodded.

"This is therefore not a matter of Law."

Severn cleared his throat. "It is not a matter for the Hawks," he replied. "Not all of the Imperial edicts stop at the borders."

The castelord nodded. He rose, walked to the table, and began to pour wine. If Severn hadn't stilled in the silent way he did when he was shocked, Kaylin wouldn't have paid much attention. But he did.

"Will you take wine? Sweet water?"

"Water," she told him.

Severn stepped on her foot.

"Water, please."

Oddly enough, the pressure on her foot didn't ease much. But the castelord did return with her water, which she took. She found a patch of very soft grass—moss soft, and almost hypnotically soothing to the touch—and sank into it, near the feet of the consort. Which, she suddenly noted, were bare.

"This is going to be tricky," she told the castelord. "And it's possible I might say something that either gives offense or crosses a line that I can't see. I apologize for both in advance; if the situation weren't so bad, I wouldn't have come here at all. Not," she added quickly, "to talk about this. I would have visited, though." She said this last to the consort.

The consort laughed. "Kaylin," she said, when the laughter had died into a quiet smile. "There is no one at Court like you. I would greatly appreciate your presence here."

"Because they'll have someone else to focus their anger on?"

She laughed again. "Something very like that, yes." Friendly or no, she was still Barrani. "You will be excused much for your ignorance of our customs, and strange though it may sound, were you to emulate the Barrani perfectly in every way, you would upset a larger number of people.

"They would, however, be less likely to openly share their displeasure." She glanced at the High Lord, and her expression lost some of its amusement. "Yes," she said quietly. "We are aware that there has been growing difficulty in the fiefs. We have some measure of protection against the possible danger of a fief failing to hold the border—but it has not been tested."

The consort's knee was at Kaylin's eye level, which, in the end, wasn't entirely comfortable. Kaylin rose. "High Lord," she said, because she didn't actually know his name, "you're of course aware of Lord Nightshade and the position he occupies in the fiefs."

"We are. We are aware, as well, of the nature of your own relationship to the fief and its Lord."

"Were you, at one point in time, aware in the same way of Lord Illien and the position he also occupied in the fief of Illien?"

Silence. It was the usual type of silence that implied, if not guilt, then a lot of hidden—and relevant—information. She kept her voice steady, and her hands by her sides, as she continued to speak. "We don't have a lot of experience with the fiefs or the fief lords. I probably have more than most people present. And I have no experience at all with Illien, because according to what I know of the fiefs, he should be dead."

More silence, but this time, she expected it.

"Or I should say, according to what I *knew* of the fiefs. Fief Law is pretty simple—if you're powerful enough, you rule. If you rule, it means the previous fief lord wasn't powerful enough to stop you."

"Which sounds familiar," the consort said, with a wry half smile.

"Should. Although to be fair, it sounds familiar in *any* culture except possibly the Tha'alani." She hesitated, and then added, "And maybe the Aerians." She took a deep breath. "I need to know what you know about Illien." She refrained from using the word *undying,* although it was difficult.

But the High Lord—the man who had been, until his father's death, the Lord of the Green—studied her in silence for a while. "Very well," he said at last. "I owe you that much, Kaylin Neya, midwife." He rose. "Follow."

She glanced at the table of food that she hadn't touched yet, and then shrugged. Severn had said nothing, and judging by his expression, wouldn't start now.

The High Lord led them from the gardens, and into the wide, tall hallways that were adorned with statues, marble floors, and living flowers. He passed through them, the consort at his side, until the halls changed in texture. Kaylin had a suspicion she knew where they were going. Nor was she wrong. The High Lord led her from the gorgeous, open halls into halls that seemed older and darker; they were also shorter. The stonework was smooth, but seemed rough and lifeless.

"This is where I first met you," Kaylin said quietly.

"Indeed."

"But why—"

"It is, of all rooms in the Halls, one of the safest."

And one of the darkest and most disturbing. Which would probably be the ideal definition of safety for the Barrani, she thought with a grimace.

He opened the single, thick door, and entered, clapping his hands twice to encourage what light there was to shine. It was a sickly light, a green-white that never really illuminated, and it was contained on a series of poles. She thought those poles might once have been home to torches, but couldn't be sure.

As her eyes acclimatized themselves to this new light, she saw the circle engraved on the floor, its carved runes both reflecting and hoarding the glow. The High Lord stepped over the circle without touching those runes, and lifted a hand when Kaylin followed; she stopped at the circle's edge. The consort's hand was on her arm to restrain her in case she hadn't gotten the hint.

Her skin began to itch, although the High Lord hadn't gestured or spoken. His eyes were now the same green as the light, which wasn't a comfort.

"You remember our first meeting," he said, turning back to face them as they stood on the circle's periphery. It wasn't a question. Kaylin nodded. "You understood what I had attempted. I know that you are not fond of Lord Evarrim, but it was Evarrim who, in the end, saved me."

It was hard for Kaylin to accept that a man who was so obviously in love with his own power could expend that power for anything useful.

"But you've seen the undying," he continued. Again, it wasn't a question.

This time, when she nodded, she added, "I'm not sure how you know that."

"It's of little consequence." Meaning he wasn't about to tell her. Fine. "You've seen—you've touched—the water of life."

Kaylin glanced at the consort, who nodded.

"But even so, you are mortal. You do not, perhaps cannot, understand the significance of our names. Our true names," he added. "They are a gift and a trap. You understood why I attempted to divest myself of my own."

She nodded because she did. The High Lord—the Lord of the Green—at least made sense, to her. She couldn't imagine why any other Barrani would try.

"What do you wish to know about Illien?"

"I think he is—was—undying."

The pause was slight, but she marked it. "He was not, when he first entered the fiefs. He was not when he first defeated the fief lord he found there and claimed the Tower as his own."

Her brows rose at his words. "Did you—did you know him?"

He laughed. The consort, standing beside Kaylin, frowned slightly. "Oh, yes. There were four of our kin who entered the fiefs, and they will never return. You have met one, Lord Nightshade. He is as he was before he fled the Court. But you have yet to meet the others. You have not, I think, met Illien."

She shook her head. "Not yet."

"Lord Nightshade is not free to return to the High Halls. It would be his death, unless the circumstances were so profoundly grim that his death would harm us all. Illien was not Outcaste when he chose to wander across the river. He found the fief. I believe, in some sense, it called to him, but that is not clear to me."

"The other Barrani?"

But he shook his head. "You will discover them in time, or you will not. I hope, for your sake, you do not."

She nodded. Hesitated.

"Ask."

"Why did they leave? I understand why Nightshade did—I can guess the fate of Barrani Outcaste, and it probably isn't pleasant. He's not a man to accept anyone else's judgment of his actions."

The High Lord nodded. "And perhaps that is why Lord Nightshade remains as he was. He did not seek the fiefs for power or knowledge. He sought them strategically." He paused for a moment, and the lights in the room grew brighter. They were still a faintly repulsive color, on the other hand.

"Illien?"

"Illien was a dreamer. Not in the way of mortals. His dreams were larger, deeper, and harsher. What we—in the High Halls—understand of the fiefs, we understand because of Illien. He went to study them, some time ago. The mortal city had failed to catch his interest, and the politics of the Court, in his own words, bored him, they had become so insipid.

"He had spent years in the West Marches, and before that, decades in the wilderness beyond the Empire. He was considered an expert, in a fashion, about the Dragons, our ancient enemies. He was not—could not—be entirely comfortable in a city in which a Dragon claimed ownership of all.

"Let me add that many of our kin sympathized with this—they are not all young, and they are not all foolish. We suffered great losses at the hands of the Dragons."

"They probably suffered similar at yours."

He shrugged. Unlike Kaylin's fief gesture, his was smooth and elegant—but it amounted to the same thing. "My father, the previous High Lord, saw the benefit of the Dragon Emperor. The Dragon Emperor does not visit the High Halls, and he does not interfere in internal Barrani affairs. He was not of a mind to intrigue against the Emperor, except as it suited his purposes in the Court political structure.

"I am not my father. I accept the Dragon Emperor and his claim." The High Lord turned, as if he heard something that even Kaylin couldn't hear. "The Halls beneath are restless," he said after a moment.

The consort lifted a hand, and he shook his head; she was slow to lower it.

"I understand why the Emperor chose to build his city here. I understand why the High Halls stand as they stand. And I understand, in some small part, the nature of the fiefs. It is why we can prepare at all." He paused. "Understand, Kaylin," he said, as he turned to face her. She took a step back, because the emerald of his eyes was now laced with dark shadows, glints of ebony. "That the holding of a true name is not a simple affair. Stories say that when you know the true name of another living being, you can compel him to the action of your desire. I believe you understand why this is not always true."

"Some names are...too big."

"Yes. But if there is balance, the binding works both ways. I remember," he added, "some part of what the Other knew. It is not knowledge that the High Halls have had before, not in this fashion. Nor would I suggest it in future," he added, with a grim smile. "But he held my name, in secret, for many years."

She nodded.

"I did not, and could not, hold his. He has no name." He glanced at her, as if testing her reaction. What he was looking for, she didn't know.

"He's—it's—an Old One. Do they even *have* names?"

"We don't know. Not even the most ancient of Dragons does. What information we once might have possessed, we lost in the shadowstorms and the wars. It did not seem entirely relevant at the time—the Old Ones were lost. They were gone."

"They're not entirely gone."

He nodded. She didn't like the color of his eyes. "Illien was undying, in the end. He was not undying when he found his way across the Ablayne; he was not undying when he took—and held—the Tower."

"Did he tell you what the Tower was?"

The High Lord laughed. It was a brief burst of sound, startling when coming from a Barrani. "Yes, Kaylin. Has Lord Nightshade never told you what his Castle is?"

"It's his," she replied with a shrug. And then, because it was important, she set the fief attitude aside. "It conforms to him. It's not entirely solid—it changes shape. The halls move."

He waited, but she fell silent. "You have described the Castle, to some extent," he said when her pause had grown long enough.

"And in your fashion, you have answered my question. Let me tell you what the Tower of Illien was, for Illien."

She nodded, glancing once at Severn, who was now utterly impassive.

"It was—as no doubt Castle Nightshade is—far larger on the interior than the exterior suggests. When he wrested control of the Tower away from its former occupant—"

"Barrani?"

"No. When he wrested control of the Tower from its former occupant, the Tower began to shift and change. He had expected something of the sort," he added quietly. "And if I were to guess—for he never put it in words—he enjoyed his early occupation. The fief itself was not of concern to Illien, not at the time. But the Tower was.

"I am under no illusion. I do not, nor would I, claim to know all that Illien knew. He was Barrani, as am I. But in part, his love was the ancient and the powerful, and he was drawn to the fiefs because they stood against the rule of the Dragon Emperor. I think he thought he might find freedom there."

"It wasn't freedom he found," Severn said, speaking for the first time.

The High Lord raised a brow. "You are perhaps mistranslating. It is a failure with the spoken word. Freedom, for the Barrani, *is* power. Without power, you are beholden to others, and you live—and die—at their whim. You are aware, Kaylin, that this City, in one form or another, has existed for a long time." It wasn't a question.

"It was occupied, but it was occupied not by Barrani or Dragon although they did live within its boundaries. We think—we are not certain—that the Old Ones made their home here for some time, mimicking the lesser mortals, as if to see what they gained from their odd communities. We are not certain.

"What we are certain of is this—the Towers, the Castles, were not created by Barrani, Dragon or any mortal race. Yet in our muddled histories, we have the odd record that indicates that the fiefs themselves, as they now exist, were not a barrier when the city was discovered. The…present difficulty…was a gift of shadowstorms and possibly the nature of the fiefs themselves.

"But that does not answer your question, and I see you are impatient."

As she was actually listening with interest, Kaylin grimaced.

"Lord Illien remade the Tower for a time in his own image, and he explored what he found within. Some of our knowledge of Old runes comes from that time, for there were parts of the Tower that were…akin in some fashion to the High Halls. Frequently, he would leave his Tower to venture into the High Halls during this period, and he would speak with one or two of his friends about his discoveries. But he traveled less and less with time. He was not Outcaste, he was not denied his role in the Court—but it ceased to interest him. Or so we thought."

"Nightshade can leave his Castle. He's crossed the Ablayne."

The High Lord nodded. "He does not leave it often, however."

"How often do you leave the High Halls?"

"Seldom," was the quiet reply. "And perhaps, in the end, for similar reasons. Lord Illien discovered, as he rebuilt his Tower, that the hold that the Tower *also* exerted over him was substantial. It was subtle, but it was always present."

She hesitated, and then said, "I don't think Nightshade views it the same way."

"Perhaps he does not."

"He *is* the fief, in some ways. That much, we know. He can be aware of almost anything that occurs in the fief if he *wants* to. I got the impression it was a lot of work to be that aware, and it requires a lot of focus. If he's homing in on the small things, he can miss the bigger ones. Well, some of them—if you wanted to storm the Castle, he'd know no matter what he was doing."

The High Lord nodded.

"But Nightshade is definitely not undying."

"No."

"And Illien wasn't." She frowned. "I don't think—"

"Yes?"

"I don't know enough. But I don't think he could have taken the Tower if he'd been undying." She frowned again. "Nightshade told us something."

"Us?"

"Tiamaris. Lord Tiamaris," she added. "He's one of the—"

"Dragon Court. I am familiar with all of the Lords who comprise it."

She nodded. "He told us that Liatt—the fief of Liatt—is held. I don't think it's held by Barrani. I think—I'm not sure—that it's held by a human. A woman."

The High Lord inclined his chin slightly.

"But humans don't *have* names. So I don't understand how—" She stopped speaking for a moment, and looked at Severn. "If he attempted to divest himself of his name, and he succeeded, he wouldn't, strictly speaking, be dead. But if it's not entirely based on name—"

"He would not lose the fief, no."

"But the fief—the fief has no name," she told the High Lord.

"You said it was Barren."

"It's Barren, at least that's what the people who live there call it. But I call Teela Teela; you call her Anteela. In either case, we're not using her true name. People know who we mean. It's the same with Barren. I think." She stopped. She was missing something, and knew it.

Swallowing, she looked up at the High Lord, enclosed by the circle and surrounded by sickly torches. "When you attempted to divest yourself of name," she asked softly, "how did you do it?"

CHAPTER 14

The consort stiffened, and turned to look fully at Kaylin. Kaylin had the strong sense that she could have asked for the particulars of their sex life and caused less offense. Not that she was tempted to try, because one of them might actually answer.

The High Lord said, after a pause, "If this Liatt can somehow name a fief, it is *not* a Barrani name, not an immortal name." She recognized a deflection when she heard it. She almost accepted it, given the fact that the consort was still staring sharply at the side of her face.

But even if it was true—and it was, she couldn't deny it based on what she knew—it was also beside the point. "The fief of Liatt," she replied, in her most reasonable tone of voice, "still *has* a name. Barren—" and it struck her as she said it that it was an appropriate name for the fief "—doesn't. Not in a way that means something to the fief lords."

"Or," Severn added softly, "to the shadows at the heart of the fiefs." He took a step forward, although he did not attempt to step over the carved boundary of the circle itself. "What is occurring

in the fiefs now—at least in the fief of Barren—has something
to do with Illien, with the name that he attempted to surrender."

The High Lord *laughed*. It was a bitter, dark laugh, and his
eyes were a green that looked like dead plants, not the heart of
a living forest.

The consort reached out, her arm crossing the circle, her feet
remaining at its edge. He did not take her hand; didn't even seem
to notice it. Kaylin did; she also noted that the consort didn't
withdraw what was ignored.

"Do you understand, Kaylin Neya, that I *failed* the test of the
High Halls? Do you fully understand?"

She nodded. "I would have failed," she replied quietly.

"You are not—you were never meant to be—High Lord."

She nodded again, but some of the edge left her expression as
his shifted. "I would have failed that test," she told him, "if I had
taken it. I would fail it now," she added softly, thinking of the
darkness of the caverns below the High Halls, in which the
damned waited in the only Barrani version of hell she had ever
heard of. "You didn't have your full name."

"It wouldn't matter. It wouldn't have mattered then. My
brother, the Lord of the West March, and my sister, my consort—"
he met her gaze, then, although he still did not touch the hand
that remained outstretched before him "—passed."

Kaylin said nothing. "You knew," she finally said. "You knew,
then, that you'd failed. But you didn't attempt to strip yourself of
your name until later."

"Until I knew that my father intended to perform the rites and
surrender the High Halls—to me. Had they come to me, the
creature that held my name would have controlled the Halls."

Kaylin swallowed. "I'm not Barrani," she said, speaking in her
native tongue. "I know it won't mean much to you—but I can't
judge you, not in this. I would have tried the same thing. Except
in my case, it would have been simpler." Suicide, in theory, was.
Give this to the Barrani: they couldn't do anything simple if something more complicated and twisted could be done in its place.

She looked at the consort. "The waters," she finally said, "of life."

The consort nodded, but the nod was not an agreement; it was an acknowledgment of the words, no more.

"All names, past and present, are there—somehow."

She nodded again. "You've seen them," she finally grudgingly added.

"The babies—your babies—they don't wake without names."

"No."

"And you go to the waters to find their names. But you don't *know* them."

"No."

"But the children—they're not dead. Before they're joined to their names."

"No." The consort shook herself, and her face lost the cool chill of anger. "They breathe," she said, her voice softening. "They can open their eyes, but they see nothing. We believe they hear little, as well."

"They eat?"

The consort lifted a brow.

"I'll take it that's a no." It was her turn to frown. "But they don't starve."

"They're not mortal," was the consort's reply.

"Do they grow?"

"No. They do not change at all. They…wait. Only when they have their true name do they begin to interact with the world."

"The undying—"

The consort grimaced. "Understand that our knowledge is limited, Kaylin. The undying are *not* children. We are not certain *what* they are. They have lived, often for centuries, and the rhythm of life does not leave them. They can speak, they can eat, they can sleep—although they do not seem to require it. They can converse and interact."

"Then why do they need the name at all?"

"It is a question that our sages have oft asked when discussing philosophical issues. It is not a question that I, as consort, and mother of our race, will ever ask." She glanced at the High Lord; her hand was steady, but still outstretched, and its silent grace was almost a demand.

He ignored it.

"When the Barrani die—if they die—their names are freed. Those names," the consort added softly, "will return to the lake of names, to the waters of life, and they will flow there, among the others, until they are chosen again." She paused, and then added, in a softer voice, "this is our lore, and this is our understanding.

"But I am not my mother, or my grandmother. I have seen the dead, and if I do not know their true names in any way the Barrani understand, I can almost sense the *shape* of them. But I cannot— I have never been able—to find that shape in the waters. I looked," she added quietly. "When my mother chose her end. When she allowed the waters to wash over her a last time. I looked for her.

"Perhaps I couldn't find her because if I did, I might choose that name for another because of my own attachment to it. I do not know. We have no gods," she added softly. "But perhaps our creators meant this as a kindness."

"The names of the undying—are they meant to return to the lake?"

The consort glanced at the High Lord.

Silence.

In the silence, for just a moment, Kaylin could hear the faint cries and pleas of a multitude of muted voices. She could, if she closed her eyes, see the dead who uttered them without hope, standing across a chasm that was bridged by a slender span of mis-shapen rock. Above them, rock, dripping over centuries into shapes that only ice took in the streets of the city; beneath them, hidden to Kaylin's eyes, different rock, fire, the glimmering of a magic that was so old it didn't truly feel magical at all.

And before them, in command of them, pulling them from the darkness and sending them back at its whim, one creature, nameless and almost shapeless.

Because beneath these Halls, in a darkness that had probably never seen light, the shadows gathered, waiting for one gap, one lapse of guardianship, that would allow them to run free. And while they waited, they held what they had taken: the Barrani who did not have the strength—if *strength* was the word for *indifference*—to walk away from the truth of their private vision of hell.

She didn't close her eyes.

"They died," she said quietly, her voice so soft even she had trouble hearing it. "Those who failed the test of the High Halls. They died."

The High Lord closed his eyes and turned his face away. It was a very Barrani gesture.

"Yes," the Consort replied, for he would not. "They died."

"But their names—"

"Their names have *never* returned to the lake. They will never return while the shadows of the Old Ones remain."

Kaylin allowed the words to sink in, to take a shape and form that intuition alone didn't give them. She waited until she could find her voice again and speak clearly and cleanly. Where *cleanly* in this case meant a whole lot of hushed Leontine invective.

"It is to prevent our entire race from meeting that fate," the consort said evenly, "that my brother is High Lord. Because of your intervention, he has the strength to ensure that we are safe while he is alive."

Kaylin nodded, still thinking. "If Lord Nightshade died, I couldn't hold his name. I couldn't hold him here."

"No."

"But the—"

"The shadows beneath the High Halls *are,* in some ways, the Old Ones, Kaylin. They are half of the face of the only gods we knew. They *created* the words. What they can do, none of the rest of us can do, and for that, we must be grateful."

"High Lord," Kaylin said, for he had still not spoken. "What did you do?"

"I studied," he replied. "For decades. I traveled, as I could, and

I learned. You have heard the stories about the undying, no doubt. The Dragons have some understanding, but it is, as is so often the case with Dragon theory, flawed."

She was grateful that Tiamaris wasn't in hearing range. Not that he would have done anything but respond with similar arrogance.

"At the height of our power, in the absence of the Old Ones, there were those of our kin who had some understanding of the tongue of the ancients."

There were Dragons who did, as well; Kaylin didn't point this out.

"Understand that to *us* language is not a simple act of communication. Not the Ancient language; it is transformative. What you say becomes what you are, and if you say it well, and clearly, and with will, it will transform the landscape around you, altering it in subtle ways.

"We came to our understanding of magic through our attempts to speak the Ancient Tongue."

Kaylin frowned. "But most magic—"

"Does not require speech?"

"Only if you're bad—Sanabalis says speech and physical gestures are a type of crutch."

"That would be Lord Sanabalis, and yes, he is correct. Magic, as it is taught and understood, does not require speech. But our attempts to harness the Ancient Tongue taught us how to approach the magic that underlies this world." He glanced at the consort. "Our names, our birthing rites, our waking into the world, were given to us by the Old Ones. We were said to be formed of stone, not flesh, until they gave our ancestors the First Names, and story says this is why we do not age as you do."

"I think I understand the difference between myth and history."

"Good. Understand that the concern of my kin has often been power. Without it, we die or we serve. There is not a man born among us who dreams—at first—of service, although in the end, many are bent that way."

She grimaced, and said nothing.

"But in that dawn, when the world was young and the Old

Ones had left us, we were powerful, Kaylin. We thought of ourselves as the new gods."

"So did the Dragons."

"Yes. They are the eldest," he added after a slight pause. "Although I admit this is not completely accepted chronology among some of my kin."

She would have let him continue, but something about the words made her raise her hand. "Why do you believe they're the eldest?"

"They have two forms. The one that you see in the City, and the form of a great beast. They breathe fire, and smoke, and ash. They bear scales that only the very, very finest of our weapons could pierce."

She nodded; she'd seen it. "They were made that way, though."

"Yes. But…it is my belief that they were made when the Old Ones were not yet themselves at war, that some part of the chaos that is shadow and some part of the order that is not went into their building. The Dragon form is sharp and it is beautiful—but it is also kin, in some ways, to the beasts that leave the shadows when the shadows find some freedom.

"But that is not to the point, and if I reach the point slowly, I am tracing a path toward it. Our ancestors played with the words the Old Ones appeared to have abandoned, and those words brought magic to us all. You have studied with Lord Sanabalis." It wasn't a question.

Kaylin nodded.

"You bore his medallion when we first met. It was seen," he added, "by the Lords of the Court, and if you did not understand it clearly at the time, they did. They could interfere with you, but in so doing, they courted the fury of a Dragon Lord. The Dragons are notoriously possessive."

Given that their most important laws involved hoarding, this was not news to Kaylin.

"Magic, when it is taught to humans, is taught differently—but some of the fundamentals must remain the same. Tell me, have you encountered the test of the candle?"

Kaylin cringed and bit her tongue to stop herself from cursing. "Yes," she managed.

"Did he not tell you to imagine—to discover—the *name* of fire?"

She nodded slowly.

"Understand that this is not a simple convention. Fire *has* a name. Different students will arrive at it in entirely individual ways—especially the humans. But the name, the naming, is part of making it *your own*. This is the legacy of the Ancients, and some pale reflection of the glory they discovered when they began to attempt to invoke the Old Tongue.

"Because they sought power, and they found it, they were content for a time. But as their power and knowledge grew, they came to understand that they had a fatal flaw, a singular weakness—the names that bound them. Those names, private and hidden, could be used against them, and all of the magic at their disposal would avail them nothing."

"You can't just *use* a name. It has to be given."

"No, Kaylin," he said quietly. "It does not."

She stared at him.

"Do you think," he added, opening his eyes and meeting hers, "that I willingly gave my name to the creature the High Halls imprisons? Do you think *any* of the damned did?"

She was silent, after that. It didn't last, but she felt that for the duration, it was a somber and qualitative silence. It certainly was compared to the first words she spoke. "I don't understand."

"No. And I am not the man to enlighten you. But some beings exist who can see names as clearly as they can read handwriting. It is not always possible, and before you ask, I am not one of them— I don't know how, or when, it works." He hesitated for just a moment, and she marked the hesitation. But when he spoke, he said, "It is my suspicion that you could do it."

"But—but—"

"Because of the marks you bear, Kaylin. And if you're about to ask me how, don't. I understand the marks little better than you claim to." He raised a hand as she opened her mouth. "I am not accusing you of lying. I believe that you have as little understanding as you claim."

"Thank you. I think."

"But our ancients grew to understand their names not as the source of their life, or even their power, but as a weakness. They learned the Old words, and they tried, in their fashion, to exist without names."

"It didn't work."

"Oh, it did. You have seen the results of it, I think, at least once." She nodded.

"They do not die as you or I understand death—nor do they live. Nameless, they exist. They are not without thought or cunning."

"Neither are ferals."

"But they are not as we are. They do not appear to feel either pain or fear, and they are therefore without natural caution." Again, he hesitated. "Do you understand why we attempted to destroy them all?"

She nodded.

But he shook his head. "I don't think you do. Had I succeeded in my attempt to divest myself of a name, my father would have had no choice but to destroy me and end his long game. He had hoped my brother, the Lord of the West March, would do so."

She remembered. "He wouldn't."

"Not until the end," the High Lord said softly. "But it is my belief that in the end my brother would have done what was necessary to save us all. I do not know if he would have done so in time. But I would have achieved some semblance of peace—I would have given my name to the void, and the shadows beneath the High Halls would have had no direct purchase over me.

"They might have had some indirect purchase. We destroy the undying," he told her quietly, "because they are hollow, and they can often be vessels for the chaos of shadow."

"When you say you would have given your name to the void, what does that mean?"

"It means that the name would leave me, or I would leave it. It would not return to the lake, because I would technically still be alive."

"Where does it go?"

He shook his head. "I am not entirely certain, Kaylin."

She frowned, then. It was a twitch. Something in his words tugged at her memory, at the facts she'd gathered and had not yet fully examined. Name. Something about true names. She looked at Severn, whose face was, as it so often was in the Barrani Court, a study in neutrality. He did not meet her gaze, but he did nod, briefly.

"Illien wouldn't have made himself an empty vessel," she finally said. "Not so close to the heart of the fiefs. It makes *no sense*. He had to know—"

"Yes."

"What was he trying to do?"

He didn't answer the question, not directly. This, Kaylin thought, with some frustration, was the problem with talking to immortals. They *had* forever. And they generally took it, too. "I told you I studied. I studied our legends and our lore. I spoke with our sages. And what I discovered in my desperate search for some solution to my dilemma was this— There were at least two, in our history, who managed to lose the names that had brought them awareness without becoming essentially empty vessels. They learned, from the errors of those who had made the first attempts, and they attempted to do better.

"It was not an option, for me."

"Why?"

"Because it involved, among other things, the study of the words of the Old Ones. Not the memory of the words, not the traces that exist in our history—or even the history retained by the Dragons—but the words of Power."

"Words of…" Almost involuntarily, she glanced at her arms. The marks on them were hidden, as they usually were, by the fall of fabric. "Power."

"Yes. I do not know if Castle Nightshade is like the Tower that Illien inhabited. I suspect it must be, but suspect, as well, that each building is unique. The buildings themselves have power, Kaylin, and it is a power that we, as individuals, do not possess."

She remembered the living statues in Castle Nightshade, and remembered, as well, that Nightshade had said that he had dared to use the Castle's power to create them. To preserve living members of almost every race in Elantra, frozen in time, until he released them.

"Two Barrani sorcerers discovered that they could, in some fashion, remake their names. They could choose, for themselves, runes and words that were never resident in the lake from which we are all, as infants, birthed. They did so, Kaylin.

"And they remained among the Barrani, shorn of life, but *living*." He glanced at the consort. "It was not discovered immediately," he said. "But when it was, it was discovered by the consort of the High Lord—she knew."

"Did she survive the knowledge?"

"You understand much. No. But at least one of them perished when revealed."

"The other?"

"He fled."

"How long ago was this?"

"Long before Elantra existed."

"You don't know if he died."

"No. We know that he could possibly live, even now. But so, too, could any one of our race from that time, in theory. We do not fear time, but many are the things that diminish us as time passes.

"What we also know, from those records, is that the two could, with time and subtlety, create the undying. Those, they could imbue with some of their power, some hidden word of their own, and those they changed thus cleaved to their masters."

"It seems like a lot of work for people who could just use their true names against them."

"The use of a name requires both power and concentration. It is not perfect control for anything more than moments at a time. Because it is imperfect, there is always the possibility of betrayal, if not in the obvious way, then in subtle. This? It required very, very little of either.

"You understand," he said softly, "why the Outcaste Dragon is a threat, to us."

She did, now. "He can create the undying."

"Yes."

"And he has."

"Demonstrably."

She shook herself. "But this isn't what you tried, in the end."

He laughed. It was a low, resonant sound, and as it filled the rough contours of this dark, strange room, the color of his eyes deepened until it was almost a green she could recognize as Barrani. "You are like a bulldog, Kaylin."

"I'm a Hawk," she replied, with a shrug. "It may not be what Illien tried to do. It may be what he achieved. I don't know what will be useful in the investigation."

"I tried to shed my name. I had nothing to replace it with. I would have made myself an empty vessel, and in the High Halls, *that* would have been a threat. I do not know who—or what— might attempt to retrieve what I sundered from myself; it was not, at that time, of concern. If the name was no longer part of *me,* whatever might somehow grasp it could not use it in a way that affected me."

"But you failed."

"My brother and Lord Evarrim interfered. It was not pleasant and I will not go into the details. They are not—I hope—relevant. Even if they are, they are not mine to share."

It wasn't the answer she wanted, but had she been allowed to do something as trivial as bet, it was the one she would have placed money on.

"Illien tried to rewrite his name, didn't he?"

"Again, I now offer speculation. But, yes, I believe that is what he did. Although you put it crudely, it is what our ancient ancestors achieved."

"But…"

"Yes?"

"It would still *be* a name."

"Would it?"

"Yes." There was no doubt at all in her answer. None.

"You are certain."

She nodded, frowning.

"Why?"

Sometimes the short questions were the biggest pain. She began to pace across the floor, avoiding the runes engraved in the rocks beneath her feet; it made her stagger like a drunk. "It's what the Outcaste did. The Dragon," she added. Her feet continued to find unengraved spaces. "And he has a name."

The silence that followed the statement was not the silence of hesitation. It lasted as long as it took Kaylin to reach a wall, pivot and pick her way back toward the circle. "How do you know this?"

"I saw it," she replied, hating the answer even as it left her mouth.

"You—you *know* his name?" At any other time, she would have taken some small and private joy in being able to actually *shock* a Barrani High Lord. Now? She wasn't even tempted, although a tiny part of her mind saw it as a lost opportunity.

"No." She grimaced. "Maybe. I *saw* it. If I close my eyes and concentrate, I can see it now. But I can't say it. I can't even begin to say it. And, no," she added, before he could speak again, "I can't talk about the Outcaste. Anything I now know is mixed up with everything I've learned from the Lords of the Dragon Court—and if they knew I was talking about it, nothing that could happen to me in Barren could be less pleasant than what they'd do. Trust me."

"I have some experience with the ferocity of Dragons who guard their hoard," he replied, with a dry chuckle. "Trust, in this case, is entirely unnecessary." But his smile ebbed from his face as he watched her. "You are a threat," he finally said. "Lord Evarrim saw truly.

"But anyone who wields power is a threat. It is the nature of power."

"Intent has something to do with it," Kaylin pointed out.

"Perhaps. Perhaps not. I will not debate the point with you." He glanced at his consort, and then, at last, took the hand she had never lowered. Their fingers, where they touched, glowed faintly in the darkness. "Illien must have attempted what our ancestors attempted. I cannot say whether he failed or succeeded. In the end, I fear you will know far better than I, or any of his kin.

"But if he exists in the Tower, now, he is not what he was when he first claimed it." He met her gaze and held it as the floor itself began to coalesce beneath his feet. "We do not fully understand the nature of the Towers—nor can we claim a full understanding of the nature of the fiefs or what lies at their heart. But Elantra exists, in some small measure, because the fiefs exist. That much, we know and accept.

"Perhaps the Towers were meant, in their entirety, for the living. Perhaps they were built with the living in mind. That must be our hope.

"You will go to the Tower of Illien, Lord Kaylin. You will find what remains. If the Tower no longer has the power that sustained the fief, you will discover that, as well. It is possible that Illien's act of transformation drained whatever magic lay resident there. If that is the case, we must prepare," he added softly. "There is power in the High Halls to withstand the dangers that come from the fiefs, if they breach the river."

"You can't put the entire damn City into the High Halls, and I'm not certain that the same can be said of any *other* building."

"There are others who also have the power to withstand the most ancient of forces. If I am not mistaken, you have met at least one, and consider him a friend."

She started to ask who he meant, and realized, before she'd opened her mouth, that he spoke of Evanton. "I'll do what I can," she told him. "But I'm already under orders to—"

"It was not a request. You are a Lord of the High Court."

And he was the High Lord. She swallowed, and then executed a bow.

But she hadn't quite finished. "One more question?"

"Ask," he said, as his feet drifted toward the floor.

"What do you know of shadowstorms?"

He stopped moving for just a few seconds. But his expression, as he watched her, was grave. "Why do you ask?" Raising a hand, he added, "I would be greatly obliged if you would tell me the question was entirely theoretical."

"I was never a great student of theory."

"If rumor is to be believed, you were never a great student of anything."

She shrugged. "I'm learning to be a better one," she said with a grimace. And then, as if she needed to justify her record, added, "I always paid attention to anything that seemed practical and important. I didn't realize just how practical some of the theoretical classes would end up becoming."

"A flaw that is common in the young."

She didn't consider herself that young, but compared to the Barrani, she knew she was almost a babe in arms. She forced herself to nod.

"There have been storms in Barren," the High Lord said quietly. It was almost a question.

"I think so."

"You are certain."

"No. I've never seen a storm. But…the Dragons were certain."

"Storm," he said softly, to his consort. "It is time."

She nodded.

"Time for what?" Kaylin asked, as he stepped, slowly, out of the circle's confines.

"For the High Court of the Barrani to convene," he replied. "You will, of course, be excused if you do not answer the summons. You have a personal duty to which you must attend on behalf of the Court. Lord Severn is likewise excused. You may tell Lord Andellen, however, that his presence will be expected."

"I'm not even sure I'll see Andellen—" She stopped, and then offered him a bow. "I'll make certain he knows."

CHAPTER 15

Tiamaris was waiting for them on the bridge that crossed the Ablayne. It was still the wrong bridge, and Kaylin hoped that it would always feel like the wrong one. The bridge to Nightshade had been, in its way, a symbol of hope when she had been growing up in the fiefs.

The bridge to Barren meant, in the end, death.

"Corporal Handred," the Dragon Hawk said, nodding as if he had expected Severn to accompany Kaylin.

"Lord Tiamaris."

No one was sporting the Hawk, today; the clothing was all practical. Even Tiamaris was wearing what was, for Dragons, almost obscenely casual: a tunic, rather than his more stately robes; flat, thick boots that looked vaguely obsidian in what was left of the morning light; an undyed shirt beneath which the thick links of golden chain could barely be seen. Obvious daggers were notably absent. Then again, until yesterday, she would have bet money he didn't bother with them; Dragons didn't generally bristle with arms that weren't attached to their bodies.

"Private Neya. Your friend was here. I believe she became impatient after the first hour had passed."

"You could have gone with her. We'd've followed."

"I do not believe she trusts me," was his reply.

Kaylin shrugged. "It's Morse. If she'd learned to trust many people in her line of work, she'd be feeding worms under some patch of weeds in Barren, if they bothered burying her at all. Was she pissed off?"

"If, by that, you mean 'angry,' I would say she wasn't pleased."

"Did she say where she was going?"

"No."

Kaylin swore. "The meeting with the High Lord took a little longer than I expected, and I dropped into the office to pick up a couple of things—including lunch."

"Was the meeting useful?"

"Hard to say." She grimaced. "Actually, what I want to say is no. But I'm not sure. I've been ordered to investigate Illien's Tower." She adjusted the fall of a belt that was, unlike Tiamaris's, snug and practical. Waterskin, knife, knife. She had also shrugged herself into a backpack into which she had dropped one round cheese, two candles—neither of which resembled the candles that she had come to think of as torture during her lessons with Sanabalis—and a large coil of heavy rope. It was the rope that provided most of the bulk.

Tiamaris raised a brow.

"Rope," she told him, as she readjusted the buckles now that the pack had settled some.

"Ah. Why?"

"Just a hunch. If we're anywhere near fighting, I'll drop it."

"If you have time."

Fair enough. It's not as if she usually carried what was admittedly an awkward pack on her shoulders during her regular duties. "I know the Tower's important," she told him. "I know we have to go there."

"It is not, however, the first place you want to visit."

"Not really."

"You want to go back to the White Towers."

"I can't figure out," Kaylin replied, as she started across the bridge, leaving Tiamaris and Severn to follow, "why Sanabalis thought you weren't a good student. You're damn perceptive."

"I can't figure out," he replied, mimicking her Elantran, "why almost all of your teachers thought that you weren't, and for the same reason."

Dragons.

"Private Neya?"

"What?"

"How well do you know Barren?"

She stopped walking. Glanced over her shoulder. Shrugged. "I can get to the White Towers from almost anywhere in the fief. Good enough for you?"

Walking through the streets of Barren without Morse as a native guide should have been easy. In some sense, it was. Severn and Tiamaris flanked her on either side, and given her own gear, and the expression she was probably wearing, they kept people at bay. The only people likely to be stupid—or cocky—enough to try to stop them were all employed by Barren. But he employed a lot of stupid people; Kaylin thought, given a sample size of two, most fief lords did.

She had thought—and most of her teachers had agreed, usually when they were pissed off—that nothing would take the fiefs out of her; they were her first home. They were where she'd learned to speak, learned to walk, learned to eat, steal, and dream.

But the truth was different. She wondered if the truth, when she arrived at it, would always be different from what she'd been certain it would be.

She saw the cautious and nervous people who didn't manage to wander off the streets in time, and she wondered what would happen to them. What might have *already* happened to them. She couldn't ask, of course. That would take time, and the familiarity of presence. The Hawks had that, and by extension, when she wore her uniform, she had it, as well.

Here, all she had were obvious weapons, and equally obviously armed companions; no one would come near her, unless she flagged them down or approached them first. If she did? She wouldn't be able to trust anything they said. Fear made poor discussions.

And she'd fed on that, in Barren.

It made her cringe, when she thought about it. She'd tried hard *not* to think about it for almost seven years. She'd been Morse's shadow. She'd been Morse's apprentice. What she'd left the people of Barren, in the end, was more death, more fear. Morse had been proud of her, then.

And—this was worse—she'd been proud of *herself.*

Severn touched her shoulder and she started. He didn't speak. She wanted to, but the words wouldn't come. She had never, ever imagined that she would walk through Barren with Severn by her side. Then again, she'd never imagined that she would see Severn again and survive it.

So many mistakes. So many stupidities. So many deaths. All of them led here. *How did you survive?* she thought, glancing at his profile. *How did you learn to live with what you did to Steffi and Jade?*

She glanced at her hands. Severn had killed them to save *her.* She had killed, as well. And why? To save herself. To be able to look at herself in a mirror again without loathing. She hadn't killed anyone who trusted her. She told herself that.

But in the end? The dead probably had families or friends to whom they'd never return. She hadn't cared, then. And now that she did, there wasn't a damn thing she could do about it.

Why was she a Hawk, anyway? To put a stop to people who were exactly like she'd been herself?

"Kaylin." Severn's voice. He still wasn't looking at her.

"What?"

"I think we have a problem."

"No kidding." She knew he could sense what she felt; knew that if he *wanted,* he could probably hear what she was thinking.

At this particular moment in time, she didn't even care. It would—it might—be a relief.

But Severn shook his head. He lifted a hand and pointed. She followed the line of his arm, her eyes widening slightly in confusion.

Tiamaris was standing, utterly still, in the open and deserted street. Before him, in the distance, she could see the swirling motion of something that looked like it should be cloud. Some glimmer of the azure of clear sky could be seen through its folds, even though it was dense and dark, roiling in the air as if it were at the heart of a maelstrom.

"Clear the streets!" She lifted her voice, raising it so it could be heard clearly. She'd learned, in the Hawks, not to shout, or rather, not to sound as if she *were* shouting; she knew how to keep her voice level and even, regardless of how panicked she felt.

There was almost no point, though—the three of them were in the streets; the streets were therefore as clear as they could easily get. They weren't entirely empty—some people had nowhere to go. They huddled in doorways or the mouths of alleys formed by the spaces between tall buildings. In this part of the fiefs, there wasn't a lot of land to go around; near the White Towers, there was more of it, but it was usually filled by whatever weeds could survive the total lack of any human care.

"Tiamaris!"

He turned to look at her, his expression uncharacteristically grim. "Yes," he told her, although she didn't ask. "It's a storm."

"Where is it going?"

"If we're very lucky, somewhere else."

She cursed in Leontine, and he raised a brow. "My luck's been crap lately, in case you hadn't noticed."

He shrugged; it wasn't exactly a fief gesture, but for a Dragon Lord, it was damn close. "You're still alive," he pointed out.

"According to Morse," she said, raising her voice to be heard, "their effects can at least be expected—" She stopped. It didn't

look the same as it had the last time. Then, she had seen something she thought was a sigil. Now?

Now she could see only the vaguely repulsive hint of swirling
colors, like a rainbow in a black sky, but ugly. She looked at
Tiamaris's stiff back, and remembered the Arkon's story.

Severn said, "I think we're about to find out where it's going."
The streets did empty. Even those who could only move slowly
found unexpected reserves of energy. But the streets weren't wide.
Kaylin didn't even remember the name of the one she was standing
in. If Elantra had its obscenely wealthy quarters, and its own brand
of poverty, the fiefs echoed it in subtle ways. There were always
people who struggled their way to the top of the heap, no matter
how much that heap looked like garbage when seen from the outside.

Tiamaris was so tense Kaylin was afraid to touch him. He didn't
look at her; he didn't look to the buildings that lined the side of
the road—as both Kaylin and Severn did. The whole of his attention was caught and held by the storm that spread across what,
moments ago, had been clear sky. Tendrils of shadow moved
against the breeze, reaching into the blue as if to anchor themselves.

She watched as they suddenly pulled themselves back toward
the center. The sky *tore* as it followed them.

What was left in the wake of shredded sky, revealed as azure
crinkled and vanished, was starlight, the shape of the moons and
the clarity of the air turning the back end of Summer, for a
moment, into the heart of Winter.

The streets were no longer empty. They weren't crowded—in
this cold, they couldn't be—but Kaylin was shocked by the sound
of moving wheels and the bells that sometimes rang when a
carriage was politely asking for right-of-way. The ruder version,
which was more common, was to ignore anyone who weighed
less than your horses.

Tiamaris's back was still stiff and still directly in front of her;
Severn was by her side. They were—all of them—underdressed
for the weather. At least there was no damn snow.

Kaylin shook her head and scanned the streets for signs of the shadow that had lain across the entire width of a watchtower. It wasn't there.

"Tiamaris?" she said quietly. Or as quietly as coach bells allowed. He turned.

"Where are we, exactly?"

He shook his head. "You see no shadow?"

"No. There's a lot of street and a bloody loud carriage. Come on," she added, stepping off the street and into the lee of a building. "Let it pass."

Severn joined her, as did the Dragon Lord; Severn, however, was looking at the street and the people it contained. He was looking at the buildings to either side of the long road—a road that was in good repair.

"Kaylin?" Severn said quietly. The second syllable tailed up, making it a question. She understood.

"I see it," she told him. "The streets can support a carriage without making cartwrights rich." As she spoke the side of the carriage went past, and she forgot what she'd been about to say. Not only could the streets support a carriage without destroying its wheels or axles, it could also support a carriage that made the Imperial carriages look plain and dowdy in comparison.

The horses were tall, and they were a uniform color that the night made look gray. Their manes were plaited, and even though the lamplight in the street wasn't bright, glints of the gold braided into those manes could be seen. The carriage itself was pale, possibly white, but that's not what made it remarkable.

"It's Barrani," she said. "It's a Barrani carriage." She frowned, and then, seeing the markings on the side of that carriage, said, "Stay here."

"Kaylin, wait—"

She ran after it. The driver, his face framed by a scarf, his hair by an oddly peaked hat, was in no hurry; the horses weren't even breaking a sweat. She pulled even with the carriage, wishing she could say the same. The windows, which were long and wide, were covered by the fall of dark curtains, and they were higher off the ground than she could easily reach.

She glanced up at the driver. "Stop! Stop for a minute!"

He didn't appear to hear her. Given the noise a carriage made just by moving, that wasn't a big surprise. On the other hand, given Barrani hearing, it was probably deliberate. Cursing, briefly, in Leontine, Kaylin reached out, grabbed one of the decorative door handles and hoisted herself up onto the step.

The carriage rolled to a stop. The driver glanced down at her, but didn't move his hands from the reins. She was standing a little too close to the doors—as in, almost plastered against them—when the curtains on the other side of the glass, and it *was* glass, were pushed aside. She couldn't see the carriage's interior, but it didn't matter.

She recognized the face that open curtains revealed.

"Nightshade," she said, softly.

He raised a brow. It was, of course, perfect; his skin was the same flawless skin he'd always had, and his hair trailed down his back and into the shadows of the carriage interior; across his brow he wore a slender circlet, at the center of which rested a sapphire. He didn't wear armor; he wore what looked like a greatcoat beneath the folds of a cloak.

Something was wrong. She knew it the instant his eyes met hers; they were green, but shading to blue in a hurry.

"Sorry," she said quickly. "I thought you were someone else." She let go of the door and stepped back, landing roughly against the stone.

Before she had taken three steps, the door opened. Nightshade stepped out of the carriage and into the street, his breath leaving a thin cloud in the night air. "You thought I was…someone else."

She nodded.

"I see." He stepped forward, and she had the choice of either backing up or standing her ground. The former was seriously tempting; the latter, given he was a Barrani, was smarter. She settled for smart.

"This is intriguing," he said softly, so softly his voice shouldn't have carried. He approached her and lifted one hand. "I am Lord Nightshade. There is no other. But I am not cursed with the fallible memory of your kind, and I have no memory of you." Blue, blue eyes, now. He reached out to touch the side of her face.

She stepped back, avoiding his hand. He let her.

"More intriguing," he said, watching her, "is that you bear my mark. I would think this a game, and a dangerous one for you, were the mark not genuine."

"Game?"

"I have marked no one. There are other ways of making ownership clear. And yet, here you are, like an accusation or a taunt."

The hair on the back of her neck rose, and her skin turned to instant goose bumps. Magic washed over her as if it were warm breath.

He frowned, and then turned in the street. Tiamaris and Severn were watching in silence. When he saw Tiamaris, his brows rose slightly—and for the Barrani that was as close to open shock as possible.

Nightshade—this other Nightshade—was utterly still, but Kaylin felt the painful tingle that spoke of magic. He did not lift hand or move lip; he simply called it. Sanabalis, she thought, would be impressed. Or as impressed as any Dragon was when confronted with a competent Barrani Lord.

"You are far from your own lands," Nightshade said to Tiamaris, his voice a cool warning. He did not touch a weapon. Nor did Tiamaris, but Kaylin felt the answering wash of magic surround him; *his* hands moved slightly, though.

"And you from yours," Tiamaris replied.

Lord Nightshade raised a brow. "I am not far," he replied, "from my kin. You are far, indeed, from yours. Why are you here, Dragon?"

The streets around Nightshade and Tiamaris did empty, then.

Nightshade, she thought, *leave it, please. Leave it be.*

His brows rose, his eyes widened, and he turned to her, paling in the uneven magelamps that adorned the street.

She bit her lip. She hadn't intended the thought to be heard—but she had never been good at hiding her thoughts from the Lord of Nightshade. Not even, apparently, when he didn't recognize who she was.

She lifted both hands, exposing the palms, as if to show she was harmless. But harmless, to a man who suddenly *knew* that she held his name, didn't exist.

The magic that flared from him then wasn't subtle, and it was painful in a more direct way: fire blossomed around her, turning the night a shade of white-orange that singed her hair.

She bit her lip to stop from crying out, and raised her hands; her skin began to glow. But it was not her magic that guttered the fire; it was Tiamaris's.

"Lord Nightshade," he said. "We are not, strange though it seems, your enemies. I would be obliged if you did not feel the need to destroy my companion." His voice was lower and deeper than normal, but he spoke perfect High Barrani.

"And if I feel the need?"

"We will damage much of the real estate in the streets," was the Dragon's reply, "and you will never have the satisfaction of answers."

Lord Nightshade stood for a moment considering the Dragon's words; Kaylin felt the edge of threat in him as if he'd spoken—but she also felt, to her great surprise, amusement. Acknowledgment. Tiamaris had scored a point.

"Very well, Dragon Lord. I will hold my hand if you will offer answers."

"I will," Tiamaris replied. "But I fear this is not the place to offer them. I am a stranger here," he added. "If you will not risk it, I will speak in the open street, but if you choose, we might repair to someplace less…public. It would, of course, be a place of your choosing."

"And what oath can a Dragon give a Barrani Lord that would vouchsafe his safety?"

"None that would be acceptable," Tiamaris replied. He glanced at Kaylin. "Not at this time. Perhaps one day, in the future."

Lord Nightshade chuckled. "Indeed," he said grimly. "If then. Come." His gaze brushed Kaylin's cheek; he wanted to say more. But he didn't.

His driver was less copacetic than Nightshade himself, but it was Nightshade—thank the gods—who was Lord, here. They exchanged a few words, and then the carriage pulled away in the streets. Which was good, as the horses became instantly skittish when Tiamaris approached them. It had never occurred to Kaylin to wonder how well-trained—or calm—Imperial horses really were; they stood in the presence of Dragons, and they did their job even when a Dragon was literally at their back.

"You sent warning?" Tiamaris asked quietly.

"There is little warning that would arrive in time, should you intend me harm," was the reply. Kaylin filed it under yes. "He was not, however, as controlled as he could be. Many of his kin were lost in the war. I will not have him embarrass either himself, or me." Of the two, Kaylin knew which would be worse for the man, and she almost pitied him. In as much as she ever extended pity to the Barrani.

"And yours?"

"All of the Barrani are my kin," Nightshade replied, and again, his words were threaded with amusement. It was very Barrani humor, however. "Come. This is not perhaps the finest part of this city, but you are also likely to cause less…surprise here. Are you familiar with the city?"

"I am familiar with parts of it," Tiamaris replied. "But it is not my city."

"No," Nightshade said. "It is not. Who do you serve?"

"The Emperor," Tiamaris replied.

Nightshade raised a brow. "Emperor? And what Lord of what Flight has styled himself Emperor among your kind?"

"We just call him the Eternal Emperor," Kaylin said quickly. She touched Tiamaris's sleeve in warning, because his eyes had shaded almost instantly to an orange bronze. Nightshade was amused. Dragons, in Kaylin's experience, had as much sense of humor as wet eggs.

Nightshade raised a brow, and then shrugged. Kaylin slid between Nightshade and Tiamaris as they began to walk down the almost empty street. She wanted to stop and to ask questions of the pass-ersby, but she didn't want to be separated from Tiamaris. Severn, who hadn't spoken a word, walked behind them all.

Still, if she couldn't stop to ask questions, she had eyes, and she could look. The buildings here didn't imply disinterest—at best—on the part of their owners; the streets were in good repair; there were no weeds, or at this time of year, shriveled husks of weeds, growing in the cracks between stones. The people were decently and warmly dressed, and if their clothing looked a little odd to Kaylin—and it did, the shoulders too pronounced and the colors too bright—they were obviously well cared for.

Having spent a winter or two in the oversized castoffs—or worse—of strangers who were clearly both wider and taller, Kaylin understood that wherever *this* was, it wasn't home. It wasn't Barren.

But the street, the *shape* of the street, was. It felt familiar, to Kaylin. She could walk it, she knew, and turn a corner four blocks ahead, taking a right; she could wind her way toward the White Towers, and the border along which the fief sat, watching for ferals—and worse. Her feet, and the part of her memory that was purely physical, knew the truth; her thoughts caught up slowly, as they often did, and arrived with a stumble.

This *was* Barren.

It wasn't, however, the Barren she knew. It wasn't the Barren that Tiamaris had investigated years ago, when he had come to the fiefs, seeking ancient knowledge at the behest of the Imperial Court. It was older, cleaner and lived in; it looked cared for.

She wondered, with a sudden pang, if *this* Barren, in *this* City, had foundling halls and Aerians and Tha'alani and Leontines. It ob-viously had humans and Barrani; it just as obviously didn't have Dragons. No Eternal Emperor. No Halls of Law. No Hawks.

She glanced back at Severn, and he met her gaze and nodded.

"How long ago is it?" she whispered.

His eyes narrowed and he shook his head.

But Nightshade had heard her. She knew that Nightshade, at this distance, would hear whatever she said. And most of what she deliberately tried not to say. His gaze, as it brushed across hers, was shuttered and cool. If Tiamaris noticed, he failed to react.

But given the absence of words, it was a pretty funereal walk. Kaylin followed where Nightshade led, tracking the buildings, the cross streets, the shape of the road that lay beneath the nearly pristine winter surfaces. They moved out of the more tightly packed central streets, and here, the landscape was entirely different to the eye; the buildings, set back from the streets, were placed at very wide intervals, and the fences that girded them were solid and obviously kept up. There were occasional guardhouses as the streets widened, passing around a central well over which a large stone statue towered.

It was not a statue that existed in the Barren of Kaylin's experience, at least not one that she remembered, and she was certain she would remember this one: it was of a Barrani Lord, armored, armed, his helm's visor raised. She had seen similar statues only in the High Halls from which the Barrani were ruled, and wondered if this particular one had crumbled naturally, or if it had disappeared when the Dragons truly arrived in Elantra. Which hadn't happened here.

Yet.

She wondered. The Arkon had said a lot about shadowstorms, but none of what he'd said covered *this*. She had expected something bad to happen; she had expected some assault on Tiamaris—and judging by his tension, so had he. She'd even expected to have to fight. Instead, she was walking down the safest Barren streets she'd ever seen, in the company of a man who was fief lord one fief over. That the streets *were* occupied said, more clearly than anything, that there were no ferals here.

Had they just somehow been thrown back in time? Had some curtain been pulled back across all of history, as if everything that had *ever* happened still existed if you scratched the surface of the here and now? No, the Arkon hadn't mentioned this as a possibility.

Then again in order for him to know it *was* one, there had to be witnesses or reporters to the event; if it had happened before and no one returned, wouldn't everyone just assume they'd been eaten by the damn storm?

What if they were stuck here, now? What if there was no way back?

As if he could hear every word she was trying so hard not to think, Lord Nightshade said, casually, to Lord Tiamaris, "What brings you to our fair city?"

But Tiamaris didn't appear to hear the question. It might have been deliberate, but Kaylin thought it wasn't, because she saw what had caught his attention.

Rising up, between the separate faces of the two moons, was a tower. Not the White Towers; they were well away from the border—and whoever lived in the here and now wasn't the fief lord because there *was* no fief. No, it was the tower beneath whose shadow Kaylin had found her first shelter within the fief of Barren.

Illien's Tower.

Except that it wasn't Illien's Tower, not yet. Illien hadn't come to the fiefs because the fiefs didn't exist. Looking around these very ordinary, if somewhat upscale streets, she couldn't imagine that the fiefs *could* exist. The half-standing buildings that often characterized the wider streets were missing entirely, as were the various odd standing structures that suggested—strongly—that whatever had once lived here, it wasn't human. Or any of the other races Kaylin knew.

"You choose an odd location," Tiamaris said quietly.

"For privacy?" Lord Nightshade replied, looking up at the tower, and the moons, himself. "I think, if we must choose neutral ground, there is none better in these streets."

"You do not occupy that tower."

"I? No."

"Who does?"

Lord Nightshade raised a brow. "For a stranger," he said, "you understand much." It was an accusation, but there was no rancor and no suspicion in it; he expected no truth from Tiamaris. "No one occupies it. But we will be undisturbed if we spend a moment upon its grounds. There is no better neutral territory in the City," he added. "Although its like does exist elsewhere."

"You are...bold," Tiamaris finally said. But he nodded, and turning to Kaylin and Severn, made clear that they were to follow.

"Are you *sure* this is a good idea?" Kaylin asked.

"I am certain it is a poor one," he replied, without any apparent concern. "But it is very unwise to attempt to use magic upon the grounds of such a place, as I'm certain Lord Nightshade knows well. We will both be somewhat disarmed."

Kaylin snorted. She had seen both Nightshade and Tiamaris fight, after all; they didn't need a whole lot of magic when they were cleaving limbs off people with either their swords or their claws.

The fence that surrounded the tower wasn't falling over. There were no gaps through which she could easily slide. Stone foundations—foundations that weren't cracked or absent—supported the thick posts that rose well above their heads.

"Your fence?" Tiamaris asked.

Lord Nightshade shrugged. "I was not personally responsible for it, no. But it is not original to the tower itself." He touched two of the posts, and Kaylin felt the familiar and distinctly uncomfortable presence of magic. She sucked air between her teeth.

"Private?" Tiamaris said.

"Magic," she replied.

"The fence is safe," Nightshade told them both. "Beyond it, however, is less...certain."

The fence posts warped beneath his hands, until they were wide enough to allow passage to even Tiamaris. Lord Nightshade nodded, and after a pause, he went in first. Tiamaris turned, then.

"Do not speak," he told Kaylin quietly. "If you feel the presence of magic—*any* magic—interrupt us immediately and make it known."

"Without speaking." She raised a brow. Severn stepped, gently, on her foot. "You don't trust him."

Tiamaris rolled his eyes, which were bronze. "Of course not. He's Barrani. But at the moment, he means us no harm. Or rather, he will not harm us personally."

"You know that how?"

"I have spoken with the fieflord," was his quiet reply. "And the Barrani are very slow to change. Come."

CHAPTER 16

The first thing Kaylin noticed—and it was a stupid thing to notice, but she was off her stride—was that there were no weeds. No wild, unkempt long grass, no thistles, no clinging vines, no burrs. It was like stepping into a different world. Memory didn't make this one.

As if to remind her of this, the Tower stood above the grounds, surrounded by—of all things—empty, weedless flower beds. Kaylin wasn't a gardener; she had black thumbs. Gardening was more of a mystery to her than magic, but she knew weeds grew everywhere there was space.

But the Tower? It was almost of white stone, and it stretched, unbroken and undiminished, toward the moons in the dark sky. What had become crumbling, broken walls now seemed to float above something as petty as time.

She felt Lord Nightshade's gaze upon her face, and turned to meet it.

"Have you seen this tower before?" he asked softly.

She opened her mouth, caught Tiamaris's sharp glance and

closed it again. But she was annoyed. *You already know the answer,* she thought, curtly, at him. *What's the point in asking the question?*

His brows rose, and she remembered that this particular Nightshade had not yet had the experience of dealing with humans for so damn long; she'd probably been enormously—and even dangerously—rude.

But after a pause, his brows fell, and his smile, which was both strange and familiar, lifted the corners of his lips. *Manners,* he replied, in kind.

Her Nightshade seldom spoke this way to her, although he could; he knew she didn't like it. This Nightshade probably knew it, as well—but as she'd started it, there wasn't a lot she could say.

"Manners," he said, aloud, "are severely underappreciated in my opinion."

"Oh?"

"Where practiced well, they remove the probability that someone in my position will be forced to go through the effort of killing someone in yours. Believe that on occasion that much death can become tedious." He gazed at the Tower.

"Are we going in?"

And then, turned to look at her. "She is not," he said, to Tiamaris, "well informed or well trained."

"No. We have chosen to find it endearing." He raised a hand before Kaylin could speak.

"Ah. That might present some problem."

"It often does. But it occasionally presents solutions, as well, if unorthodox."

"You show surprising flexibility for one of your kind."

"I am not considered old, by my kin."

"Ah." His gaze left Kaylin's face slowly. "Why have you traveled here?"

Tiamaris heard the sudden edge in Nightshade's voice. His stance shifted, but he did not otherwise move. "You are aware," he finally said, "of the shadowstorms?"

"I am." Lord Nightshade's brows actually rose.

Tiamaris nodded. "They are here," he said softly, turning to gaze toward what was, in Kaylin's time, the heart of the fiefs. "Or they will be, soon. We did not intend to visit you here," he added softly, "but we were interrupted in our journey by one such storm."

"Impossible," was the flat reply. "You do not bear the taint."

"And has shadow become so predictable that you can, with certainty, know what is either possible or probable, Lord Nightshade?"

The Barrani looked as if he would speak, but turned to Kaylin instead. She tried to think of something harmless, and ended up with a very strong image of pork buns because she was, among other things, hungry. Which caused him to raise one brow. And, to her surprise, laugh.

It was a wild, electric laugh; the hair on the back of her neck rose at the sound—and the feel—of it. "She believes you," he told Tiamaris, without looking away.

"She should. She traveled with me."

Kaylin started to speak, saw Tiamaris's face and stopped. But the hair on the back of her neck didn't settle down, and her arms began that awkward tingle that spoke—strongly—of magic. It wasn't Nightshade's; she was almost certain of that.

"Tiamaris," she said softly.

He froze. Nodded.

She pointed up to the tower's height. There, in the moonlight, clouds were beginning to gather.

Nightshade gazed up, as well.

"We didn't bring them with us!" Kaylin said quickly. She turned to Tiamaris.

He shrugged. It was a tense, tight motion. "We have no records of the City at this time, or very few of them. The Barrani would have more, if they were accessible. I'm not aware that they rely on records for their history."

"Records?" Lord Nightshade said quietly.

Kaylin grimaced. The shadows were coalescing; they looked dark against the moonlight, and they seemed to travel quickly—

but that high up, she had no idea how windy it was. They didn't quite look like the storm that had swept them off the streets of the Barren she knew and into these ones.

"Kaylin Neya," Nightshade said, and this time, she did look down. "I have tired of this game. You know me. I know you. I do not yet know why. But you speak of time, and you speak in riddles."

"Not on purpose, trust me. It takes too much effort. Look— I've seen the High Halls."

His brows rose a fraction.

"Because of *your* interference—and no, before you ask, you have no idea what I'm talking about—I passed the test of the Halls."

His brows rose again. This younger Nightshade seemed infinitely easier to surprise.

"So I know what lies there. In the High Halls. I *know* why the High Halls stand where they do. But the rest of this?" She threw an arm wide. "In my time—and it is time, I think—it doesn't exist. Not like this. Not even the Tower."

"The Tower...is gone?"

"Oh, no. The Tower is there—but it doesn't look like this. And in my time, it's not empty. Not in theory. This—this City, these streets—the Barrani rule here?"

"Who else?"

"And the heart—the heart of this City?"

His eyes narrowed, then, and his gaze flickered across Tiamaris's face. "What do you know of this place?"

"Nothing much. Except this. We *can't* get to the heart of it. Whatever lies in the center of the City, we can't touch. It's surrounded by shadow, and by the things that come out of the shadows. It's like the caverns below the High Halls, but run wild."

"You cannot lie to me," he said softly. It was half a question. She felt the tail of it rising.

"I don't see the point in trying," she replied. "I don't know why we're here. I don't know what sent us this way, or why, and before you ask, I certainly don't know how. But where *we* are—where we were—there's shadow, and it's going to spill out into the rest of the City. The High Halls will be safe," she added, and then stopped.

His eyes were very blue when they met hers. "But?"

Tiamaris was stepping on her foot. Not literally, but his expression would have frozen water at fifty paces.

"But I might not be?" Nightshade said quietly. He glanced, not at Tiamaris, but at Severn, who hadn't moved. At all.

"No."

Nightshade moved, then. He moved so damn fast she barely had a chance to take a step back. But she did; it wasn't nearly enough. He caught her wrist, pulled her forward, and raised his hand to touch her cheek. The mark, where his fingers traced it, burned. But it was heat without pain; she drew one sharp breath at the shock of it, and exhaled slowly when her skin didn't shrivel and blacken.

And then he lifted the wrist he held, and he unbuttoned the cuff of her sleeve while she watched, almost hypnotized. Severn stepped in, and Nightshade released her instantly, raising his hands and taking a step back. But her arm remained where he'd raised it, and gravity tugged the heavier fabric down just a few inches.

Enough, really, to reveal the edges of the symbols that spread across most of her body. She felt his surprise, then; he contained its physical expression perfectly, but he couldn't keep it from her; she wasn't even certain he tried.

He looked at Tiamaris, whose expression was about as open and revealing as Nightshade's. "She bears the marks," he said softly.

"She does. Will you now listen to her?"

At that, the Barrani Lord offered a very wry smile; it was almost remarkable. "I would have no choice if she insisted," he said. "But I do not think she will."

"It is not generally in her nature, where whining and badgering will do in its place."

"There are no storms here," Lord Nightshade finally said. "Not now, not yet. We have had some trouble in the West March, and in the plains—but some of those troubles you are no doubt familiar with."

Tiamaris nodded. "But storms do come," he said.

"When?"

"What year is it, in your reckoning?"

"Demetrad is the Lord of the Flight that is our greatest concern."

"That is not much of an answer."

"It is not. It is, however, true."

Tiamaris frowned. "How much of the land does my kin now hold? How much is held by the High Lord of the Barrani?"

Nightshade began to gesture, and then stopped. "Perhaps," he said, glancing at the Tower's height, "this was not such a wise choice of venue. I think, however, that there are few choices that would be safe for either you or your unusual companions."

Kaylin said, quietly, "There are no shadowstorms here?"

Nightshade agreed.

"None? None recorded?"

"None."

"But you have records of the storms' existence elsewhere."

"We have had some difficulty with the storms. As," he added quietly, "have the Dragons, if rumors are to be believed. They do not trouble us here."

She nodded, holding that thought as she moved on. "Who lives at the heart of the fiefs?" When he raised a brow, she grimaced. "At the heart," she said, "of this City, now?"

He glanced at Tiamaris. It was Tiamaris who replied. "No one."

"But if there are no shadows—"

"There is still danger, Kaylin. The unknown in the heart of this City has teeth. It draws blood and destroys life. What we explored, what we searched for—it was known because it had been previously approached during the absence of the darkness."

She'd seen that darkness. She hesitated, glanced at Nightshade, and let it go. "But in the here and now, you have people who are exploring it?"

Nightshade nodded slowly. "You are concerned that they dabble in things that pose a threat to us all."

"They're probably Arcanists. They always do."

"Arcanists?"

"Sorcerer," Tiamaris supplied.

Nightshade nodded. "Continue."

"They're doing something now."

He raised a brow. "And you know this how?"

"I don't. It's a guess. They're doing something now, and it's already started whatever chain of events leads to the City as *we* know it."

"And who rules the City as you know it?"

"The Eternal Emperor."

He raised a brow, but he did not press her further. "Why do you assume that something is happening now?"

"Because we're here."

"Ah. Mortal reason." There wasn't more than the usual Barrani condescension in the tone.

She lifted a hand and pointed. The clouds that had gathered had gathered solely above the Tower. But they weren't the swirling chaotic dark of roiling shadow; they were—seemed—gray and silver. No wind moved them. She thought no wind could. But they had come anyway.

"Kaylin?" Tiamaris said softly.

"You can't feel it?"

"Not without using spells." He didn't even lift a finger.

"I think," she said, looking up at the cloud at the Tower's height and feeling the stretch of exposed throat begin to ache as she did, "we should move."

"I concur," Nightshade replied. He made his way to the fence, moving both quickly and gracefully enough that none of his movements suggested the clumsiness of forced flight.

They followed, and stopped a foot from his back; his hands were spread out along the fence posts, but they weren't moving.

"Please tell me that you haven't tried to open them yet," Kaylin said to his stiff back.

"Are you required to believe it?"

She swore, spinning with far less grace than Nightshade had so that she could once again crane her chin up and look at the clouds. They were now shining as if made of new steel. "Tiamaris—"

"It's not shadowstorm," he told her, in a tone of voice that provided exactly no comfort.

"Then what the hell is it?"

"I fear we are about to find out."

The clouds parted, then, as if they'd been waiting for exactly that comment. Lightning—or something that would have been lightning if lightning was slow, thick, and solid—groped toward the Tower's height.

When it touched the Tower, it changed. The light that had appeared as a slow-moving liquid suddenly stiffened, and for just a moment, looked like a hand, tendrils becoming fingers that gripped—and held—tight. The clouds, with their odd flecks of light, stiffened, as well, losing all motion, all sense that wind might have any effect on them.

Those clouds now bled into the Tower, light trailing down its walls as if it were, indeed, rain; as they did, they began to dwindle. But the clouds could almost be forgotten; the Tower glowed, bright and silver, as if it were in the running to become moon number three.

"So," Tiamaris said softly.

Nightshade glanced at his profile. So did Kaylin, but something dragged her eyes skyward again, toward those shrinking, condensing clouds. Her skin ached, but no surprise there; so did her jaw, but that was because she'd clamped it shut.

The clouds had thinned so much they were simple tendrils now, and they were fast being absorbed by what, on the surface, looked like stone. But as they moved, they teased themselves apart into separate strands. Those strands, thin and pale, glowed now with the same steady light that touched the Tower walls. They moved, rising as if pulling against the gravity the Tower exerted, dancing, not by the grace of wind or breeze, but deliberately, as if each turn, each slow twist, was a predetermined step.

And it was. Kaylin saw that as she watched.

"Kaylin," she heard Severn say. She lifted a hand; she didn't look down. She knew that she had to see this; if the Arkon's memory crystal was somehow still functioning in this shadow-born version of their past, she had to allow it to capture her vision as perfectly as possible.

So she watched as the individual tendrils continued to weave. Some, she saw, divided into two or three strands; one would cease its motion, and the other two would carry some variant forward. This happened again and again until all motion stilled. When it did, she saw, clearly, what those strands had been doing: they had been writing, in light, a very complicated rune. A word.

It shone there, as clear as glass, light illuminating it from within. It looked…familiar. But even as she tried to identify it, it began to fade. She felt a hand on her sleeve, on her arm, as she tried to memorize the intricate lines and strokes. It was a lost cause, and normally she gave up on those immediately; it saved effort.

Here? She was mesmerized until nothing at all could be seen but night sky and moonlight. Only then did she look down.

Nightshade was standing in front of her—directly in front of her. He had rolled the sleeve up her arm, and exposed to light, glowing in the same way that the rune in the sky had, were the marks on her arms.

"I didn't do that," she told Lord Nightshade softly.

He nodded. "What do you think was done?"

"I don't know. Something."

That produced a very dry chuckle.

"Enough," Severn said quietly. He stepped in, but did not touch Nightshade. They fenced with stares for a minute, and then Nightshade let her arm go, dropping his own to his sides. "So," he said softly to Tiamaris.

Tiamaris was staring at the Tower. Nothing about it appeared to have changed, and even the light which illuminated it faded as they watched. "It has started," he said quietly.

Nightshade, this Nightshade, had no knowledge of the fiefs because the fiefs didn't exist. But he had never been, frequently to Kaylin's regret, a fool. "What do you think caused this?" he asked.

Tiamaris considered his words with care. "Something, or someone, in the heart of the interior, has caused a disturbance."

"And this?"

"I would say that this…" and here he gestured toward the Tower "…is our—your—last line of defense."

"Against?"

"The ferals," Kaylin broke in, "for one. They'll come. I don't know when."

"Ferals?"

She cursed. "They're like hunting dogs. Except larger. Smarter. They're black, or so dark a gray it's almost the same. They don't come out during the day." Which no longer applied in Barren, but she let that go. "They hunt in packs. They kill whatever they can find in the open street."

He raised a brow, and she cursed again, this time in Leontine. "No, they wouldn't be able to kill *you*. But it's not you they'll hunt. It's us. It's people like me." She hesitated.

"Can they be killed?"

"Yes."

"Then this does not sound like a disaster."

When he put it like that, it didn't. It certainly didn't seem like more of a disaster than street gangs and drug dealers and loan sharks. She turned to look between the tines of this very well-kept gate, to the equally well-kept streets beyond them. How would it happen? How would the City go from this—where no one looked as if they were starving or prematurely aged by a life on the streets—to the fiefs she'd been born in?

"There will be more than her ferals," Tiamaris said softly. "I do not know what form it will take, but I am certain, Lord Nightshade, that you will recognize it when you see it; you or your kin. There is a reason the High Halls stand where they stand. A reason, in the end, that the capital of the future Empire will *also* stand here. That reason lies in the ruins and the buildings that your kin now explore. And that we also do, to our lasting regret."

"Could we stop them?" Kaylin asked them both.

They stared at her.

"Could we go out—now—and head toward the center of the City? Could we find them and stop them before—before—"

"Before what?"

"Before they release or invoke whatever it is they must have to cause things to change so damn much."

"It is centuries, Kaylin," Tiamaris told her gently. "There are those who live here in relative wealth. How long do you think they will stay once the ferals come?"

"But it's—it's their home."

"They will find another. They will still be wealthy, and they will be alive." He watched her. "It will not happen overnight, but it *will* happen. I think it has already happened. The start."

She started to speak, and stopped. "Because of what just happened to the Tower."

"If I guess correctly, there are six such buildings, ringed by the river. They have all been touched by similar clouds. They will all…wake. Soon." He glanced at Nightshade, and then back. "Even if we go now, and we are against all odds successful, you delay, you do not prevent. There are always men of power—in any race—who will be drawn to what lies at the heart of our fiefs."

"Why?"

"I do not know why they—"

"Why were you?"

He raised a brow. His eyes had shaded from gold to bronze so slowly she hadn't really tracked the change. But in the end, he merely said, "I am not considered of significant power among my kind. I was sent to investigate."

"And the Outcaste?"

"It was different."

Lord Nightshade lifted a hand. "I believe the time for your conversation is at an end," he told them both softly.

Kaylin didn't even need to ask him why.

The Tower at their back had suddenly developed something that looked suspiciously like a door.

It was not a terribly *fine* door. The frame that contained it was solid and blocky, one piece with the stone of the Tower. There were no letters above it, or, as was often the case in parts of Elantra, adorning the wall to either side. In fact, it looked as if the door had been added as an afterthought. Given that the door seemed flat, rectangular, and plain—the type of door behind which someone like Kaylin or Severn would live—it might have been. It had a doorknob. The hinges were on the inside. It seemed—at this distance—to lack a keyhole.

Kaylin glanced at Severn.

"No," he said quietly. "It wasn't there before." He'd spoken very little since they'd arrived on this cold, night street—but she was used to that. Severn had never been much of a talker. He looked at the door.

So did Kaylin. "Tiamaris?"

The Dragon didn't seem surprised. He didn't, on the other hand, seem amused or curious, either. Nightshade did. "An invitation?" he asked softly.

Kaylin said, "How? No one's home. Not yet."

The door swung open.

The universe, on occasion, had a very irritating sense of humor.

"I think it unwise," Tiamaris said.

"No kidding," she replied, adding a few Leontine words for good measure. She had slid into Elantran, which caused Nightshade to raise a brow. *He doesn't understand me,* she thought, with surprise. He looked so similar to the Nightshade she knew, the fact that centuries had passed had seemed almost unreal.

But he wasn't her Nightshade, not yet. She wondered, briefly, when he had learned to speak Elantran. And wondered, as well, if Elantran even existed in this City at the moment. If it didn't, where had it come from? The Dragons certainly hadn't introduced it.

"Severn," she said, still speaking her mother-tongue, "two things."

He nodded, waiting.

"This is a very, very bad idea." When he raised a brow, she grimaced. "And I don't know if we get out—or get back—any other way. For a value of out," she added, "that doesn't end with our corpses. Nightshade's said that the Tower takes a master—always. This one doesn't have one yet."

"You think it's already started to search."

"There are two people here who could easily control it." Nightshade was frowning. She *knew* that he could understand the emotional gist of what she said, but knew, now, that the words themselves would elude him. It wasn't exactly privacy, but she'd take what she could get. "So, yeah, I think it's looking."

"You don't want either of them in the Tower."

"I don't *know.* I don't even know if this is real, or if this is some sort of illusionary effect of the storm. I've daydreamed for years about changing the past." She broke off and looked away. "But not *this* damn far back."

He still waited. When it became clear that she'd retreated, momentarily, from words, he said, "I don't think the Tower is speaking to either Tiamaris or Nightshade."

"Please do not tell me you think it's speaking to me."

"To you," he said, "or to me. Look at the door."

"I really hate magic," she told him, and spit to the side. "It is so goddamn *creepy.*"

"You noticed."

"That the door has no doorward? Yeah, I noticed. I also notice that my arms are still glowing. And I *do not* want to be stuck here." She hesitated, and then approached the open door slowly.

"Private," Tiamaris said sharply. It was a relief. She turned to look at him. He stepped past her, and toward the open door; the door didn't slam in his face. It hung open, as if whatever had animated it had retreated. He paused in the frame, and then turned back.

"There are bodies here," he told her quietly, and in an odd tone of voice.

"Bodies? Multiple?"

"Three."

"Race?"

"Human."

She frowned. "How did they die?"

"From this distance? Not of magical causes. Blood loss, or possibly lack of oxygen."

"How can you tell?"

"I can't at this distance. But I've seen enough death to recognize the state." The words were slightly clipped. Kaylin gritted her teeth. "Severn?"

"With you," he replied. They approached the Tower door, and almost ran into Tiamaris's back.

"Either you let us in," she told him, in her most reasonable tone of voice, "or you drag them out."

"I prefer the latter, at the moment." Again, his tone of voice was unusual.

"Fine." She stepped away from the door, and when she was well away, he walked into the Tower. She was holding her breath, and realized it only when he reappeared. Dragons looked mostly human, but they were stronger; he didn't have to make three trips. He wasn't particularly careful, but there wasn't much reason to be careful—not here.

Years of training, on the other hand, made Kaylin want to snarl in frustration; Teela would have broken one of her arms if she'd dragged corpses this carelessly out of the area in which they'd been found before the Hawks had gotten everything recorded. The Hawks, she thought, that didn't exist, even as a concept, yet.

But she understood why he'd been so hesitant the minute he laid the bodies on the ground. It was their clothing. There was nothing fancy about it, nothing terribly expensive—and that was fine with Kaylin; even the fancier streets here didn't preclude the poor—they practically *demanded* it. But it was *familiar* ratty clothing. It was fief clothing.

She hesitated, and while she did, Tiamaris turned the bodies over.

"Kaylin?" Severn's voice. She heard it, but didn't look, didn't acknowledge him. Swallowing, she knelt by the side of one of the corpses, her hand hovering above his open eyes.

Tiamaris said, "You know these men." It was not a question.

She was silent for a long moment. "Yes."

"Who were they?"

"I didn't know them well. They worked for the fief lord."

Tiamaris waited more or less patiently—for a Dragon. Kaylin continued to stare. "Barren. They lived in Barren," Kaylin finally managed. Her voice had thickened; the syllables seemed to stick to her throat.

"They died in Barren?"

She nodded. "Seven years ago, give or take a few months."

Barren thinks you're ready.

She closed the dead man's eyes, and rose.

"Why are they here?" Tiamaris asked. He didn't ask it of her, but she answered anyway.

"The Tower. And if this is its idea of conversation, it can go straight to hell."

CHAPTER 17

Barren thinks you're ready. Morse, her lopsided grin, her hands on dagger hilts, the points toward Elianne. She stared at them, wondering, dully, if this were the day Morse would kill her. Gray day, cold and almost wintry, although there was no snow. But the day didn't matter. The time didn't matter.

She was in Barren. Morse was waiting. She lifted her hands, and Morse reversed the daggers, placing both of their hilts into her palms. Her smile was still there. The side of it was that purple-yellow of fading bruise. Where the bruise had come from, Elianne didn't know. She didn't ask. If Morse wanted her—or anyone else to know—they'd know. They'd probably have bruises of their own at the end of the conversation, but they'd know.

"Who?" she asked.

Morse nodded. "Start with Sorco. You know him?"

The name meant nothing. Elianne hesitated, but didn't let it show. "Not by name," she finally said. "He travels alone?"

"No." Morse waited for questions. Elianne didn't have any. She understood what Barren meant by ready: this was a test. "He'll travel with two others. If you can separate him, fine. You're only on Sorco. If you can't…"

"Are you going with me?"

"No." Morse shoved her hands through the short brush of her hair. "*Are* you ready?"

"Yes."

Morse raised one brow, and then shrugged; the shrug was more pronounced. She was irritated. "You've got seven days."

"Seven *days?*"

"Barren figured seven days was long enough. At the end of seven days, he'll either send someone else or go in person."

"He'll send you, you mean."

Morse exhaled. "No. That's exactly what I *don't* mean. You're mine, as far as Barren is concerned."

Elianne closed her eyes. Swallowed. "Everything in Barren is his," she said quietly.

Morse said nothing, and when Elianne opened her eyes again, she saw that the older woman was staring at the wall. Her hands were fists. "Fine. What's *mine* is your training. I found you. I thought you might be worth something. He's not testing you, here."

But he was. They both knew it.

"He's testing me."

Morse would pay if she failed. How, and for how long, Elianne didn't know. Didn't ask. "You can't come with me," she said, voice flat.

Everything in Barren belongs to me.

She checked her sleeves, made sure they were fastened. They had no buttons, but they did have strings sewn—badly—on the inside of the wrists. She'd gotten good at tying them with her off-hand. Morse believed you could train yourself to use either hand efficiently; the strings were one of the ways in which Elianne pursued this.

Morse lived in a building that was close to what passed for a market in Barren. No, it was a market, but it wasn't the same as the market in Nightshade. It was sparser, grayer, dirtier. She checked the mental image of Morse's map. This was not Sorco's beat.

His beat lay elsewhere. Closer to the river, where Morse said the real money was. Closer, Elianne thought, to the bridge.

Of course it's closer to the bridge, Morse had said with a sneer. *Where do you think the money comes from?*

It had never occurred to her to wonder, in all her years in Nightshade. But she understood it, now. It was a bleak, bitter knowledge. There were people on the other side of the river who came to the fiefs. What they did in the fiefs they could not do in the rest of the City; not without getting into trouble. Whatever trouble meant, there.

"We need their money," Morse told her grimly. "So the rules are pretty damn simple. Don't fuck with them. Don't scare them off."

The streets didn't open up as she approached the river; they were still narrow and in poor repair. Only by the river streets themselves had any effort been taken to insure that they were safe, and if you saw clean, well-repaired streets, you knew you were taking a chance. She'd never come this close to the river, not in Barren. In Nightshade, she and Severn had gone, on warmer days, to look at the bridge and to try to see what lay beyond it.

But they didn't belong there. They'd never tried to leave.

And why? *Why?* As if to find an answer, she now followed the road that led to the bridge from Barren. It wasn't the same bridge, of course; it didn't even look the same. It was flatter, slightly wider; the height of the curve didn't mark the midpoint between real life and dream. There were no guards on either side. There never had been, that she knew of.

Two days, she lingered by the river streets, watching the big houses. There were three; they were probably brothels. Or some combination of a brothel and something else. It was true: men came from the bridge, crossing into Barren as carelessly as if the bridge were just another damn street. They came in the late afternoon; they would leave before it got too dark.

At the end of the second day, pushing sunset, she finally caught sight of three men who didn't look much like outsiders. Not like the other customers, and not like the guards who did keep an eye out for important people who might need to make their way back across the bridge to real safety.

Promising.

One man was clearly in charge. Hair and height were right. He approached the closest of the big houses, followed closely by his two men. Knocked on the door. She couldn't hear what was said, but it didn't take long before the door opened fully and he was let inside. His men trailed him like awkward shadows.

She waited for them to leave. The sun sank. Sunrise and sunset marked boundaries for the ferals. Sorco—if it *was* Sorco—had two armed guards; he could afford to take risks. She couldn't.

Come on. Come *on*. She watched, feeling the air cool. Shadows lengthened; she could feel the minutes stretch; could feel her stomach begin to knot, not with the familiar pangs of hunger, but with an equally familiar fear. It was a long way home, and even at a dead sprint, she wasn't going to make it.

Sorco—if it was him—didn't emerge. Clearly, whatever skimming involved it probably *also* involved partaking. She took a deep breath, counting days. She had some left, and if she wanted to keep it that way, she couldn't stand here, watching as the street darkened around her. She marked the house. If Sorco was drunk or cocky, he'd leave before dawn. If he wasn't, she might have a small chance of catching him on his rounds—but to do that? She had to be alive.

She turned and ran.

The moons were high and clear. The streets were deserted. She could hear the slap of her soles against cobbles, some of which were so poorly placed, they caused her to stumble. It didn't matter; she injured nothing and rolled to her feet. Dignity wasn't important in the night streets of the fiefs.

A third of the way home, she heard them. She froze. It wasn't just fear, although fear was sensible; she had to listen. Ferals had howls that meant, as far as she was concerned, boredom. Or hunger. With ferals it was pretty much one and the same. They had howls that meant other things. Anyone who had lived in a room with warped boards as a window shutter got familiar with the sound of their calls. They howled when they sighted—or scented—quarry; they howled in clashing voices when they were trying to run it to ground.

Less often they howled in pain, because some of their quarry—at least in Nightshade—were Barrani, and were perfectly capable of taking down a feral or three without losing limbs. Or life.

They did not howl when they were feeding. They snarled or growled, and Elianne had only heard that a couple of times, because it was a quiet sound. Occasionally those snarls turned into actual fighting; it was the only time the ferals seemed to work as less than a perfect team.

She listened, trying to pinpoint direction. The one good thing about ferals—or the one stupid thing about them, depending on your point of view—was that they never seemed to shut up. They could howl all night. Severn had taught her how to listen, how to figure out which way was safe—or safer, at any rate—to run.

She froze again, and tried to rid herself of the sudden memory of night streets in Nightshade. Severn had taken her by the hand, he'd led her into the middle of the street just beneath their one-room hovel, and he'd told her to close her eyes. Just that. And she'd done it.

No more no more no more.

But she stood in a totally foreign street, without the promise of safety a door and a few yards away, and she closed her eyes and did what she'd learned to do then. Listen. Just…listen.

When she opened her eyes, she stared bleakly at the streets.

The ferals were running between her and the only home she had. Had she known the streets—and the yards, the alleys, the doors with poor locks and no crossbars—better, she might have been able to run in a wide circle, coming up far enough behind where they were roaming that she could make it in one piece. She didn't.

But standing still was worse. She thought, briefly, and began to run again, moving at a diagonal—and away—from the howls.

The only good thing about the run? Halfway through it, she developed a very strong dislike for Sorco.

In the end, she wound up at a familiar street, with a familiar, fallen set of gates, a familiar opening through which she could slide, if she turned sideways. It was still cold, but she was better dressed for it now; Morse had money, and if she bitched about spending it, she spent it anyway. Elianne could hear the ferals at her back. She couldn't tell if they were getting closer because she didn't pause to listen; she just kept going until she passed near the ruins of an old tower.

There, she stopped, found the opening in the fence, and slid into the stiff, dry grass. She didn't lie flat, didn't curl up on her side; she crouched, her knees coming up to her chin as she curled both arms around her lower legs. She drew a long knife and held it, more for comfort than protection; this lasted about ten minutes, because even in the grass, she could feel the air's bite, the touch of wind.

Here, though, she could close her eyes; she could listen.

They were closer. She waited five seconds, counting breaths, and then she heard the sound she most hated: they had caught living scent. She prayed it wasn't hers.

The ferals were closer, now. They were howling like a storm. But a storm was just water and a light show; unless you were really, really unlucky, it couldn't kill you. With the ferals, the opposite was true, and Kaylin had never been lucky. She waited silently, gathering and stilling all movement until she was barely breathing. Closer, yes. Closer.

The howl suddenly shifted and changed.

She didn't see the ferals first, though. That was the worst of it. She saw *Morse*. Morse, sweating in the cold, her short brush of hair almost gleaming, her hands gripping knife hilts and pumping air as she tried to lengthen her stride. Morse was heading *to* this Tower, and the Tower's fence.

If Elianne were unlucky, Morse would duck in here, and the ferals would follow. Two against the ferals was better than one—but honestly, in a space like this, not that much. Elianne *knew* this. Knew it. If you'd asked her, she could have written a test on the *smart thing to do* when ferals were hunting someone else. And unlike most of Morse's tests, she'd've passed that one, first go.

But that would have involved thinking, and what she did next involved no thought at all. No memory. Nothing but instinct. She shot out of the grass like a startled animal, and she sprinted to the fallen gate, the slender passage that had led her, twice, to safety. She passed her knife from right to left hand—that much, she had the sense to do instinctively—and then she reached out, with hand and voice.

"Morse!"

Ferals ten yards behind, Morse running full out. But Morse was good at picking up little details, even in an all-out sprint to save her own neck—because some of those details might be relevant to the saving. She saw Elianne, saw the arm she extended, and she zigged toward her, only barely losing speed.

Elianne caught her wrist—Morse hadn't dropped either knife, and wouldn't—and yanked hard, praying that Morse would *fit*. Morse was larger, wider, more muscular—and being stuck in the fence for even a minute would be a gruesome death. But being heavier gave Morse momentum, and being desperate did the rest; she barreled through the opening and the fence creaked so damn loudly, Elianne thought half of it would fall over.

"What the hells were you doing out at this time of night?" Elianne shouted. She had to shout, just to be heard. The sound of her voice drove the ferals into a frenzy of teeth and snarling howls. It would have chilled her blood, had any of it still been running.

"Being a fucking idiot," Morse shouted back.

She looked at the fence—at the precariously *leaning* fence—

for a minute, and then sheathed one of her long knives. Bending, she started to root around in the grass. She came up, after a minute punctuated by snapping jaws and howling, with a rock the size of her palm.

Elianne stared at her.

Grinning like a madman, Morse headed closer to the fence; the ferals began to try to *leap* it as she cleared the thickest of the grass. She snarled back at them, and then she threw the rock. It smacked one of the ferals square in the middle of the face, and he howled in rage. Real rage. In the moonlight, his eyes looked red.

"Morse, what the hell are you *doing?*" Elianne screamed.

"Pissing them off. Here, grab a rock!" Morse shouted back, in obvious delight.

Elianne stared. Morse repeated this, ranging a little farther for heavy enough rocks as she did. On the fifth throw, she paused. "What the hell are you waiting for?" she shouted, grinning.

Elianne hesitated for another minute, and then she heard Morse laugh. It was an odd, high laugh, unlike any other laugh she'd ever heard from Morse, and she found herself hefting a rock that seemed to have leapt from the ground to her hand as if by magic. She had to get nearer to the fence to throw hers; she didn't have Morse's bulk or musculature.

Over the snapping and snarling and howling of enraged and frustrated ferals, Elianne watched Morse bend, lift a rock and throw it. Morse had to shout to be heard, but after a while, it didn't sound like shouting; she was giddy but calm, and she was precise.

Elianne cleared the fence on her fourth attempt. It was hard to tell whether or not the rock did any damage when it hit—but it was also impossible *not* to hit something; the ferals didn't seem to care enough to get out of the way of the rocks.

"What the hell," Elianne said, grunting as she threw, "were you doing *outside* at night?"

"Taking a walk," Morse answered, notably grunt-free as she also let a heavy stone fly.

"Taking a walk *where?*"

Morse cursed, and turned, pausing as she did. "You didn't come home, idiot."

Elianne closed her eyes. She wanted more, and she knew Morse would never give her more. So she grabbed stray words instead, making a sentence out of them. "I found him," Elianne said, her voice dropping.

"Found who? Oh, Sorco?"

"Yeah."

"He's dead?"

Elianne grimaced, and bent and found another rock.

"So he's not dead," Morse said, bending to do the same. The rocks flew over the fence in unison; Morse was definitely the better throw.

"Barren's going to be pissed, isn't he?"

"Probably."

"What'll he do?"

For a moment, the gift of glee deserted Morse's face. Elianne had no words to describe what was left in the gap before her expression closed into the familiar sneer. "Sorco's not dead. I didn't kill him. He didn't say much about ferals. Let's see if we can kill one."

Elianne found her laughter. The fence was going to hold. They were going to make it. In the morning, they'd eat, and they'd plan. She'd find Sorco. She'd worry about his guards later.

Morse had come out—at *night*—for her.

Elianne would have bet against that ever happening. She would have bet that Morse, seeing the last of the sun, would have shrugged and gone to sleep. One less mouth to feed, if Elianne was gone. One less test to worry about passing. But she was here, now, and she was teaching Elianne how to throw rocks the size of her fist.

Elianne's arms tired long before Morse's did. But although it was cold, and the breeze was biting, she felt the echo of familiar warmth at the base of this deserted Tower, the ferals singing their raging, chaotic chorus. She couldn't sleep, and she didn't want to sleep.

Here, they played like the children they weren't.

★ ★ ★

In the morning? The ferals retreated, their howls dropping to whining as the sky steadily paled. Only after they'd gone—and Morse was certain they weren't coming back—did they leave the overgrown grounds that had provided such unexpected safety—and such unexpected joy.

CHAPTER 18

"Kaylin?" Severn touched her shoulder and she jumped.

Sorco's body—and it was Sorco—lay in front of her. The last time she'd been this close to it, she'd been checking to see if he was still alive.

You can botch things, you get too nervous. You can think you're done, when you're not. You need to think and be aware.

He'd been alive enough that his eyes, wide with shock, searched for some sign of her face, but not alive enough to understand what they saw when they hit it. He wasn't alive now. But…he wasn't dead by much. She'd seen enough corpses over the past several years to know.

He certainly wasn't seven years dead.

"Kaylin?"

She looked up from her crouch, her hand still against his cold skin. "Sorco," she said roughly. "He was one of Barren's collectors."

"Seven years ago?"

She shrugged. "Whatever that means, now." She glanced up at the Tower, as if to make her point.

He nodded as she rose, wiping her hands on her thighs. Too much memory, here.

"How—or why—do you think they're here?" he asked. Tiamaris and Nightshade had retreated from speech entirely.

Kaylin snorted. "How else?" was her despondent—and angry—reply. "Magic. As usual." Her arms ached.

Sorco was dead. On the surface of things, she was fine with that. She'd been fine with it the minute she was certain it had happened, although the reasons then had been different. He would have killed her—or sold her—just to alleviate boredom. He'd probably killed countless others before she'd been sent to take him out. He wasn't worth tears or nausea or guilt.

But then? She'd felt the stillness of that nausea as it grew with the realization that she had done this: she had killed a man. The blood on her hands had been—mostly—his. She had taken him down by surprise, Morse's advice; he had never really seen her as much of a threat. Scrawny street urchin, too much fief in her.

She had cut off his ring finger. Because it had a ring on it, and Barren wanted the ring as proof. That was it. The body, she'd dragged all the way to the Ablayne. She'd meant to push it into the water. She hadn't. She wasn't sure what the corpse would do there. Bodies in wells made the water undrinkable. Maybe it worked the same way for rivers.

Maybe it didn't; maybe it only poisoned them subtly.

She left the body by the shore. It wouldn't be the first corpse to turn up there, and even had it been, Barren would only laugh; there, by the one symbol of freedom the fiefs had for anyone whose only experience of power was fear, she'd left proof of his strength. But Morse wasn't pleased.

She had the apartment door open before Elianne had even cleared the stairs.

Morse took one look at her and stepped out of the way. Elianne swallowed, opening her mouth to tell Morse what had gone down—but Morse didn't ask. Instead, she pointed toward the large room in which they both ate and strategized, and nodded to the table; it was more or less empty. So was the chair.

Elianne took the chair; Morse remained standing. She didn't, however, remain still; she picked something up off the table, glanced at Elianne and shrugged. She handed Elianne a glass full of amber liquid.

"Drink."

"What is it?"

"Just drink it, Eli."

Elianne took the small glass in both hands, waiting. Waiting for questions. Waiting to make a report. Waiting for pride or joy or even anger. For *something*. Morse gave her silence, and this damn glass. At any other time she would have asked Morse where she'd picked it up—it was heavy, clear, entirely unscratched. Worth money.

Today, money belonged in another life.

She drank.

And choked. She managed not to drop the glass, but the same couldn't be said of the contents, which spilled down the front of her shirt, mingling with dried blood. It had been too cold by the river to try to wash it out.

Her eyes watered. She was half afraid that she'd just let Morse poison her. But Morse wasn't smug enough. She wasn't even amused—and Morse usually found people's discomfort amusing.

"Drink."

This time, she sipped. Morse nodded. After a few minutes, she left and returned, carrying a tunic. Holding out her hand for the glass, she handed it to Elianne.

Wordless, Elianne took it and changed, abandoning her chair. Her face felt flushed and warm; her hands were shaking. She untied strings, loosened sleeves, stood for a moment in half-naked silence before she remembered what she'd been doing. Then she pulled the clean clothing over her head and her shoulders, letting it fall. Morse took the old clothing away.

Clothing had been a problem for Elianne for all of the life she could remember. Finding it. Finding anything that would fit.

Keeping it for as long as she possibly could. Finding clothing for Steffi and Jade.

Her throat tightened; she gagged.

Morse was there, just behind her. But Morse didn't touch her, and didn't speak. Elianne expected a lecture. About the clothing. About *anything*. Morse surprised her. There were no lectures.

Just the gift of silence, because silence was cleanest, safest; you could hide in it without ever having to lie. And if there were no lies big enough to hide the truth, there was no need for truth.

Truth was just words.

Kaylin stepped away from Sorco's body, retreating from the past as if it burned. It did, but she'd almost gotten used to the sensation. She half wondered why people were so damn keen on memory; hers never seemed to do her any good.

"The other two?" Severn asked.

She shook her head. "His guards, I think. I didn't—I don't know how they died." It was true. She hadn't killed them. Just Sorco. She stretched, drawing night air into her lungs. Then she turned to the Tower. "A conversation?" she said quietly.

"I believe you said it could go straight to hell."

"It probably has," she replied, with a twist of lips that might have been a grin on a different day. "Which is about where I am, at the moment. Come on. I want to see what the follow-up is." She nodded in the direction of Sorco's corpse.

He raised a brow. The night drew the red from it, leaving only the deeper browns behind.

"You're going in?"

"Pretty much. I *really* want to hit something, and my best shot at that has to be inside." She glanced at Tiamaris and Nightshade. "Because I'd also like to survive it."

"Private Neya," Tiamaris began.

She turned.

"I think it unwise."

"Oh, it's unwise, all right. But I don't think we're going home through any other damn door. You can wait outside if you want," she added, without much hope.

He didn't dignify her offer with a reply. She glanced at Nightshade, who offered the courtesy of one raised brow. "So," she asked him, just before she turned and entered the open doorway, "did you ever learn anything about time in your magical studies?"

He offered her a rare smile. "Yes," he replied. "I learned that it passes very, very slowly when I'm bored."

She laughed. She had no idea how much younger this Nightshade was because he looked exactly the same—except for the uniform. But she felt for just a moment that she liked this one better.

The Tower, from the outside, looked like, well, a Tower. Not really wide, lots of height, things that looked like arrow slits trying to pass themselves off as windows climbing the walls in spirals. It was too much to hope that the inside of it would bear any resemblance to the outside, and Kaylin didn't waste the effort.

"At least there's no damn portal," she said to Severn.

He chuckled.

He had let her enter the darkened Tower first, but he hadn't been far behind; he certainly wasn't far enough behind for the door to close before he'd gotten two feet across the threshold. The door, which was remarkably obliging when compared to Kaylin's past experiences with Castle Nightshade, did not slam shut until Tiamaris and Nightshade had entered the Tower.

It did, however, close on the last few inches of Nightshade's cape. Capes, apparently, didn't follow the rest of the Barrani code; this one was jammed in the door, and no amount of graceful tugging would actually free it. Kaylin helpfully drew her dagger and gestured toward the taut fabric.

Nightshade raised a brow. Reaching up, he unfastened the cloak by its clips, and shrugged it off his shoulders. "It would be ruined, anyway," he said, when she stared at him. Years of less than optimal pay warred with personal pride. It was a short war, and the outcome was not in doubt; she picked up the end of the cape and cut it free. It was long enough that she could have it cut down and actually use it for *something*. It didn't take her long to roll it up into a much less bulky version of itself.

She slid her pack off her shoulders and wedged it inside.

Tiamaris was staring at her. Nightshade, one brow raised, was doing the same. She felt no pressing need to explain herself to either, but had the grace to flush slightly. She was in the *damn* fiefs; what did they expect?

Better, of course.

Oh, well. They wouldn't be the first people she'd disappointed in her life. She stood, shrugged, and walked past them. The lights went on.

They were in a room that was, in Kaylin's estimation, larger by about half than the outer walls implied. It was stone; the floors, stone, as well. No marble, no gold, nothing fancy—but it was solid work. There were window seats, and the windows themselves had been carved out of stone; they contained no obvious glass at this distance.

There was light in the room. But it was like sunlight in an open courtyard—there was no obvious source. No torches, no chandeliers, no brilliant glass. Nothing. She glanced up at the ceiling. Oh. Well, that would be the problem. There didn't appear to *be* one.

She glanced up, and up again. While there didn't appear to be a ceiling, there also didn't appear to be a sun. Heaving a sigh, she looked at the walls. Besides the windows, there seemed to be a suspicious lack of anything that resembled a door. Sadly, this included the one they'd just passed through to get here. She could see where the door must have been, because jagged blue cloth hung from between the gentle curve of the stones of one wall.

"This," Kaylin said, as she headed toward the closest window, "has not been my day."

"Interesting," Lord Nightshade said to Tiamaris.

"You've never explored the Towers?"

"It was not considered entirely safe," was the reply.

Tiamaris raised a brow, and then, to Kaylin's surprise, laughed out loud. Which caused Nightshade to smile. She thought she'd never understand either the Dragons or the Barrani, because as far as she could tell *this* Nightshade had been in one war or another with the Dragons for a long damn time.

Without thinking, she said, "Do you still have *Meliannos?*"

The temperature in the room banked sharply in a downward spiral. But Nightshade's brows rose slightly in surprise, and she felt the undercurrent in a connection that somehow still existed. "No," he said softly. "I do not *yet* have *Meliannos*. I am... surprised...that you know the sword's name. It is not often that mortals express so much interest in such things."

She almost bit her lip. "Never mind," she said, failing to meet Tiamaris's steady gaze. "I was just thinking out loud."

"You were failing to think," was the Dragon Lord's clipped reply.

"You really did have Sanabalis for a teacher," was hers.

Nightshade waited for an appropriate break in the conversation—such as it was—before he spoke.

"Are you truly from the future?"

"I don't know. It looks like it." She shrugged. "What we said is true. We're having some trouble with shadowstorms in a city that looks a lot like this one will when things have gone to hell and been partially spit back out. We entered a storm—or it hit us—and when we emerged, we weren't in the same place. Or the same time."

"And we need to get back."

"You could do it the long way. Ah, I forget myself. Your companion, however, could."

"I don't think his boredom level is much different from yours, and he's already been here and done it." She had, by this time, made her way to the closest of what she had thought of as window seats. Looking at them up close made her revise her opinion, and her shoulders drooped slightly.

"Kaylin?"

"Portals," she said with a grimace. The ledges were actually stairs; the windows were actually empty, gray spaces that looked a lot like a door but without the obvious things like wood and a handle. Or a knocker.

"I concur," Tiamaris said. "What did you *think* they were?"

"Windows, if you must know."

"To where?"

"Your eyes are probably better than mine. They looked like windows to me."

Those eyes, a steady shade of gold, narrowed. "Do not attempt to see what you desire to see," he said quietly.

"If I did, I wouldn't be looking at a big, round, empty room with no ceiling, no sky and no egress. I'd be thinking of—"

Tiamaris stepped, hard, on her foot.

"Pain, clearly."

She counted nine portals in total.

Which was unfortunate, because everyone *else* counted eight. They didn't split up to examine the room; Tiamaris didn't think it wise, and for once, they were in agreement. The entire place gave Kaylin hives. Severn, silent, was watchful. "Where is the ninth?"

"Here," Kaylin said, pointing to what was obviously another tall, narrow arch. The steps here were curved, as if well-worn, but also flat and wide; she could sit on them. Her butt would probably get cold; the Tower did not radiate warmth.

But Severn shook his head and looked at the Dragon Lord and the Barrani Lord. They both frowned. Tiamaris lifted a hand, and then closed it and dropped it before he had cast the spell that was at his fingertips.

"You think we have to take this one?"

"I think," Tiamaris replied, "that you are intended to do so."

"Thanks, but if it's all the same to you, I'll give it a pass. I'm not going anywhere in this place without at least two of you."

Nightshade raised a brow.

"No offense," she told him, "but we already have one of you back home; two of you would be a little much to handle. If you get lost here, we're even. If they get lost here, we're screwed." She had been speaking low Barrani, which was easier for her; she had had to descend into Elantran for the last word.

He repeated it, and she grimaced. "It means—"

"I take the meaning."

She took a deep breath, turned, and said, "All right, let's try the first door to the left."

The door to their immediate left was a bust. Kaylin approached it first, and tried to touch it; her hand bounced off the gray of its slightly luminescent surface. As if there were, in fact, glass of a quality so fine that it could not be seen at all. "Figures," she muttered. She turned on heel and approached the next door, with the same results.

Seven doors later, she was staring at the portal that only she could see, and remembering, glumly, that there were whole days in which staying in bed was the best and most viable option. "I don't suppose you can see any strange marks on the floor that I missed the last fifty times I crossed it?" she asked Tiamaris.

"Not with the naked eye, no."

And anything else was a risk. Kaylin stared at the door that she knew appeared to be a flat but curved expanse of wall to everyone else in the room. "All right," she said, straightening her shoulders. "What do you want to do now?"

Tiamaris glanced at the wall out of which blue cloth could still be seen. "I am not entirely certain that we will be able to open the...door...that we entered. Nor am I certain," he added, "that we will be able to follow you. If," he added, "the portal that you can see and we cannot is more active than the others."

"I'm not sure I can ascertain that—"

"Without passing through it, no. Nor can you be certain that it is not, in fact, a one-way portal."

She glanced at Severn; she didn't need to ask him what he thought; the *no* was written clearly across the lines of his face.

"If we can assume anything at all about shadowstorm," Kaylin asked Tiamaris, "can we assume we're here for a reason?"

"No."

"Those bodies—"

"No. The Tower and the storm are not the same."

"You're the senior officer, here," she told him, glancing at the portal. "What's your call?"

He snorted. She could see the smoke leave his nostrils. He walked past her, closed his eyes, and touched the wall. Kaylin watched his palm traverse stone—and watched it reach the lines of window. "Can you feel it?"

Tiamaris continued his entirely physical inspection, and then nodded.

"I hate to sound like I'm directing a field trip of orphans," Kaylin began, "but maybe if we all hold hands we can get through without losing anyone."

"And maybe," Severn helpfully suggested, "whoever is directly behind you will only lose an arm."

"Thank you," she told him. The thought had, of course, occurred to everyone. "I think it's either take the risk, or let me go through on my own."

He offered her one of his rare smiles; it was both edged and genuine. "That," he said, stepping forward and offering her his hand, "is playing by fief rules."

"Why, thank you." She took his hand. It was surprisingly warm in a room that was gradually becoming chilly. She turned to face the door as Severn held out a hand to Tiamaris. Tiamaris grimaced, but took Severn's hand; it took him two minutes to extend his own to Nightshade.

Nightshade looked at all three of them, and shook his head. "I have often been criticized," he said, as he slid his perfect hand into the Dragon's wider palm, "for my impulsiveness."

"A trait, sadly, that we all have in common," Tiamaris replied.

Severn coughed. Kaylin laughed. "Not all of us," she told the Dragon Lord. "But Severn has other burdens to bear." And she smiled at him. It was pained, and shadowed, but it was genuine.

She took a deep breath, and then, testing the strength of

Severn's grip, took a step forward. Her foot disappeared instantly from view, and she put as much weight on it as she could. "We're not going to fall instantly," she told Tiamaris.

"You're not," he replied. "Go."

She walked into the gray, flat surface of the portal.

"Why do you care about all these damn kids?" Morse asked.

Elianne turned to look at her mentor. "What do you mean?"

Morse smacked the side of her head. "Don't give me bullshit. I'm asking a serious question, here."

"Why makes you think I care?"

"You've gotten into three fights this week. All three of 'em have been with our people." She glanced at the crowded street. It was midday, and they were on the way to the White Towers. It would be hours before they had to worry about heading back home to avoid ferals. But it would be less than an hour before they had to talk to Barren.

"They picked the fight."

Morse raised a bisected brow and lifted a hand. "What did I just say about bullshit?"

Elianne stopped herself from shrugging. "How'd you notice?"

"I've got eyes and they weren't closed. Look, Mullet—" which wasn't his real name, but Morse didn't have a great memory for the names of people she viewed with contempt, "kicked the crap out of the boy with the bucket the other day."

"He *broke* the damn bucket. You think they're just going to steal another one in this part of town?"

Morse's smile was thin. "Probably about as easily as he's going to do his job with a broken arm. That was nice work, by the way."

"He did most of it." Morse's turn to shrug. "Kebbs."

"Which one was he?"

"The one with no hair."

"Oh. The one who tore the shirt off that girl?"

"That one."

"She was six."

"And that's not a guess."

"I asked her." Elianne glanced away. "All right, yes. I don't care enough to give them all my money or offer them a place to stay."

"You don't have one, that's why."

"But I don't mind making their lives a little easier."

"Why?"

Elianne didn't want to have this conversation. Morse did. "What harm do they do? What do they have? A bucket. A shirt that they can barely afford to replace. A bunch of stones and a stick."

"And you had so much more?"

Elianne frowned. "What does that have to do with anything?"

"Maybe nothing. Look at me. I don't give a shit."

"I'm not asking *you* to give a shit." She saw the expression twist Morse's mouth, and took a breath. "If they were rich, if they *had* everything, it wouldn't *be* my problem."

"It's not your damn problem now. You're *making* it your problem."

People were now beginning to clear the streets to the side and ahead of where Elianne and Morse had stopped. "Does it matter?" Elianne said, struggling to keep her voice even; Morse's hands were now forming loose fists. From loose to tight was only a matter of seconds. "I'm *doing* my job. I'm getting *good* at it."

"You put two people who were *also* doing their jobs out of commission for a couple of weeks."

"They weren't doing their jobs then."

"They can't do their fucking jobs *now*." Morse slapped Elianne. Or would have; Elianne dodged. Morse wasn't serious enough to try again. "You don't think he'll hear about this?"

"They're going to crawl back to Barren and tell him they were taken out by *me*?"

Morse opened her mouth and snapped it shut; Elianne heard her teeth. "Your point," she finally managed. "But you've got to stop this." She started to walk, and Elianne began to follow, trying to gauge what a safe distance was. She usually knew what would throw Morse into a mood; she hadn't seen this one coming.

"You care about this shit, it'll kill you. One way or the other, it'll kill you. You can't be careful, you care too much. You can't do your job in the best way, or the safest—for you. You'll take too many risks."

"I didn't."

"Not yet. But what happens when you piss off enough people—"

"Stupid people—"

"They won't all *be* stupid. They'll be self-serving, cruel, malicious—yeah, all of that—but you can't count on stupid just because they do things you don't fucking like!" She drew air across her teeth, and Elianne moved to the side. "And you'll piss them off. They'll know. They'll know enough about you to know where your own weaknesses are. You don't think they'll use them?

"You don't think they'll use them so they can take you down? They might not kill you. Not yet. Not if they think Barren'll be pissed. But they'll hurt you, and you're letting them know *how*." Her face was red enough that the white scars stood out, like broken, brittle strands of old webbing.

Elianne stopped talking. Her own anger turned sideways and slipped away, leaving her stranded with Morse's and nothing to stand behind. She had never seen Morse this angry. She never wanted to see Morse this angry again. She tried to speak, swallowed the words, and trailed after her, like quivering shadow.

Because she knew—even then, she knew—that she could not make it, not yet, without Morse. If Morse turned her out, she was as good as dead. Or possibly, thinking about the houses closest to the river, worse off.

"I should *never* have taken you on. I should have known better." Morse, by herself, had now cleared the streets the way a small squad of Barren's men on a bender might have. When she wheeled and turned on Elianne, Elianne leapt back. "You need to decide what it is that you want. You want to learn how to kill a man? I'm your woman. You want to coddle fucking urchins? Run across the goddamn bridge and crawl up the steps of some fucking church!"

★ ★ ★

Kaylin's foot touched bridge.

She couldn't see it. She could see the gray and shimmering light of this particular portal, and while she didn't much care for it, she didn't much care for *any* magic. Gray was better than pitch-black, and at least it wasn't winter-cold. It was also thin, like a veil or a curtain, rather than a big, heat-sucking void. She wondered, briefly, if Nightshade could change the entrance to his damn Castle so it didn't chew her up and spit her out so badly anytime she visited.

Then again, she hadn't actually gotten to the other side of this one yet.

Severn's hand tightened around hers, and she took another step forward. More bridge. And it *was* a bridge; she was certain of it. It was the bridge across the Ablayne. She still couldn't see it, and she walked slowly because of that, testing the planking beneath her feet to make certain it would support her weight.

What had felt thin and veil-like continued to hamper her vision. She reached out once, with her free hand, and touched rail. If she listened, and she did, she could hear the movement of the river beneath her feet.

"Kaylin—"

She turned. She couldn't see Severn; if it weren't for his hand on hers, she wouldn't have known he was there. That, and the sound of his voice. But she *could* see, stretching out from the bridge, the backward streets of Barren. It was *her* Barren. It was not the Barren into which they'd walked a scant hour or two ago.

The streets were empty; the sun was low across the horizon. Ferals, if they ran, would be all but gone. All-but not being safe enough for most of the people who cowered behind doors or closed shutters, just as Kaylin had done for most of her life.

"Okay," she said out loud. "I get it."

"Get what?" Severn replied, his voice rising slightly in concern.

"What do you see?" she asked, shunting the question aside.

"You."

"Anything else?"

"Mist. Grayer and denser than the usual riverside variety."

"What are you walking on?"

After a long pause, he said, "We're endeavoring not to answer that."

She chuckled. "I'm walking," she told him curtly, "on the bridge over the Ablayne."

"Barren's bridge."

"The same."

"Which way are you headed?"

"Out. To the City. I think. I can't actually see what's ahead of me. I can only see what's behind." She paused, and then grimaced. "Which technically doesn't include any of the three of you." She turned and saw gray; it was as if the portal—or what had moved within its stone frame—was constantly moving just out of range. But as it did, it revealed bridge, that old and bitter symbol of hope and failure. "Halfway there," she told them softly. "I'm going to keep moving."

Severn squeezed her hand twice. *Yes.*

She continued walking—more quickly this time—until the bridge sloped toward the far bank, and the streets of the City itself. Only when her foot hit stone did the mist begin to clear.

CHAPTER 19

But the mist cleared across a cityscape that was entirely unlike the Elantra Kaylin knew. She turned to look back at the bridge. It was gone. So was the river, and the familiar bend of run-down buildings that housed the affluent on the wrong side of the Ablayne. Severn, on the other hand, had now appeared, his hand still clutching hers. So, too, had Tiamaris and the other Lord Nightshade. They were, to a man, as white as alabaster.

She frowned, studying their faces for a moment. Severn's was set in familiar, neutral lines. They offered no comfort, but asked for none. He didn't speak, and she knew, by the set of his lips, that he wouldn't unless she pushed it. She didn't. Tiamaris's eyes were almost red, and she had never seen his skin so pale. One of his hands still held Severn's, the other, Nightshade's, but he didn't seem—at this moment—aware of either anchor. He was staring past Kaylin's shoulder, his lips thinned, the inner membranes of his eyes raised high.

Nightshade's eyes were a blue so deep it was almost midnight. Tendrils of perfect, Barrani hair framed his face as if breeze moved them, although the air was stale and still. He, like Tiamaris, looked past her. Only Severn met her gaze, but only Severn seemed to be watching Kaylin.

Clearly, she didn't see whatever it was they saw. She would have asked Severn to let go of her hand, but she wasn't certain he would do it. Instead of asking, she turned back toward what should have been the City that was joined by a slender bridge to the Barren of her youth.

But that Barren? It was gone, as well. She had no idea where she was. She would have asked Nightshade what his first encounter with his Castle had been like, but this Nightshade had no answers for her, and she didn't feel up to his questions.

Her hands were trembling. She would have forced them to her sides to hide that fact—but one of them was in Severn's. He didn't speak. She was grateful for the silence.

She looked at the remains of the entirely unfamiliar City to which the bridge had brought her. There were—or had once been—streets, but they were gone. So were the buildings that lined what had once been road, although some walls were still standing at various crumbled heights. Here and there, some hint that those walls had once owned roofs existed. There had been gates of some sort, fences of some sort, but even those were gone; poles or posts remained, as if they were markers.

As if, she thought, the whole of the City she could see was one large and untended grave. She began to walk toward the broken streets, beneath the gray and murky sky, and felt Severn's hand tighten. It made her feel as if she were one of Marrin's orphans.

"We might as well take a look around," she told him, her fingers beginning the painful tingle that happened when they were basically being crushed. "Severn, what do you see?"

"What do you see?" he countered. He *was* tense.

"A whole lot of broken," she replied. "Broken streets, buildings, bits of leaning fence posts. I think—I can't tell—but I think I see statue bases in the distance. No statues. Some of the rubble on the ground is probably wall."

"The sky?" he asked, in the same tight voice.

She frowned. "It's gray."

"Cloudy?"

"No, just gray."

"Time of day?"

"I can't tell from the shadows; there aren't enough. I'd say it's afternoon. It's not cold enough to be morning at this time of year."

"What time of year?"

Now, she frowned. "Spring? Fall? I...don't know. It's just one
of those gray days. No rain. No sun." She hesitated and then said,
"What does the sky look like, to you?"

"Black."

"Black?"

He pressed her hand twice, and she nodded. "Stars?"

"None."

"Moons?"

"None."

"Severn, when you say black—"

"He means shadow," Tiamaris replied. "We see shadow, Kaylin."

"And not just darkness."

"Unless 'just darkness' roils with the hint of unpleasant color,
no. Do you sense magic?"

"You mean, more magic?"

He grimaced. "That was perhaps not the most intelligent of
my questions. But, yes."

She shook her head. "Honestly, Tiamaris. I see a broken cityscape. It is definitely not Elantra. It might—possibly—be the City
that Lord Nightshade knows."

"It is no City I know," the Barrani Lord replied. "Unless much
has changed since we entered the Tower. It is no City that is safe
to explore."

Severn said, "It's unlikely to be a City at all."

"Ahead of you," Kaylin replied, frowning. "Tiamaris, when
you entered the Castle in—in the other fief, what did you see?"

"The first time? I will not speak of it."

So. She squared her shoulders. "You didn't *try* to take the Castle."

"No."

"But you were tested by the damn thing anyway."

He said nothing. A lot of it. "It would be nice if tests like these varied at all."

"Meaning?" Severn asked.

"A little less darkness and gloom, a lot less accusation." She grimaced. "Way less Barren." She began to walk toward the distant, broken streets, and this time, her companions followed.

After the silence had gone on for long enough, Severn said, "What do you think you'll stumble across next?"

As the answer was rubble, and she'd hit it with her toe hard enough she almost hopped up and down, she answered in brief, curt Leontine. She felt, rather than saw, his smile. But when she had worked her way past the worst of the fallen stone, she said, "Probably more bodies." It was a noncommittal answer, or it was meant to be. It would have been a *lot* easier to be able to use both of her hands; she couldn't. Their only vision was filtered through her, and they were afraid they would lose it the minute the physical contact was gone.

There they were. Partly obscured by the rubble, the fallen walls, the shards of oddly sharp glass in this devastated landscape. She saw the outstretched arm first, blood trailing across it from wrist to elbow like wet webbing. Bending, she saw that the hand was missing a finger. She had no idea whose body it was; she would have had to remove stone for an hour to see if anything was left of the face. But she knew it was one of hers. One of her targets. One of her kills.

Like Sorco's hand, she had probably removed something from it: a ring. Barren liked some proof that the work had been done. He also had some way of detecting whether or not the item was genuine; Morse had made that clear on Kaylin's first outing. Whatever else she did—succeed or fail—attempting to lie to Barren and pocket whatever it was she'd taken would not end well.

She walked, slowly, the rhythm broken only by the turn in the street, the large piles of rock it was better to avoid than climb over. She saw a broken leg, another arm, a twisted hand. It was as if the streets had opened to swallow just enough of the bodies that they could be held in place, by cases and pedestals made of debris, for her inspection.

How many? she thought, as she walked. How many *more* could there be? The past answered. It told her she would know if she cared to take a good, hard look.

"What did he do?"

Morse shrugged. "Does it matter?" She glanced at Elianne, and then swore. "You gotta stop asking."

She stopped asking Morse. *Barren wants him dead. You kill him. End of story.* And it was the end of the story—but Elianne wanted the rest of the story, as well. She always had.

Morse even understood why. Her sneer was one of Elianne's strongest visual memories of life in Barren. *You think it's cleaner somehow, you killing for money, if they did something? You think it squares it away so you can sleep at night?*

Elianne had laughed. It was loud, brittle laughter, and it fooled no one, but Morse let it go. Elianne didn't. She asked. She found out. She had to be careful who she asked; Morse blackened her eye the one time she found out. Elianne understood the lesson Morse meant to teach her: be more careful. She'd learned.

The streets were growing colder as Kaylin walked them. She walked them too slowly, but she couldn't force herself to move faster. Blaming Severn, Tiamaris, and Nightshade came and went; she knew damn well her speed and their awkward human chain weren't connected. She had to look at the limbs, or the hands or the occasional bleeding face. She had to see them. She wasn't sure why.

Or maybe she was. She'd only lived in Barren for six months. She'd had time to get good—to think she'd gotten good, she amended—but she hadn't had time to lay down a carpet of corpses that could easily cover more than a few City blocks, when lined up like this. And there was a lot more space than a few City blocks stretching out toward the gray and dim horizon.

It was too much to hope they'd be empty.

The next body she discovered was not buried. Nor was it lying across the ground like so much refuse. It was on display, pinned to crossed beams, its chest cut by shards of sharp glass. The blood had stopped running, but it was still red, still damp.

"Kaylin?" Severn said.

She was silent. This man, she hadn't killed. But she knew damn well how he'd died. Everyone in the fief knew it. Everyone in the fief probably had some idea of why. He'd interfered with the money that had crossed the bridge over the Ablayne. He had killed an outsider, and left his body close enough to the bridge that it could be seen.

The people who lived across the river were used to a soft, safe, easy life. Death scared the crap out of them. When they were scared, they took their money and the business that would have been illegal in their own homes, and they crossed a *different* bloody bridge. Or they stayed home.

What everyone else did not know was that Kaylin had been assigned *this* death. Her first failure.

Finding information about Paul Moroes, and finding Paul Moroes were heading in the same direction: nowhere. Barren had sent his enforcers into the streets, where they met with the same luck, although they terrified more people.

Lost, as she seldom was, in thought, she was surprised when someone shouted at her. Her hands dropped to her sides, but not to her weapons; the voice belonged to an older woman.

"What d'you think you're doing, standing like that in the middle of the street?"

Elianne turned, and saw the speaker clearly. She was, as her voice suggested, older; she had lost a few teeth to those years, and her eyes were sunken into the wreath of lines that was her face.

"Don't you know it's dangerous for a girl your age, here?"

Elianne glanced at the river. At the people on the far banks. She started to shrug, and then stopped herself. "Is it?" she asked, instead. "You're here."

"It's not dangerous for me," the old woman replied, indicating the whole of her body in one sweeping and dismissive gesture. "But you'll get yourself a few years of trouble. Go on back home, girl."

Instead, Elianne knelt in the street, over the bloodied ground.

"Aye," the woman said, noting the blood. "But *that* kind of trouble won't hurt you."

"Someone died here."

"Someone deserved it. It ain't enough that they've got laws and freedom, over on their side of the damn river; they got to come down here and cause trouble. Well," the old woman said, her smile growing edges, "sometimes they find it. That one," she added, pointing to the street and the absent corpse, "he hurt a girl from down here. He hurt her bad. But her brother was home, and he came out hunting."

"When—when did the girl get hurt?"

The woman frowned. "A week ago, maybe less. It was—oh, no, it was five days ago."

"Days?"

"Aye, happened at end of day, before sunset. Girl wouldn't have been out, otherwise. But she shouldn't have been alone."

Elianne nodded slowly. She didn't ask the girl's name, and she didn't ask the man's; she had them both, and didn't need them. "You're heading down to the out-towner stands?"

"Aye. So was she."

"Mind if I keep you company?"

"I'm not much guarantee of safety," the old woman replied, handing Elianne a worn, empty basket.

She had the information she wanted. She knew the *why*. The information she needed—where—was still out there, in someone else's possession, and clearly, Barren's offer of both reward and possible punishment had failed to get those other people to pass it on. The old woman, Arna, wasn't an idiot; Elianne didn't try to ask her where Paul Moroes was. She, like anyone who'd lived in the fiefs, tended to sharpen her suspicion; there was a lot to sharpen it on, and Elianne wanted it blunter.

She spent two days dogging Arna's shadow. She carried water from the well, because it was *just* warm enough that you could get water; she carried empty—and slightly fuller—baskets. She carried sheets and clothing to the very cold running water of the Ablayne, and she listened to Arna chatter, gossip, and rant. Only at the end of the second day did she ask about the incident—but she didn't ask about Paul; she asked, instead, about his sister.

"She's your age. Maybe a year younger. You're twelve?"

"I'm thirteen," Elianne said, her smile freezing in place for just a second.

Arna chuckled. "At my age? There's not much damn difference, girl." But the chuckle quieted. "She's home. We're not sure she'll make it past winter.

"Come on. I'm to stop there today, and if you're up to carrying a bit, you can keep me company." She had a sharp look to her face as she said it, but it wasn't a suspicious one; it said *Purpose,* with capital letters.

Here, now, Kaylin looked at the body of Paul Moroes. The other bodies weren't immediately visible, but it didn't matter; like all good ghosts, they haunted her anyway. "Severn," she said quietly, clutching his hand.

He nodded.

"Unwind the weapon chain; attach it to me. I need to—I need both of my hands." He didn't ask her why. She knew he wouldn't. Most days, she took the silence for granted. Today she felt it as the gift it was. She transferred her free hand to his shoulder, in order to hold on to him; they both didn't like what might happen here if they were separated. He unwound the weapon chain with care.

When he had passed the blade at one end of the chain around her, the links followed it with a cold musicality as he let the chain play out. Seen this way, in the endless gray of a sullen sky, it looked slender, decorative. She touched the links; they were warm with his body heat.

When he had finished, she lifted her hand from his shoulder, and turned to the corpse of Paul Moroes. She didn't ask him questions; she didn't beg his forgiveness. She said nothing at all as she began to cut him down.

"Private," Tiamaris said curtly, "is this entirely necessary?"

"Is what necessary, Tiamaris?"

"Whatever it is you are doing."

She ignored the question. There was only one sensible answer to it, and she didn't much care to give it. No one liked feeling like an idiot.

She should have told Arna that she didn't want to go. That's where it should have ended. She even knew it, at the time. But she told herself that if she could make a favorable impression upon Sana and her mother, she'd have her best shot at getting to Paul Moroes, and she kept her growing uneasiness to herself as she followed in Arna's steps.

Sana's grandmother was a woman named Kora. She looked as if she was about the same age as Arna, but she was a good deal less talkative. "Put the basket on the table, girl," Arna told Elianne, as she unwound a ratty great scarf and dumped it on a chair. "We're not staying long," she added, speaking to Kora. "But I thought there was a good chance you didn't head out today, and you need to eat."

Kora's lined face was pinched and shadowed. "Aye, we all need that. But the food won't help my granddaughter," she added bitterly. "We've tried. Gods know, we've tried." She covered her face a moment with both hands, and then pushed the curls out of her face with her palms. "Sit," she told Arna. "You can fill me in on any news I shouldn't miss."

"Let me say hello to your daughter."

"She might be sleeping," Kora replied. "I hate to wake her."

"Sana?"

Kora shrugged. It was not a fief shrug; it was a gesture used in place of all the words that you couldn't say. "Aye," she said. "You can see Sana. Maybe—" She took a breath, and inhaled the rest of the words.

But she lead Arna to a very small hall, and from it, to a room. The door was slightly ajar. She opened it and entered. Elianne, whose hope that she'd been forgotten was dashed by a determined Arna, entered, as well.

Kora's daughter was, indeed, asleep. Like her mother, her face was creased and shadowed, but sleep deprived it of the edges and the unutterable weariness of the older woman's expression. She was curled over a chair just to one side of the bed that occupied the far wall—where far, in this case, was a matter of ten feet away, if that.

But the girl in the bed? Her face was not so much gray as black and yellow. One eye was swollen almost beyond recognition, and the lid remained closed. The other, bruised, was a slit through which Elianne could just barely see awareness. Sana was awake; her mouth was slightly open, and she was drooling.

"You take a good look," Arna whispered, bringing her lips to Elianne's ear so that Kora wouldn't hear what she had to say. "If you're not careful, that'll be you."

CHAPTER 20

If you're not careful. She closed Paul Moroes's eyes. They had left his eyelids intact, so she could.

"Kaylin." Nightshade's voice. "There is a danger here. You do not perceive it."

She raised her face, looked across at him. The wind moved his hair across the perfect blue of his eyes; he ignored it. "What danger?" she asked quietly, her voice remote.

"You expose too much weakness."

Her laugh was brittle, harsh. "And you're going to take advantage of it? Here?"

"No. Not here, and not I. You stand in a building that not even the wise understand, and in our limited experience, these buildings test all visitors. Not everyone who chooses to enter is allowed to leave, if they even survive the attempt. Their bodies are not found.

"I...am not entirely aware...of the significance of what you see, but I am aware of what you see in a way that Lord Tiamaris and your human compatriot are not. No building offers the same test, but this one is in keeping with the tests that are known."

She shook her head. "This isn't about the Tower. It's about me."

"That," he replied, "is the nature of the Towers. You must move, Kaylin. You cannot afford to stand here."

"No. No, you're right." She was still crouching. Her knees were beginning to feel it; the air here was damp and cool. The street was still a fractured display of broken things, especially in the square in which his body had been discovered. There were no shovels, here. No pickaxes, nothing with which to dig into the unyielding ground.

She had left him, once, untouched, just as she had found him today. As if the intervening years had never happened. Today she cut him down, arranging his body to give it whatever dignity the dead cared for. Maybe, she thought, bitter now and angry, the *next time,* she would actually bury him.

It was impossible to see Sana and not understand what had driven her brother to the act of revenge that would be his eventual suicide. It was *exactly* what drove Elianne herself. Arna had meant to scare Elianne. Elianne was beyond fear of that type. She'd seen worse. Worse, because Jade and Steffi had died.

But this injured stranger hurt her in ways that she didn't understand, not at first. She could barely bring herself to speak to the girl. Barely. She kept her distance, though, as if the injuries were somehow contagious. Sana couldn't actually speak; her voice came out in a thin squawk. She had trouble closing her mouth properly, which is why she was drooling.

"She was in worse shape," Arna told Elianne on the way out, "when they found her. She'd dragged herself half down the street, her legs broken, and one arm. We weren't certain she'd survive." For the first time, Arna hesitated, and then said, in a lower voice, "and we're not sure Paul will, either." It was the first time she'd mentioned his name.

Elianne should have felt some triumph at the sound of it; she didn't. She should have asked what Arna meant, should have pretended she thought Paul was also injured. She couldn't. She was hollow, nauseated, and frightened. But she couldn't go home until she'd gotten enough of a grip that she could look normal; Morse would notice, otherwise, and she'd ask more than Elianne could reasonably answer.

"Did you kill him?" Severn asked, as she began to pick her way over rubble again. The question was a shock; not even Nightshade's voice had felt so foreign.

She had no answer to give him; no answer but movement, although movement separated them only as far as the chain stretched. She didn't remove it, but didn't offer him her hand. She'd had enough of people, now; people, Dragons, and Barrani.

Morse had known. Kaylin had never been one of nature's natural liars, and although she'd developed some skill at it during her weeks in Barren, that skill was a thin veneer over years of the exact opposite experience. She'd expected Morse to be angry, and she was—but the anger was a strange anger; it involved no fists, no slaps, no kicks. Instead, it involved a towering wall of silence.

These streets were mercifully unlike any streets she had ever walked before. "No," she told Severn. It sounded like yes.

Paul Moroes had been a shock, Kaylin admitted that. But once she had seen him, she had lingered by his side, showing him the respect that no one in the world cared about, anymore. Not his sister. Not his mother.

Not Arna, either.

It wasn't long before she found their bodies, mixed in the rubble, the way she'd known she would. They hadn't been killed in the same way that Moroes had; they weren't on public display in the open streets. Paul's crime had to be *discouraged,* Morse had said. But their crime? It was the usual. Death was fine.

Only death was fine.

"You know," she told Severn, when she could speak normally again, "I *hate* these places." Turning to Nightshade, she added, "I am never going to complain about your portal again for as long as I live—"

And stopped.

"Tiamaris, is he going to remember all of this?"

"The Barrani are famed for their memory."

"He never mentioned it to me."

"Perhaps he had some reason for his silence." He said it in a tone of voice that implied that Nightshade's silence, and her lack of it, were strongly connected. He wasn't pleased with her at the moment.

Then again, neither was she. Reaching out carefully, she took Severn's hand. "I went to Barren," she told him, "because there was nowhere else for me to go. I didn't even realize I'd crossed the border. I found Morse, and Morse promised she would teach me how to kill a man. It was the only thing I cared about.

"But Morse? She worked for Barren. She trained me so that I could do the same thing. Work for Barren. I did. For six months." Her fingers tightened as she spoke, as if she were afraid he'd pull away. "He told me who to kill, and I figured out how. I killed them," she added. "The bodies in the first door that opened were the bodies of the first men I killed."

His hand tightened around hers, but he didn't speak a word. Didn't really need to. "And the rest of the bodies?"

"The rest of the bodies, until the man I cut down, were bodies of people I'd killed. For Barren."

"All of them?"

She frowned. "Yes, I think. I didn't stop to dig them all out, and not all of them could be identified by their arms or legs." She shrugged.

"These bodies?"

She flinched. "These…were different. The man who was nailed to the posts? I was supposed to kill him."

"You didn't."

"I…no. I didn't. I *understood* what he'd done. I understood why. It was what I would have done. What I wanted to do. It would've been like killing a part of myself. I thought I could do it. But I couldn't." Her voice dropped. "I left him a message, with his mother. He understood what it meant. I think he—he might have tried to move his mother and his sister. I don't know.

"But Morse—or someone who worked for Barren—must have been following me. I wasn't as careful, then. Not then. They must have heard what I said to him. I did *try*, Severn. I tried to kill him. But I couldn't. We fought. I was injured. He was injured. I told him—I told him to clear out. I told him to cross the bridge."

Severn looked away. He did not withdraw his hand.

"Yes. They heard that, too," she told him quietly.

"What happened?"

"Moroes died."

"And you?"

"I lived, more or less."

"Kaylin—"

But he didn't have to tell her; she knew. The shadows were gathering in his vision, but they were gathering in her chest, as well, constricting breath and words and thought. She had never told anyone about Barren. She hadn't even told Morse, and Morse was kind enough—or brusque enough—not to try to guess. Morse didn't offer sympathy, and she didn't hold out hope; she offered life, and it was the life of a person who ends anyone else's, on command.

"He didn't have me killed," Kaylin said, surprised at the sound of her own voice. "He didn't even sound angry. He sounded sad. And quiet."

"You do not have to say this," Severn told her. "Not to me."

"But I do," she replied, keeping her voice even and her hands still. "Because if I don't, we don't leave."

"You're guessing."

"Yes, she is," Tiamaris said. "But as is often the case with Kaylin's undereducated guesses, this one is, I believe, correct."

"If I'm right," Kaylin continued, "I'll see other bodies. Other victims, not of my knife, but of my stupidity, my carelessness. People who died by chance, by being in the wrong place, by seeing the wrong damn thing. I didn't wield the knife, and no one paid me, but I did kill them.

"I think," she added, "that's why you can't see what I see; I've never let you. It's dark, it's horrible—it's everything *I believe about myself.* The Tower is speaking to me, yes. Bit by bit, it's unraveling all the lies of omission, even the ones I told myself. Maybe especially those. It's pulling out the things that I kept hidden because I couldn't stand to think about them.

"I don't know who I am, Severn. I don't think I've *ever* known who I am. But I know who I *want* to be, now. Maybe that's all I'll ever know. What I *was* is so large in my own mind I can't break through it if it's hidden. And I keep it hidden because I'm afraid. Of what it says about me. Of what it'll say about me to people whose opinion I actually care about.

"I'm not proud of it," she added. "But I can pretend I accept it—as long as I never have to acknowledge it. And *this,*" she said, throwing her arm wide, "is what it is. It's too big. I need to let it be what it *was.*

"Barren never called me an idiot after that. He—" She shook her head. "I knew I'd failed. I knew I'd failed Morse."

"And Barren?"

"Until then, I honestly didn't give a shit about Barren." She sucked in air. "After, I knew what I was to him. I knew I was his. I understood Morse better." She looked at her hands, turning them so the palms were visible. "I knew I didn't deserve more, Severn. When we lived in—in the other fief, I had hope. I had you, and I believed in you. When you killed the girls, it shattered."

He flinched then, for the first time since she'd started.

"No," she told him, gentling her voice. "This is *not* about you. This isn't even really about the truth, because truth is so damn slippery. It's about me. It's about what I—as a thirteen-year-old—believed. I wanted to believe there was a reason for what you did. But I *couldn't.* And because I couldn't, the only reason I had to go on was you. In a twisted way, it was you."

She turned toward the ruins surrounding her on all sides.

"I thought, if I killed you, the nightmares would stop. But they were worse, because I was killing. Me. I thought I could just kill Barren's thugs, and that would be all right. I could justify that, to myself. But when Paul Moroes and his family died…I lost that.

"They aren't the only ones who are here," she added softly. "But they're the first. They made me understand just how worthless I was." She lifted a hand and pressed it to his mouth, which had opened, sealing in the words. "They died because I was an assassin and a coward—they were neither."

Straightening her shoulders she glanced at gray sky; lightning streaked groundward in the distance, from the roil of green-gray cloud. "Storm coming," she told him softly. "It would have been different, if I could have accepted what their deaths taught me about myself. I couldn't. So I hated the Emperor."

Tiamaris cleared his throat, and she grimaced. "I hated him anyway. It was safe to hate him—he didn't care about the fiefs; it wasn't as if he'd launch himself out of the safety of his palace and fly down to burn me to cinders. I hated the Halls of Law, and I hated the fact that they were supposed to protect people like Paul Moroes, but *didn't,* just because he lived on the wrong side of the Ablayne.

"I hated them for not doing what I couldn't do. I hated them for not stopping *me.*" She looked at Severn. "Yes, I know it doesn't make sense. I didn't make much sense, then.

"Mostly, I hated the Hawks because those were the officers I saw. I saw Swords, on occasion, but not damn often. We never saw Wolves. Just the Hawks, patrolling the far banks."

"Where you patrol now."

"Where we patrol now, yes." She hesitated, and then said, "After Moroes killed the stranger, the Hawks clung to the banks near the bridge. They couldn't prevent people from crossing, but they could stop them, inspect their cargo if they had any and question them. So people stopped coming to Barren. They probably crossed the bridges to every other damn fief. Except where the walls are. I imagine those were harder.

"None of which mattered to Barren. He tried sending his men

out to case the bridge, and to offer the possibility of threat—but they couldn't touch the Hawks, and they knew it. I went a couple of times, but I hung back, watching."

"He sent you across the river, then?"

"Not immediately, no. I think he tried bribing the Hawks first."

Severn raised one brow. "I bet that went over well."

"How much are you betting?"

He laughed. It was almost a shock of sound, even though it was his usual, low laugh. She wanted more of it, but at this moment, she didn't have the energy or the creativity to draw it out.

"It didn't work. I think Teela broke someone's arm; I *know* Tain broke someone's jaw. Not that they have anything against the concept of bribery; they just felt the amount was insulting. Then again, they'd probably find *any* amount the merely mortal could offer insulting, and at least *I* grew up in a fief where insulting the Barrani was a life-shortening proposition.

"It was after that, that I left Barren. But before that, I was sent out to kill. Barren made some of the hits 'invisible' hits. People weren't supposed to know it was him, so they couldn't know it was me. Looking back, it was practice, of a sort. I learned how to scale buildings, how to use ropes and grapples and any old thing that might support weight. I learned when to do it.

"Sometimes," she added, with a shrug, "I worked at night. No one's careful at night except the people who are down on the streets. I didn't know Barren as well as—as the other fief. But I knew it well enough. I was almost always in the same area. Morse didn't like it," she added. "But I was beyond caring at that point.

"I stopped asking what they had done. The victims. My victims. I stopped asking questions, because I didn't want to know. Knowing, needing to know, had only killed three people—or four—who'd done nothing to deserve it. I think—I think that's what Morse was trying to tell me when she got so angry." She inhaled, and in the silent space of breath, she heard distant thunder.

"I was never as good as Morse. But I would have been, had I stayed. I don't know if I would have ever been as scary." She exhaled. "I would have been hunted, in the City, had I lived there. I would have been a dead man had I crossed the bridge, if the Hawks had any idea of what I did.

"And Barren ordered me to cross the bridge, in the end. The Hawks still lingered, choking off his money. He had trouble, near riverside, from the men who ran some of his operations, because they weren't making enough money, either. They wanted him to do something about the Hawks.

"He decided to send them a message." She shrugged. "I would have been just as happy to hit the men who were giving him trouble; I think Morse was sent to take out at least one of them. But that wasn't for me. He never trusted me," she added softly. "I—I don't know that he ever trusted Morse, but he trusted her to kill them.

"Me? He sent me across the river. Morse argued with me. I didn't have much to say." But she did, and she could remember the conversation, playing out as if the years had unwound the moment she had entered the Tower. "Well, not much that was useful," she added.

"I don't know why he sent me. I know that he didn't intend me to survive it." She shrugged. "I didn't really think about it, then. Later, yes. But even if I had, I don't think I would have cared."

The thunder was closer now.

"Kaylin," Tiamaris said. "The shadows are moving. I can see some light, now."

"Is that a good sign, or a bad sign?"

"It's generally safest to assume anything you see in the Tower is ambivalent. You see a storm of some kind, as well."

"Yes. It looks natural. For a value of natural that would give hives to the harbormaster." Her grip on Severn's hand tightened, and she realized that she had been speaking to Severn. It didn't matter who else might hear.

He turned to look at her. "You can see me clearly?"

"Yes."

"Can you see the rest of the City?"

He frowned, his eyes narrowing in something that was like a squint, but more subtle. "Not clearly. And it's not much of a City."

She shrugged. "It's what's *left* of a City. Is that better?"

"Is there a way out?"

"How should I know? We're surrounded on all sides, as far as I can see." She frowned. "You think I should know because it's all fashioned on my experience somehow."

"It's fashioned on the way you hold on to your experiences."

She nodded. "Can I make a way out?"

He laughed. "I think only you can."

"Ugh. Welcome to my life." She tried to smile, and found half of one; it was awkward.

"I told you," he said quietly, "I don't care what you did when you ran. I half expected you would die—" He looked away. "Because you weren't in Nightshade. I looked. I knew everywhere you might go. You didn't die. Whatever else you did doesn't matter to me."

"It matters to me," she said quietly.

"Yes, and it should—but I'm not you."

"I noticed." And sometimes, she was grateful for it. "It's different, for you. You wouldn't change anything. And me? I would change it *all*." She took a deep breath, and wiped dust off her hands. "But I can't."

"No. You can only do what the rest of us do—move forward."

"Tell that to the shadowstorm."

He laughed again. It helped.

"I'm not sure what we do next," she said.

"Get wet."

She grimaced, because the thunder was much closer. "We might be able to outrun it."

"Not unless you've gotten noticeably faster in the past few hours."

Had any of the standing structures had reliable roofs, it would have been no problem; they didn't. Ducking behind walls helped with the winds that the storm dragged in, but made it much harder in other ways. Tiamaris and Nightshade were still blind; Severn, less so—but his vision was dim compared to Kaylin's.

It would also have helped if the storm had been a natural one. The thunder and lightning weren't particularly ominous; the wind, however, was. It was, for one, as cold as winter wind, which made being soaked to the skin much less pleasant. The cold, however, wasn't as much of a problem as the force of the wind itself, which made it hard to stand upright. When they managed, stray rocks and flying debris hit them, knocking them off balance.

"If you can't see the City—"

"We can see the storm," Tiamaris replied curtly.

"But there's nothing in it that should be able to hit you; there are no rocks, walls or rubble where you're walking—"

"Congratulations. You have now been exposed to the logic and causality of the merely magical." He grimaced, and tried to wipe the edge off his very wet expression. "We do not doubt what you see. And given the number of flying items and the distinctly heavy weight of their blows, I do not believe that the shadow itself is attacking. Shadow usually takes a more ambulatory form."

"Meaning?"

"There are rocks, and we can't see them."

Severn, however, could. His vision had been clearing as the minutes passed. He couldn't see as far as Kaylin could, but at this particular moment, it didn't matter; visibility was less of an issue than trying to get out of the damn wind.

They'd stopped briefly to get the rope out of her backpack. It gave them a bit more freedom when linked to each other— though they still stayed close for fear of being separated.

Tiamaris, cursing, gave up and armored himself. Kaylin had seen him do it once before, in non-Dragon form—in Dragon form, armor wasn't really optional. Scales grew out of his body, enveloping—or shredding—cloth; they looked, when they finished emerging, like a very ornate set of strangely interlocked plate. The lower membranes of his eyes were high, but she could see that they were now bronze; he was no longer worried. Or angry.

Nightshade and Severn didn't have that option, and neither Nightshade nor Tiamaris had been willing to risk magic in the Tower. In the end, Kaylin weaved around walls as much as she could, trying to orient their passage so the walls provided a break from the flying stones.

She had crossed one familiar bridge to get here, and it had led to unfamiliar terrain, populated by corpses that only Kaylin could see and recognize. But they were half buried by this damn rubble in places they hadn't died. So: the rubble, the ruins, the stretch of uninhabited land—those were all somehow her.

And right now—she heard Nightshade grunt, and she felt the sharp pain in his left forearm through the bond of name that shouldn't have existed this far back in the past—what she needed was a solid structure in the middle of what was, for all intents and purposes, a desert or a wasteland.

She managed to find a corner of thick stone that rose into the sky like a wedge on two sides, and she drew Severn, Tiamaris, and Nightshade behind it. It helped, but the windbreak was small, and the noise of rock striking rock—and Tiamaris, who kept his broad back to the outside of the group—was loud enough that she would have had to shout to be heard, if she'd had much to say.

What do you damn well want? she thought, cursing in Leontine. *What do you want from me?*

The storm answered, and the answer was about as much use as she expected it would be. Rock struck her shoulder, sending her into Severn's chest. Clearly, questioning the Tower's motivations was not on the list of useful things Kaylin could do.

"I don't have a choice, Morse. If I don't go, I'll suffer for it."

"If you do go, you'll die."

"Tell me Barren won't kill me if I stay."

Morse shrugged. "He won't kill you if you stay."

"Say it as if you believe it."

"He *won't* kill you."

Elianne met, and held, Morse's gaze. Given the expression on the rest of Morse's rather reddened face, this took effort. She did stand far enough back from her that she could avoid either a snap-kick or a fist if it came to that. Morse wanted to hit something; she didn't want to hit Elianne. When Morse got angry enough, it didn't matter.

"I *want* to go," she said, more forcefully. "The Hawklord is perched at the height of his damn Tower while the rest of us are living in the dirt on the ground. I want him to have to deal with the ground."

"Why?"

"You know why—his damn Hawks are still lurking by the bridge. It's costing us—"

"That's why Barren wants to send a message. Why does it have to be you who carries it?"

"Because I'm good?" Elianne snapped, stung.

"Because you're stupid," Morse snapped back.

Fair enough. Kaylin wiped water out of her eyes, and pushed wet strands of hair to either side of her face. She had a bump on her forehead, and her arm now ached. If they couldn't get out of this storm, they would die here. Everyone, she thought, but Tiamaris.

There was enough flying debris that it was hard to see the sky clearly; it was impossible to see what lay across the broken horizon. She kicked the wall in frustration, and her foot slid across slick ground, unbalancing her. Severn caught her.

She looked at the ground beneath their feet, and frowned. It was wet—everything was, even Tiamaris—but it was the wrong consistency; nothing else had caused her boots to slide. Severn looked down, as well, and then he nodded.

"Help me clear the junk out of the way!" she shouted, because she had to shout to be heard.

He began to kick stones and dirt out of the way; the dirt was now mud. To her great relief, he didn't also kick a random exposed limb; there was no corpse where they were standing. But there was something that looked suspiciously like a very well-crafted trapdoor.

A trapdoor in the middle of the open air, in a howling storm, in the corner of the only standing walls at this edge of what had probably been a very large building. Down had not been the direction she wanted to go. But up required a building that was actually standing and in good enough repair that the floors hadn't rotted. Something like that might exist in the ruins of this City, but if it did, it was far enough away that it wasn't likely to offer much haven. Kaylin didn't believe in coincidences. Or miracles.

She did, on the other hand, believe in magic, and she expressed that belief in four official languages, until Tiamaris told her to stop.

Severn and Kaylin between them began to search along the seams of the door for anything that might be used to pull it up, which was awkward, because they were still linked together by the rope.

"What are you doing?" the Dragon Lord demanded.

"We're trying to find a way down. There's a—sorry—trapdoor of some kind under our feet."

"Made of stone?"

"Not usually, no."

"It feels like stone, to me," he replied, slightly testily. His eyes were now a bronze that was a little too dark for Kaylin's comfort—not that there was much comfort to be had at the moment.

"It's not stone—or at least it doesn't look like stone to me," was Kaylin's sharp reply. "I slid across it when I took too large a step."

Tiamaris nodded. "Move aside," he told her.

She started to argue, and decided there was no point. "There's not a lot of side to move *to.*"

"Then flatten yourselves as best you can against the wall. I would ask that you do the same, Lord Nightshade, but the risk is yours to take."

Kaylin could see the bare hint of Nightshade's enigmatic smile. He was Barrani, but his apparent concern for dignity and the appearance of power was absent; if it weren't for the gash across his cheek—a gash that was already fading, it had been so shallow—she would have sworn he was enjoying himself.

I am, he replied.

She swore.

And I believe that I will continue to do so for at least a little while longer. Do you know that I have never seen a Dragon Lord in human form take armor? I am aware that it is done—but it is seldom done. I have, as has Lord Tiamaris, ventured into Towers such as this—but never with this effect; they did not test me.

Because they weren't activated yet, Kaylin thought.

This Tower is strong, he said, his voice soft and smooth, because he didn't actually have to struggle to make it heard, *or you are.*

I cannot quite decide.

CHAPTER 21

Tiamaris, adorned by water, shone even in the gray and overcast light. Lightning, like gods blinking, flashed briefly above, and his armor left an afterimage in Kaylin's vision.

"Private?" he asked, as he positioned himself more or less above the patch of ground that had nearly dumped Kaylin on her backside.

She nodded, grimaced, and said, "Yes, there. More or less."

"More would be preferable."

She let Severn guide Tiamaris into the center of what did appear to be wooden slats, and nodded—which Severn at least could see—when it was time to stop fussing with his position. After which, Tiamaris took two steps backward. Rocks pinged off his armor.

He looked just beyond his feet, and his lips turned up at the corners in what was, for the Dragon Lord, an almost unpleasant smile. Kaylin pressed her back into what was left of a wall, dragging Severn with her; Nightshade stepped back, away from the wall's protection, the odd, fey smile still adorning his face.

The Dragon *breathed*. Steam rose instantly from the ground

around the circumference of the cone of flame that left his mouth, and Severn cursed in sharp and pointed Leontine as the wood in front of his feet began to blacken. The flames rolled up to the edges of Tiamaris's feet, but he wasn't apparently troubled by them.

She glanced at Tiamaris's face, which was once again impassive, and then took a tentative step toward the hole he'd made in the flooring. "There are stairs," she said. "Going down. Why is it *always* down?"

"Is it?" Nightshade asked, raising a dark brow.

"Welcome to my world," she replied, as she placed one foot on the first step. "There's a bit of light farther ahead; there's not a lot of light, otherwise. I don't suppose you'd care—"

"We'll use magic if there's cause," Tiamaris replied. Which meant, essentially, no. "There's light—and water—from the hole. It will do for some time. Walk," he added, "with care."

She would have told him she always did, but she was no longer certain it was true.

The stairs, unlike the trapdoor, if that's what the flooring was, were solid stone, and they went down in a spiral that hugged one smooth, central pillar to Kaylin's right. They were wide enough to fit two abreast, but they had no rails, and the pillar was the only wall available. On the other side, to Kaylin's left, it was dark. Dark enough that she couldn't immediately look down to see the length of the drop if she happened to misstep.

They walked down single file.

"What does this look like to you?" Kaylin asked Tiamaris.

"Stairs," he replied. "Solid stone. There is one central supporting pillar."

They were—finally—seeing the same thing. She started to say as much and then stopped and looked at the surface of the wall beneath her palm. "What's—what do you see on the wall?" she asked him. She could see, in a spiral that paralleled the stairs themselves, a line of carved runes. They weren't Elantran; they weren't regular enough. But the lines, strokes, dots, and curves of these runes reminded her, vaguely, of Barrani. Or, she thought, with less joy, of the marks on her skin.

He turned to look. "Besides your hand?"

"Very funny. And I thought Dragons had no sense of humor."

"We don't." He frowned, and the frown deepened as he stared. "Yes," he finally said. "I see the runes."

"Tell me they aren't following my hand."

"They can't be. Either you're carving them, somehow, as you walk, or you are uncovering them by touch. Neither option is particularly comforting," he added, as he reached out and touched the wall. His hand rested on the rock about a foot above where hers had touched it, and her touch was very easy to see, given the words that seemed to run in its wake. She watched Tiamaris's hand move the length of three steps as he descended, which was awkward, given the room on the stairs. She had to back up, and she felt Severn's grip tighten as he followed.

Tiamaris frowned, and retraced his steps. His hand remained against the surface of the wall as he descended again. He did this four times, and then he studied the wall in silence.

"Yes," Lord Nightshade said, although Tiamaris asked no question. "There is an impression."

"It is not—quite—the same."

"No, and it is not as deep or as refined. But it *is* there." The Barrani Lord, not yet Outcaste from the High Court, raised his own hand; it hovered above the smooth surface of unblemished stone for just a minute, and then fell once again to his side. "I think I will not repeat the exercise."

Tiamaris nodded, as if he were barely paying attention—in Kaylin's opinion, because he was. "Can you read this, Private?" he asked her quietly.

"No. It's not—"

She stopped. She couldn't read what she had left behind on the wall. She could, however, read what he had. It was High Barrani, and the runes were rigid and uniform, although they weren't deep.

"Severn?" she said, after a moment.

"I can't read them," he replied.

"But it's—"

"Yes?"

"It looks—to me—like High Barrani."

"Interesting," the Dragon Lord replied, for Severn merely nodded and remained silent. "I cannot read what I in theory placed there. What does it say?"

"Umm."

He raised a brow over a bronze eye.

"It's not exactly a sentence."

"What, exactly, is it?"

"Words. Associative words," she added quickly, as the brow rose slightly higher. "I think… *Flight. Wind. Fire.*" She hesitated again, and then, in a more firm voice, said, *"Breath. Stone."*

"I…see." He lifted his hand, and let it drop to his side.

"Good. Because I don't. Is this supposed to be a description?"

"In all probability."

"No mention of hoards, if that's any indication of completeness."

"It is, and I wasn't aware that you understood that concept."

She ignored the small dig at her academic reputation, in part because she was still staring at the shallow marks in the wall left by his hand. "What do they look like, to you?"

"Gibberish," he replied.

"And mine?"

"Those," he replied, "look very much—to my eye—like the marks." He glanced at Nightshade, and then shrugged.

"Did any of this happen to you when you tried to enter a Tower?"

"No. But as I said, the experience of breaching a Tower is unique—no two Towers will be the same."

"And no two visits?"

"If you can enter—and leave—a Tower in one piece, the second visit will be relatively benign."

"Relatively?"

"The second time, it's only external things that will try to kill you. A statue will start to move. The ceiling might dislodge a chunk of stone over your head. The carpets will rise—slightly—to trip you."

"So if I came back here—"

"If you can leave," he interjected.

"Then I wouldn't have to go through this again?"

"No."

"Good." To be fair, she never intended to enter another Tower again for as long as she lived. If she got out of this one.

Neither Severn nor Nightshade touched the walls on the way down. Kaylin half regretted it; she was curious, now, to see what the walls would say in the wake of their touch. Not, however, curious enough to actually ask them to try it.

She did, however, have to touch the wall again, and this time she could feel stone shifting and flowing beneath her palm, as if it were a slow-moving, very thick liquid.

"If these were the High Halls," she said to Severn, "we'd hear ferals, soon."

"These are not the High Halls," he replied, "and I *believe* that discussing them is forbidden by the Lord of the High Court."

"Yes, but—" She glanced at Nightshade and reddened. "Sorry. Thinking out loud."

Nightshade raised a brow. "I am familiar," he told her quietly, "with the High Halls, as you are no doubt aware."

She nodded. "But there's a Tower in the High Halls—" and stopped.

He didn't miss a step, but his gaze sharpened. "There is," he said at last. "It is not thought of in the same way as the Towers here are. It is part of the Halls, and it serves a function."

"A test of Name."

"Indeed. You have seen them." It wasn't a question.

She nodded.

"And you are here."

She nodded again, and then added, "Humans don't have true names."

"So it is said. But of you, Kaylin Neya? I feel that it is perhaps less true than you know. If you have passed the test of Name, and you are here—and I admit the thought is strangely dissonant—then you have some experience with the nature of these buildings. But the High Halls do not serve the same function as the Towers. It was not thought that the Towers served any function at all, although I am revising that opinion as we progress. Continue to be cautious."

She was peering into the darkness to her side. "Tiamaris, what can you see?"

"In the darkness?"

She nodded.

"Darkness. If there is shadow, there, it is not moving now."

"Good. Because I think we're almost at the bottom."

"Oh?"

"There are no more words being written. The wall has stayed smooth for the last five or six steps."

They did not reach the bottom; the stairs seemed to descend in the same spiral, wound around the same pillar, for as far as the eye could see. Not that it could see that far. They did, however, reach a door that was slightly recessed into the curve of the central pillar itself. It was neither wide nor particularly tall, which in this case meant that Kaylin could fit quite comfortably through its frame, and everyone else would have to crouch.

The door, however, appeared to be made of stone, and if there were any hinges or handles, they weren't immediately obvious— where immediate was a matter of long minutes spent pressing against seams or grooves.

"Down?" Kaylin finally said.

"No," Tiamaris replied. "In as much as the Tower serves as guide, I would say that this is the only door we will find, no matter how long we walk."

"It's not much of a door."

"It's not much of a Tower, if you speak of simple architecture. Figure out how to open it. We'll wait."

She was almost surprised. "Was that an attempt at humor?"

"It *is* possible."

She laughed. "Severn, help me push."

Pushing did not, in fact, yield any better results. Kaylin stared at the door for a long, long moment, and then she swore in Leontine. Lifting her palm, she placed it flat against the center of the door, at shoulder height. The door began to glow.

"It's warded," she said. "Can you see it—"

"Glow?"

She nodded.

"Yes."

"Good. It doesn't appear to be opening. I think it's an *old* ward." Old wards required keys; they were usually—although not always—words. New wards were more complicated, and they were written—or rewritten—to recognize the hands pressed against them. Or to allow all hands to activate them, or a specific subset of hands—divided along racial lines, in many cases; divided along age or gender, in others.

This was apparently due to great advances in modern magic and magical theory. Clearly the Tower was not interested in keeping up appearances. Kaylin began to speak. She tried several obvious words—open, entry, passage—in all of the languages she knew. She tried several less obvious words when she'd hit the point of frustration that usually devolved into cursing. Nothing worked.

"If I may make a suggestion?" Nightshade said quietly.

She glanced at him, bit back all sarcastic retort, and nodded grimly.

"I believe the words you might require were given to you on your walk here."

"Given—" Her eyes rounded slightly. She looked at the trail of runes that had appeared on the Tower walls in the wake of her hand, and cringed. "I can't read them," she told him. "*Tiamaris* can't read them. The Arkon probably could—"

Nightshade's eyes had shaded from green to an odd shade of blue. It was not quite the sapphire that spoke of anger in the

Barrani, but there was some element of concern in the color. "The Arkon? You *know* the Arkon?"

"That's too strong a word. I've met him, yes."

"And he might be able to read what you've written. Before you ask," he added, because she was about to, "I cannot."

"Then we are so screwed," Kaylin replied. "Unless anyone else has any ideas."

Tiamaris cleared his throat. "I believe," he said quietly, "that I might. Your hand, Private?"

"My hand? Oh." She withdrew it, and the light from the door faded. Backing down the stairs, she made room for Tiamaris, who was still covered in dragon plate. He placed his palm roughly where hers had rested. "You might wish," he told her, "to cover your ears."

She took his meaning immediately, and grimaced, lifting her hands to cover her ears. "It never helps," she told him, although she tried anyway. Dragon voices were *loud*. And if she'd had any hope that she'd misunderstood him, he dashed it instantly.

He spoke in his native tongue. She felt the syllables of each word reverberate in the air around her; it also felt as if they were shaking the stairs. Severn caught her arm, and drew her toward him, a few steps down from where Tiamaris now confronted a closed, hingeless door made entirely of stone. Nightshade chose to stand a few stairs above the Dragon Lord, watching—and listening—with care. She didn't ask him if he understood what was said; she knew he didn't. She could feel elements of his frustration war with his fascination; the fascination won.

"What are you saying?" Kaylin asked Tiamaris, when he paused.

"I am attempting," he said, without taking his eyes off the door, "to repeat the words that you said were engraved by my touch in the wall."

"I don't think they were in Dragon."

"How would you know?"

"I can't read Dragon." She had not, to the best of her knowledge, ever seen it written.

He laughed. "Lord Nightshade couldn't read what was engraved by my touch, either. Nor could the Corporal. I couldn't read it, and I assure you that inasmuch as my native language has a written form, I *am* conversant with it."

"You want me to go back up the stairs and repeat what I read?"

"No. My memory is not *that* poor."

Dragons.

"Put your hand on the door, Private."

Wall she wanted to say. She didn't, because he was in a foul enough mood he'd probably step on her foot—and break it. Instead, she placed her palm on the door. It began to glow again, and she allowed herself the luxury of a single Leontine word.

He placed his hand *over* hers, enveloping it completely. She grimaced; she could only cover *one* ear, and she knew, from the way he drew breath, that he was about to speak Dragon again.

He did. It was just as painful, but this time, she felt the words reverberate throughout the whole of her body, as if she were a badly designed gong, and each syllable was a clapper. As they did, she *understood* them. Dragon wasn't an official language—in part because the Emperor was rumored to have a strong aversion to the mangled babbling of any other race's attempts at producing the linguistic sounds. These were not, therefore, words that she knew the way she knew Leontine, Barrani or Aerian.

I could read them.

Yes. But she could no longer remember how; she could not clearly recall what they looked like, and she should have—her training was not so poor that something that significant should have slipped away in an immediate fog. It didn't matter. She listened to words that she knew, even if she didn't actually *recognize* them.

Flight was there, for a moment, and she knew it as if its gift had always been hers. It wasn't the industrious flight of bees, or the swift and sudden grace of bird's fall; it was freedom, dominance, majesty.

Fire was breath, heart, voice; it wasn't power, not in the way that mortals feared. That was tooth and claw and scale; that was the whole of their natural form. And yet they walked as almost-humans, speaking in their slight, quavering voices, forsaking birth and…life…and war.

Stone was not the rock of the quarry, or the rock of the buildings in which the Emperor lived and from which he ruled; it was not the stone of the Aerie, either. It was not—in any sense of the word—stone as Kaylin understood it. Birth, she thought; flesh. The beginning of life. Tiamaris's voice broke over the syllables, he spoke them so harshly.

It should have been finished then. She waited for silence, the flat of one palm covering one ear to dampen the bass that was shaking her body. It didn't come. Instead, Tiamaris continued to speak, and she regretted her earlier, flippant words, because she felt the truth of the word that slipped beneath her conscious understanding of language.

Hoard was all desire, all love, all focus. She could feel it as dream, bright, sharp, and bitterly unfulfilled, and it felt deeper, stronger, and lonelier than *any* dream she had ever—in waking—given all of her thought to. Shifting her gaze away from the door for the first time, she looked at Tiamaris's face. What he had been unwilling to consign to the wall, he now offered the door in its stiff and implacable state.

"Don't," she told him, raising her voice to be heard, although she wasn't sure by who. "I understand what it wants, now. I understand what to give it."

His hand tightened, crushing hers. "You have given it enough, in your openness and your ignorance." He spoke, of course, of the corpses and the ruined, lifeless cityscape. She accepted it.

It stung anyway. But she knew that it wasn't meant to; she saw the concern in his expression so clearly, he might have been Severn. "I can do this," she told him, trying to lift her hand in order to force his away from the glowing surface of the door. She saw that in the light, the stone had begun a slow swirling motion. "Tiamaris—I have a name. I can—"

"No." He spoke in Dragon, and looked above her head to Severn, who hesitated for a moment before he reached up to touch her shoulders.

"I will not give it my name. I am not afraid to give it anything else." This, Tiamaris said in Elantran. He didn't even pretend that he believed she couldn't—or shouldn't—understand him.

"I've already—"

"Yes. How much *more* can you expose?"

When she failed to answer, he offered her a rare smile. "I know who I am, Kaylin. It has been many, many years since I have feared it."

She wanted to tell him that she felt no fear. But he was willing to take a risk in full knowledge that she had taken only blindly; she couldn't bring herself to dishonor that determination with a lie. She forced her hand to lie flat against the surface of the door; it was no longer the cold, smooth gray of stone. Light moved beneath it, as if it were made of glass.

He continued to speak, but the words were grim and harsh; he had forsaken all hope of hoard, and this was in his voice. He had told her once in a different time that there were reasons so few of the Dragons served the Emperor, and she understood now why. Had serving the Emperor meant the death of her dreams and her hopes, she would—like so many of Tiamaris's kin—have died.

But he served, and he served in ways that she was not competent to serve. He had given up so much; she dreaded taking lessons to learn how to keep her mouth shut. She had never felt so small and so petty before.

No, she thought, as the door began to glow far more brightly, that wasn't true. But each return to that self-awareness always struck her like this. *I'm not worthy*. And the only way to change that if it was so unpleasant? To *become* worthy. Which was a lot like work, but worse.

She opened her mouth to speak because the silence she was in was so bitter, and bit back words with effort; they would have been spoken to make herself feel better; they wouldn't have helped Tiamaris.

But he didn't seem to need help. He spoke and she cringed until the moment the door, now shining beneath the combined touch of both of their hands, shone so brightly she had to shut her eyes.

Which was good, because the damn thing shattered.

She heard it crack, and she heard the timbre of Tiamaris's voice shift and tunnel into a single syllable that reverberated throughout her body; she had only enough time to stiffen before she felt the surface of what had once been stone break beneath her palm—and beneath his spread fingers. Glass—if it was glass—drove itself into her hand like sharp, misshapen teeth, and she let loose a volley of Leontine.

Severn caught her wrist as Tiamaris lifted his hand.

"I would think it inadvisable," Nightshade said quietly, "to offer the Tower your blood."

It was nice to know that Barrani Lords were consistent in their ability to offer helpful advice. Kaylin stopped herself from snarling, largely because Severn was removing a large shard of glass. "It's not the first Tower I've bled in," she snapped, before remembering that he didn't—yet—know.

But he did, now. She cursed him in four languages, and in silence, and he smiled. It was a thin, blue-eyed smile, but he was genuinely amused.

"She is not the only person," Tiamaris said drily, examining the tips of his fingers, "who has fallen foul of that advice. It is," he added, glancing at Kaylin, "good advice."

"I'll try to avoid cracking solid stone doors in the future," she said with a grimace. Severn was bandaging her hand. She didn't ask him with what. It wasn't a deep cut, and it had looked—for the seconds it was exposed—like a clean one.

"If you're finished?" the Dragon asked Severn. Severn raised a brow. "I believe the door is open."

"It's unlikely to close soon."

Given that it was a gaping, slightly jagged door-shaped hole, Tiamaris nodded. But Nightshade said, "It is a Tower."

They moved.

Because it was a Tower, Kaylin didn't expect much continuity between what was on one side of the door and what was on the other. Which was good, because there wasn't any.

Grass spread out before them like a well-tended carpet. The bits beneath their feet were crushed by Tiamaris's weight. The sun was high, and the sky was the clear azure that happens only on a perfect day. In the distance, trees stood like windbreaks, and the sounds of a river could be heard at their back.

Kaylin turned. Sure enough, there *was* a river. It had one rickety, wooden bridge above it in a distance that was almost as far away as the trees, but in the opposite direction. "You can see the grass?" she asked, with just a trace of anxiety.

Tiamaris nodded.

"Severn? Nightshade?"

The Barrani Lord did not seem to be offended at the lack of affixed rank. His eyes were a mix of green-blue that meant alertness, but offered no danger.

"Yes," he said quietly—for their benefit, not hers. "I can see grass. There are trees in the distance, and a river."

"Do you recognize the river?" Kaylin asked him.

"Yes."

"Good. I don't."

He raised one brow. "Do you not?"

"I've never traveled outside of the City."

"You wouldn't have to," he replied quietly. "It is the *Abiliani.*"

"The what?"

He raised a brow, and the strangely pronounced word suddenly came into focus. "It's the *Ablayne?*"

"I believe that is how it is often pronounced by your kind."

She stared at him for a long moment. "Do you even remember a time when there was no City here?"

"No. Nor do I believe Lord Tiamaris does."

She glanced at the Dragon Lord.

"He is correct," Tiamaris replied. "But we are all, now, in the Tower. What we see reflects some amalgamation of the Tower and ourselves."

"Where do we go from here?" she asked him.

"The trees," he replied.

But Severn was gazing beyond the trees. Beyond, and above. She touched his shoulder to get his attention, and instead of looking at her, he lifted a hand and pointed to the Southern Ridge. It was part of Elantra, but the buildings and the horizon they made usually obliterated most of its majestic rise. Here, nothing impeded the view of the sharp, stone cliff with its almost invisible caves.

"They're not far," she told him quietly. "But we don't have much way of scaling the cliff face."

"We'll worry about that when we get there."

It was a pleasant walk, as they'd dispensed with the rope linking them. It was not even, in Kaylin's experience, particularly grueling; her daily patrols covered more distance, if not more ground. No one spoke, but no one felt the need to speak; there was nothing on the horizon for as far as the eye could see that posed much of a threat. The grass bothered Kaylin, though. It continued, the perfect representation of a rich person's lawn, in its green stretch. There were no flowers, no weeds, no stones—nothing to break it at all. There was also no sign of what had done the work to keep it in such an unnatural state.

She knew it wasn't real; she just wanted *more* reality. Not that she was grading the Tower's presentation, but still. Severn, judging from his minute frown, had noticed; Nightshade, as guarded as any Barrani stranger, seemed above noticing, and Tiamaris? It escaped his attention. The Southern Ridge did not.

Nor did the shadows that began to flit across grass as they approached the foot of the cliff. Kaylin looked up instantly, squinting against the sunlight that blanketed the cliff face. She could see nothing in the sky that cast those shadows, but they continued their movement, from one side of the ridge to the other.

They weren't uniform, and they weren't entirely regular, but she recognized them; they were what sun and distance made of Aerian wings, of Aerians in lazy flight. There was no stop and start; the Aerians that she couldn't see except in the afterthought of cast shadow, were patrolling the ridge from above. They never patrolled it on foot; there was no point. No one approached the ridge from the ground.

No one, she thought with a grimace, sane.

"Are there stairs?" Lord Nightshade asked.

"Are their Aerians, in your time?"

"There are."

"And they live in your City?"

"No. Our City does not extend this far. They live...separate from it."

"The High Lord accepts that?"

"Let us just say that the structural changes required to affect a difference would significantly alter the shape of the City he rules. He has not—yet—decided that it is necessary."

"Do they cause him any trouble?"

"None."

"Beyond the irritation of their independence."

He glanced at her, and smiled. "Beyond that. But for a man accustomed to the absolute obedience that comes with power, that is more than enough. In my world—and not the Tower's—they are not friendly. They are not actively hostile, but you will find no easy way up to the aeries."

"The Aerians," Tiamaris said quietly, "would never agree to serve those bound to land."

Nightshade nodded. "Nor would we, had we their ability. It is not in our nature to serve."

When they reached the foot of the cliff, they stopped. The sun had neither risen nor fallen during their walk, as if it were an artist's perfect rendition of the object, and not the object itself. Like props, Kaylin thought. She walked to the base of the cliff, where rock gave way suddenly to grass, looking for some sign of stairs or a path cut into the side of the stone; she wasn't terribly surprised when she found none.

Because this cliff could be climbed. It could be—with difficulty and not a little risk—climbed by her. She began to walk again, looking for the best place to start, and watching the possible hand and footholds become smaller and smaller as they ascended. Shrugging her shoulders out of her pack, she knelt, untying her regulation boots. She knotted them together by their laces and dropped them into the pack.

Remembering, as she did, another climb, a different impossible height to scale. At the top of it waited the last assignment she had accepted from Barren—the one that had caused the last big argument with Morse. She was careful, even in thought, not to call it a fight, because Morse did *not* lose fights, and Kaylin had walked—not limped, not bled—out of the apartment that had been their home for six months. Her face had been white and red with the imprint of Morse's open palm and her own anger.

That had lasted as she'd walked into the intermittent flow of people in the streets of Barren, evaporating only as she approached the bridge. She stood to one side of it, near the bank of the river, looking across at the outer City. Barren's men had been told she was passing through; they weren't to hassle her—but she wasn't to linger. It looked bad.

She hadn't much cared what it *looked* like, then. She'd probably picked a fight with his thugs just by walking halfway across the damn bridge four times before turning back, but it was a fight she could more or less finish if she had to, so it didn't frighten her.

The City did. She wasn't sure why. Maybe she thought they would notice that she didn't belong. Maybe they would notice *why*.

But…maybe they *wouldn't*.

The second thought had frightened her more, but she couldn't have said why.

Severn joined her, and she startled. "Climbing?"

"I can, yes. There don't seem to be stairs or portals. I'm not complaining about the lack of portals," she added quickly, just in case the Tower was listening.

Severn chuckled. He'd been scanning the rocks, as well, but he said nothing, merely waited for Kaylin to find her first hand-hold and start.

But as she did, the hair on the back of her neck began to rise, and she froze, one foot on the ground, and one already rounding to accommodate both her weight and the uneven surface of a large rock.

CHAPTER 22

Tiamaris roared, and the wind that howled and whistled fell silent, as if in embarrassment at the inevitable comparison. Kaylin's foot found solid ground as she turned; her hand still touched the cool surface of rock.

Tiamaris looked at her, and then craned his neck, briefly, toward the height of the cliff, where the aeries could barely be seen from their vantage. "I do not think," he said, with a very odd smile, "that that will be necessary." His eyes were gold, and they shone.

She started to speak, stopped, and then said, "Lord Nightshade, I'd advise you to move." The Barrani Lord was perhaps ten feet away from the Dragon Lord. He raised a dark brow, and then glanced at Tiamaris. When he backed away, he moved slowly and gracefully, but he did move, although Kaylin could feel his stiff reluctance to take advice from…mortals. He came, however, to stand between Kaylin and Severn, the cliff face at his back.

Tiamaris stretched his arms to the sides; wind caught his hair, pulling at it as if it were a small, nagging child who wanted attention *now*. He felt it; his smile shifted, becoming, for a moment, indulgent. "Private," he said, "this is the heart of a Tower. It exists in the gap between worlds.

"There is no Emperor here. There is no law."

She knew what he intended before his body began the shimmering and vaguely terrifying process of shedding humanity in favor of the primal power of the true Dragon form. "You have—I am told, with frequency—spent many years cajoling any Aerian unwise or unfortunate enough to stand his ground to take you up into the air."

She winced. "They're exaggerating."

Tiamaris fell forward, his hands splayed flat against the unnatural grass in the lee of the great, stone cliff face. Those hands grew, changing shape and texture. The mail of gauntlets that were entirely composed of scale gave way to scales, and to claws, each much longer than his fingers had been. His neck stretched as his body did; his legs, like his hands, seemed to absorb the bronze plates that had been greaves, and anything bootlike or bootshaped moved fluidly away from his midsection, transforming as it did into the hind legs of a giant lizard.

Not that she would ever *use* that word where he could hear it.

Wings unfurled from his back, breaking through his shoulder blades as if they had just fled jail time. They went on forever, catching sunlight and reflecting it in a spray across the short grass Tiamaris was crushing simply by existing.

He roared again, and in some ways it was a comfort—it was almost the same sound that he had uttered to get her attention the first time. Deeper, yes, and rumbling—but it was recognizably his voice. And when he lifted the jaw that had opened on that roar, he swung his massive head toward her. His eyes were the size of her fists. Or maybe Severn's.

"Come, Private. You like to fly, and you have *never* flown like this." He lowered his neck, stretching it so that she could approach. She did, but she hesitated. "I don't—I can't—ride," she finally confessed. "The Aerians carried me. But horses tend to throw me just for the fun of it. Or step on my feet when their trainers aren't looking."

He chuckled. The ground shook. "They tend to run screaming from me. I will not throw you. I will attempt to catch you
if you fall."

She looked pointedly at the mess his claws were making of the
ground. "You get a lot of practice catching things you *aren't*
trying to kill?"

"No." He laughed at the sour expression that didn't quite hide
her growing excitement. "Climb up on the back of my neck.
Avoid the pinions. They move."

"What—what about the others?"

He snorted, and a plume of smoke wafted in the air in front
of his nostrils. He ate it. "I will barely feel their weight, if they
can hold on. Come—we are meant to reach the top."

"Is it wise, Lord Tiamaris, to play into the Tower's demands?"

"Never," the Dragon Lord replied gravely. "But the Tower has
not yet heard ours. Come, Nightshade. The air is alive with magic.
Can you not feel it?"

"I feel it," was the quiet reply. "But it feels wild, and the taint
of shadow is strong in it."

"It is strong," Tiamaris replied, "in all of the living, be they
immortal or no. Let us see what waits above."

Lord Nightshade nodded, but he let Kaylin and Severn find a
place on the Dragon's back first.

"Kaylin," Lord Nightshade said, as he joined them. His voice
was quiet. It was almost inaudible. Had he been any other man,
she would have missed the sound of her name. But she turned,
craning her neck to the side to meet his gaze; his eyes were the
clear blue of sky. It was not a color she recognized in Barrani eyes,
and she had no ready translation for it.

"The Tower is not yet done."

She would have snorted, but he was Barrani; she contented
herself with a nod instead, as the flesh beneath her moved. Her
hands tightened. Here, the scales were small enough they felt
smooth as snake's skin; they looked slippery, but that was sun.

Tiamaris was no longer entirely bronze, but the red of the night in the fiefs was absent.

"When it is, there is a choice to be made."

"How do you know?"

"It is the nature of testing, and this Tower appears to be testing you. You, and the Dragon Lord."

"But—"

"He is at ease, here."

He wasn't, but she didn't say as much.

"Your choice will define the Tower. Be wary. Let it *be* your choice."

"And not the Tower's?"

He nodded. "You have left blood here. Unwise, but perhaps necessary." He spoke again, but this time she lost the words to the roar of Dragon and the breathless harmony of the wind his flight caused.

It didn't matter. They rose. She could feel the shift of Dragon musculature beneath her legs, and the smooth, supple surface of scales beneath hands that gripped too tightly. She could see the world shrink into a sea of green, and regretted bitterly the lack of City streets and tall buildings, because she had always judged her height above the ground by their size.

Tiamaris roared and roared, his voice a rumble that shook them all, defying both wind and gravity. Kaylin had never liked the sound of horns; they made her think of cows trying—and failing—to be musical. But she thought that this was what horns wanted to be: this arresting, this momentarily all encompassing.

The cliffs rose forever. Tiamaris followed them, but only barely; he didn't seem eager to land. And why would he? How often did he have the freedom of the skies? He spoke to the land from above, and his voice traveled, bouncing off the cliff face and into the darkness of the approaching Aerie.

But eventually, he turned toward it. It was not built in a way that would allow Dragons easy access; he might have been able to walk in, with his wings furled tightly across his shoulders. There was, however, a long path to the rounded and carved entrance—

again, it was meant for Aerians, who were human in size and shape if you ignored their wings. But if Dragons were power and majesty, they were also graceful. He made the landing, and a spray of loose pebbles flew, wingless, in arcs behind them, toward the ground.

"Is this," he asked, when he had resumed his human form, complete with the bronzed plate scales, "the Aerie that you're familiar with?"

She nodded. "They built the cave mouth so that it looked like an arch. It's not a bear cave."

"You've seen a bear cave?"

"Figure of speech."

He chuckled. His eyes were a glowing gold. "Shall we enter, then?"

The cave face that presented itself vanished the minute the last of the light did. Fire, appearing in brief gusts, and always aimed down or away from the group, provided illumination for Kaylin until the moment Tiamaris decided that he was not a walking, intermittent torch. Then there was light, and it was a mage's light. She felt the sharp shock of Nightshade's surprise and disapproval.

Hers was louder. "Tiamaris—"

The Dragon snorted. "The passage we are in continues for some way. If we are not to be here all week, some light is required for both you and the Corporal." He lifted a hand and traced the cave wall; Kaylin half expected to see words follow in the wake of his touch. These walls, however, didn't change. "Where does this go?"

"I don't know. I only came here a couple of times, and I wasn't given free run of the Aerie. They thought I'd take a wrong turn and dump myself off the ridge, which Cliff said would be severely career limiting. But…I don't think any of the passages were this long. There should be branches into other caverns and nesting zones."

As if it could hear her words, the cavern now blurred; speech blurred with it, as if time itself had suddenly unwound. The strangest thing about the distortion was Tiamaris's light; its glow was a steady warmth that did not shift or change at all. When it was over, the tunnel was as she remembered it from her previous visits, more or less. Nightshade was staring at her so intently her cheek warmed. Unfortunately, it was the one that bore the mark he had not yet placed there in his own time. "Where," he asked gravely, "should we now go?"

Tiamaris looked at Kaylin. "Private," the bastard said, "the lead is yours."

She chose, after passing two branches, to veer to the right. It was arbitrary; she honestly didn't remember where anything led—but if she hadn't entirely lost her bearings, right was central; left eventually led to the small windows and openings that were seldom used except in emergency—fires being one. War, although she wasn't aware of any major wars fought by Aerians, being the other. In either case, she didn't want to give the Tower any ideas.

The inner passages led to living quarters, such as they were; the widest part of the inner cavern would be several stories high, like a set of connected apartments around an inner courtyard—but missing one exterior wall. The Aerians might have valued privacy, but they didn't actually *have* a lot of it.

But the nesting area was a smaller series of rooms with lower ceilings and sandy floors; it maintained heat. Why they needed heat, she wasn't certain; she understood that this is what chickens and other birds wanted—but Aerian babies were born the normal way. More or less.

Tiamaris caught her shoulder just before the passage widened. "Something," he said softly, "is not right here. Lord Nightshade?" Tiamaris, hand on the wall, turned to the Barrani Lord.

Lord Nightshade nodded. "I sense them," he said softly.

"Sense what?" Kaylin asked.

"The shadows," was his quiet reply. "You cannot sense them, Kaylin?"

"I—" She closed her eyes. But her skin had been tingling slightly since before Tiamaris had gone Dragon; nothing felt different to her. "No." Eyes still closed, she reached out and touched solid rock. "I feel the Aerie." She turned, as she so often did, to Severn, and opened her eyes. It was dark in the passage, but Tiamaris's spell still brought shape to the gray.

"I see the Aerie." His voice was soft; he didn't trust what he saw.

Fair enough. In this place, trusting what you saw was probably death. She continued down the passage. Tiamaris stepped beside her as it widened, and they walked two abreast, following its gentle, upward slope. She frowned, and slowed.

"Private?"

"I don't remember the passages sloping up like this."

"That," he replied gravely, "is unfortunate, because I do."

"You've been in the Aerie? But how did you get—"

"Not the Aerian one. *Aerie* is, in fact, a more general word." His smile, in the scant light, was all teeth, and they looked preternaturally sharp. "I was born in one."

"This isn't—"

He lifted his head and fire spread itself in a thin, orange veil across the nubbled height of the ceiling. Above their head, writing appeared in glowing, gold letters. They were Barrani words, but they weren't sentences; they were single runes. Sun. Wings. Claws. It looked like a child's vocabulary.

Her eyes narrowed slightly as the letters dimmed.

"They're sensitive to heat," Tiamaris said, also gazing up. "And were meant to encourage the very young to use their breath. Learning to do so, and exercising the ability, is onerous for the young, and the young are famously lazy."

"But these halls are people sized."

"Their breath is not the only ability they were encouraged to use," he replied. "And many games were played in mazes such as these, and just beyond. Hiding, if you will. One of the old Dragons who was famously indulgent used to chase us. We'd lie in wait, thinking ourselves very clever while we planned ambush after ambush.

"You cannot imagine how cramped the smaller tunnels became," he added, in a tone of voice she had never heard him use.

"And during one of those occupations, a number of hatchlings became stuck. There was quite a ruckus before they pulled down a small part of the wall."

"The hatchlings could pull down a *wall?*"

"Not an entire wall, no. But enough of one." He lowered his gaze. "These halls remind me of those ones. I do not think it accidental."

"But it's the Southern Ridge."

"Yes. And I think that no accident, either. Let me make a suggestion. When the halls are familiar to me, I will lead. Where they differ, we can confer." He led. She followed.

The halls were an amalgamation of a Dragon's memories and a human's, and the human memory was sketchy, at best. Kaylin took mental note of the shifts and changes, puzzling her way to something that she hoped would resemble an explanation at the end of their walk.

When they reached the foot of the stairs, however, she stopped. There had been no stairs—that she could recall—in the Aerie. "Tiamaris?"

"I believe, if you study them—" and here, he brightened the magical light "—you will recognize them. The guardrails—and attendant guards—are absent, and the walls are entirely wrong, but the design of the steps, the width, and the height, you should know."

She didn't spend a lot of time studying—or measuring—staircases. She usually ran up—or down—them, in a blind rush to get somewhere else. Instead of telling him as much, she backed up, jostling Severn and Nightshade as she did. "Sec," she told them, and she made a direct run at, and up, the stairs.

And yes, steps beneath her boots, she *did* recognize them. They were the Tower stairs in the Halls of Law. She had run up them, late, more times than she cared to remember; she had all but crawled down them after interminably long debriefings in which she felt about as appreciated as a cockroach, albeit in better shape. She took the turns the same way she always did; she didn't stumble and she didn't find that they opened up into any strange passages.

But she did stop before she reached the top, and she turned to glance back. Tiamaris looked like thunder would if it had a face.

"*What* do you think you're *doing?*"

She mumbled an apology. "I wanted to see if they were the right stairs," she said, by way of explanation. If he'd been her teacher, she'd have failed the course on the spot. "But you're right—these are the stairs to the Hawklord's Tower."

"Which we do not currently inhabit. You have no idea what could have met you on the stairs on your run up." He didn't raise his voice; he didn't have to. The stairs rumbled with the force of his words.

She mumbled another apology. He glared. But he joined her, and he allowed her to walk a step—not more—ahead of him. She climbed; everyone else followed. But they followed in silence, like natural shadow, until they reached the flat landing in front of the Hawklord's doors. The doors were familiar; they were well cared for, but showed age as if age were majesty. And they sported the doorward that she had come to hate during her first week here.

No, not here. *Not* here.

She lifted a hand; it hovered above the ward that crossed the closed door.

"Kaylin—" Severn caught her wrist. "Look at the ward."

She did. "It's the doorward."

"Not to my eyes. Lord Tiamaris?"

Tiamaris frowned. "Private," he told Kaylin softly. "Let me open the door." It wasn't a request. On any other day Kaylin would have agreed with alacrity.

"You think you can safely touch this ward?"

"Ah. No, you misunderstand me." He lifted his arm, drew it back, and drove it into the planks. It took him five attempts to break through the wood, the door was that solid. As he was pulling what remained off the hinges, Kaylin said, "Well, that works. I don't suppose I could get you to try that when we get back home?"

He offered her the glimmer of a smile. "You could," he said, with some satisfaction. "It's not as if I depend on the salary."

★ ★ ★

When the door frame was clear, except for stubborn, sharp splinters, Tiamaris shone a light into the room. It was, more or less, the room Kaylin remembered, at least at first glance.

The dome was there, its stone petals closed to the sky; windows let in the endless sun. The long, oval mirror that the Hawklord used to access records stood where it always stood, and as Kaylin entered the room, she caught a glimpse of her reflection, and froze.

The room in the reflection wasn't the room she was standing in.

For one, it was darker; the light was less natural. Flickers of firelight made long and trembling shadows by glancing off standing structures—the mirror, the chair, the recessed desk, the shelves against the curve of the rounded walls. The room was empty.

She knew this because it had *been* empty when she had first seen it, and it had been night. She hadn't dared to make the climb during the day; the Aerians patrolled the sky, and if they were careless because they expected no trouble, they weren't exactly blind. She had watched them for days. She had watched the building for days, as well. She had even gone into it—albeit from the public entrances that led to Missing Persons.

The Halls were crowded enough that she could leave Missing Persons without much difficulty, but bypassing the guards standing in front of any other set of closed doors became instantly too difficult; she didn't want them to take note of her. She had tied her hair in pigtails and divested herself of any obvious weapons, in order to appear younger. This was rewarded by "Are you lost?" or, worse, "Are you lost, dear?" rather than snarling or suspicion.

But if she were honest—and she clearly had trouble with that, which was ironic given how bad she was at lying—she could admit that she'd *wanted* the climb. She'd spent weeks practicing. She could scale the outside of the tallest building in the City, and she could *make* it. They'd wonder how she'd gotten in.

Getting down was always harder, but she'd worry about that later. Always later.

She could see that in the face of her reflection—her reflection, seven years younger, and hungrier in ways that she couldn't clearly remember. Oh, she remembered the fact of it—but it had no teeth, now; it didn't make her bleed.

She studied her younger self. Her eye was bruised; she'd forgotten that; her cheek was rubbed raw, probably by sliding down stone. Her hands were at her sides. But her own hands were empty; her reflection's bore daggers; when she lifted a hand, her younger hand rose, as well, blades glinting briefly. The blades were flat and small. *You've come here,* she thought, *to kill the Hawklord.* But the Hawklord was not yet in the Tower. Her reflection turned to the door, and then shrugged and moved out of Kaylin's field of view, to find a place to hide.

She hadn't come here to challenge him, after all; she'd come here to kill him. How she achieved it didn't matter. It wasn't about bravery or honor, just death. Death and her own survival.

She let her hands fall, and turned to Tiamaris. Tiamaris stood to one side of the mirror, his back toward its reflective surface. He was staring at the Hawklord's chair. As he did, Kaylin thought the chair shifted in place, the lines of it becoming taller, wider and more severely grandiose. What had been wood—albeit it finely oiled and expensive—glittered with something brighter and shinier. Gold? Gold leaf, at least.

This is not the past, she reminded herself. Because in the past, the Hawklord didn't occupy a throne. No one occupied this one, now. It sat like an invitation or a promise.

"Understood," Nightshade said quietly. He glanced at Lord Tiamaris.

"The Tower is not subtle," Tiamaris agreed, although he was tense. "But it is newly invoked, newly infused with whatever power we saw; subtlety, where it exists, will come."

Lord Nightshade's gaze trailed over Kaylin's face. "I am curious," he finally said. "What does the Tower offer to tempt you?"

"I'm mortal," she said with a grimace. "Powerful things don't bother to tempt us when they can squash us flat without effort.

This is a perfect example. Tiamaris—Lord Tiamaris," she added quickly, "gets a throne. I get a reflection of my younger self that's a lot more real than I wanted to see."

He surprised her. He laughed.

"You," she said, with slight heat, "get amusement at our expense. So far, only the Corporal is out in the cold."

"And he's more than content to remain so," Severn added.

Lord Nightshade lifted a hand and touched her cheek, covering his mark with the tips of cool fingers. "You do not fear me." There was a trace of surprise in his voice.

He meant the touch to be discomfiting, and it was. She stood her ground in spite of that. "I did, once," she told him, since she was in the Tower and the Tower seemed to demand as much honesty as she could offer. "I was terrified of the shadow of your Castle."

"My...Castle?"

Dammit.

Severn shrugged; Tiamaris looked momentarily impassive.

"Castle Nightshade," she said. "In the fief of Nightshade, where you rule."

"And you lived in this fief of...Nightshade?"

"For almost all of my life until—until—" This, she would not share, not yet. Maybe not ever, although her Lord Nightshade knew. "Until I had to leave. When I left, I came here, to the fief we call Barren in my time. This Tower is Barren's Tower."

"And the fief?"

"The fiefs are what's left of the interior of the City. Or the ring around the interior. They're divided into six parts; the parts aren't even, and I've no idea how the division was decided."

"The Towers decide," Tiamaris said. "Private, you speak too much."

"I know. I do." She turned to look at the mirror again. "I'm not sure why you get offered a throne and I get offered the truth."

"We are offered," Tiamaris told her, "some part of what we know, and of what we hide."

"You hide thrones?"

He smacked the back of her head, but lightly enough that he might have been human. "Come away from the mirror," he told her. "Come look at the throne instead."

It was a welcome invitation. "Is there something wrong with it, other than the fact that it's a throne?"

He didn't answer, and it was the wrong kind of silence. She walked across the room, cutting in front of Tiamaris, until she stood three feet away from the throne itself. "I wouldn't sit in it," she said, and as she did, something beneath the surface of the bright and shining throne moved, curling slowly in on itself, like a snake pressed beneath glass, but not quite crushed.

"No," he replied. "But it was not meant for you." He came to stand by her side. He did not, however, approach the throne. "What will happen here, Kaylin?"

"You're asking me that as if you expect me to have an answer. If the throne is for you, and the mirror for me, you have just as much chance as I do of predicting what comes next."

The Dragon's smile was thin and strange, because none of the rest of his face seemed to move. "The Tower is attempting to have two conversations at once, with predictable difficulties. But I believe that it is not yet aware that it is speaking to two distinct entities."

"I'm not going to like how you know this, am I?"

"Probably not. You appear to still be sane." He lifted an arm, and drew her gaze up to the closed aperture of the Hawklord's Tower. She watched, squinting, as it began to open. It let in, not sunlight, as she would have expected from the light that poured in through the windows, but night—a night broken by stars, and the hint of silver that was moonlight. One moon; the other lay hidden by the curved petals of roof itself.

But she lost that, and the night sky, as she saw what descended through the opening. The first thing she saw were wings. She had never seen black wings on an Aerian before, and decided then that she'd been happier for the lack. Flight feathers almost gleamed in the light Tiamaris's spell still shed, as if they were edged, and waiting to cut.

It was only the wings that were black; the figure that descended was robed in gray, and its hands were almost alabaster, they were so pale. One ring gleamed on the slender fingers of the right hand; it was green and gold, and large.

She recognized it instantly.

She'd worn it that morning to the High Halls. She stopped breathing as the figure descended; it landed directly in front of the throne itself. The robes were hooded, and as the figure touched down, it lifted graceful—impossibly graceful—hands to push the hood aside.

It needn't have bothered; Kaylin knew whose face she would see.

CHAPTER 23

It was, of course, her own face. Her face, but paler, and completely unscarred and unbruised. Something as common as a pimple had never touched that skin.

Tiamaris caught Kaylin's wrist as she moved. Since she'd had no intention of moving, it came as a surprise, and she pulled at her wrist, which was about as useful as pulling at rock and hoping the bits stuck between your fingers would come off in your hands. "Wait," he said.

She nodded, but he didn't release her wrist.

In the sudden night of the Tower, the figure nodded almost regally, and then, folding her wings, took her place upon the throne. Kaylin snorted, and the figure's almost impassive reflection of Kaylin's living face turned toward her.

"Aerians," Kaylin said, "don't sit in high-backed chairs. They can't."

"It is," the not-Aerian replied, "a special chair." Which was creepy; it spoke with Kaylin's voice, but without any of Kaylin's usual inflections; it sounded too damn smooth, too chilly. "Why are you here, Elianne?"

Tiamaris's fingers tightened. They would, Kaylin was certain, leave bruises. Bruises were better than this. She started to say, *I'm not Elianne,* but she couldn't. "I'm fine, Tiamaris," she told the Dragon Lord. When he didn't respond, she added, "Can I have my arm back?"

"I'll break it," he whispered, "if you do not act with caution."

She nodded, and he let go. Rubbing her wrist, she thought, yes, definitely, bruises. But she looked at the figure on the throne as she did, aware that she had still not answered the question. Looking around a room that was, except for the throne and the wrong version of her, familiar, she said, "I'm here because you called me."

A slight frown creased the pale, perfect mirror of Kaylin's face. "I think you misunderstand the question. Perhaps I did not ask it correctly the first time."

"No, I understood it the first—"

"Why are you here?"

This time, she spoke with the voice of Lord Grammayre, the Hawklord, and *his* voice shook the Tower.

Why are you here?

She had watched him from the top of the aperture. She had timed things perfectly, but if she hadn't, she would never have come this far. All she had to do now was wait, drop, and kill. He wasn't— according to Barren—a mage; he was just an Aerian.

Just an Aerian. Barren had made it seem as if Aerians were something less than men—but Barren had made her feel as if she were less than one, as well. In the dark of this almost-night, she could hear Barren's voice, Barren's words; she could feel hands that would leave bruises and the subtle scars that she would only understand years later.

Fief truth: survival was all. Well, she'd survived. She'd killed, continued to kill, for Barren. She didn't question him, anymore. When he'd assigned her this kill, she'd crossed the bridge, scuttling across the Ablayne like a terrified spider. Only Morse had questioned her decision. Only Morse had fought it. But she'd fought with Elianne, not Barren, and Elianne was therefore here.

Some part of Elianne had expected every single person she met here to be happy, cheerful, grateful for the lives they had never had to lead. That part was to be disappointed; she could live with that. But she had also expected the people here to see, clearly, what and who she was, what she'd done on the other side of the river— as if she bore obvious marks across her brow.

They didn't, of course. They barely even saw her, they were so wrapped up in their own lives. She had passed between them in the open streets, except when she failed to notice them in time—the streets here were more crowded than she was used to on an instinctive level. Some had apologized, some had cursed her—it was really no different.

But when she'd finally arrived at her destination—a small inn, owned by a man to whom she'd given a letter and received keys for a room and no questions—she had made her way to the Halls of Law. There, for the first time, she had seen the Aerians in flight. She had seen them leave the ground; she had seen them land. She had seen their wings fold and open as they gained height or lost it rapidly.

The Hawklord is just a man with wings. Nothing special.

But he had to be, to command these. He *had* to be, to be one of them.

That had been her first mistake. She made up for the lost time by studying the Aerians and their flight patterns as they skirted the height of the Tower, and she marked the changes of their guard.

Barren had given her the climbing gear she would use on this mission. He had made clear she was not to lose it until the Hawklord was dead, after which she was to lose it immediately and in a place it was unlikely to be found. Which meant, Elianne thought, across the Ablayne. Maybe she'd drop it in Nightshade.

The night was cool, and the sky was cloudy; everything had gone to dark gray. She tried to find her anger, as she waited. She tried to find the bitter envy and resentment she felt for the people on the right side of the bridge, because the man beneath the aperture roof protected them, watched over them, and offered justice for the wrongs done *them*. Who had ever done that for the fief of Nightshade or the fief of Barren?

She had seen examples of Nightshade's justice, hanging in public cages. She had experienced examples of Barren's in private.

Anger eluded her, even so. She felt tired. Resigned. Her sheaths were strapped to her thighs; she had enough rope to guide her fall, and she wore open-fingered gloves on her palms so the rope didn't burn on the way down.

Ready, she thought. *I'm ready.*

She took a breath, and as the Hawklord finally moved, she *moved*.

The height from the ceiling to the ground wasn't insignificant; it didn't have to be. The only people who used the roof as if it were a door had wings; height didn't bother them. It didn't bother Elianne, either. She dropped rope, and she dropped herself almost immediately after it, landing in a head over feet roll, knees bent into her chest so that she could unfold herself into a standing start.

He was already facing her when she stood, daggers out, her muscles gathered to leap. But he held no weapon, and he didn't attempt to leap out of her way; his eyes were the color of sky that hasn't quite faded into night.

"Why are you here?" he asked. His wings twitched slightly at his back, but he didn't open them.

She wanted to say *Why do you think I'm here?* because she had daggers in either hand and she obviously hadn't come up the stairs. But when she opened her mouth, the words that fell out were, "To kill you or die trying."

He nodded, as if he'd expected no less—but he must have assumed she was a child, because he didn't move. He waited, his eyes taking in both her face and the daggers in her hands; because he waited, she was frozen for a moment, watching not his face, but the folds of his wings. Alone among the Aerians she'd watched for days, he possessed white wings, angel wings, and they flexed slightly as he at last unfurled them.

"What have I done," he asked calmly, "that I deserve death?"

Too many words crowded into her mouth then; she spit, because she had to to draw breath. What she should have said—that Barren had ordered it—wasn't even in the running. The anger she couldn't quite find when she had watched him in silence from above now broke through, and she found herself shouting, while her hands shook around dagger hilts, all the things that she could have hated him for.

He was impassive; he watched, he waited, and—without comment—he listened.

All the deaths. The deaths she hadn't been able to prevent. The deaths she'd caused. All of the rage and the pain and the fury because *someone* should have cared, *someone* should have *been there,* and *he* sat hunched on the wrong damn side of the river, on the side of the river where he wasn't *needed.* Her breath was ragged, and her sides heaved as if she'd just run across the whole of Barren, a feral pack on her heels.

She even mentioned the ferals, because the ferals didn't hunt on this damn side of the Ablayne. She might, in her rage, have accused him of cooperating with the ferals—she couldn't honestly remember. Her mouth had slipped entirely free of her conscious control, and it spouted words she would have died before she'd let slip anywhere else.

Or, given the nature of the words, directly after.

Only when her silence had lasted half a minute did he raise a hand, turning his palm toward her almost gently. "Are you done?" he asked quietly.

It was not the question she expected, and she felt the line of her shoulders slump, as if the strings that had been supporting them had unexpectedly been cut. "Yeah," she said. "I'm done here."

And she was. All the words. All the effort. All the months of killing for Barren, a man she both hated and feared—they were over. For a moment she couldn't remember why she'd started, and when she did, her throat closed over the words. It was almost over. It would be good, to have an end.

Elianne found her legs again, and they not only held her up, but bent, tensing as she began to move, to circle, to seek the easy, quick opening. His wings extended fully, and she saw them arch slightly, as if he meant to push off, seeking the obvious advantage of height.

No, you don't. Shifting dagger weight in one hand, she threw the knife at the stretch of the pinion. She was a good aim. But it missed. Somehow. She didn't throw the other; instead she slid a hand down her thigh and rearmed herself. She wasn't Morse; she still favored her right hand, but she could kill with her left.

If she was facing one of Barren's thugs gone bad.

Facing this man was different. The anger had left with the words, and in its place was nothing; she was hollow, and she felt it as a lightness that was absent any joy. She found her pace, moving, almost dancing; she struck him once with the edge of her right blade, and left a shallow scratch that separated his robes.

He still hadn't bothered to arm himself. Like Elianne, he was done with words; unlike Elianne, he hadn't had to shed many of them to reach that state. Twice more, he let her close; there was no third time. Instead, he lifted both of his hands in a clap that sounded like thunder, and light flared in the Tower.

It was a bright light, but it suggested fluid, not air, and it swirled around her as if it had weight. That weight, untouchable but not untouching, folded itself around her limbs, locking them in place. She felt a moment's smugness as she thought *not a mage, Barren?* Which was stupid, but last thoughts were like that. She couldn't look down, but she could see, in the periphery of her vision, a ring of bright light around her, a circle in which she was enclosed.

The Hawklord folded both hands and wings as he watched her.

She waited in silence. She offered no further threat; the words would have been pathetic without the ability to move to back them up. Instead, she waited. As she did, her arms and her legs began to ache. She thought it was the magic itself, but realized, after a moment, that it was her *skin*. The marks were making themselves felt.

He frowned, as if he could feel it, as well—and for all she knew, he could. His hands did a complicated dance in the air, a deliberate series of gestures that flew by so fast she could get nothing else from them, and his frown deepened. Her left arm rose entirely of its own volition—or his—and he approached her cautiously, first removing the dagger from her frozen fingers and setting it, with care, against the stone floor.

Having done that, he now unbuttoned the wrist of her shirt, and folded it up, until it reached the faint bend of her outstretched arm. The marks on her arm lay exposed to his eyes, as if she were parchment; what they said to him, she didn't know. To her, they were now a bright gray-blue, and they pulsed as if they were alive.

"Records," he said. It was the first time she had heard the word spoken in that tone.

The mirror at his back came to life, the way the light of this circle had, as if everything in the Tower responded to his command. But the images that flickered in the mirror were familiar to Elianne; they were marks.

Ah. Marks and bodies. Corpses. Children her own age, or not much younger. Faces she vaguely remembered. Faces she knew. None of them were her own. But he didn't watch faces; he spoke again, and the images shifted until all that was in them were marks, like these, against pale, bloodless skin.

"So," the Hawklord said. And then, after a pause, "Who sent you?"

It made no sense, and she was silent for a long moment.

"The answer," he told her softly, "can be gained in two ways."

She nodded; it was pretty much what she expected. But she didn't particularly feel like being tortured solely to protect Barren. "Barren."

He frowned. "Barren?" And then his eyes widened slightly. "You refer to the fief lord?"

She couldn't shrug, although she wanted to. "Yes."

"Why? I mean," he added, watching her expression, "why did he send you?"

She tried shrugging anyway; nothing moved. "You're causing grief at the crossing."

"Grief?" Again, his frown; it was as if she were speaking a different language that he could understand only with effort.

"Your Hawks are patrolling the only bridge that crosses the Ablayne into Barren. It's scaring people off."

"A man died just before the foot of that bridge."

"He died on the wrong side of the river for you. You don't care about the fiefs, remember?" Her cheeks felt hot.

"It is not that we don't care. What is your name?"

Elianne said, without pause, "Kaylin. Kaylin Neya."

One white brow rose in a subtle arch, but he nodded. "Very well, Kaylin. It isn't that we don't care. Our jurisdiction in the fiefs is limited by the nature of the fiefs themselves."

Of course. Of course it was. "You're saying we deserve what we get there?"

"I will not speak for the others. You, however, appear to kill men at the behest of a crimelord. What would you now say you deserve?"

There it was. The truth of the words, the truth of his question. His eyes were ash-gray. She wasn't certain what it meant. Barrani eyes shaded between green and blue, where blue meant death. Clearly the Aerians were different, and not just because of their wings.

"I deserve," she told him, "whatever I get. There's no justice, there's no fairness. You can kill me. If you kill me," she shrugged. Or tried. "I won't be the first. And at least I had some chance." She couldn't keep the bitterness out of her words, which was fine; it was the pain she begrudged him, but he got that, too.

"So you don't believe in justice."

She could spit, because she could talk. She did. This caused a ripple of distaste to mar his calm expression, and she was petty enough to find satisfaction in it. "Do you?" she asked, in as scathing a voice as she could find strength to use.

His smile was an odd smile; it was neither cruel nor smug. Instead, it seemed to reflect some of the pain she herself had revealed. "Yes," he said quietly. "It is why I am the Lord of the Hawks."

She snorted. "Barren's the Lord of the Fief, and he sure as shit doesn't."

"No. But not all Lords rule for the sake of power." He glanced at the mirror, in which marks were frozen so perfectly it might have been a framed painting. "We do not always succeed in our attempts to find—or uphold—justice. But if we fail to try at all, what is left? The only justice that exists is the justice we attempt to make. The only fairness, the same.

"But I consider it worth the attempt." He turned to face her again. "Is this your attempt to find justice?"

"Yes."

"I see."

"No, you *don't*. I had to do this—all of this, this whole life—because I need to be strong enough to kill a man."

"To kill a stranger?"

"No! To kill someone who—"

"Hurt you?"

She swallowed. Hurt her? Gods, yes. Nothing that had ever happened in her life had hurt her as much, not even the dim memory of her mother's death, her inexplicable desertion. But she said, "No. Not me." And she tried to turn her face away. Something held her fast—held her without bruising—and she fought it, biting the inside of her cheek until it bled. Some things, she didn't share. Not with Morse. Not with this beautiful, terrifying stranger.

Not with anyone but Severn, and Severn—

Her arms and legs felt raw; she couldn't move them and didn't try. But she turned her face, by slow, agonizing inches, away from the Hawklord's inspection.

"And will you find the choice you've made worth it, in the end?"

"How the hell should I know?" She should have shouted; she whispered the words instead, as if they were broken prayer. "It's not the end yet." But it was. She would not kill this man; she couldn't. Barren had been wrong; he *was* a mage. He did have power. Kaylin understood what was done with power, when you had it. Maybe laws existed on this side of the river—but not for people like her.

Was it worth it?

No. *No.* Because her dead were *still dead,* and joining them, people who had done nothing at all to deserve it. Kaylin was never going to be strong enough to protect any of them. What had she become instead? Weak enough to lead the men who would kill them to where they were hidden, and safe. To Paul. To his mother, his sister, and Arna.

I didn't kill them! I didn't mean for them to die!

But it didn't matter; they were dead. Who else would she kill just by walking past at the wrong time? Who else would she fail to defend because she was terrified and powerless? If she had even been home, would she have saved Steffi and Jade? Could she have?

Yes. *Yes.* She cried out in wordless fury. All of her words were trapped on the inside of her head.

Eli, you're the worst liar I've ever met.

She felt something brush her cheek; not fingers, but the tips of wings. Startled, she turned to look at the Hawklord again; it was easier to move her head this time, although her body was still frozen in place.

"No," he told her, as she met his gaze. "I do not mean to harm you. Even if I wanted to make you suffer, could I cause more suffering than you are causing yourself?" But his wings ceased their motion, as if he could tell that she found it unbearable. He stepped back.

Watching her, he raised his arms; the motion was swift, but somehow spare. Whatever was holding her in place suddenly vanished; she was standing in the center of a circle carved in the stone floor, and she watched as its light guttered. She had one dagger; the other, he had retrieved, and as she lowered her arm, her sleeve fell over the marks that had changed her life.

"What will you do now, Kaylin?" he asked quietly.

So, too, asked the apparition that now sat in a throne that had never existed in the Hawklord's stone tower, its high back at odds with the fold of black Aerian wings, waiting and watching in a way that felt familiar. She spoke with the Hawklord's voice, with the nuance that implied both curiosity and hope, but her eyes were now flat and shiny, as if they were made of perfect, polished stone.

Kaylin glanced around the room that was so much like—and so much unlike—the Hawklord's tower. "You're not the Hawklord," she told the figure.

"No." This was now spoken in Kaylin's voice.

"You're not me, either. Not even close to me."

"I am close," the figure replied, "to what you might become, should you desire it. The flesh of the Tower has not yet been shaped, and it is waiting." Ebon wings unfolded, unhindered by throne. Or reality. "Have you not dreamed of flight all your life?"

Kaylin stared at the wings. And then she turned to look at Severn, who waited silently by one wall as if he understood all the memory, all the rage, and all the bitter sense of failure that had dogged her steps since she'd crossed the bridge—both bridges. All bridges, really.

"I didn't kill him," she told the seated figure, although it was obvious.

"You couldn't. You know that now. You might have understood it then, had you tried. You didn't—and wouldn't—think about it. Why?"

Kaylin laughed. It was a bitter, shaky laugh, but she had already decided that what the Tower wanted—or what it wanted from her—was honesty. "I didn't think because I was thirteen years old, and a fool. I came here, or my version of here, to kill him and leave Barren's message. Not more, not less."

"You failed."

Kaylin shrugged. "Story of my life."

But the warped mirror-image was not satisfied. *"Why?"* it asked, and this time the walls and the floor of the Tower shook.

"Kaylin," Lord Nightshade said, when the tremor had subsided, "might I suggest that you answer the question?"

Kaylin nodded. "Why did I fail?"

The not-quite Kaylin inclined her head, and her wings twitched; it was a disturbingly familiar gesture.

All of the excuses that she'd used until now failed her. They were just that: excuses. She faced herself, seeing shadows in the wings that were extended, and she said, "He was what I wanted. To serve. Or to be. He was—all of the Aerians were—like that little bit of dream that just won't die, no matter how hard you try to kill it.

"And I didn't want to kill it."

"You came to kill."

"Yes."

The woman now rose. And smiled. "So," she said, in a voice that was neither Kaylin's nor the Hawklord's. "You thought to die in its place, in this room. To fail, and to die."

"I never had the courage to kill myself," Kaylin replied. "I didn't even have the courage to die fighting, not when it counted." She thought of Paul. "I had enough courage to fail. I thought death at his hands would be clean. It was more than I deserved."

"And he failed to kill you. Instead, you gave him whatever information you had, and you chose to serve him."

Kaylin shrugged. "He pays me."

"Does he pay you enough?"

"He pays me enough." She kept the edge out of her words. Whoever this woman was, she was beginning to get on Kaylin's nerves, the way bad office gossip did. Or Sergeant Mallory. "Not that it's actually any of your business."

"You chose to enter the Tower."

"So? I choose to enter the Library—it doesn't mean the Librarian gets to disembowel me and read my bloody entrails." Not unless she tried to steal something or ended up breaking something, but that didn't seem relevant at the moment.

"If the Librarian chose to do so, and you had no means of preventing him, why not?"

"Because the Law is the Emperor's, and he expects his citizens to uphold it."

"You are not in your Empire now."

"I'm in yours, is that the idea?"

The woman laughed, and her wings suddenly bent; she pushed herself up and off both throne and ground so quickly she might never have been there at all. But the air was alive with her; she seemed like dark light. No Aerian hovered the way she did now.

"No, Kaylin, that is not the idea. You are in a Tower, and the Tower is not—yet—complete. What it does while it struggles is not dissimilar to what *you* did while you struggled," Tiamaris said. His voice was muted, but clear.

"With what?"

"With your life."

Kaylin shook her head. "I'm not done struggling with that," she said quietly, trying to get her mind around the concept of a Tower's emotional drama.

"No. Nor is the Tower. It will find what it seeks."

Kaylin nodded slowly. "It will," she said, and this time, her voice lost the edge of irritation. "But I'm not it."

The Tower spoke, then. "You bear the marks, wild one. Complete us, and you will find everything you need here."

"I'm not so good with understanding what I need," Kaylin replied. She glanced at the throne, and then up at the perfect, black wings of someone who looked almost like her. "I'm not even good at understanding what I want—it gets so confused. I know my daydreams," she added. "But you can't live on those, or in them. You're a daydream, to me. This throne isn't even part of what I—" She frowned. "Not since I became a Hawk. It's not what *I* dream about. It's even ugly."

"Take it. Make of it what you desire."

Kaylin looked at the empty throne. It was a fancy chair. It didn't even look comfortable. "I don't want it," she said quietly. "You don't understand." As if a Tower could actually understand anything. Kaylin had, on bad days, talked to the walls before—but this time, they were instigating the conversation. "I don't want—I've never wanted—to tell other people what to do. I've never wanted to control their lives. At most I've wanted to protect the lives that were—and are—important to me. Not more, not less.

"Whatever you're offering, it's not for me. I'd have to be a different person to take it."

"But you could turn the Tower into a shelter."

Kaylin almost laughed, but it would have been on the wrong edge of crazy; she bit it back. "I admit I haven't seen many Towers," she said, when she could speak clearly again. "But shelter is not high on the list of what they *do*. A fortress isn't a shelter. A fortress isn't a foundling hall. It isn't a midwives' guild. It isn't anything I understand, anymore."

"You're a soldier."

"No. I'm a groundhawk. I uphold the Emperor's Law, and when it's been broken, I try to find the person who broke it and put him someplace where he can't break it again. I don't fight wars. I talk to people who also don't fight wars. I don't want more authority over their lives than I already have."

"If you have power—"

"If I have that much power, it's all my responsibility. Every single life I control becomes more my problem than I ever wanted it to be. What you're offering—I don't want. What I want, you can't offer."

"And you do not desire these people to do your will?"

"No."

"Do you not think you know better than they what is required?"

Kaylin snorted. "We *all* think that. We also have days where we think we're the only person who's doing any damn work. That's *normal*. I can even say I know what's best for me, and mean it. But I clearly don't, if you look at my life to this point. I try to learn from the mistakes. I try every damn day not to screw up. You know what? I fail a lot. Hopefully I fail less than I used to.

"But I can't have that kind of power if I'm going to screw up everyone else's life with it. I've already destroyed so much with no power at all."

The stranger's wings folded, and she fell; she hit the ground as if she, like the floor, were made of stone. Neither of them cracked, but the ground shook with the impact, and Kaylin fell to one knee in an attempt to avoid falling any other way. The throne listed to one side; part of the flooring had fallen, there, as if it were now made of cloth.

"We have waited for you," the stranger said, and Kaylin flinched. The voice was no longer hers, and no longer the serene and distant voice of a greater power. It was—and gods, this was so unfair—a child's voice. As the stranger rose, her wings cracked, falling to either side like a fine veil of ash. Her skin lost the patina and hard shine of alabaster; it became, instead, the dark of bruising. She no longer looked like Kaylin, which was a mercy of a sort.

She looked, however, like a child.

CHAPTER 24

She heard Severn's intake of breath; it was as sharp, as immediate, as her own. She couldn't even be certain it was for a different reason, and she raised both hands, as if to ward off a blow.

To ward it off a different way, she said, "Don't do this. I know you can look like whoever you want, and I know you know more about me than you could without magic. I'm fine with that.

"You take either of those faces, either of those forms, and I will find some way to bring you down, brick by brick. I don't care how long it takes."

The transformation stopped, as if it were part of a heated conversation that had not—yet—turned irretrievably ugly. The face was a child's face, yes, but it was not Steffi's and not Jade's. This child now turned to Severn, who had not moved.

"You killed them," she said, in a child's voice. "They trusted you, and you killed them."

He didn't blink, didn't flinch; he refused to play the Tower's game. "Yes."

"You saved her," the child continued, surprising Kaylin. "And she hated you for it."

"Yes." His expression was harder and smoother than the walls.

Kaylin wanted to deny the words. She couldn't. What she said instead was, "I don't hate him now."

"You waver in your purpose."

"I learn more, as I get older. If that's wavering, that's wavering. Killing him wouldn't bring them back."

"Would you bring them back?"

"Yes. But I can't. And you can't."

"No. I can kill him, though."

"You can try," Kaylin replied, with a little heat.

"I can kill him," the Tower repeated, with the stubborn certainty of a child. "But you can stop me if you take the Tower." And the slyness.

She should have been afraid—for herself, for Severn. Instead, she felt frustrated and annoyed. It was a familiar feeling; she had to suppress it frequently in her visits to the foundling halls. The children there were similar; cocky, arrogant, in your face. They had so much to prove, and they wouldn't understand, until years later, that the people they needed to prove it to were themselves.

She'd been there. She knew it wasn't pretty. She couldn't *remember* being as insecure and stupid, but maybe sometimes memory was kind, although she would have bet against it if someone had asked.

"I can't stay with you," she told the girl, gentling her voice and—with effort—capping her irritation.

"Why?"

"Because I also have other responsibilities." *You might not be aware of what that word means.* "You won't be alone forever."

The child stared at her.

"Someone will come. Someone who can survive your tests—"

"My tests?"

"You test people who walk through your doors."

"Test?" the child said again, looking very sincere in her confusion.

"What you did to me, when I walked in." She sucked in air;

the confusion, like complete cloud cover, didn't so much as break to allow a glimmer of illumination through.

"What did I do? I spoke with you. It was hard. I tried to show you that I understood your pain."

Kaylin managed to keep her jaw from hitting the floor only because she'd spent so many years helping Marrin deal with found-lings of all ages.

"Most people," she finally managed to say, "don't want that much understanding."

"Why?"

"Because they don't understand or admit to their own pain. It makes life a lot easier." Taking another breath, she said, "Look—" and stopped. "What is your name?"

This time, the expression on the child's face was completely clear: she was shocked. Her eyes rounded, and her mouth opened slightly. "I have no name," she replied, as if the words were an ac-cusation. "You *know* that." As if the accusation might be missed if it were too subtle.

"I'm sorry," Kaylin replied, "but I didn't know. I wouldn't have asked, if I had."

"I'm waiting," the child said, after a long pause. "I'm empty, right now. When I'm not, I'll have a name."

Kaylin frowned. "You'll have the same name as the person who lives in the—here."

The child nodded. Kaylin resisted the temptation to make up a name on the spot, but only barely. Given the names some of the kids chose for themselves—Dock came to mind—she was sure she wouldn't do lasting damage.

But the child said, "Name me, if you want."

"I can't give you my name—"

"You're not even using your own name," was the reply.

"Yes, I am."

"No. You're Elianne. You're Kaylin. You're *Erenne*. You're *kyuthe*. It's all broken—you won't put it all together."

"I don't *need* to put it all together. And those are all things that other people call me because it's convenient for them. Humans don't have names the way Dragons or Barrani do. Or maybe Towers."

"Tower?"

Kaylin looked at Severn, who shrugged the up-to-you shrug. Then she turned to Tiamaris and Nightshade, both of who were watching the girl as if she had a terminal—and communicable—disease. "Tiamaris," she said, in a tone of voice that suggested Lord was both superfluous and entirely overly respectful.

He raised a brow. "Yes?" When she frowned, he shook his head. "This is more speech than I have ever heard from a Tower, Private Neya. If you are about to accuse me of withholding vital information, believe that it was entirely a by-product of ignorance."

"Nightshade?" she said, managing a slightly more subdued tone.

He did not take his eyes from the child, but did answer. "The Towers, as you call them, have always taken poorly to intrusion and to the use of magic. What they are, and what they were, we do not entirely understand. They are old," he added, in a tone of voice that implied that compared to Kaylin, even he wasn't.

She looked back to the girl, who did not seem at all old now. Then she walked over to the circle in which the girl stood, and she knelt to bring their eyes to about the same level, leaving her hands, palms flat, in her lap. "Did you understand what you saw in me?"

The child—dammit, no. "I'm going to call you—Tara."

Severn's silence changed, but he said nothing. He recognized the name she'd pulled out of thin air—because it was the thin air of a past in which they had both been, for all intents and purposes, children. Her mother's name.

"Tara?"

Kaylin nodded.

"What does it mean?"

The Tower's avatar—if that's what it was—had taken the shape and form of a human child. But it wasn't a question that human children asked; it was probably a question asked by Dragonlets or young Barrani, not that she'd ever really laid eyes on either. *What does it mean?*

But the Tower was, in theory, much older than either the Dragon Lord or the Barrani Lord who were present; old enough, and unschooled enough, that even her use of the word *name* meant something completely alien to Kaylin. Kaylin understood enough to know that she had to answer carefully, which was a pity, because she'd come up with the name on the fly, as she so often did.

But really, was it so hard to answer the question that the Tower had asked?

She glanced at Tiamaris and Nightshade, and winced. Yes, because it was embarrassing. Anger, you could expose. Rage. Even pain. But there were some things you protected, because you weren't quite strong enough to endure the mockery that was certain to follow.

She grimaced again. She wasn't thirteen and bereft of a home anymore. She wasn't that girl, even if twinges of her reactions remained.

"Tara," she said slowly, "means many things, to me. I don't know if you'll understand all the words I use."

She only *looked* like a child; she didn't bridle at all.

"It means home. It means hope. Warmth. Safety. It means love that asks nothing." It means, Kaylin thought, loss. She didn't say that.

But the Tower said, "Loss?"

Kaylin winced. If she hadn't had experience with Nightshade's ability to read her thoughts through the questionable gift of his mark, all of her hair would be standing on end.

"Why?"

"I'm human. We don't like—no, let me try that again. What we think, what we do our best *not* to say out loud, is private. If we wanted other people to hear it, we'd say it. Out loud. When you answer my thoughts like that, you're ignoring my attempt to maintain any sense of privacy, and you're exposing things to anyone else who's listening."

"You don't want them to hear us?"

Kaylin froze. When she spoke again, she spoke slowly and carefully. "No, I'm fine with it now. Please don't do anything they'd regret later. Which is beside the point. I was telling you—"

"What *Tara* means."

"Yes. But loss? When you have something special, when you have something good, you sometimes don't recognize how important it is until it's gone. When it's gone—when it's too late—you realize what you had, and you miss it. That's loss, pretty much. And it's that loss that's in the name, for me. In a better world, I would never have had to experience it.

"And if I dwell on the loss, you won't understand *why* the loss was so bitter. So stop reading my mind and stop interrupting me."

"May I read your mind if I don't interrupt?"

"Since I can't stop you anyway, yes."

The child smiled, and Kaylin, still kneeling in front of her, spoke as softly as she could about her mother—or about what she remembered. She had been young enough when her mother died that she had few solid memories now, and one or two of those involved her mother's infrequent temper. She hesitated, and then shared those, as well, wincing but grinning as she did.

"But I am not your mother."

"No. That's not what the name is supposed to mean. It's what the name means to me, and I want you to take the good parts of it—or all of it—and make it something different, something of your own."

"What is your name?"

"You already said I don't have—" She stopped, and then held out her hand. The child took it in both of hers. Kaylin did not feel up to explaining the manners behind a polite handshake, because they really made no logical sense when you got right down to it. "My name is Kaylin."

"Kaylin."

"Yes. It's a name I chose for myself. It was meant to be a lie," she added. "But it was a lie I wanted to believe so badly, I've been busy ever since then trying to make it my truth."

"Can you make truth of a lie?"

"I don't know. When I was your age—I mean, the age you look—I would have said no. Now?" She shrugged. "Time will tell. I'm happier than I was, I think." She hesitated. "You can make up a name, if you don't like the one I gave you. I just wanted some-thing to call you because I'm used to talking to children who have names—or at least names as I understand them."

"These things, in this name, are they good?"

"To me? Yes. They're some of the things I want, and I want them enough to try to build them, even on days when I'm cer-tain I don't deserve them."

"It is important to be loved?"

If Kaylin could have handpicked an audience for this discus-sion it would never have included the Barrani Lord and the Dragon. It might not have included Severn, but that was less certain. But as she met the girl's gaze, she was caught by it. In some ways, the Tower was—as Tiamaris had said—newly wakened. It was, in whatever ways a mystical creation of walking gods could be, in its infancy; it had confusion and uncertainty, even if it also read minds and cut to the heart of the worst of your fears and self-loathing just to expose them.

"It's important. For some people it's too important. For some, it's never been important enough. It's not magic—it doesn't make you a god or anything. It doesn't cure the world of evils, and it doesn't keep you fed. But…it takes the edge off of everything—envy, resentment, insecurity. More, it makes it easier to give to, or to care for, other people in turn.

"I'm not good at explaining things," she added. "I've never been good at it. But even if I don't remember her well, I re-member that she loved me. I don't know—I guess I thought of her name because she *was* my home, and you're a—a Tower. A building. But you could *be* someone's home. Just not mine.

"And if you're going to be a home for someone, a good home—not a home with ferals and evil multi-eyed bastards in the basement—would be better."

"Tara."

"It sounds sort of like Tower," Kaylin offered. Tara's hands tightened, briefly, around hers.

"You won't stay with me," she said.

"I can't."

"You can. You won't."

Children were always perceptive when you least wanted it. Kaylin nodded, her expression carefully neutral. She wasn't talking to a child, but had to remind herself forcefully of this. "The City I care about—the City I was born into—hasn't happened yet." This would have confused a real child; Tara simply nodded. "I'm not sure how I got here, and I'm not sure how I'll get back—but I have to go back. We're fighting a war with the shadows that live in the heart of—of this place."

"Fight them now," Tara said. "Fight them. I'll help you. It's all I've been waiting for. You cannot imagine how long." If something that was essentially made of stone could look sly—clumsily sly, like a foundling—she now did. "You can do more damage here. You can change things now so that your City won't be facing the dangers they face without your intervention."

Kaylin met, and held, her odd, colorless gaze. "Truthfully?" she said, after a long pause. "Can you tell me that and mean it?"

She thought the child would lie. But she *knew* it would be a lie; it was that obvious. The child's gaze slid away from hers, as if it were oiled.

"No, then," Kaylin said. "Tara, I'm sorry. I can't stay here, and I think you already know that."

The worst possible thing—for a value of worse that didn't involve mutilation, torture, or the end of the world—happened, then. The child began to cry. Silent tears slowly filled her eyes and rolled, unhindered, down her pale cheeks, catching the odd light in the room and transforming it, for a moment, into isolation and loss.

Very few of her co-workers came to Kaylin with their crises; that was left to Caitlin, or each other. Their heartbreak often seemed so inexplicable to Kaylin, her response was always practical—and people were quick to point out that logic and emotion weren't the same thing. Which, conversely, she already knew.

But other people always seemed to be so steady or stable compared to Kaylin, at least in her own eyes.

The Tower was not a person. Not a child. But it was not yet old—if it matured the way living creatures generally did—and it was clearly afraid of being left alone. Of being, Kaylin thought, deserted. It was a fear she understood because she had feared it, and it had happened anyway.

For a moment she wanted to stay, just to quell that pain. It tugged at her in a way threats never could.

But Severn chose that moment to touch her shoulder. She didn't even shrink away; it steadied her. Nothing bad, she thought, would happen to this Tower. It, unlike so many of the other lives she had destroyed just by wandering through them so carelessly, would remain standing when all of the other buildings had fallen into the half ruins so common in the fiefs.

"But I will fail," the Tower told her, the tears still wet on her cheeks. "You have told me that."

"No, I—"

"If the shadows have broken the confinement, and they have only done so in my demesne, I have failed."

"How can *you* fail? You're a Tower. The man who took responsibility for you—and for the rule of these lands—failed. He failed utterly. But you?"

The Tower looked up at Kaylin, and then took a step back; her arms were extended because she had not let go of Kaylin's hands. "It is time," she said quietly, and she looked up toward the closed dome. On cue, it opened.

Above them, the sky was an angry shade of what might have been gray. Kaylin's hands tightened—around nothing. The girl still stood in front of her, but she was shining and transparent now, like a ghost.

"Tiamaris, is that—"

"Yes," he said, his voice soft. "She has summoned the storm."

"Tara, did you—"

The Tower nodded. "It will take you," she told Kaylin, "where I cannot go. But I will remember you, Kaylin. I will look for you in the streets of my City. You fight what I fight; you can't help it. You were made, like me, to stand against it." She turned her face away so that Kaylin could see the small, snub nose in profile. Her eyes were glittering like opals, but the rest of her face was still all child.

Kaylin reached out to touch her face. Not to grab it, not to force it to turn, but to touch it. Her fingers felt warmth without texture, and Tara turned to look at her, her eyes widening in surprise. "We'll come for you," Kaylin said. "We'll come for you, if we can."

Tara hesitated and then nodded. "If you can, and if I can allow it. But I will look for another, now. I will find someone who will make these lands strong."

Kaylin started to speak and bit back the words. A lecture on the nature of strength had no place here, but it was work not to give it. Instead she swallowed the words and nodded. "Remember me, if you can. Remember what I said."

"I will. I do not think I am allowed to forget anything."

She lifted her arms, and the sky descended, eating away at the lines of the open roof as if it was corrosive.

Kaylin grabbed Severn's hand and levered herself to her feet as the child vanished. "We're done," she told Tiamaris. He gazed at the falling sky and grimaced.

"An unfortunate human idiom."

"That's not what I meant—"

"No. But meaning is often decided by your intended audience. Lord Nightshade?"

Magic, hidden until this moment, flared in the room. How much longer it would be a room wasn't clear; darkness now dribbled like ink down the rounded curve of the Hawklord's Tower walls, taking stone with it as it fell.

Kaylin.

It was Nightshade's voice, but her name felt almost tentative as it touched her. She nodded; she rarely spoke to him this way if he was actually standing in the room.

The Tower will look for you.

"I know. It already has, once. I didn't understand it, then."

And I, little one. I will look for you, as well.

She said, with just a trace of bitterness, "I know. I don't know if this changes anything. I don't know if it's always been in the past. I don't understand what's happened at all. But…I know." Severn was holding her hand.

"Private." Tiamaris's voice was steady.

She swallowed. "I think—I think we're meant to be in it."

"It is not to my liking."

"No. Maybe you could stay. You'd be a lot older by the time I saw you again."

"Or perhaps simply dead. Most of my kind are." His smile was vivid and brief. "I do not regret this," he added. "I regret none of it." He looked around the Tower as it dissolved into the primal storm.

"You're not afraid of—"

"No. Not *this* storm. Come. Corporal, Private." He glanced once over his shoulder at the Barrani Lord. "You are welcome to join us."

"I think not. Whether or not you fear it, it is what it is—primal and wild. If it is bent to a will, the will behind it is not to be trusted."

"The Barrani never trust."

"Indeed. I will find my way out of the Tower," he added. "It will not be the first time, and I will be unburdened, now, by the frailty of mortal companions."

"It is not so troublesome a burden as we were taught," Tiamaris replied, surprising Kaylin. "Or perhaps, in spite of that, it is not unwelcome in the end. You might find that the Empire, when it arrives, will surprise you." He paused, and the rest of the words he might have said were lost as the shadows spoke.

They spoke in a language that Kaylin both recognized and failed to understand; the words pressed into her skin on all sides, as if a drunk scribe were attempting to leave his mark on living parchment. Light flared in the darkness, and if the darkness was described as shadow, it was all the wrong word. Shadows were things light cast. What existed in this darkness was not static, and it was not the by-product of standing beneath, or beside, light; it was like a living forest in a gale that moved first one way and then the other, with no recognizable pattern behind it.

But when they spoke—when it spoke—light answered; blue light, limned in a silver-gold nimbus. She knew what the source of that light was: the marks on her arms, her legs, the back of her neck. She could see them rise, like slender serpents, from her skin, swaying in the black wind as if to devour it—or be devoured by it.

Which, given they were part of *her* arm, was damn uncomfortable.

Three times the shadows spoke; three times the light that was her marks flared. There was no fourth time. Instead, the storm broke, and as it did, it retreated over broken stones and dead weeds, slowly unveiling the warped facades of buildings that had been old a hundred years ago. No faces peered out of the windows, but then again, the windows were boarded or shuttered; it was the fiefs, after all.

She looked immediately to her right and left, and found she was bracketed by Severn and Tiamaris. The sky above returned to something resembling normal.

"That," Tiamaris said, "was enlightening. And costly, if I am not mistaken."

"Costly?"

"Costly. Come, Private. We were ordered to investigate Illien's Tower."

She almost laughed. "Haven't we already done that?"

"If you feel you have a report that would satisfy either the Arkon or the Emperor, yes."

She spoke a few choice Leontine words. "I'm not really ready to go back. I'm hungry, tired, I've only just left, and I wasn't certain we'd all make it out."

"I am not at all certain we will all make it out a second time. As I said, the choice is yours."

She looked toward the heartland. She wasn't close enough to the border that she could clearly see the White Towers, Barren's home.

"Yes," Severn said, in a much quieter voice than the Dragon's. "It's the Tower or Barren. The Tower or the border."

"I'm not sure the border will hold much longer."

"It won't," Tiamaris said, voice flat. "That much must now be obvious to you. What the Tower did was a last act of desperation. It has, I think, little left to offer."

If they were at the border when whatever contained shadow broke, they might be able to save some lives. Tiamaris, at least, could fly. Kaylin wasn't entirely certain *what* she could do, but the curse and the gift of these damn marks would almost certainly make some damn difference.

Not as much of a difference, she thought, as the Tower. Or Castle Nightshade. Or any of the other buildings that had, if she had understood all she'd heard correctly, been created to contain and withstand what lay at the heart of the fiefs.

"All right," she said, sucking in air. "Tower first."

The streets were empty for the time of day. Empty enough that it made Kaylin wonder if the storm had delivered them to yet another time and place. "Were we even *in* the Tower? Was it all an artifact of the storm?"

"I will leave that to the theorists to decide," was the Dragon's reply. "But if you are uncertain about our location—and time—don't be."

"Why?"

"The Emperor is close," he replied curtly.

"You know that?"

The smile that touched the corner of his lips failed to touch his eyes. "Yes, Kaylin. I, and all my kin. Take comfort from that fact if you can."

"I can," she said. *Can you?* She didn't ask. She didn't understand Dragons at all.

Or perhaps, just perhaps, she did. What had his choice been, after all? To serve or to die. What had hers been? The same. And she'd done it, because she'd seen no other damn choice. It had never occurred to her to judge him, and it was probably suicide to pity him.

"Tower," she repeated, because it was safest.

The difference in the Tower was immediately obvious, perhaps because they'd just left it. It looked like a standing ruin, albeit a ruin of stone, surrounded by a sea of weeds and a fence that made leaning and falling synonymous. In spite of the last fact, there were very few gaps in it through which to fit a Dragon Lord. Kaylin had found her way in once, and found her way in again with ease. This time, however, she held on to Severn's hand as she made her way into the weeds, and he followed her lead in silence.

She paused. Where there had been a door in the past, there was nothing now.

Nothing except a hole in the wall, and standing in that hole, Lord Nightshade. He was leaning against the standing stone, and it clearly supported his weight.

"What are you doing here?" Kaylin asked. "Why are you not in Nightshade?"

He smiled. It was not an entirely pleasant expression, but that was to be expected from a Barrani smile. He turned to Tiamaris. "Lord Tiamaris," he said, bowing. The gesture was both respectful and familiar, something only a Barrani could carry off. "You have been missing for hours, and in those hours, there have been further difficulties in the fief of Barren."

Tiamaris nodded. "I had noted the change of the sun's position." He said nothing else.

Then again, he didn't have to; Kaylin was there. "What happened?" she said, her tone sharpening. She started to add more and stopped as she looked more carefully at the Lord of Nightshade's face. It was pale, but not in the flawless way of normal Barrani skin. Had he been human, she would have said he was exhausted.

"You shouldn't be here," she said, voice flat.

He inclined his head. "But here," he replied, "is where the fief will stand—or fall. What is left of Barren in the wake of the breach, I will not venture to guess. Look, and look carefully, Hawk."

Kaylin frowned, as his gaze grazed the sky. She looked up, as did Severn and last, Tiamaris. It wasn't unusual to see Aerians on patrol in the skies above the City; the heights were part of their beat. But these Aerians—and she recognized their wings in the distance, they couldn't be anything else—weren't flying above the outer City—their path was too low for that.

They were flying over Barren.

"How bad is it?" she asked softly, watching the skies.

"Bad enough," Lord Nightshade replied, "that the Dragon Court is rumored to be preparing to take wing, as well."

Tiamaris said, "Come, Kaylin. We have no time."

"Should we—"

"No time. The Emperor will not summon me back from the Tower, regardless of what the Court does or does not do. It is the Tower that is at the heart of the danger, and it is to the Tower that I was sent." He started toward the opening in the rounded, thick wall, and Nightshade slid to one side.

"I have delivered what word I can," he told Kaylin. "And I will deliver, as well, one gift." He lifted a hand, and he cupped her cheek. It was the cheek upon which he had placed his mark, and where his skin touched hers it burned and it froze simultaneously. Magic at work. "I would go with you," he told her, as he let his hand—which was smooth and unblemished—fall away. "But the boundaries are not stable, between my fief and this one. I stand upon the boundary," he added.

"You're standing in the fief."

"Yes. But I have no power, here. All of the power I can bring to bear holds the boundaries fast."

"Nightshade is safe—"

"No, Kaylin, it is not. Not one of the fiefs is safe if Barren falls, but it will be Nightshade and Candallar who will crumble first."

"Candallar?"

"The fief to the other side of Barren," he replied. "It is not, in size, the equal of Barren or Nightshade, and it is narrower, but its defenses hold."

"The fief lord there was rumored to be—"

"Barrani, yes. I have heard the rumors."

"Is he?"

"It is not relevant. What is relevant is this—Illien was the fief lord of these lands, the last true fief lord. What Barren is, his name implies. If Illien chose to escape his name in the way of the foolish, you must find out why the Tower still holds his memory, or why he still holds the Tower."

"But we—"

"I saw what you did, when you first ventured here. You have returned. If anything of that Tower remains in this one, find it. Wake it."

"I can't—"

"No. You are bound to me. Even when we first met it was true, although I did not understand the reasons for it. The Tower cannot take what you cannot offer."

"Lord Nightshade," Tiamaris began.

"Lord Tiamaris. I leave you now. Kaylin—"

She had started to enter the darkness, and turned. "You're worried," she said, half surprised.

"I am concerned, yes. Given the circumstances, I do not think it a sign of undue weakness. Be careful, in the Tower. Be careful with your wishes, be careful with your fears. Expose as little as you possibly can."

Severn, who seldom spoke when Nightshade was present, said, "If the fate of the City depends upon that, we're already doomed; what the Tower saw when we visited it a few hours ago—in subjective time—will give it everything it needs, if it intends harm."

"It is not perhaps the Tower itself that is the concern. The will of the Tower is not the only will present when the Tower is active."

"The Tower *isn't* active or we wouldn't be in this mess," Kaylin snapped.

"Is it not?" Nightshade replied. "Touch the walls, Kaylin. Trace the circles on the floors." He stepped away from the gaping hole itself. "It was not a simple matter to gain entry."

"We walked in through the gap in the fence."

"Yes. I...did not. And I fear that leaving will take some effort. I will leave," he added, "while you enter. One of us will have a less difficult time because the attention of the Tower will be split." He nodded to the Dragon Lord, and to Severn.

Kaylin lifted a hand to her cheek. Then she grimaced. "Haven't we done this before?"

"Last time," Severn offered, "there was a door."

CHAPTER 25

There was dust on the floor; it was undisturbed by anything but the edge of Nightshade's cape. Small shards of rock added texture to the walk, as did the visible webs of industrious spiders. There was no light. Kaylin glanced at Tiamaris, and the Dragon shook his head.

"It is still a Tower. Magic here is unsafe."

"Even more so than it was the first time," Severn added quietly. They turned to look at him as he knelt and examined the floor. When he rose, he glanced at them both. "If I understood everything that's been said to date, this Tower is starved for power, for magic. The use of magic will draw its attention because it requires magic to fulfill its mandate."

Kaylin grimaced. "You not only didn't fail magical theory," she said, as she began to edge her way into the darkness, "you probably got the highest mark in your damn class."

"Which is your way of telling me I'm making sense."

"Pretty much." She stood in the door frame, listening. Silence. She spoke a word. A name. Silence. She spoke a different name, with the same results. Nobody was home. She bent and touched the surface of the floor that the outer light could still reach. Severn bent to sweep the dust away, and she caught his wrist, pressing it tightly in warning. He stilled.

"What is wrong?" Tiamaris asked.

She shook her head. "Nothing. But…"

"Is the Tower speaking to you?"

"No." That would be too damn easy. The building was as silent as most deserted buildings; the walls muffled the sounds of the nearby street, which wasn't hard, given how deserted it was. "You?"

"No. If we exchange words, I believe you will know." Tiamaris glanced at her arms.

"It's like a crypt in here," Kaylin said. "Can either of you see any doors?"

Mindful now of the dust that Kaylin had prevented him from disturbing, Severn began to walk along the rounded wall. He walked full circle, some of it in darkness, and came back to them. "No doors," he said, to no one's surprise. "Nothing that looks like it might be either a window or a portal, either. The dimensions on the inside of this section of Tower appear to conform to the dimensions on the outside.

"There are no stairs. It's possible there might be a trapdoor under the dust along the floor."

"The floors are stone."

"The floors that we've examined in any detail are."

Kaylin completed her own circuit of the interior wall. He was right; it was what you'd expect if the building were entirely as it appeared. Except for its lack of stairs. Or a door that led into the rectangular part that jutted out the side.

"Any ideas?" Severn asked.

"Yes."

"I was afraid of that."

It wasn't possible to walk across the dust without disturbing it, but Kaylin made certain they walked carefully as she surveyed the floor. She couldn't walk on her toes, and didn't try, but she sec-tioned off a large part of the floor—verbally, as she'd brought nothing with her to do it the regular way—and then she began to brush the dust away.

She did it carefully and methodically as Severn and Tiamaris watched.

"Private, what are you doing?"

"Writing," she replied. She was. She had no ink, of course, but the dust itself was useful for that. Tiamaris took a breath, but no words followed. She lost track of time as she worked, writing first the large, crossed strokes of a *T,* followed by the steeple of an *A,* and the rather more difficult rounded *R.* The last *A* was slightly squashed by the perimeter left by careful feet.

When she had finished, she motioned to Severn.

But Tiamaris and Severn were already conversing, in low enough voices that she'd missed them while she worked. "Severn?"

It was Tiamaris who answered. "What have you written, Kaylin?" The quiet hush of his voice made her instantly uneasy.

"Her name. The name I gave her."

"Not your name."

"No. I think you'd recognize my—" She stopped. He'd also recognize the name she'd given the Tower. Turning, squinting into the pale light cast by a missing wall, she saw the floor. The dust had been cleared, all right—but the letters she had thought she was making and the ones that now existed in the temporary medium of age were in no way the same.

She'd seen complicated religious mandalas that were simpler, albeit far more colorful, than this. "I did that?"

"Yes," Tiamaris said. "Surprising, isn't it?" If he'd been Severn, she would have kicked him for the tone of his voice; she considered it, but it was a bad deal. She'd probably break her own toes without leaving so much as a bruise.

"I don't suppose you can read it?" she asked instead.

"No."

"Recognize it?"

"Yes."

"The Old Tongue."

"Yes. But I will say this—it is of a piece. Whatever you wrote, it has a cohesive overall meaning."

"How can you say that if you can't even read the language?"

"Look at it."

She did, although it was more of a glare. Over her shoulder, Tiamaris's voice continued. "The Arkon and Sanabalis have some experience with the written word—but it is scant experience, and much of it is secondhand. I have more firsthand experience with the written word, and very, very little with the spoken; the Arkon considers it a failing. Of mine," he added, in case this wasn't obvious. "There is some visual component to the written word, and in the case of stone or stand-alone carvings, some dimensional component, as well. Where the words combine in a specific way, there is an overall harmony to the whole." When she failed to speak at all, he sighed.

"If a wall is made of brick," he added, "it is a wall. If you throw bits of wood and copper and wax into the whole while you're constructing it, it is something else entirely."

"This," she said, looking at the complicated pattern of lines, curves, and dots, "is a wall?"

"I hope," he replied, "for the sake of this City that it is either a key or a door, but yes, you grasp the general idea."

When the breeze began to move through the opening in the wall, Kaylin barely noticed; she was, for the moment, as tired as she might have been had she spent the entire evening with the midwives. But the breeze became wind, and when she turned to look into the open streets, she found that she could no longer see them. They'd disappeared, and she hadn't noticed. In their place? A window, of sorts. The glass—if it was glass—was murky, but it looked solid enough that wind shouldn't have passed right through it.

She dug her fingernails into her palms, because pain sometimes pushed her into a state of wakefulness.

"No," Severn said quietly. "It's not a natural wind. You're all right?"

"I'm fine." But she grimaced. "I feel like I pissed off the general drillmaster and I've just finished running his forty damn laps." Raising her hands, she tightened what passed for a knot of hair as the breeze blew tendrils into her eyes. It was, she discovered, always at her back—but that wasn't the most striking thing about it.

The wind lifted the dust. Both the dust she had cleared and the dust she had obviously painstakingly left in place. But it didn't scatter the writing; it didn't obliterate the work she'd done. Instead, the dust and the space where it had been pushed out of the way rose as a single piece, as if both dust and space were now solid.

Tiamaris frowned like a classroom teacher, as if this sort of thing happened every day, and he was intent on *marking* it. When the wind had stilled again, the entire mandala was facing them and slowly—very slowly—rotating. He watched it intently, his frown deepening.

"There is," he said, as he moved, taking small and precise steps, "a distinct aesthetic to the writing. Have you noticed it?"

"No. I don't exactly spend long hours staring at the backs of my legs or the insides of my arms." To make a point, she held up her sleeve-covered arms.

"Ah. Well." He shrugged. "If you look at the words you scribed—in an admittedly unstable medium—you can see where the lines are slightly off, the spacing is off, the placement is crooked. It's much the work of a beginner."

She turned to look at Severn, who saw the expression on her face, and offered a very fief like shrug in response.

"But here—can you see this, Private?"

Any response that came to mind would have been considered career-limiting. Biting her tongue, she watched as he carefully lifted a hand and began to touch the dust. Some of it clung to his fingers; if the rotating structure before them looked solid, it wasn't: it was dust and the space that wasn't dust.

He frowned, and began to massage the dust, moving as the runic pattern rotated. If it had taken Kaylin a long time to write the initial words, it took Tiamaris just as long to fiddle with them. Longer, really, and to Kaylin's eye, he was making no damn difference. But to his own, he was, and given that she'd thought she was writing elementary letters, she left him to it.

When he finished, he stepped back. He was paler, and he was sweating. She couldn't recall ever seeing him sweat before.

"It's done," he said, his voice a hushed whisper.

"Tiamaris?"

He glanced at her, as if surprised that she were standing beside him.

"Lord Tiamaris," Severn began. Kaylin never heard what he'd intended to say, because light flared in the darkness of the Tower's confines, and it was, in shape and size, the entirety of the pattern that she had written and Tiamaris had slowly nudged into shape. Dust became ethereal gold, and the lines, the dots, and the squiggles that were so distinctive, hardened in place, as if they had always been seeking a form.

She still couldn't read it; neither could Tiamaris. But they both felt its voice as if it were song or story, and they were held in place by it.

Severn Handred was not. He touched them both, left hand on Kaylin's shoulder, right on Tiamaris's, although neither Kaylin or the Dragon liked to be touched much, and he shook them gently. "Lord Tiamaris," he said, in a tone of voice he might have used on one of Marrin's foundlings, "I believe that Kaylin made the door and you have unlocked it. We have little time, if Lord Nightshade is to be believed."

They both turned to look at him; Kaylin actually shook herself back to reality first. She watched Tiamaris with real concern as he slowly did the same. He was not particularly pleased by said concern, and his expression chilled into the glacial.

He did, however, nod to Severn. "Indeed," he replied. "Private?"

She grimaced, and then realized that all of her hair was not, in

fact, standing on end; her skin wasn't so tingly it felt raw. "It's—
I don't think it's magic."

One dark brow rose. "You think it natural, then?" And she'd
thought Dragons weren't as capable of sarcasm as the Barrani.

"No…but it doesn't feel like magic to me. Or to the marks—"
she bit back the rest of the words. "Never mind." Taking a deep
breath and ignoring, with effort, every word of warning Nightshade had left her with, she stepped into the runes.

They were a portal, but it was a portal unlike any she'd experienced, which was just as well; she was likely to get only one meal
today, and she didn't much feel like losing what was left of it. If
anything was; it felt as if she hadn't eaten for days. Where the usual
trip through a portal involved darkness and dizziness followed by a
painful and disorienting ejection, this time there was light, and it
was gentle, as if emitted in its entirety by golden dust.

Where usually she lost all sense of up and down, in this transition she could feel the ground beneath her feet, and when she
looked to either side, she could see both Severn and Tiamaris. Her
voice—because she was Kaylin, she had to try to speak—was soft,
the sound diffuse. But it was clear.

"Severn?"

He nodded. "I can hear you."

"Is this different for you from a normal portal?"

He nodded again. "I don't think it *is* a portal." He turned to
look back, and so did Kaylin.

"There's no door," she pointed out.

"No. But there's a path. Portals don't generally offer those."

"It is not part of the general mechanics of a portal," Tiamaris
added. "But the Towers bend the mechanics of magic as we currently understand them."

Or as Dragons did, at any rate. Kaylin paused and knelt. The
floor felt strange; it had give. She thought it might be a very thick
carpet, but when her hand touched smooth, cool stone, she
changed her mind. "Where are we?"

Tiamaris was silent for an uncharacteristically long time. "I am not entirely certain," he said at last, which was hardly worth breaking silence for.

"It feels...like...flesh. Flesh with stone skin."

He nodded. "I noticed. Take the path, Kaylin. Let us follow where it leads."

It led nowhere, as far as Kaylin could tell. The comfort that she'd first taken in the soft landing—as it were—gave way, step by step, to an uneasy sense that she would never again get her bearings. The floor continued to give slightly with every step she took, but she could feel no walls when she stretched her hands out to the sides, and without walls, there were no doors.

No, that wasn't true. The words she'd written had become a door. But it was a one-way door that led to a stretch of faintly illuminated nothing. She stopped walking and after a few seconds, so did her companions. "You didn't encounter anything like this when you went to Nightshade's Castle, did you?"

"Nothing as harmless, no. And at the time, it was not Castle Nightshade."

She wanted to ask whose damn Castle it had been, but didn't; this wasn't the time or place for it. "So this isn't like the other traps or resistances you encountered?"

"No. I would not say that this *is* a trap, if my opinion is to count for much."

"What would you say it is?"

"The Tower has very little power, Kaylin. I would guess that whatever it does have, it husbands it. It gives only what is necessary."

"What would this have been, if it had more power to give?"

"This may come as a surprise to you," he replied drily, "But I am not an Ancient. Nor am I, human philosophy aside, a living construct."

"Which means you don't know."

"Which means, as you so succinctly put it, I do not know."

She blew hair out of her eyes because it was better than the alternative, which was a loud, long rant in Leontine. Leontine did not, at the moment, seem like the right language for this Tower. Then she sat down in the middle of what was a very narrow road, and wrapped her arms around her folded legs, resting her chin on her knees. "I can't believe she did all this—"

"It is not a she—"

"Just to lose us here. She might have only had the power to bring us this far, but this has to lead somewhere."

"You feel we are approaching it incorrectly."

"Yes. It's my life," she added with a grimace, "so I can't possibly get it right the first time."

What was a door, in this place? She had seen the basement of part of Castle Nightshade, and she had seen the writing on the floors and ceilings of the one room in which she'd first heard the voice of the Old Ones. "Tiamaris, does every Castle have writing in it?"

"The Old Tongue?"

"Yes. The marks."

"It is our suspicion that every Tower possesses them, yes. I did not encounter them in Nightshade."

"I did. And if Illien owned this Tower, he probably found them here."

"Why do you say that?"

"Because when I was in Nightshade, I heard the Old Ones. They spoke to me."

"Did they speak to Lord Nightshade?"

She frowned. "No, I don't think so. I don't think he was expecting what happened. But that's when he—" She hesitated, and then said, "When he let me read his name. I needed to hold on to that. I'm not sure what would have happened, otherwise. I don't think they were ever meant to speak with mortals." She thought, for a brief moment, of the Leontines, their creation and their corruption.

"Why do you feel that Illien found such a room?"

"Because it was only after he had lived in the Tower for a while that he began to attempt to shed his name. I think he could understand some of what was written. He was supposed to be like that."

"Ah. You think what was written was inimical?"

"No. I think it was inimical to him." She closed her eyes and then, opening them, began to unbutton her sleeves. Severn helped; his fingers brushed her wrists in the low light. He rolled them neatly up until they gathered at the bend in her elbow. "I thought so," she said softly.

They were glowing. "Severn—look at the back of my neck, will you?"

He nodded. "Yes," he added, from behind her back. "They're glowing. They're not blue, and the light isn't harsh."

"It's like the light in this tunnel, isn't it?"

"Very."

"Grab my shoulders," she told them both.

Severn did as she asked; Tiamaris hesitated. "What are you attempting?"

"I'm not sure."

He raised one brow.

"They're glowing," she told him. "That's always meant something before."

"You've used the power before."

"Mostly unintentionally."

"That brings me little comfort, Kaylin. What do you intend now?"

"To use it intentionally," she replied.

She closed her eyes. In the dim light, everything went dark; she could hear breathing—hers, Severn's. Tiamaris, if he was breathing at all, was utterly silent about it. She listened for a moment longer, and then she let it go, concentrating instead on seeing. With her eyes closed.

The marks on her arms were glowing. The marks on her legs were glowing, as well; she could even detect the faint luminescence of the marks that traced part of her spine from her back to the base of her skull. They didn't speak to her, of course; she couldn't read them. But she could look at them. With her eyes closed.

They looked very much like the runes she had accidentally carved.
There are no accidents.

Who had said that? She thought it might be Marcus, but she
couldn't clearly remember. The runes she had carved in the
medium of dust were far fewer than these; she tried to count them
and lost track, in part because they began to move, growing
brighter as they approached the edge of her field of vision,
dimmer as she turned to look. And she did turn, or felt that she
did; in the end, it didn't matter, because in the end, they surrounded her, glowing in that same pale way as the light in these
strange halls did.

She wondered if Tiamaris would see any harmony in the way
these runes lined up, or if he would attempt to nudge them into
a slightly better formation; it didn't matter. He couldn't see them.
And they felt right to her. But she turned toward two—if it was
only two—that glowed more brightly than the others, and
reaching out, she touched them.

They were hot, and while the heat didn't burn her figurative
hands, it was on the wrong edge of painful. She held on anyway,
using the grip to lever herself off the ground. Without opening
her eyes, she said, "Follow me."

They followed. She felt Severn's presence by her side; she couldn't
feel Tiamaris, but she heard the rumble of Dragon breath. It was
loud and deep, disturbing in such a small space. She opened her eyes.

The darkness was gone, as was the endless narrow path; they
had walked from it into a room the size—and almost the shape—
of a cavern. It was not, however, a natural cavern, because everywhere the eye could see, runes had been carved into the surface
of stone, some of it curving its way to a height several stories above
their heads. The floor was carved with runes, as well, but unlike
the strokes and deep grooves that reached upward, these lay in a
series of concentric circles, which very much implied that the base
shape of the room was circular.

Kaylin took one step and stumbled; Severn caught her arm.

"I'm fine," she told him, righting herself.

He said a very loud nothing. "What did you do?"

"I looked for the right words. I think—I think I found them."

"That," a new voice said, "is not all you have found. Welcome to my home."

In the center of the room a man had appeared. He was hard to look at, not because he was ugly or intimidating, but because he should have been beautiful. He was tall, as all Barrani Lords were tall, and his hair was a sweep of black that trailed down his shoulders like the finest of cloaks. His skin was pale, his cheekbones high, his shoulders both broad and slender.

But his eyes were all of black; they showed no trace of the blue that meant anger or the green that meant contentment—not that contentment in the Barrani was a sure sign of safety. Kaylin stopped herself from taking a step back and schooled her expression. This, she was certain, was Illien; he was not—quite—alive.

"Lord Illien," Tiamaris said, tendering the standing Barrani male a deep bow.

"I was," the Barrani replied, after a long pause. "I was called Illien by my kin. You are not, I think, among their number."

"No."

"But the world has changed much. I bid you welcome." He raised both of his arms in one sudden, sweeping gesture, and the runes along wall and floor began to glow a livid, ugly red. His arms then fell to his sides; the red, however, didn't diminish.

It began to pulse, as if it were alive.

Don't stand on the floor, was Kaylin's first thought. Her second was, *where the hell would you like us to stand?*

But Tiamaris threw up one hand in a brief, sharp gesture, a twist of fingers and palm in the air, and when it was done, Kaylin's skin developed the usual goose bumps and raised hair. She also developed a distinct lack of weight, and buoyed by the Dragon Lord's magery, left the stone floor, hovering a foot or two above the ground.

Illien—the man who had once been Illien—nodded as if he'd expected no less; he wasn't shocked, surprised or annoyed. In fact, he had no facial expression at all, which was why his face looked so disturbing. That, and the fact that he was sort of dead.

"I will take nothing from you," he told them all, in a flat, neutral voice, "except what is needful. You need feel no fear."

"Fear is entirely voluntary in this case," Severn replied.

The Barrani Lord looked through Severn. This wasn't uncommon, but usually it happened because Severn was merely human; in this case, Kaylin had the distinct impression it was happening because what Severn said made no sense to him. If anything did.

"Do not fight the Tower," Lord Illien told them, and his arms moved again, almost a blur to the eye given how still he was otherwise standing. The floors and the walls didn't change; the air did. It swept across them all like the edge of a storm, slamming them toward the rounded curve of walls, and the runes that waited there, continuing to pulse as if they were alive.

Tiamaris gestured. If he was slow—and compared to the dead Barrani Lord he was—he was timely; something invisible, and not terribly soft, inserted itself between the walls and the people who were rapidly approaching them; they bounced, and landed once again in midair.

Kaylin almost told Tiamaris to drop them because she couldn't fight while dangling. But Illien hadn't moved, and any fighting she was good at didn't seem relevant. He did, however, frown. Or almost frown. His face lost some of its total absence of expression. She couldn't call it composure; Severn, to the far right, was composed.

"The Tower," Illien said, in a slightly different tone of voice, "is mine. It is *mine*."

"It is yours," Tiamaris said, in a tone that indicated no agreement, "only so long as you can hold it."

"I can hold it," the Barrani Lord replied, "forever. You do not understand, Dragon Lord, if Lord of anything you be." Dead or not, he was still Barrani; something in Tiamaris's expression indicated weakness. It was a weakness that not even magic was required to exploit. "Is that why you are here? Are you without purpose, Dragon Lord? Have you lost your hoard?"

Tiamaris said nothing for a long moment, and then he opened his mouth. Kaylin had time to shout a word of warning—no more—before the room was wreathed in flames.

Kaylin's hair singed, which she expected.

The walls screamed, which she did not.

If runes could bleed, these did; the ugly, livid red now looked like blistered flesh when skin has been seared off. Tiamaris fell silent at once, and the flames that had left his mouth guttered, but the room smelled pretty much like it looked; it took effort not to wretch. Still caught in the grip of Tiamaris's magic, which hadn't faltered, Kaylin looked to Severn; Severn was watching the Barrani Lord.

"Lord Illien," he said quietly, in the silence Tiamaris left.

"Tiamaris," Kaylin said, ignoring him. "Let me go. Keep Severn away from the runes—keep yourself away—but put *me* down."

Tiamaris hesitated for just a moment, and then nodded. She settled—slowly—to a ground that groaned in pain. She couldn't comfort it—it was a damn floor. But she overrode her intense and unexpected squeamishness, and knelt carefully.

"Tara?"

The word seemed to make no difference to the floor's expression of pain. It would almost have been easier had it opened eyes and a gaping maw, because then it would make sense. Briefly.

Severn, however, ignored her. "Lord Illien," he said again. "You were once considered a sage. One of the wisest of your kin."

Lord Illien was silent for long enough she wondered if he'd heard Severn, but eventually he nodded. He looked neither pleased nor flattered. "I was."

"For years, you studied the words of the Old Ones. They brought you here."

Something like blue light flickered in the black of his eyes. He nodded again. Even dead, the Barrani were capable of suspicion; it was their rest state.

"It's our guess that every Tower has a room such as this, and you must have visited more than one Tower before you chose to take up residence here."

Again, light flickered, pale streaks in the darkness, like the trail left by falling stars. Illien did not answer the question.

Severn waited until he was certain there would be no answer before he continued, "This is not the only Tower that you visited. There would have been few Towers that would be closed to you."

Lord Illien nodded.

"Was this the last?"

"No. It was the first."

"And you returned to it."

"It is not relevant," was the cool reply. "I have seen what lies at the heart of *Ravellon*. There is no escaping it."

CHAPTER 26

The Dragon Lord shook his head. He had remained silent throughout, neither adding nor disagreeing. Now he said, "Have you found the freedom you sought, Lord Illien?"

"I am free," he replied after a pause. "And the Tower is mine."

"The Tower was built to serve a purpose."

"Yes. But it has served. It can no longer function as it did. I would have let it feed. I have let it feed before, content to wait. I have eternity, and Ravellon will arrive sooner or later. It is reality, Dragon Lord. This," he added, lifting his arm in a slow, wide arc, "is the daydream of senile gods."

"And the mortals?"

"Who can say? They should never have been here at all. You've seen that. The Old Ones corrupted what they touched. But the humans? The winged ones? This is not their world. It is ours, and we are chained—*chained*—like the most base of dogs." Light now, blue, deep blue, the color of anger or danger, shone in his eyes. It was still there, somehow.

In Illien, it was still there. Kaylin had seen no signs of emotion in the undead Barrani she'd encountered in the fief of Nightshade months ago. But Illien had been no fool, and he had had some understanding of the Old Ones, their language, and what he intended for himself; the others had been shades and shadows; animated corpses.

"What lies at the heart of *Ravellon?*"

For the first time, Illien smiled. Kaylin thought it was both the most beautiful smile she had ever seen, and conversely, the most repulsive. "You will see," he told Tiamaris.

But Kaylin had heard enough. "And what of the Tower?" She rose, settling her hands on her hips in a pose the foundlings would have recognized.

"It is mine."

"The hells. You chose this Tower for a reason. You made that clear. *This* one was different. And it's still different. You knew that, then," she added. It was an accusation.

"It is mine."

"And what in the hells is *left* of you that you think you can lay claim to *anything* else?"

"I am what I was," he replied. "But I am not bound. I cannot be chained. Not even by the Tower itself."

Kaylin shook her head. "The Tower—"

"Yes. This Tower was different. I do not know why. But it can no longer take from me what it required. A gift," he added, "of knowledge and planning."

"You will kill it—"

"It is not alive."

"How would you know life? You've given up yours!"

"And you, mortal, are you so swift to judge me? You were never born to the chain of word and command. You were given the breath of life and thought by the simple expedient of birth. No lake holds the name that someone else bestows upon you. No single word can force you to do what is against your very nature.

"I am," he added, "what you are."

She shook her head. "You're not."

"How so?"

"We die. We age, and we die." And then she stopped speaking for just a moment, and she *looked* at Illien. There was no power in her gaze; no magic, no unconscious use of the runes that lay glowing across her skin—but he flinched for the first time. Dead, she had called them, when she had first seen them.

"Tiamaris." Her voice was soft. "He has no name."

"No. I believe that is the point of the undying."

"He has no power."

"He demonstrably has power, Private."

"No power of his own."

Tiamaris stiffened.

"The power is mine."

"No, it's not. It's no more yours than your name, now. The power you use—"

"It is the Tower's power—"

"No, it's *not*. It's not the Tower's. The Tower's power comes, in part, from names—from Old names. You have nothing to give the Tower, and that's why the borders have all but crumpled."

"The Tower," he said again, "is mine."

"Is that what you were told? That everything would still be yours?" It was a guess. He didn't give her the satisfaction of an answer, not in so many words. But she was tugging at the thread of an answer anyway, and she followed it. "The lake," she told him. "The lake you sneered at. It's not a real lake. It's not anything like that—but it's life. It's the life of the Old Ones.

"And it's the life of the Dragons, the Barrani, and the Tower. You were the children of gods. It doesn't matter what we are—your names are eternal. You can be destroyed, yes—but the name isn't destroyed with you. It continues. Our magic—those of us who have it—is tied to our bodies. It withers us, consumes our life. Yours doesn't.

"But you've given up the source of your power."

"I have power."

"It's not yours. It's not a power that the Tower can use. The

Tower has taken power—somehow—from those who have it, but it's not a power that can sustain either the Tower or the poor sod who—" She stopped for a moment. Barren.

"It's trying to feed," she told him.

"It cannot drain me, anymore."

"It didn't drain you—"

"I could not *leave*. Do you not understand?" Again, strands of blue in those eyes.

"And you can now?"

"As I please. I do not need the Tower."

"The Tower," Kaylin said with heat, "doesn't damn well need *you*." She launched herself across the red and blistered ground, and it rose like a wall of scored flesh to prevent her from reaching Illien. Kaylin managed to stop before impact. But she lifted a hand—her palms bare—and she touched runes misshapen by the unnatural rise of the floor.

If the Tower was hungry, as she knew it must be, it devoured nothing; she felt no pain, no loss of self, in the simple contact. The runes which were a livid, blistered red felt like…injured flesh, no more, no less. She'd seen a lot of that in her time. It had no face, of course, and no mouth with which to utter whimpering sounds of pain; it didn't sweat, and it didn't bleed. Well, maybe it bled.

But to Kaylin Neya, it felt alive, and injured. There was no shadow in it, no darkness, no malice.

"Tara," she whispered.

The ground shook.

Tiamaris roared before she could speak again. The hair on the back of her neck rose, and she knew, before she turned, what was happening. As he had done once before in the vast confines of the Tower's artificial freedom, he did now in its cage: he assumed the great, scaled form of myth, of legend.

She turned, her palms still touching Tara, as if to offer comfort by sheer presence, and she saw the last of his transformation: the elongation of jaw, the growth of fangs, the unfolding of webbed, glittering wings. He was red, as he had been once before; she had never asked him about the variance in color and what it meant. If it was similar to eye color, the Barrani Lord was in trouble.

The room was huge. She'd thought it, coming in, but she had proof now: Tiamaris stretched his wings, tip to tip, before he bunched them behind his shoulders and they didn't hit wall. Or floor. He pushed himself off the ground, and in this room, all surfaces adorned by reddened glyphs, he looked almost kin to them.

He breathed. Fire plumed from his open mouth, but this time, it was a tight, tight cone, similar to the one that Sanabalis might use to light a damn candle when he wanted to show off. It struck Illien, who remained standing in the flames as if they were merely weather.

Fire had killed the undying she'd encountered twice before; fire did not touch Illien. But the Tower, beneath her flattened palms, shuddered, rippling as if in agony.

"Tiamaris, stop!" she cried. "You're hurting *her!* You're hurting Tara!"

The fire banked; the Dragon landed. He said, "I will kill him, Kaylin," and the ground shook, not as if it were in pain, but because his voice was like an earthquake. Except in the air.

Had Tara been a real child, and not a building too vast to measure, Kaylin would have gathered her in her arms and turned her back to Tiamaris and the fight itself—which, in the case of unknown magic, was a big risk. As it was, Tiamaris breathed again, but this time, on the ground, the cone was short and aimed entirely at Illien's chest.

Fire wrapped itself around that chest like an orange, translucent hand—but nothing burned; not Illien. Not, thank the gods, the ground.

Severn, silent, had unwound his weapon chain from its berth at his waist. He glanced at Kaylin, whose hands were still pressed against the only part of the floor that had risen, like rock formation. She nodded grimly, and he began to navigate the runic surface of the floor, almost exactly opposite Tiamaris's chosen point of first contact.

Illien lifted his arms, a sweeping, sudden gesture, and the lights in the room flared white. Cursing, Kaylin closed her eyes.

The sound went out with the lights.

She opened her eyes immediately, but the sound didn't return, and the light was a shimmering gold that transformed the people she knew: Tiamaris, Severn, and Illien. Tiamaris wavered in her vision, his Dragon wings and tail almost transparent. At his heart, she saw the man—or his human form—that she'd worked with. Severn was Severn, although his weapon was a bright, solid shape that was hard to look at.

And Illien? His outline existed, dusted with light, but it was pale and ghostly; of the three he was hardest to see.

He is dead.

She turned at the sound of the familiar voice, and saw Tara.

But this Tara was not the child she had met hours ago in her own subjective time. This one was a woman, older than Kaylin; she was so gaunt and thin she looked as if she were starving to death. Her hair was pale, and her eyes were the same shade of gold as the light; the same shade of gold that had illuminated the path taken to reach Illien.

She smiled when Kaylin's eyes widened; there was something about the lift of her lips that was subtle enough to be Barrani. Not that Teela's smile was particularly subtle. "You return," she said to Kaylin. She spoke in High Barrani.

Kaylin nodded. "The border defenses are falling. The shadows—"

"Yes. I've seen them. You are safe here," she added.

"I'm not. He—his name—"

"He surrendered his name."

"No—that would be service, and servitude. He did something else to his name—"

The Tower nodded. "He did. He was unhappy here. I did not understand why." She turned so that Kaylin was looking at her face in profile; her chin sank slightly as she spoke. "He said he could not leave, but that was not true. He left. He left often." She glanced back at Kaylin.

Kaylin was, admittedly, distracted; Tiamaris had closed with Illien and Illien pushed himself off the ground, and away. Not back, not toward Severn, but *down*. She could see him, but only barely.

Tiamaris's massive jaws snapped at empty air, and then he looked down. Kaylin couldn't see floors or walls from this strange vantage; she could see only the people—as if all else was stage dressing, or less. But she knew, from the way Tiamaris lifted his head, that Tiamaris and Severn were seeing the room itself. Illien had somehow gone through the floor, and only by breaking it could they reach him.

She had no doubt that Tiamaris *could* break stone; she had seen him do it. But he hesitated before he attempted to destroy this floor. She felt a surge of uncomplicated gratitude, and she turned to the Tower, because the Tower had said something that urgently needed clarification.

"Tara," she said, voice low, "what did he do to his name? The others—the other undying that I encountered—weren't like Illien."

"No. They are sundered entirely from the name that gave them life. They did not understand the strength that the name signified; they were driven by their fear of its weakness.

"But Lord Illien understood the strength in a name. He came to Ravellon and its crumbling edges, and he began to search. To learn."

"He came to you."

She nodded.

Kaylin hesitated for a minute and then said, "And you spoke with him. As you spoke with me the first time."

Tara nodded.

"Did you speak to the others the same way?"

"No."

"Why this one? Why Illien?"

"I knew he would take the Tower." She wrapped her arms around her chest tightly and then met Kaylin's gaze. "It is not easy, Kaylin Neya. To be a Tower. To have the responsibility. I was just…a place, to the others. I was just a source of power. They understood the boundaries of this building," she added, gazing around in what looked like darkness to Kaylin. "They understood that they were to hold it, to defend it, with their lives.

"But it was not a matter of fealty. It was a matter of desire. They were supreme if they held the Tower."

"And the Tower?"

"I was—the word for it is difficult—lonely. I do not know if the other Towers labor under the same difficulty. They were not wakened by you. What I wanted—" She shook her head. "But it is ruins, now."

Kaylin saw Tiamaris thrown back, through the air; saw his wings flatten against what she assumed was a curve of wall. She saw Severn leap and roll as if to avoid either a collision or a magical blast. She knew she should be there.

But she was here. "No," she said, trying to keep her voice level, "what you wanted was important."

"He talked to me," Tara whispered. "He tried to talk to me. I knew…how to answer. I knew I shouldn't. It was many years before I did. He asked me questions," she added. "He asked me about the shadows, about Ravellon, about my goals.

"He sat there," she told Kaylin, pointing. Kaylin couldn't see what she pointed at in the darkness, but it didn't seem to matter. "He sat there, almost every day, for many years. And one day, Kaylin, I answered."

Kaylin's breath cut across her teeth as Tiamaris roared. She couldn't hear it; she could only see the shape of his neck, the way his head rose, his jaws opened. And she could, once again, see Illien; he was moving beneath Tiamaris.

"What happened, then? Why did he seek to lose his name?"

Tara's gaze slid away. "It was my fault—" she began.

Kaylin wanted to grab her by the arms and shake her. She didn't, but better, she didn't even try. Golden, diffuse light sharpened and brightened for a moment, and Tara staggered, falling to her knees. Kaylin could hear, as if at a great remove, the timbre of a Dragon's roar.

She reached for Tara then. Her hands passed through the Tower's shoulders and arms.

"He is strong," Tara said, struggling to rise. "Even as he is, he is strong."

"Tara. *Tara.*"

The woman looked up. She made no attempt to rise. "It's my fault," she whispered. Kaylin felt the words as if there was no space between Tara's lips and her ears.

"What, exactly, is your fault?"

"I wanted to keep him," she whispered. "I wanted to keep him forever."

"But—but that's the way the Towers work, isn't it?"

She shook her head. "We cannot *choose*. We can test, we can protect, we can hide where necessary—but we cannot choose."

"You chose him."

She shook her head. "He chose *me*. He understood that I was different. He was powerful, Kaylin. Of his kin, one of the wisest. His knowledge is deep. He chose me, but I could not destroy the Lord of the Tower. He challenged the Tower Lord—"

"Who was the previous Lord?"

She frowned. "I...do not remember."

"And the Lord before that?"

The frown deepened, as if it were a fracture line under pressure. "I do not remember."

"What do you remember of your life before Lord Illien?"

The Tower was silent for a long, long time, and the silence carried the faint echo of the crackle of Dragon fire. At last, the Tower said, "I remember you."

It was not the answer that Kaylin had hoped for. "Why?"

"I don't know."

The Tower had existed for a long damn time. It had been awake for less, but that less was also a long damn time. What Kaylin tolerated or expected from children and what she expected from adults, was almost entirely different. But she understood loneliness, and she understood the ways in which it could, over time, drive you insane. Or drive you to places that were, in the end, far worse than being alone.

"What did you do?" she asked softly.

Tara flinched, and when she looked up, the left corner of her mouth was swollen and bleeding. "I wanted to keep him forever," she said.

"Tara—"

"I brought him to my heart, and I tried to teach him to read what was written there. I thought if he did he might change the rules enough that I *could* keep him."

Severn was bleeding. Ice had driven itself into his arm and splintered; water mingled with blood as it fell. The wound wasn't deep, but it was also not the only one he'd taken; it was just the most recent. He was fast enough in the red, pulsing light, to avoid death; his chain was fast enough to deflect almost anything the Barrani Lord sent against him. But Illien—if he was indeed Illien—seemed to vanish and reappear at will.

Tiamaris had the advantage of height; he seldom made contact with either wall or floor and the room itself was so cavernous he could manage small leaps as if they were flight. If he was injured, it wasn't obvious. He was, however, angry. The Wolves, like the Hawks, learned early that anger was not an emotion that helped one survive contact with an enemy intent on killing you.

Illien was above rage, or beyond it; he was above the petty pleasure of triumph that power often bestows. He wasn't human, of course—but Severn had seen enough Barrani to know he wasn't Barrani, either; they had a ferocious pride in their ability, and an overweening arrogance when displaying it. He appeared, he cast whatever spell he had prepared, and he vanished.

The light in the room shifted, as if to give warning. Severn swung the chain in a circle in front of his chest, moving with it as he glanced over his shoulder. The walls of the cavern—no, the runes in the walls—began to dim.

"Severn!" Tiamaris cried. His wings folded as he landed.

Severn backed toward him, watching everything—wall, ground, the air encircled by both. The Dragon lost wings, absorbed scales; the neck shrunk, and the jaws began to fold into themselves. As it had before, armor emerged from folds in his skin—scales plating themselves into a roughly man-shaped defense.

Severn couldn't watch Tiamaris closely; he could hold his back, that was all. The Dragon Lord said, "Stand close."

"How close?"

A circle appeared on the floor, bisecting the runes that were laid there. "Within the circle."

"Lord Tiamaris—magic—"

"I judge it worth the risk," was the edged reply.

Kaylin would have asked what the purpose of the spell was; Severn was not Kaylin. Instead of asking, he said, "The risk to the Tower is not minimal if I understand everything we've seen."

"The Tower is failing," was the quiet reply. "If we do not survive, if we do not unseat Illien, it *will* fail. What we've seen in Barren will be nothing compared to what we will see, then, and it will not stop at the Ablayne. Do not leave the circle," he said again.

Severn stilled the spinning of his chain. *Kaylin,* he thought, as he felt the ground ripple. *Whatever it is you're doing, hurry.*

Kaylin heard him; his voice was so clear he might have been standing beside her, his lips pressed to her ear.

"What did you teach Illien?" Kaylin asked Tara, trying to keep the urgency—and the panic—out of her voice.

Tara's face was bruised now; her eyes were swollen. "I told him how the words were written."

"What?"

"They were laid in stone, the way they were laid into the first stone: the Dragons. The Barrani. They were inscribed into the Tower, and they were told to sleep until they were needed. You were to wake us, I think," she added. "Chosen."

"I am not the only Chosen—"

"No. But there is always one. Always." She coughed, and the

cough continued for a while; her lips were red and wet with blood. Kaylin had seen that type of cough before; it was never, ever good.

Dammit, Severn, hold on—I'm trying.

"The words," Kaylin said urgently. "How were they laid in stone?"

"How are they laid in the sleeping newborn? No hand crafts those children, but they require the strength of the word to open their eyes; to think, to breathe, to *be*."

Kaylin shook her head. "What did you tell *him?*"

"I told him that. I am alive, as he is alive, and I serve, as he serves."

She cringed. No Barrani she had ever met reacted well to being called a servant.

"I showed him the makers," she added.

"You…showed him the makers."

"Yes. I remember them. Before the long sleep, I remember their voices and their words and their song." The sentence was broken in three places by wheezing.

Goddammit, Severn, tell Tiamaris to stop whatever the hells he's doing!

It is not, sadly, Tiamaris.

"Tara. *Tara*. You don't—you can't—you don't have much time left."

She looked up then, and she lifted shaking hands toward Kaylin. Kaylin reached down automatically and caught them in her own— but this time, Tara's hands were solid. Or possibly this time, Kaylin's hands were ethereal.

"I know," Tara whispered. "Not much time. But it's better. I failed. Come, let me show you what he saw." She pitched forward with a grunt and Kaylin tightened her grip around hands that were very cold. "He doesn't want you to see," she whispered. "But I know who you are, and you know who I am. He can't stop me."

"Does he know I'm talking to you now?"

"Of course."

"Is he going to try to stop you?"

"There is only one way that he can," was her reply. An actual cut appeared across her forehead.

Yes, Kaylin thought, with growing anger. *And he's trying to do it now. With our help.* She wanted to kill him.

"No, don't," Tara whispered. "It's my fault."

Kaylin started to answer, and the light changed sharply. She could no longer see the shimmering forms of Tiamaris and Severn moving around her like golden ghosts. Instead, she could see a room—which looked a lot like the one they had entered to greet Lord Illien—which was covered in runes.

The runes were carved and precise, but there was a flow to their lines and curves, the way the dots meshed or completed a pattern that reminded her of Tiamaris's speech about harmony and placement. No chisel had carved these, she thought, and as she did, she turned. And there they were: larger than life—literally—working in a room that dwarfed Kaylin and the avatar of the Tower, but that suited their size. They were not human, did not look human; nor did they appear to be Barrani or Dragon. But they had two arms, two legs; one had wings with iridescent webbing that were folded across giant shoulders. She could not see the face of the creature that owned those wings.

But she couldn't clearly see the faces of those that walked: there were three, and they paced the room with care, examining the walls, the floors—and the two small women who now bore witness. They were brilliant, on the edge of painful to look at, they were glowing so brightly.

Chosen, one said. He was tall, and broad, his face was long, his cheeks high; of the three he looked most like the Barrani, although they fell short of the quiet confidence, the certainty of power, he radiated.

His companions turned as he spoke the single word, and Kaylin now saw that the owner of the wings had a long face, as well—but it was almost Draconian in form and shape.

This is the only life we are capable of sustaining.

Tara turned to her, her eyes now sunken and black, her skin sallow. "This did not happen," she whispered.

You will touch this youngest of our seven children, and you will be there

*when she wakes. Understand what it is that we do; understand what it is
that quickens her.*

Kaylin nodded. Her mouth was too dry to manage speech,
which, given her ability to offend her superiors, was probably a
damn good thing. Her arms began to ache. Her legs. The back
of her neck. It was a familiar pain.

The man—god?—then bent until one knee touched the surface of the floor. He traced the runes that were carved there with
care, his brow furrowed slightly in concentration. Light began to
fill those runes; the same blue light she had seen once in Castle
Nightshade's forest of a basement.

It spread slowly, and as it did, the other two began to do as he
had done; they did not kneel, but instead moved to sections of
the covered wall, touching them, concentrating on them. Gods,
Kaylin thought, in labor.

The runes across the wall came to life slowly, the light filtering
evenly across the whole of its curved surface. She watched the light
spread, until no surface was not touched by it, and then she turned
again to the three. She drew a sharp breath.

The light that had illuminated them was all but gone. They
were glowing, faintly, but the harshest of their brilliance had been
shed. It had, she realized slowly, become one with the runes. It
was *their* power. No, she thought, as they came to stand together,
it was their life.

Their life that gave the words life.

Their life that had given the Tower life.

You will touch this child, the man who had first spoken said. *What
you touch, you will change. Because you are alive. And she, too, is alive.
Life cannot long be contained or confined, although we have tried. It is
our nature to try.*

*It is your nature to grow. Grow in a way that does not destroy life, and
we must be content.*

"This didn't happen," Tara said again.

*But decide, Chosen. You have influence in this story. Choose wisely.
Choose quickly.*

I didn't ask for this, Kaylin thought.

No more did they, he replied. *No more did we. Not all events of significance, be they birth or death, are in our hands.*

Kaylin turned to Tara, who was staring at her creators. At, Kaylin supposed, her parents. "Tara," she said quietly. "What did you show Illien? What did he see?"

"Not this," Tara whispered. "This didn't happen."

"It doesn't matter. They're gods. Gods break all rules."

Not all, Chosen, the creature with a graceful variant of a Dragon's face said. She couldn't tell if it was smiling or not; that many exposed teeth never looked friendly. *But where we can, we try.*

The first god to speak said one sharp word, and the air crackled. But the Dragon god did not seem ruffled. Kaylin turned her back on them because looking at them demanded too much of her attention, and she needed what she could manage to pull together.

"What did he see?" she asked again.

"He saw the words graved. He saw the words given life."

"He saw the gods? The Old Ones?"

"He saw the creators, yes." She staggered. "He's coming, now," she whispered. She was afraid—not resigned, not tormented by the certainty of her own failure, but fearful.

"He has other things to worry about."

Tara shook her head. "Not while I live."

I was afraid of that, she thought.

You weren't. You weren't even thinking it, Severn replied. It was like having another voice to give her unwanted second thoughts.

Kaylin started to respond and then stopped because the walls began to crumple, and the floor began to fracture. She had forgotten that she was holding Tara's hands until they turned to ice in hers, the sudden cold almost blistering her skin. "Don't leave me," she whispered, eyes wide and haunted by bruises.

"I won't. But you need to let go of my hands."

She shook her head. "I let him go," she said. "I let him go, and he found a way to leave me."

"He hasn't left you. He's still here."

But Tara shook her head again as the stone of the rounded room fell; there were no longer any struts to support its weight. Dust rose, glittering like motes caught in sunlight, and in the haze of those motes, she could see the figure of a man.

"So," he said, arms folded across his chest, "now you know."

"I know she let you go. Why did you return?"

His laugh—the first such sound he'd made—was bitter. Not ugly, not quite that, but it was the only thing he'd said or done that hinted at the emotions she associated with the living. "She let me go? Is that what she told you?"

Tara, hands now numbing Kaylin's, stared at him in defiant, angry silence. "I let you go," she said, voice shaky. *"I let you go."*

"She owned my name," Illien continued, as if she hadn't spoken. "She owned it. She knew it. She *used it.*"

Kaylin's eyes widened and she turned to Tara. "Is this true?"

Tara didn't answer.

Kaylin now remembered why any smart person avoided getting involved in anything that looked like a lover's quarrel, although admittedly the circumstances didn't permit that much discretion. "Tara," she said, trying to shake her, which was hard, given the grip on her hands. "Is this true?"

"He wanted to *leave!*"

"Tara—"

"He wanted to leave." Her voice fell.

"She had what she needed," Illien continued, the laughter gone, his face once again smooth and unreadable. "She had the power to sustain her. I was not aware that I supplied it—not immediately. Did you watch what she showed you?" His demeanor was entirely different.

Kaylin, understanding that Barrani lied as naturally as most people breathed, watched him like, well, a Hawk. But she nodded, her arms now painfully cold.

"She did not show you all," he said. "Or you did not understand it. You understand the harmonics inherent in the patterns of the runes as they are laid out?"

"I'm sorry, but no."

"I...see. She will attempt to drain you, you know."

Kaylin looked down and saw that Tara's face was looking less bruised and less swollen.

"It is not the first time it has happened. I do not believe she will kill you."

"Barren," Kaylin whispered.

"The petty human mage?"

"Sounds about right."

"Yes. Some years ago."

Kaylin looked away. "You should have killed him instead."

Lord Illien said nothing. Her elbows were numb. She couldn't see the marks on her arms, and wondered what they now looked like, if they remained there at all. She had dreamed for years of getting rid of them, but this wasn't the way she wanted to do it.

"I am not the Lord of this fief. The fief has no Lord."

Tara said, "You *are.*" And then she stopped. "I have power," she told him, as if it were a promise. "I have power. I don't need—"

He looked through her.

Kaylin, however, looked down. Tears tracked their way across the face of the avatar, and as they did, age literally melted.

"Pathetic is it not? I am not the author of this decay, this destruction. But I will it. In no other way will I be free."

"You didn't give your name to the Darkness."

"No. I would have, but I was not—then—desperate enough. It doesn't matter. She cannot stand long against what waits in Ravellon. I went to Ravellon," he added. "The once. I wanted to understand the nature of life and the nature of Words. I understood enough of them to enact a change. I thought I understood the purpose, and the binding, of the old words. They are not the only language," he added. "Do not venture into Ravellon or you will be unmade.

"But when I understood the making and unmaking of life as the Ancients might have told it, I began to...revise."

"And she knew."

"She held my name," he replied. "She held it truly and completely. I could hide nothing from her when she bent her will toward me, and she watched in terror. She understood, late, what I attempted; she understood that I was reshaping, reforging, the word within me, the name itself. I thought it would free me of her. But she did the unexpected, the unforeseen.

"She changed with it, in order to continue to hold it. But she could not change much without destroying some essential part of her nature.

"She did," he added softly. "She remembers what she was but she can no longer achieve it; we will die here."

"Let her go," Kaylin whispered.

He laughed again, and it was bitter. "I let go centuries past, little human. My name is not what it was, and it cannot support life—not the life of the Ancients, not the life of my kin. I wanted knowledge, and knowledge I received."

"But you came to the Tower the first time, and it's to this Tower that you returned. Why?"

His gaze flickered for just a moment, eyes blue-green amidst striations of black. "I thought…I heard a voice. No other Tower spoke, not to me."

CHAPTER 27

Kaylin looked at Tara as if Tara was not attempting to drain her of whatever power she had. There was no triumph, no guile, nothing malicious, in Tara's expression; there was fear, pain, and a horrible desperation. Desperate people did stupid things. They did worse than stupid; they did ugly, ugly things that scarred—or destroyed—whole lives. Maybe they learned something from it, if they survived. Maybe they let the guilt of survival eat away at them from the inside, hiding from their own truths.

No one knew this better than Kaylin.

Why, then, did she have to fight the urge to kick the avatar? Why did she have to remind herself of what she herself had done, without the knowledge or the power the Tower had?

Because, she thought bitterly, it was so much easier to hate other people for making the same mistakes you'd made—because you didn't have the time to hate yourself if you did. And it was time to be done with it, because it *wouldn't help anything*.

"You came to her because she spoke."

"I heard her voice, like an echo, in this place. Like," he added softly, his expression growing remote the way expressions did when people stared off into the distance, "the essence of loss or sorrow. It was a child's voice, but it was an ancient voice."

Kaylin nodded, and Tara's breath—which she had not heard until now—was sharp and painful, like a deep, clean cut.

"She spoke to me, eventually. I listened. I decided, then, to stay."

"The Tower had a Lord."

He shrugged. "If he could hold the Tower against me, yes. He could not. It was a difficult fight, but it was challenging. Little was challenging then, but you do not understand why challenge interests the immortal. We grow bored."

And trading boredom for damnation is such a good idea.

"I learned much in my time here. I learned about the nature of magic, and the nature of worlds. I learned about the nature of life, of our concept of life. I explored," he added. "And it seemed at that time exploration was not desertion." He did not look at Tara.

Kaylin did. She seemed transfixed.

"They will destroy the Tower, now," he added softly. "Your companions. The Dragon, the darkchild. They will destroy the Tower, and we will be free."

"They *won't!*" Tara shouted. "I have power now—"

"They will," he said quietly. "There is no one left to defend it. Not you, not I. The power you might once have taken from her, you cannot take now."

Kaylin's numb arms argued against his words, but Tara's eyes widened in panic as Illien continued to speak. "You can destroy her. She is presumably mortal. That is all." He turned to Kaylin. "What will you now do, Chosen?"

"You made no deal with whatever lies in the heart of Ravellon."

Illien shrugged. After a pause, he said, "There is no negotiation possible with the power at the heart of Ravellon. I ventured into Ravellon—that much is true."

"And I'm expected to be able to tell that you're speaking the truth how?"

"I am here. I did not risk existence and sanity to free myself from the grip of one master in order to become puppet—and less—to another, especially not an unknown. I failed," he added. "She is bound to me, and I to her. I am free of her compulsion. I am not free of this place."

"What would you have of me?"

"Death," he replied. "True death. I have not achieved it."

The Tower whispered, "I'll die if he dies."

"That," Illien replied, "was a story you told yourself. It was never the truth."

It was a story that Kaylin had told herself, as well. "Tara," she murmured.

"In the end," Illien continued, speaking to Tara, "I have never been able to give you what you feel you need. I was able to give you only what you required to function."

The Tower looked up. She was crying. Not weeping; not sobbing. Just…crying. "I'm sorry," she whispered to Kaylin.

"So am I. Lord Illien?"

"You understood what she showed you?" he asked, as if it were only barely a possibility. She'd had teachers take exactly that tone of voice before, but she didn't bridle. Instead, she nodded.

Tara grunted in pain.

"I believe your companions are now attempting to reach you." The color of his eyes was a braided mixture of blue and black. "Time, now, to have an end."

"The world will fall into shadow if you—"

"Is it possible you believe that I care? One way or another, mortal, that end is coming. Were I whole, were I not encumbered by the ties I chose to accept and chose to break, even I could not long stand against it."

"I could have kept you safe!" Tara said, her voice rising.

"And what force could keep me safe from you?"

"I would never have hurt you! I wanted to keep you safe!"

"Safety," he said sharply, "is illusion. It has always been illusion." As if it were an old argument.

Kaylin could no longer feel her hands, and the bones in her

forearms were aching. But she could see, and she could see clearly. The room. The shape of the floor, the rounding of the walls. The contours of Tara's cheeks, the wetness of them some echo of any tears Kaylin had ever cried in her childhood. She saw the Old Ones flicker past her vision like ghosts going about their business, uncaring—or unaware—of observers.

She heard their voices. She could no longer understand their speech—if they had spoken at all—but the texture of those voices, the rise and fall of syllables, their distinctly individual tones blending and harmonizing as they worked, calmed her. Tara's eyes widened slightly.

She turned to look just over Kaylin's shoulder—at what, Kaylin couldn't tell because she couldn't move at all—and shook her head. The voices grew softer, as if the speakers were finally moving away.

These things, in this name, are they good?

To me? Yes. They're some of the things I want, and I want them enough to try to build them, even on days when I'm certain I don't deserve them.

It was a shock to Kaylin to hear her own voice, because she didn't recognize it at first; she might not have recognized it at all had the spoken words not been so clear, and so clearly Elantran. The words weren't level; they weren't soft; they weren't mysterious and ancient.

But they were confident, and they were spoken with that little bit of heat that's on the right side of temper. They didn't clash with the voices of the Old Ones; they didn't clash with their meaning; nor did they shout over it. They blended, her words; theirs.

She understood, then. *I did this, Tara. I did this to you.* But…she hadn't called the storm that had taken them to the moment of the Tower's awakening. She hadn't called the storm that returned her to her own time. Tara had done that. But Tara's knowledge was the knowledge imbued in her—written in her foundations—by her creators. It was more than confusing.

Kaylin pushed confusion to one side. It didn't matter. What she'd done in her own bumbling way was to give the Tower a name that meant something deeply personal—to Kaylin. She had given her a definition of home that meant something deeply personal—also, sadly, to Kaylin. They were things that Kaylin remembered so clearly, and still wanted so badly, no matter how hard it was to believe in them.

And Tara had taken them in, blending them with the imperatives of unknown and unknowable Ancient gods. No wonder she was broken. No wonder. How can you want human things and still be immortal and unassailable?

She felt the cold as she turned just her head to look at the walls. They were gray, stone walls; the livid red of Illien's Tower had left them, but so had the soft, blue glow of the Old Ones. She saw cracks in those walls, and wondered if the cracks were literal. It didn't matter.

Severn.

She felt his surprise; felt the sudden surge in worry.

No, don't. I'm fine. What you're doing—whatever you're doing—stop it. The Tower will break. Tell Tiamaris—the Tower will fall. It's on the edge of existence now, and if we break it, we don't have the power or the knowledge to build it again.

Where are you?

In a room. In the same room that you're in, by look and feel. I think it's the real room, she added. *The one we saw was Illien's illusion.*

Illusion?

He wants to destroy the Tower. Or rather, he wants Tiamaris to do it. He was goading us. He was playing on our fears.

There was a pause, and then Severn said, *Well, he is Barrani.* Another pause. *Tiamaris asks what you would have him do. He is…not himself.*

Tell him to come to me.

The pause was longer. *Kaylin, he's not—*

I don't care. I don't care if he's gone Dragon again. You know how to talk to him, and I need you to do it. He's been in a Tower before. If he thinks, he can figure out a way into this one. I need him here.

Why?

Because he knows something about ancient runes and the Old Tongue, and I need his help. I need to—to realign things. I need to harmonize what's already written.

Meaning you need him to do it.

Something like that.

Silence. Then, *He's thinking.*

Is he breathing? I smell something burning—

That, too. But he isn't melting stone, if that's any consolation.

Lord Illien frowned. His eyes were darkening as he watched Kaylin. "You've stopped them, somehow."

"It's not in our interests to destroy the Tower."

"And it is in your interest to allow the Tower to relieve you of your power?"

But she wasn't afraid. She felt cold, yes, but she did not feel as if she were losing anything but heat. And when Tiamaris suddenly arrived in the heart of the Tower—inches from the huddled and wretched avatar who would not let go of Kaylin's hands—even heat returned.

His eyes were red. She'd thought she'd seen Dragon red before, but realized that she'd been mistaken, and she understood Severn's hesitance now. But Tiamaris's inner membranes were up, and his movements were minimal and very tightly controlled.

Severn stood by his side. He nodded at Kaylin, but it was a clipped motion; his attention caught by Illien and couldn't be pried away.

"So," Lord Illien said, gauging the Dragon's mood in much the same way Kaylin had, "you fail, here."

"It is your failure we attend, now," was Tiamaris's brittle reply. The air eddied around his face, the way air does on a very hot day.

Illien nodded, and folded his arms loosely across his chest. "And how, now, will you compensate for my failure?"

"Not him," Kaylin replied. "Me." She still couldn't free her hands, but she didn't need them. "Tiamaris, look at the room. No, *look at it.* Listen, if you can."

He drew breath, and she was afraid, given his expression, that its expulsion would be accompanied by flames. He closed his eyes completely; no one spoke. "I hear nothing," he finally admitted.

"I hear words," Kaylin told him. "I don't understand them, but I've heard similar words before. Sanabalis once told a story using only those words."

"You could see his words."

"I can almost see these ones. They're engraved in the floor at your feet, and in the walls around us. There are cracks through some of the runes."

"What would you have of me, then?"

"Look at the runes, if you can't hear the words. I can't move."

He glanced at the avatar for the first time, which didn't help the color of his eyes much. "Tara," he said, which surprised Kaylin.

It surprised the Tower, as well; she looked up, her skin still bruised and wet with tears. "I remember you," she said softly.

He nodded. "You gave me the gift of flight."

"I can't fly."

"No." His lips curved a moment in a smile and the red of his eyes lost a little of its livid intensity. "But you had wings, for a moment, and so did I."

"They weren't mine," Tara told him. "They were hers." And she nodded in Kaylin's direction.

"I definitely don't have wings." Kaylin said.

But Tara didn't argue, and didn't seek to clarify. "I'm broken," she told them both, and she turned, once again, to look at Lord Illien.

"So is he," Kaylin told her, gentling her voice. Tara hesitated for a moment, and then she opened her hands enough that Kaylin could pull away. Kaylin turned her hands around and caught Tara's instead, which was hard, given her own felt like stone mittens at this point. She pulled Tara to her feet. "Come," she said. "Walk with me."

Tara nodded. Illien remained where he was standing; Tiamaris joined them. Severn did not; he simply watched Illien in silence. Which was smart.

"You know this room," Kaylin told Tara. "And you know what was written here. Can you show us?"

Tara hesitated.

"Show us the words as they were when they were complete. Show us the words as they were when you first woke."

Tara glanced at Tiamaris, as if she were nervous. Kaylin shook her head. "I'm not an Ancient," she told Tara. "I'm human. I live for a brief span of years, and I die. Everything I learn will die with me. He's lived for longer than I have, and he'll live forever if nothing manages to kill him. I need his help."

"It is wrong to need help," she told Kaylin.

"Then I'm destined to be wrong." Kaylin drew breath, held it, and expelled it without adding any colorful words. "Look, if we were meant to *be* Towers, we wouldn't need you."

She frowned, and Kaylin realized the metaphor made no sense to her. "We're not meant to stand alone," she added. "If we were, there wouldn't be any other people."

"But people betray you."

"That," Kaylin said, with some annoyance, "is Illien speaking. The Barrani don't *have* a word for trust."

Tara hesitated. And then she said a phrase that Kaylin didn't understand. Tiamaris, who had been silent, looked at the avatar. "Private," he said. "Repeat the word."

"Repeat the what?"

"The word."

"All that was one word?"

His eyes had shaded to orange, and simmered there when he turned them on her. Kaylin took a step back—a small one, because she was still attached to Tara—and then, haltingly, she began to pull syllables from short-term memory.

Tara watched her, and for a moment, her face lost its look of strained desperation. Like a child who suddenly realizes that someone else might—with effort—be capable of understanding them, she began to fill in the gaps provided by Kaylin's decidedly mortal memory. When Kaylin got a syllable wrong, she shook her head and repeated it; when she got it right, she nodded, as if to encourage her.

Illien said, "What is the point of this futile exercise, Dragon Lord?"

Tiamaris snorted flame, which caused Kaylin to wince. The Tower didn't seem to notice. She did, however, notice that Kaylin's attention had been diverted, and she frowned and pulled on her hands. Or rather, pulled at her own, which Kaylin still held.

Kaylin mumbled an apology, and Tara made her start from the beginning again. This time, Kaylin managed the syllables more quickly, stumbling on fewer. When she had them all in place—and she thought there were twenty of them—Tara made her start it *again*. This time, she watched intently as Kaylin spoke, her eyes unblinking gray windows through which the faintest hint of internal luminescence shone.

But when she'd finished this final time, she saw the gray, misty wreaths of a moving, living *word*. It took shape both before and behind her, terminating lines curving around the three of them, dots and crosses and delicate loops adding something to the way they now stood, almost huddled together.

"What does it mean?" Kaylin asked Tara softly.

"It means…trust?"

Kaylin turned, then, and saw the word, absent three living people at its core, embedded in the far wall. It shone silver in the gloom. "That wasn't one of the words they wrote," she told Tara faintly.

Tara didn't seem to hear her, and she turned to Tiamaris. "Tiamaris—"

He lifted a hand, as if her words were gnats in serious danger of needing to be crushed. She started to argue, but she stopped when she heard Severn's voice; the sound of it made her hair stand on end.

"We've got trouble!"

Turning, she saw a wreath of black, black shadow, like the grease from tribal torches, climbing up through the cracks in the floor. At its center, immobile as a pillar, stood Lord Illien.

★ ★ ★

"Illien, don't—"

Tara tugged at her hands, and Kaylin tightened her grip. "It's not him," she whispered. "He's not doing it."

"Tara—"

"It's not him."

Kaylin opened her mouth again, and Tiamaris stepped on her foot. "Continue what you have been doing, Private. I will deal with Lord Illien and the shadows." He glanced once at Tara. "I will endeavor not to harm him," he told her, after a brief but significant pause. *"Private."*

She stared at the coalescing shadow, and saw it briefly as an absence of light, where the darker shades formed something akin to words. Shaking her head, she said, "Tara, quickly. Come."

Tara was staring, as well, with something like hunger on her face—not the hunger of greed, but the hunger of starvation.

I don't understand, Kaylin thought, tugging the avatar. *I am in so far over my head I can't see sky. Do you want to die? Do you want only what Illien wants?*

And does it matter?

One rune now lived—if that was the right word—in the curved surface of wall. The others were guttered, their shapes lost to dim light and poor memory.

I don't know what you wanted me to do, she thought to the Ancients. It wasn't quite a prayer. She turned to Tara, and then to Tiamaris's back; his arms were lifted, and light raced down them like liquid. The avatar was staring at his hands.

"Tara, please."

"What do you need from me, Chosen? I—" She took a step toward Tiamaris, or tried. Tiamaris was also in the same direction as Illien, who stood, wreathed in shadow, almost oblivious to its presence. Illien gestured and rose toward the ceiling's height as those shadows coalesced, amorphous lines becoming sharper and sharper as they watched. Stalks, eyes, and multiple legs formed, hardening and solidifying, until what they now watched was similar to a creature that Kaylin had already encountered in the streets of Barren. "Tiamaris—"

He roared. She shut up, and tried to concentrate over the sound of fighting. Tara pulled at her hands again; her eyes were wide and they no longer looked like human eyes. Or Barrani eyes, for that matter. "Let me go," she said. "I have to stop it—"

"You can't—you don't have the power."

"I *have to try*. It's what I am." She swallowed, and then said, "It's what I *should have* been. It's what I should have done."

Kaylin hesitated for just a second, and then she did let go. Her hands were still heavy and clumsy with cold, and Tara's face and body still bore bruises and superficial wounds. "Tara—"

"No," she said, voice low. "I can't take your power. He was right. Just your life. I won't kill you, not yet." And then she turned and she left Kaylin, with her imperfect damn memory, by the walls and the empty runes.

Kaylin was left in the near dark; there was no silence. She heard blade skitter off stone or chitin, and flinched. It was hard to pick the echo of syllables out of the air; they were tenuous and soft, if constant; the roars of a Dragon overwhelmed them every time she thought she'd fixed them in mind. She had no small child—or no grown woman, for that matter—encouraging her in her halting, stumbling progress, and after what felt like hours—but was minutes, if that, combat time, she threw up her hands in frustration. And fear.

She had never been good at sitting still and thinking her way through a fight; she had always relied on instinct. *Think, dammit.* Think.

She'd heard Sanabalis tell the Leontines their genesis story, and when he did, words formed. Severn hadn't been able to see them; she had. But she wasn't Sanabalis; it had taken her twenty minutes to repeat one word, and it would have taken half a life if Tara hadn't been at her elbow, urging her on.

But…she'd written in the dust, in this Tower. She'd written

Tara's name, or so she'd thought. What the dust and the Tower and the ancient magics that had created it had made of their translation of her efforts, Tiamaris had been able to see clearly; so had she. But it wasn't what she'd thought she was writing; it wasn't what she'd labored over.

She glanced at the endless carvings on the walls and floors, her eyes drawn to the sight of the multi-eyed creature who was shooting beams into it. The creature shouldn't have been able to stand, let alone walk, its limbs were so mismatched. But it had three jaws that she could see. Not three heads; that would have been too biological, too expected.

Light of various different colors were absorbed without apparent effect by the stone, but stone melted at least once, and Tara doubled over in pain at the impact. Staggering, she regained her feet, and Kaylin froze, one hand extended to her curved back. Tara knew.

Finish what you started, Tara said, her voice for the moment the *only* sound in the room. *Finish it. The creature cannot destroy me, not yet, but it is trying.* When she finished speaking, silence was left in the wake of her words. *Yes,* she said, hearing Kaylin's thoughts. *I can do that much. I can still do that much.* And then, in a softer voice, *Illien.*

Except *Illien* is not what she said. Kaylin heard both the superficial name and what lay beneath it, and they were discordant sounds, each syllable struggling to free itself from the rest, each clamoring for supremacy.

Illien, Tara said again. It was a plea. If heartbreak had a voice, it was hers. And Illien turned toward her, as if dragged. For just a moment, his expression was the gaunt, gray look of a man who has been hunted to ground and has only enough energy left to face his pursuer.

Kaylin, Tara said, voice more urgent now. *There are more. The shadows have taken the narrow path from the center. They are coming. I cannot—I cannot keep them out.*

What do you need?

Power. But yours is not available.

Why?

I do not know. Do something. Do anything. I will fall here, and he will die.

He wants to die, Kaylin thought.

I've given everything I have to prevent that, Tara replied.

You don't care what he wants.

I care about him!

You don't care what he wants. Kaylin turned away, and then turned back, and all the while, the livid spray of light from eyes that girded a misshapen, shimmering body continued to strike. Nothing stood in their path; Tiamaris and Severn were far too fast, and Illien, floating above the creature, seemed to attract no attention at all.

He's my whole world, Tara continued.

Kaylin looked at her, and then, finally, turned away. Her mother had been her whole world. When the world had ended, Severn had stepped in to take her place. And when Severn destroyed their world? She had fallen, stumbled and destroyed things as she tried to figure out how to stand on her own. She had lived with the guilt, and it had almost devoured her.

Were it not for the strange mercy offered her by a man she had been sent to kill, she might never have found a way out. Yes, she had done it to herself, and no, she didn't *deserve* salvation. But sometimes you got what you didn't deserve, and it was time now to live up to that single act of compassion. She hadn't taken the job to defend the blameless. Or even to defend the helpless, although those were usually the people who called in the Law. She hadn't offered the Oath of allegiance with the qualifier, "the law only applies to people I approve of and like."

Good damn thing.

You want the same thing! You want the same thing I wanted—

Yes. Yes, Tara. And I only hope that I never think destroying myself will give it to me. You loved him the way I loved my mother. But he's not your mother. He's Barrani. He probably doesn't even have children of his own, and if he did, there's better than half a chance he'd wind up killing them in some stupid political war. What you wanted, he couldn't give you.

He listened to me. He heard me.

Yes. But that's a far cry from love.

"Kaylin!"

She pulled herself out of the argument at the sound of Severn's voice, and turned. And then turned again. Was that what this was about? Was this about love and need and how the two *aren't* the same? She flinched once, as if struck. Her skin began to tingle, the way it did when magic was in the air. The hair on the back of her neck did its familiar upward reach.

The marks on her arms were glowing so brightly her eyes narrowed in an instinctive squint. She briefly considered removing her pants and decided against it; she knew the marks there would be the same. Crouching, she placed her palms flat against the floor; felt the indentation of stone beneath them where letters had been carved.

She had climbed her own Tower.

Why?

She'd believed the dead needed revenge. And that she needed to be the one to deliver it. She'd walked through the darkness, rewriting her life and her beliefs without even realizing what she'd given up in the process. People were dead because of it.

She'd come to the pinnacle of the Hawklord's Tower, and in the end she had failed to kill him. She had failed to truly try. Because no matter what she'd said or done, some part of her still wanted hope, still wanted to believe that *other people* could do the right thing, could live the right way, even if she'd failed. Because it meant it *could* be done.

He offered her that hope. Balanced between hope and revenge, she'd chosen hope. If it hadn't gone entirely smoothly since then, she'd never regretted her decision. And it *had* been her decision. Her choice.

She had proven that she was so *bad* at making choices up to that point, no sane god, no sane universe, would have allowed her yet another chance to screw up. But if there was no inherent justice in life, it worked both ways: sometimes you got the opportunity you didn't deserve, and what you made of it was defining.

Kaylin lifted her hands, palm out, exposing the insides of her arms, where the sigils lay. They seemed, as she watched them, to be moving, the familiar curves of lines extending and softening, the small dots and hatches contracting and expanding again in slightly different configurations. She couldn't discern pattern, or the harmony Tiamaris had insisted existed; it was almost as if she were watching the lake of life in the heart of the Barrani High Halls.

A miniature lake.

Yes, Chosen.

She looked up at the sound of the voice. Saw nothing except for the lifeless engravings in the curve of the ceiling above her. She wasn't a god. What they had written, she couldn't write. She wasn't a Dragon Lord, and she wasn't a Tower, whose existence was somehow tied to the heart of a darkness she had never seen, not even in nightmare. Fiefling, Hawk, midwife and unpaid babysitter, she took a deep breath and reached out for stone walls.

Nothing happened, except for the roar of a Dragon's fury, which shook the ground she was standing on. She touched the wall again. Still nothing, but this time she added a colorful Leontine phrase.

Think, dammit. How did you reach her in the first place?

With words. But she'd never been good with words—not like Severn, who, on the rare occasions he spoke, said the right thing. She had trouble saying what she meant; what she said instead often added to her troubles rather than alleviating them. And writing—rewriting—someone else's life seemed a disaster in the making.

But it had to be better than the disaster that loomed if she didn't.

She bent her head, closed her eyes, and finally knelt against the ground. Shadows whispered in the darkness; she heard them as if their hissing were language, another form of speech, a different set of choices, a different set of consequences.

Help me, she said, to the ghosts of the Ancients. There was no answer, but then again, they were gods.

CHAPTER 28

Tara. She had given the name to the Tower because it was hard to talk to a child made of walls, halls, joists, vast windows and changing spaces. The name was a confinement, a way of looking at things that didn't normally speak and reducing them to something—or someone—that Kaylin could pretend to understand.

She gave up that pretense now. What Kaylin was and what Tara was were not the same, and were never meant to *be* the same; without Tara, the City would fall. But Tara didn't *see* the City; in the end, she couldn't. She couldn't move; she saw only what the fief lord saw, and perhaps not even that, anymore. Why, in the end, must she live in isolation and misery to defend something she couldn't see, couldn't touch, couldn't interact with?

Start there. Start with why. Behind closed lids, she saw the lake beneath the High Halls; saw the words there, moving so quickly their shapes barely had time to catch the eye before they were gone. She reached for them carefully, trying to pierce the surface of form to find what she needed. She'd renamed a High Lord with less intent. Words came, but they didn't cut or burn her hands; they were light, like dust motes in sunbeams. They were delicate, almost translucent, like the ghosts of words that might have been. She drew them in, and she held them as she thought of the City itself.

Good things came first. Evanton. The Halls of Law. The Southern Stretch. The Tha'alani. The Leontines, and in particular, their complicated Pridlea, the heart of their kind. But the rest followed, because it *was* a City. The banks of the Ablayne. The brothels. The merchants who tried to get out of every possible tax the Emperor levied. The men—and women—whose existence was reason for her employment: con men, thieves, murderers. Worse. It shouldn't have worked, this City, this mix of people, good and bad—but it did, more or less.

And it relied, unknowing, on Tara and her kind. So: duty. Responsibility. A little bit of pride in being able to live up to a task that was so huge and so important. She didn't try to speak to the how of it, because she had no hope of truly conveying or understanding that. What she did understand was that you worked with what you had, be it a rusty knife or a bleeding fist; what you did with what you had was what counted.

Words stilled as the thoughts took shape and form. She gathered them and moved on; she couldn't clearly say how long it had taken. She wasn't dead yet, and the ground hadn't turned to melted rock beneath her legs, which was always a good sign.

When you had a duty, and you failed it, what then? Guilt. Grief. Regret. Self-loathing. These were harder to find, and she searched a long time because it was important. You had to see them, you had to name them, if you wanted to escape them. She struggled until she found the right word for flawed; it felt like the word for *life,* for just a moment. She knew she would never be able to repeat it to Tara, not even with her help.

But once done, she could offer acceptance. The past was the past. The future was still open, and it was still possible to find the strength to return, changed, to your calling. Hiding the past, pretending it had never happened, wasn't accepting it—and Kaylin had done that for years.

She accepted it here and now. She had done what she had done. She was not—would never be—proud of it, but the thirteen-year-old girl that had stupidly, foolishly, desperately destroyed so much was gone. She would never be that girl again; she understood the costs too damn well. Time, then, to let her go.

All the while she thought, she worked, the deliberate choice of words and runes becoming repetitive, like people said knitting was. Kaylin had only tried it once, during someone else's arrested labor, and she had somehow managed to end up with far more stitches than she'd started with, which caused no end of amusement to the rest of the midwives, and the expectant mother's mother.

She hadn't Tiamaris's eye, but she no longer saw the runic patterns as carvings; she saw them, instead, as a surface beneath which meaning lay. It was the meaning she now sought, as if it were small wells of light in the gloom and the red-tinged shadows, and when she reached them, she drew them out, wedding them to her narrative of what it meant to be alive.

Of what living meant, of the way it shored you up and the way it wore you down; of what love meant—yes, love, because in the end, it defined so much of Kaylin's life, both by presence and absence—to those who lived, and floundered, and fumbled and fell flat on their butts, and then got up and tried again. These were Tara's people, whether she knew it or not, and they lived in the streets yards away from the fence that circled her; they were the people she had, unknowing, been set in place to protect.

Are they? the more analytical part of her mind asked. She often resented it. She resented it now.

Does it matter? These are the people who live here now, and these are the people who need her. And we all need to be needed. We need to be useful. We need to know what our role and our responsibilities are.

She's not human.

No. But she can do what we can't.

And what can we do for her?

This was the worst part of the analytical mind. Kaylin knew enough about people—of any race—to know that you couldn't ask them to work for free. They had to get something out of the experience, or the work stopped. Things broke down. No one except maybe a mother—and even then she wasn't certain—could give and give and give without getting something in return; it was like having leeches you couldn't remove. In the end, there would be nothing left of you but an empty husk—if you were lucky.

What, she asked herself, her hands stilling, can we *give* to her in return for what we're asking? How can we appreciate what she offers if we don't see it, and don't understand it? How can we speak to her at all?

We aren't meant to, she thought. It was a slow realization. We were never meant to speak with her. The fief lord was. And is. The Lord of the Tower is the interface between the Tower, the anchor of the Ancients, and the people who take root around her.

But this fief lord was not that bridge. All he left was a gap; he showed how sharp and bitter the divide was. When she completed whatever it was she was doing, would there be any room for him at all? No, she thought. He could not love the mean streets and the meaner mortals that managed to scrape out a living beneath his windows. He could not—as Nightshade did not—care for them.

But Nightshade existed.

Illien did not.

Why?

She shook her head. It didn't matter. In the end, it didn't matter. Nightshade's Castle was not Tara, had never been Tara; what he loved—or hated or claimed or owned—was not here. It wasn't relevant. Here, she had offered the Tower a glimpse of ideal, and idealized love. Idealized because it was gone; it was what loss made of her early life.

She could change that, now. She could almost see the way to do it. She could reshape the words, shifting their meaning until they resembled what she thought the original purpose of the Tower had been. She even started to do so. But she couldn't. She *couldn't*.

This Tower—*this* Tower—was awake. It was alive, in just the same way Kaylin was, if you made allowances for the lack of limbs and the ability to move or breathe. This Tower...

Wasn't, she realized, a Tower. Not in the metaphorical sense of the word. Not an island. Not a stone fortress. From the moment she had touched Kaylin, or Kaylin had touched her, she had ceased to be some magical, mysterious construct that was at a remove from her inhabitants. She couldn't live alone for all of her immortal existence. She couldn't function in complete isolation.

And she knew it, the way Kaylin at *five* had known it. Isolation meant death; like any living thing, death was something to be feared. Tara had turned that knowledge into some sort of weird and broken way of relating to the Tower Lord, wedding her reason for existence to her awareness of her own emotional needs.

But for the City, lack of this Tower was death. It had already begun.

Kaylin found that she had arranged the white haze—for it was that, now—of words in a ring around her, as if she had touched the spirit of the walls and drawn them toward her, condensing their size and shape. She understood what the mix of runes meant—to her—although she lost her own words for them as soon as they began to move.

But she understood, as she stood at their heart, that they were not yet complete, and she understood, as well, what was missing at their center. She paled, drew breath, rose. Turning, she saw the room that existed beyond the work she'd done; her arms and legs ached, as if she'd been carrying sandbags on an endurance run devised by the most sadistic of the Halls' many trainers.

The shadows were there. The creature that had arrived through the cracks—literal and emotional—in the Tower's armor was now a twitching and burning mass. Tiamaris was not in his Dragon form but he didn't need to be to burn things. Severn was standing to one side of the Dragon, favoring his left leg. But he didn't look at her; he looked, instead, at what should have been a corpse.

Out of the smoke that rose from this carcass, another creature was taking shape and form. It moved like mist or fog, which was a problem for the Dragon and the Hawk.

But the mist sparkled as if the particles it were composed of were made of obsidian, and it headed straight toward Kaylin.

It had no head, no body, no obvious limbs, nor did folds of mist open to reveal eyes. She watched it glide through the space between Severn and Tiamaris, passing unharmed through the wall of Severn's moving chain. She heard Severn shout, saw Tiamaris turn, and saw Tara lift her arms, as if in denial.

Kaylin tensed as it approached the words she'd formed. It slowed as it approached, as if it saw the words as a wall or a barrier. Circling, in as much as slow-moving mist could, it attempted to seep between the spaces in the words itself.

It shifted what was there, nudging a line to the side, a stroke or a dot to the center. She had seen Tiamaris do something similar, and she had let him. But the Dragon had not attempted to alter meaning; he had attempted to make it clearer, somehow.

"Kaylin—what is it attempting to do?" the Dragon shouted.

"I don't know—I don't think it can change the meaning of these words."

"Not the meaning, no," Lord Illien said. He had been silent for the whole of the battle, on either front. "But the meaning that you have laid out does not exist in isolation."

Kaylin's eyes narrowed just before they widened in alarm.

"Yes," Illien said softly. "The pattern is not complete. The shadows will seek to complete it, now. If they can, they will control the shape of the whole."

"No—that's *not* the point of these words—"

"Point or no, Chosen, the Tower is, and was always meant to be, armor. Armor is donned, it is worn. You cannot turn armor into the man that wears it. No more can you make it a soldier or a leader. It is what it is, if it is to serve its function." He nodded, his face once again completely without expression. "But I can no longer stand in the space you have left. I cannot complete your pattern in any way.

"Neither can the shadows."

"You do not understand the nature of shadow," he replied. "Watch it now. Can you not see what it is forming?"

She watched. The mist had condensed, and what was left was something that should have looked serpentine. It didn't. It looked like black, black ink, and it was flexing itself into lines, and those lines pressed themselves against the exact shape of the lines Kaylin had pulled from the memory of stone.

She felt the sudden intrusion as a painful, cold pressure against her skin, and looked at the insides of her arms; nothing was touching them. It didn't matter. She felt the line she had drawn retract and shift under the pressure of this very unexpected attack, its shape changing as it shrunk and pulled away. She saw the word go with it, changing its form, and slowly altering its meaning.

Reaching out, she grabbed the line in her hands—and her hands went numb almost instantly. It was a familiar numbness. *Tara,* she thought. *Illien. What did you do?* The line was not malleable, but she could bend it, stretch it, force it—while she held it—to maintain something like the same shape.

But it *wasn't* the same damn shape. She knew it, and wondered if this certainty was what Tiamaris had meant when he talked about harmony and pattern. She wrestled with shadows here, felt the cold, and realized, bitterly, that she had wrestled with shadows for most of her life.

And that she would continue to wrestle with shadows for the rest of it, no matter how long that was. She took a deep breath. What was the option? It was wrestle or give up.

But you're tired. You're exhausted. You'll do nothing but struggle until you die.

Yes. She grimaced. *But I know what the alternative is.* Fingers numb, she peeled the shadow back; it clung for a moment to her fingers, crawling up her hands like a living glove. But when it reached the edge of her wrists, it stopped, and she heard the faintest of hisses as it suddenly withdrew.

She realized as it did that it was not a single thing; sleek lines, bright dashes, gleaming, hard dots, had attached themselves to parts of her work while she had struggled with *one damn line*. Yes, struggle was inevitable. But there was stupid struggle and smart struggle. She didn't even reach for the blackness, this time.

She knew what to do to drive it out.

She was afraid to do it. What Tara needed, she wasn't certain she could give. Yes, she could work—without pay—for the midwives. She could supervise the foundlings, take them on tours of the office, teach them to read and write, in as much as she was capable. But in both of those cases, she helped people who needed her help, and then she got to go home. Home, where she could relax and worry about what *she* needed—which, admittedly, was usually food and enough sleep to make her very late for work.

Taking the Tower—and that was the only alternative, the only way to defend it—meant that *this* would be home. Tara would be hers, to care for, to defend, to protect; there would be no place to retreat.

But she would *be* here. The fiefs would be standing. The rest of the City would be safe for a while.

She whispered Tara's name, and then, she whispered her own. Elianne. Kaylin. These two came easily: the one that she had been given at birth by the woman after whom she'd so carelessly named the Tower, and the one that she had chosen in haste and without thought, which she had taken for her own, and grown into.

But when she tried to speak the third name, and the most recent, she found her tongue almost too heavy and too thick to utter the syllables. *Ellariayn*. The name she had taken from the High Halls. The name by whose grace she was a Lord of the Barrani High Court.

A name she could give to the Tower that would allow her to hold it. She would *be* Ellariayn, a mortal with an immortal name. She would be fief lord. Illien would no longer matter. She knew it.

The shadows knew it. They pressed in against the words she had so carefully constructed and drawn—out of memory, out of experience, out of empathy—and they stained them and attempted to twist their parts so that the runes had a meaning far, far different than the one Kaylin had intended. She knew it because, even changed, they *did* have meaning, and that meaning was also a part of her experience and her truth.

She couldn't deny that truth; she accepted it. She accepted, as well, that the parts of her that had broken would never be whole and unbroken again, but they were foundation; she built on them. She tried to learn enough from them to understand other people better. She wasn't always good at it. Most days, she was damn bad. But…she tried, and that counted for something.

She struggled, now, to *give* the Tower the third of her names. But it was a name that didn't feel like it was truly her own; she'd never lived in it. She barely acknowledged it.

But the shadows did. They couldn't take it; they tried, but this was a true name; it wasn't given to them. They struggled; she saw their frenzy; felt a hint of something that might be anger or fear or some blend of both. She worked through it; felt pressure, like a hand against her mouth.

The syllables were hard. She pushed them out, stumbling on vowels or the harsh clash of consonants. She had never thought of the name as long, but this? It was like telling a story when you could only barely remember what happened. But as the syllables emerged, she felt the lines of her chosen words hardening and developing a clarity that diffuse light couldn't give them—and, more important, that shadows couldn't eat away.

She felt them take shape, felt the structure underlying their composition grow denser. She saw—for just a second—the shape that her name was meant to fill; it was the last gap, the last hole, in the wall. She drew breath, and stepped toward it.

She wasn't expecting the Dragon that materialized in the center of the construct; she certainly wasn't expecting to be knocked off her feet—and most of the way toward the far wall—by the swing of his massive head.

Severn was in front of her before she'd fully gained her feet. She turned almost wildly toward Tiamaris. His scales were red, tinged now with bronze, and infused with the glow of the runes Kaylin had built. They lit up the underside of his massive jaw as he lifted it and roared.

The shadows splintered at the sound, shattering as they fell away from the whole of the pattern. Tiamaris roared again, and a storm of fire left his open jaws.

Illien, still floating in the air above the ground, froze there, his wide eyes the color of sapphires. Beneath him, Tara froze, as well, her gaze caught between the fief lord who had changed the nature of his existence in an attempt to escape her, and the Dragon Lord who had entered the ring of words from which he might never again be free.

Between these two, there was Kaylin, and it was Kaylin who caught and held Tara's gaze. Stone didn't cry, but Kaylin already had some experience with Tara's tears. These were quiet; they traced her cheeks in the odd light. Her face was still bruised, but at this distance, the bruises looked like shadows.

"Tiamaris!" Kaylin shouted, turning away. "You don't have to do this!"

He turned as the runes began to glow, free from the constraint of shadow. He roared again; she thought that might be his answer. But she understood, as the roar grew in volume, extending until it shook the ground, the walls, and the runes themselves, that that was *not* what he was doing. He was speaking his name.

It was a long damn name, but he didn't falter once, and he didn't appear to need to struggle with anything but breath. She saw the runes begin to separate, to leave the formation she had made of them; she saw them move slowly away from him in an expanding circle. Glancing back at Tara, she saw the Tower's avatar begin to smile. It was not a triumphant smile, nor was it fearful, but there was an element of surprise in it.

It was, Kaylin thought, so entirely peaceful it was in its own class of beauty—because at that moment, for the first time, the avatar *was* beautiful. She raised her hands in front of her face, examining them, and as she did, all scratches, all bruises, all obvious signs of injury began to fade as if they, like the shadows, had been dispelled by the roar of a Dragon.

A Dragon.

"Tiamaris—you don't know what you're doing—"

His roar didn't shift or change, but the glance he gave her should have been impossible in his current form, it was so obviously derisive. He knew. He knew exactly what he was doing— and as was so often the case, he was doing a better job than Kaylin had in her attempt. The runes continued to move, and as they did, for just a moment, Kaylin could *see* the small lines, the small hatches and crosses, that seemed to touch Tiamaris from every single one of them.

As they moved away from him, she saw their shape change; they moved not in a ring, but a sphere, expanding until they touched walls that were now completely blank. No engravings had been writ upon their surface; no runes, no circles, no complex designs; they were solid, smooth rock. They weren't the walls Kaylin had studied in her attempt to somehow fix the Tower. She wanted to ask Severn what he saw, but his back was toward her; he trusted her there, and clearly trusted nothing else in this room.

The roar stopped. The sigils didn't. But Tiamaris, still a Dragon, lowered his massive jaw. It was hard to tell, given the size of that jaw and the size of the teeth it exposed while open, what his expression was. But it didn't matter; he didn't turn it on Kaylin. He turned it, instead, upon the Tower's avatar; she was shining, now, as if she were a ghost, or a human vessel for diffuse, gentle light.

"Interesting," Illien said softly. "You understand, Lord Tiamaris, that had she taken the Tower, this fief would be all but unassailable? You might have seen a power to rival—"

"She did not want it," he replied. "Like you, she would have taken it, and like you, she would have failed the Tower."

"The Tower? I failed the Tower? The Tower failed me."

Flame wreathed the Dragon's muzzle. "You do not know what you want. Either of you. You," he said, nodding at Kaylin, "with your doubt and your fear, and you," he continued, turning to the

Barrani Lord, "who chose this place as your own because you were *bored*. It has always seemed to me that the Barrani were almost mortal in the weakness of their focus."

Illien was Barrani enough to find Tiamaris's observation offensive; Kaylin was self-aware enough to accept it.

But Tiamaris, his deep quake of a voice gentling, said, "It is not enough to accept responsibility for another life as an act of fear or duty, Private."

"You serve the Emperor," Kaylin pointed out.

"That was never simple duty. When you see him, you will understand. If you survive that meeting, you will have to come and tell me what you saw. I will not be there to see it." His wings extended slowly.

"But—"

"I *want* this, Kaylin. I have never wanted anything but this. This is *mine*. Nothing but death will take it from me."

"You've been to other Towers before—"

"They were not mine. This is." He lifted his head again, and spoke a single word in his native tongue. She recognized it, although she shouldn't have. It was the Dragon word for *hoard*.

Tara seemed to recognize it, as well, but she had the advantage of being a Tower. She stood transfixed for a moment, and then she whispered a word that Kaylin couldn't understand. It was followed by words that she could, however.

"It was you. It was you I heard."

His eyes were golden, bright, incandescent. "Yes. It was me. It was both my emptiness and my desire." His voice shook the ground, but managed, conversely, to be gentle. "Now come, Tara. There are shadows and invaders in my domain. Their presence does not please me."

"I—I can't."

"You do not wish to join me?"

She did. Only a moron could have asked that question. Kaylin was wise enough to keep this opinion to herself.

But he shook his head. "You do not understand what Kaylin

intended. You cannot leave *me*. That she could not change. But she thought you capable of learning to love the people your very existence protects if you could walk, and live, among them. Today, however, you—and I—will fly." He waited.

She stared at him for a moment longer, and then she made her way across a floor that was now, once again, defined by carved runes and symbols. She did not look at Illien; Illien watched her.

"Come," Tiamaris said again, and he lowered himself to the ground—or as close to the ground as something his size could get. Kaylin thought—although she wasn't certain—that he was larger, in Dragon form, than he had been any other time she'd seen him.

Tara climbed up on his back, and Tiamaris then turned to face Kaylin and Severn. "You two, as well," he said. "Come. There is work, now, to be done."

"You're not—you're not going to fly?"

"I am," he said, voice rumbling in something that sounded suspiciously like the Dragon equivalent of a cat's purr. "This is mine, now, Kaylin. I will fly these skies, and if the Emperor wishes, he may come in person to contest the aerial territory. *Come.*"

She glanced at Illien.

"He will not leave the Tower yet," Tiamaris told her. "He cannot."

"But he—"

"He is, for the moment, my guest."

"If you can hold me," the Barrani Lord said quietly.

"Do you doubt it?" Tiamaris shrugged, as if Illien's doubt were insignificant. "Tara?"

She nodded, and the ceiling opened, as if the stone were the cleverly designed aperture of the Hawklord's tower. The sky appeared, azure against the darkness of the previously enclosed space, as the walls unfolded.

"Kaylin. Severn. Climb." He paused, and then said, "Am I more terrifying than the Hawklord? Kaylin, you love to fly. You begged, pleaded, cajoled, and nagged the Aerians to take you flying. Come. Fly."

She looked at Illien once again, and then glanced around the room. No trace of him remained in it except he, himself. "Go," he said, lifting a hand almost carelessly. "I consider myself in your debt, to some degree. I will wait."

She didn't trust him.

"Go, while you still have time. Nothing new will enter the fief, but nothing that is already here will leave it untouched."

She turned, then, and crawled her way up Tiamaris's back, lodging herself between the others in a position suspiciously close to the place where his wings joined the rest of his body. He flexed them and laughed when she jumped.

Before she could say anything, his body tensed beneath her, and he pushed himself up and off the ground, heading for a collision with the open sky. The Tower fell away as if it were a veil; what lay beneath them, when Kaylin had opened her eyes again, was Barren writ small.

Tara, seated in front of her, shouted something; the wind carried it back.

"They're people," Kaylin shouted back. "Isn't that what they looked like to you before?"

"No!"

"Well, what did they— Tiamaris! Stop here!"

He roared, but the sparsely crowded streets were already emptying, and no one had time to spare to look skyward at a new threat when the threat they faced was so much closer. People were fleeing—as they could—from something that looked, at this remove, like a feral pack. Except for the part which had them roving in broad daylight.

The ground rushed up to meet them. As far as flight went, this was almost exactly like falling, except the landing only tossed Kaylin off the Dragon's back and into the streets; it didn't kill her.

The ferals—which weren't ferals, seen up close—tried, on the other hand. They were larger, for one, and while the bulk of their bodies resembled giant dogs, the resemblance ended there. Kaylin personally discovered that their tails were both prehensile and barbed when one wrapped itself around her leg and sliced into her thigh.

Tiamaris snapped the creature in half.

The others, like ferals, were too stupid to know when to run, which was good; they were also too stupid to stop hunting, turn around, and face what was otherwise certain death. Bodies lay beneath them in the street. Most of them had long since stopped moving.

But Tiamaris made certain that the only additional corpses would be theirs; he was so fast, and so light given his size, that Kaylin only had time for defensive maneuvers; all the offense was delivered by the Dragon. It was glorious and brief.

Tara clung—literally clung—to his back for the entire fight; only when the sound of the not-quite-ferals had been silenced did she straighten her back and look around her. Her eyes were wide and shining, the latter no trick of the light.

"Not yet," Tiamaris told her, in a voice that was so gentle it seemed impossible that it came from a Dragon's mouth. "There is more—much more—to do. But we have time," he added. "Come, Kaylin. We go to the borders."

She glanced up at the sky. "There might be trouble," she said softly.

"Here?" He snorted. Smoke came out of his nostrils in tufts.

She pointed. In the distance, in the air, she saw what the rest of the City—fief or no—must have seen: the extended wings and graceful necks of Dragons in flight.

CHAPTER 29

The Dragons were high enough above the ground that Kaylin couldn't place their colors. She didn't try. She could see numbers: there were three. Three to one.

Tiamaris, however, elongated his neck and nudged her—where nudged, in this case, meant knocked her over. "Climb," he told her grimly. "We are needed."

"Where are we going?" She glanced again at the sky as Severn wound his chain around his waist and joined them in silence.

"The White Towers. There is a man who calls himself the fief lord. He needs to be disabused of the notion." All of the smile in the words was in the tone, and none of that smile was pleasant.

It caused the shadow of a similar smile across Kaylin's lips, but it was tenuous, and it broke when Severn's hand gripped her shoulder. She shifted, turning to meet his glance, and was jerked backward when Tiamaris left the ground. He was clearly unaccustomed to passengers. Then again, he hadn't had to watch Kaylin grow up.

And even if he had, to give in to her desperate desire to escape the confines of gravity would have been his death. Looking over her shoulders to see the circling Dragons above, she wasn't certain it wouldn't be his death now. He didn't care. She felt the ferocity of a savage joy in the freedom of his flight, and she thought she would never understand Dragons or the Dragon Court.

But that Court remained at a distance, circling. She noted with heat that they didn't attempt to land or help the people who were running in the streets. Later, maybe, she'd have a few words with at least one of them. Now? She went where Tiamaris went, landed where he landed, and managed not to lose any more clothing to the unpredictable placement of limbs, jaws or tails. She did get her hair singed twice, but unpredictable placement of small eyes that shot magical beams was a bit trickier.

The streets nearest the White Towers were already pretty damn empty of anything but the shadows; here or there, those shadows had dissolved, or staved in, walls. Tiamaris caught them all as he moved toward the border, and she wondered if he now had the same connection to Barren that Nightshade had to his fief. She didn't ask; there wasn't time.

He cleared the streets around the building. He cleared the streets around the watchtowers, and then, with a roar, brought the watch-towers down. They were, as far as Kaylin could tell, deserted; she didn't look too damn closely. She had never—would never, she admitted to herself—cared as much about Barren's men as she did about the rest of the people. Possibly because she'd been one.

She let the air whip strands of hair out of her face as she watched, passenger to destruction.

When it was over, Tiamaris flew a few wide arcs above the White Towers, roaring as if he was his own herald. Kaylin couldn't be certain if he was announcing his arrival to the denizens of the fief, or his defiance to the Dragons who still circled high above. He landed at last in the empty streets, at which point Kaylin, Severn, and Tara slid off his back.

Kaylin had pretty much decided that Dragons were to be classed with horses in terms of riding: never again unless her life—or livelihood—depended on it. She stepped away from Tiamaris into the street itself. Glass shards caught the sunlight and sent it straight at the unwary eye; bodies caught something less tangible. Kaylin stepped over them, bending here and there to check for a pulse she didn't expect to find. She took care with the corpses that no longer looked human—or animal, if it came to that—but they weren't moving, either.

Severn was doing the same; they moved up the length of the street, working in tandem, and found nothing alive. Sometimes this was good, sometimes it was bad. But it came to an end when they reached the White Towers. Some obvious—and involuntary—changes had been made to both the landscaping, such as it was, and the architecture. Half of the fence was still standing; half of the guardhouse was still standing. In the case of the guardhouse, it was the lower half.

The walls had seen fire—most of it Dragon—but they had seen something else, as well; some part of the front facade was no longer made of stone.

It was hard to tell *what* it was made of; it looked almost opaline, or it would have if opals were twisted and vaguely repulsive. At the core of this section of what had once been wall, light shone, pulsing as if it were an exposed organ.

Tiamaris glanced at it, and then furled his wings. "A moment," he said to Tara, who nodded as she began to approach the section of wall that looked so wrong. He shed the size and majesty of his Dragon form, donning instead the armor of its scales. When the last of the scales had slid out of his skin and into place, he walked toward Tara.

"The wall," he said quietly.

She nodded. "It is…still alive."

"Can it see me?"

She nodded again. Kaylin didn't ask *with what,* although she had to clamp her jaw shut to trap the words. "I can close its eye," Tara told him softly.

"At what risk?"

She hesitated, and then said, "I don't know."

"No?"

She bent and touched the ground with the flat of both palms. "I can do this, now. I could not, before. I...am no longer certain what is possible. This...is not my world."

"Leave it, then. We have time, later, to discover what is possible and what is not." He walked to the door and lifted his head.

"Crossbows," Severn said quietly.

Kaylin nodded. "At least three. Probably four or five. The buildings across the street are still standing."

"And their aim can be trusted at this distance?" Tiamaris asked quietly.

Kaylin shrugged. After a pause she said, "Mine could be."

He shrugged, but he would; the bolts probably wouldn't hurt *him*. On the other hand, the streets were empty enough that they wouldn't hurt noncombatants, either. She watched the door, scanning the shuttered windows. "He won't come out," she finally said.

"He will send someone."

She nodded. "If anyone's still alive in there." She glanced at the wall.

"People on the other side of the wall are still live," Tara said quietly.

"Unchanged?"

"They have not been altered by the shadow, no."

"Then I know who we're waiting for," Kaylin told them. She dropped one hand to the hilt of a dagger and waited for the door to open. It took another ten minutes, and when it did, it opened to the sound of shouting, but the person who stepped out—on her own—was familiar. Kaylin even managed a tired grin.

"Hands full?" she asked Morse.

Morse's grin was a slightly more bitter reflection of Kaylin's. "Those who still have working hands, yeah. You're here to see Barren?"

Kaylin glanced at Tiamaris, then shrugged. "He is," she said, nodding at the Dragon Lord.

It wasn't the first time Morse had seen Tiamaris, but this time she really looked. She didn't even shrug when she turned her attention to Kaylin again. "Street's clear."

Kaylin nodded. "Pretty much all of them. We had some trouble with what might once have been ferals on the way, and he kind of burned what was left of the standing watchtowers to ashes, but there were no—" She grimaced. "Nothing that looked human was in the immediate vicinity."

"That Hawkspeak?"

Kaylin shrugged. "You take information any way you can get it, if you trust the source."

Morse offered Kaylin a slow smile. "That so? Whoever taught you that was no fool."

"No. She wasn't. What are you going to do?"

Morse shrugged. "I was sent to find out what he wants, and to take a look around. It got a lot louder when he arrived," she added, with a thin smile. "And then it got a lot damn quieter. I think Barren hoped he'd be dead." She glanced at Tiamaris, but still spoke to Kaylin. "What's he want?"

"Want?" Kaylin asked, momentarily confused.

Morse snorted. "He's not here to be neighborly."

"He's here to kill a few nightmares and save a few lives. Not that there were that many to save this close to the border."

"Your idea?"

"No. I had no problems with it, if that's any help."

"Not really. It's not news, either." Which was Morse's very polite way of saying *shut up.* "You working for him?"

Kaylin understood all of the question. "No."

"No."

"I work for the Lord of the Hawks."

"Hawks don't come here. The Law doesn't come to the fiefs."

"There's only one law in the fiefs," Kaylin replied, as if by rote. Then she shrugged, as well, and nodded at Tiamaris. "And it's going to be his."

"He's a Hawk."

"He's a Lord of the Imperial Dragon Court. Or at least he was. He was only moonlighting as a Hawk. Will Barren come out?"

Morse laughed. "Would you?"

Kaylin grinned. "Don't try anything stupid. The Dragon doesn't owe me anything."

"The Dragon," Tiamaris interjected, "owes you a great deal, Private Neya. He does not, however, extend the debt to sparing the life of would-be assassins."

Morse nodded. "You can come in. Usually we tell visitors to leave their guards at the door, but in your case it seems pretty pointless. You don't have a weapon?" she asked Tiamaris.

"I had a sword. I never used it."

"Got it." She stepped out of the doorway, opening it in the process. "We weren't expecting guests," she told Kaylin, voice heavy with the usual Morse irony.

"It's a bit of a mess?"

"Understatement."

The transformation in the outer wall was the biggest change in the White Towers, but some of the shadows had leaked through, and part of the floor was both uneven and constructed of something that looked like shiny stone. Kaylin didn't test this by actually walking on it, and neither did anyone else; they tread around it only after Tara pronounced it safe in her softly modulated voice.

But they trudged the familiar path up the stairs in silence. Morse was in the lead, and Kaylin kept an eye on her hands. She didn't appear to have problems turning her back on Kaylin, and by extension Tiamaris.

Being Morse, she'd failed to acknowledge Severn or Tara.

The stairs were scorched and blood had seeped into what passed for carpets, but the bodies had been cleared away, or at least dumped into an adjacent room; the only open doors in the halls were the set Kaylin was most familiar with. She felt the line of her spine stiffen as they approached them.

Barren was waiting. He had four men in the room, and Morse

joined him, taking up a position that was almost formal—for Morse—to his right and one step behind. He didn't look pleased to see his visitors. Too damn bad.

It occurred to Kaylin as she watched him that it was over, for him. He had never truly been fieflord; he had called himself fieflord, and everyone who lived in the fief had obeyed him as if the words were true—because he could kill them, and did. *Even me,* she thought. *No. I was worse. I helped him. I was part of what terrified people. And killed them.*

Because she had been afraid, too. Fear was like that; a disease—or worse—it crippled and destroyed not just one life, but the lives of everyone it touched. She could remember, watching him, why she had been afraid. She hated it, but she felt the fear as if it still lived inside of her, small but hidden.

She looked up, met his gaze, and saw him measuring her; trying to see how much of her he still had in his grip. "You went to the old tower," he finally said, speaking to Kaylin.

Kaylin turned to Tiamaris, to make a point; the Dragon's eyes were a pale orange. He wasn't angry, yet; he was, however irritated. Barren wasn't born in the fiefs; he had to know there was a cost to irritating Dragons. "She did." It was the Dragon who replied.

Barren turned to him slowly, as if Barren, and not Tiamaris, were still fieflord. "You met its occupant."

"I," Tiamaris replied, "am now its occupant."

Barren's expression was shuttered and impassive; nothing escaped it.

"You are the reason," Tiamaris said, breaking his silence, "that this fief stood so long against the borderlands. Both your power, which you gave involuntarily, and your foresight, which you applied in your choice of residence and the building of the watchtowers, formed a surprisingly effective guard against the shadows that lie at the center of the seventh…fief."

Barren nodded carefully. If he'd been a cheap, stupid thug, he would have been grinning by this point; he was a suspicious, cautious man. A cruel one.

Tiamaris then waited. Having been a Dragon's student for the better part of a few months, Kaylin understood the pressure that silence could bring to bear.

"What do you propose?" Barren finally asked. "This is not the Empire."

"No."

"The Eternal Emperor has never had an interest in another Dragon Lord ruling territory within his domain," Barren continued, his expression completely neutral. Kaylin understood why, now. He thought he had a chance; the Dragons could fight it out, and Barren assumed that the Emperor would win.

It was a good assumption; the Dragon Court belonged to the Emperor.

Tiamaris nodded. "You misunderstand the Emperor. He has never had an interest in any others ruling territory within his claimed domain. The fact that I am Dragon does not change his opinion. The fiefs have been allowed to stand because he has never chosen to claim them as his own.

"None of us are interested in fighting a war that will cause our own destruction." He paused, and then said, "The Emperor has never fully tested himself against the power of the Towers that sustain the borders. It would be an interesting contest."

Kaylin remembered that she needed to breathe about a minute after his words sunk in.

"You intend to fight him if he comes."

"The fief," Tiamaris replied, "is *mine*."

Barren took a moment before he spoke again. "As a Lord of the Dragon Court, your time was of great value. The minutiae of day-to-day life in the fief—"

Tiamaris lifted a hand. "If you mean to offer me your services, I'm afraid I cannot accept them. You are known as fiefLord here, and your obvious presence in a role of power would confuse the issue of rulership. I mean to leave no one in doubt."

Barren looked slightly surprised for the first time since Tiamaris had entered the room. "Why did you come?" he asked.

"To acknowledge your contribution to the fief," Tiamaris replied. "In recognition of that fact, I will allow you—and your men—to exit the building before I destroy it. You are free to go where you will. You will not remain within the boundaries of my fief. I believe," he added, with the barest hint of an edged smile, "that you are familiar with the boundaries."

Before Barren could frame an answer, Tiamaris turned to Kaylin. "If that is acceptable to you?"

She looked at Tiamaris, started to speak and stopped. He was fief lord. Not Hawk. Not a member of the Imperial Court. Laws and rules were defined by one man—or woman. How they upheld their laws was their own business, because the Law didn't come here.

He could give her Barren. Barren, the man.

"He injured you, if I am not mistaken, in his tenure as Lord here." She swallowed. Nodded.

Barren didn't try to argue with Tiamaris; he wouldn't. He wasn't afraid of Kaylin. He had nothing to fear from her. His men still stood around him, willing to follow his orders as long as it wasn't too damn costly. The words of the new fief lord had not yet sunk in. "Well?" Barren said.

Her knuckles were white as they rested over the pommel of her dagger. She could kill him. It would silence at least one of the memories that haunted the worst of her nights. But...she had walked into Barren. She had been so focused on guilt and loss and anger, she had given her allegiance to a man who had never—would never—be worthy of it. She'd paid. But she wasn't the only one.

And killing him for the sake of the dead wouldn't ease her guilt or her culpability in their deaths.

"Elianne," Morse said. Her old name. Kaylin looked across to Morse, who was standing where she always stood. Her face was shuttered, her expression remote; she wasn't pleading for Barren. But she was asking for something. They hadn't lived together long, and Kaylin had been so self-absorbed she couldn't put two plus two together to save her life; she'd survived by accident and luck. But she wasn't a thirteen-year-old on the run anymore, and she understood, suddenly, what it was. It changed things.

It changed nothing.

Kaylin drew breath before she turned to Tiamaris. "No," she said quietly. "His life's not mine to take."

"Very well," Tiamaris replied. "You are free to leave." He reached out with one hand and caught Severn's shoulder tightly. "You will not hunt in my domain."

Barren's eyes widened.

"We are given leave to hunt where we will," Severn replied.

"Indeed. But I will be forced to kill you, an act which I would regret. If you need to hunt him, you will hunt him after he leaves the fief, not before."

Severn was silent for a full minute before he nodded. Until he nodded, Tiamaris didn't release him. But Severn wasn't stupid; he wasn't impulsive. He would not try to kill Barren in the fief. Not now. She didn't have to worry about Severn.

So Kaylin watched Morse instead. Morse's expression didn't change at all when Tiamaris refused Severn his arguably legal right to execution. Morse understood that Severn was a dead man if he even tried; you didn't piss off a Dragon and survive, not when he was standing fewer than ten feet away.

Barren turned to the four men in the room. Nodded curtly. They formed up around him, like a small human shield between Barren and the Dragon. Morse joined them, standing slightly apart the way she usually did. She didn't look at Kaylin.

Barren didn't waste breath arguing with Tiamaris, and he had never been fool enough to meet him head-on. Even if he'd still had the magic Tara had drained from him, he wasn't that type of stupid. Which, Kaylin though, was a bitter disappointment. But she'd made her decision, and if it was bitter, it was still hers; she'd live with it.

And who will die because of it? There were whole days she hated having anything that resembled a conscience.

But sometimes, it asked the right question at the right damn time. She barely saw Morse move. One minute, she was walking in her cautious, cocky way toward the double doors to one side of Barren's back, and the next, she was at his side, the flash of steel in her hand brief, the blood that gushed from the whole of his suddenly open throat less so. He didn't even have the chance to turn, to face her; he toppled backward, the whole of his body crashing to the carpet as if it were already in rigor.

But it jerked there, his eyes glazed and unblinking.

The four men froze; Morse killed one before he'd managed to turn to face her. That was Morse. The other three closed on her, and Kaylin started forward; Severn caught her, dragging her back, as Tiamaris roared. There was fire—literal fire—in the breath that left his mouth. He wasn't particularly careful about the floors or the carpets, but then again, he'd already said he was going to burn the building to the ground.

He was only slightly more careful about Barren's men. At least one of them screamed. Morse was out of the fire before it hit her would-be assailants, but she didn't even try for the door. She watched Barren. She watched Barren die.

"Tiamaris," Kaylin said, urgent now, "take Tara—"

But Tara shook her head. "This is the one who hurt you," she said to Kaylin, in a voice as cold as any Kaylin had ever heard her use.

Great. She had made friends with an overprotective and somewhat cold-blooded Tower.

"I will watch him die."

It wasn't for Tara's sake that she wanted Tara out, and Tiamaris turned to her, raising one dark brow to make clear that he understood.

"Severn, let me go."

"Kaylin—"

"Please. I won't do anything stupid."

He bent slightly and whispered a single word in her ear. *Don't.* Then he let go.

She walked quickly toward Morse, putting herself directly between Tiamaris and the woman who had, for better or worse, found her in the streets and taken her home. But she stopped just shy of her, because she had never seen Morse like this before. Her face had gone from cool neutrality to blank, and her eyes were almost as wide and glassy as Barren's. Her hands were red and wet; the blood hadn't even gone sticky yet.

But Morse, like Kaylin, couldn't just be touched. She couldn't be hugged. There was no easy way to offer her comfort. No way at all, really, but this. "Morse."

She looked up at the sound of her name.

"He's dead."

Morse nodded, but it wasn't a fief nod—it was too automatic, too empty, for that.

"Morse—"

"Will the Dragon kill me, now?" Morse asked, in the ghost of her former voice. Something had left her; Kaylin wondered if it would ever come back.

"No," she replied, with more certainty than she felt.

"He should."

"Morse—"

Morse shook her head. She pushed Kaylin to one side with no force at all and stumbled over to Barren's body. There, she knelt, staring at his open eyes, his still face. Kaylin thought, then, that hatred was corrosive, but in some ways, if you had nothing else, it could sustain you. It was poor sustenance, but sometimes poor was better than nothing.

Nothing, however, was what she said. She didn't ask Morse why; Morse wouldn't have answered. But she crouched a little distance away from Morse, over Barren's body, and she waited in case Morse asked for anything.

Morse didn't. She didn't cry; that would have been too easy.

Tiamaris walked quietly across the room. Kaylin rose, turning to face him, but his gaze was on Morse, and his eyes were almost entirely gold. Light from the windows cast his shadow across

Morse; she looked up as it touched her. Her eyes were dull, almost gray. She said nothing.

Tiamaris seemed to expect that nothing. He turned to Kaylin. "I accept your choice, in this," he said softly, "but the White Towers must be destroyed if we cannot, in safety, diffuse the changes in its structure."

"You said—"

"Yes. That was also true. There is not always a single reason to do something—often there are many. Morse," he said.

She looked up at the sound of her name. If you weren't watching her face closely, she might have been looking at Tiamaris. "Yeah."

"Tiamaris—" Kaylin began.

He lifted one hand, and she swallowed her words—which wasn't hard; she hadn't quite figured out what to say.

"He is dead."

"Barren's dead." Morse's voice was wooden, almost without inflection.

"You served him."

Morse said nothing.

"You killed him."

She nodded.

"It's over. What will you do now?"

"Now?" Her eyes focused, slowly, on his face, and as they did, her expression hardened. She shook herself, looked once at Barren, and then stood. But she rose clumsily, as if she were drunk. "I'm done here. You want to kill me for countermanding your orders, you can—"

"You were not under my orders," he replied quietly. "Or you would already be dead."

She nodded. There was no display of bravado left in her, although she'd never been one for displays of stupid to begin with. Or maybe she had been, to begin with—Kaylin hadn't known her, then. Didn't really know her now, if it came to that. Morse didn't get close to people. She didn't let people close to her, either.

It was why Kaylin had been able to walk away, in the end. Maybe that had been Morse's way of being kind.

"You don't want me," Morse told Tiamaris, after a long silence. "I was his muscle."

"So was Kaylin. She now works indirectly for the Emperor. But perhaps you feel that the change in rulership will not be to your liking. It will be reflected, in the end, at all levels in the fief of Tiamaris."

"How?"

"I dislike the lack of organization and the lack of basic laws within Barren. I intend to establish both. The laws will follow closely the Imperial laws. You may not be familiar with them," he added. "But if you intend to remain in this fief in any capacity, you will learn.

"There will be one or two significant departures from Imperial Law, the most obvious of which will be the lack of an Emperor. But there will be a basic core of guards who see that my laws are upheld. I will not require your services in the capacity of assassin. If I believe someone merits death, I will kill them."

"Just like that."

He nodded. "I will also see to the ferals."

"The ferals?" Morse grimaced. "Why?"

"Because the fief is mine, and nothing hunts in it without my permission. If they are not, indeed, dumb beasts driven by hunger, they will learn."

"Why are you telling me this?"

"I do not think there is a home for you across the river."

Morse shrugged. Her body lost its unnatural stiffness as she did. She nodded in Kaylin's direction. "Because I'm not soft, the way she is?"

"You took her in."

"I taught her," Morse snapped, with more than a little heat, "everything she knows about killing. The rest of the shit she picked up came from someone else—blame it on them."

But Tiamaris was unwilling to let Morse have the point; Kaylin wanted to kick him. He didn't understand the fiefs. "You were not happy when she returned."

"Barren wanted her here. He didn't tell me why. Anything he wanted, he wanted to strengthen himself. And I," she added, glaring pointedly at his corpse, "had no interest in seeing him strengthened. I was waiting," she added, and this time her voice lost some of its edge. "I've been waiting for so damn long."

"The fief was falling. The people—"

She shrugged. "If the shadows hadn't killed them, Barren would have, sooner or later. Killed them or destroyed them and left them standing. He was good at that."

"You are alive."

"I know how to stay alive. Always have." The bitterness, the self-loathing, in the words was so familiar to Kaylin she felt it as her own. It hurt.

"And are you willing to take the risk of keeping other people alive?"

Kaylin sucked in air. *Tiamaris, you bastard.*

Morse, however, wasn't Kaylin. She rallied. "You pay me enough, there's no damn risk I won't take."

Tiamaris smiled. It was a thin smile. "We will have time to discuss your definition of *enough*. Will you serve?"

Morse shrugged. "I have to swear some fancy-ass oath of allegiance?"

Kaylin cringed.

"No. For the moment, the only witnesses present would not appreciate the gravitas of a more formal oath. I will, however, take whatever oath you offer that would be considered binding."

"Binding?"

"That has meaning to you."

She froze. "And if I don't have one?"

"You are free to leave. Provided," he added, "that no one here has a grudge that would prevent it." His smile was thin, but there was genuine amusement in it. Kaylin didn't like it, much.

Morse stared at him for way too long. Then she turned to Kaylin. "How on the level is he?"

"About money?"

"About anything."

"He was a Hawk."

"That means nothing to me."

"You couldn't bribe him. You couldn't kill him. You couldn't get him to break his word unless you managed either the first or the second."

"You know this how?"

Kaylin shrugged. "He has my back. Any fight we've been in."

"He was in charge?"

"Not always. Didn't matter. He faced down an older, bigger Dragon."

"An older— What, they fight?"

"In the fiefs. There's an Outcaste Dragon in the fiefs."

Morse tensed. Turned to Tiamaris. "This isn't over yet?"

Tiamaris said nothing.

"Fuck it. All right, I'm in. If you want me, I'm in. I'm not *good* at keeping other people alive. They don't fucking listen. They do what they think is fucking *right*. They get themselves killed. I'm not good at it. So you have to know what you're getting, because I don't want my ass fried for their kind of stupid."

Tiamaris raised a brow.

"I'm saying I'll try. I'm saying I'll give it what I've got. But I'm not swearing any damn oath that says I'll succeed at it."

"You'll uphold my laws."

"You're the fieflord. You want to make little old ladies the queens of the street, it's your go."

He raised a brow. Kaylin bit her lip to stop from laughing out loud.

"If we have resolved the current issues," Tiamaris said, after a long pause which pretty much said *I will work with the materials at hand,* "there is some work to be done. If you would all leave the building, your first assignment, Morse, is to escort Private Neya and Corporal Handred to the Ablayne."

Morse nodded.

"We cleared the streets of obvious danger on the way here," he continued. "There may be more subtle difficulties that can only be apprehended at street level. Watch for those. You've had experience with some of the forms shadow can take. Report anything unusual that you find."

"Where?"

"Pardon?"

"Where do you want this report?"

"Ah. Take it to my residence. The Tower at which you first found Kaylin."

Her eyes widened almost imperceptibly, and then she nodded crisply. It wasn't quite a fief nod; there was more than just grudging respect in it.

The destruction of the White Towers, however, had to wait, because when they exited the building, taking care to avoid the entire section of a wall that was no longer stone in any way, they came face-to-face with a small delegation of three, standing in otherwise completely deserted streets.

None of them were the Emperor. Kaylin would have known Sanabalis anywhere; she recognized Diarmat. She didn't recognize the third immediately, although he was also a Dragon. Severn helpfully whispered the name Emmerian. They did not approach Tiamaris; they waited. Tiamaris nodded in greeting, but it was a stiff greeting, and it was silent.

Kaylin walked to one side of the former Hawk; Severn walked to the other. Tara stayed a few feet from the end of the White Tower's path, watching them all with open curiosity; Morse stayed with her. Which was fair. In a fight between one Dragon and three, any nonimmortals were going to be delicate window dressing at best.

"Lord Tiamaris." It was Sanabalis who spoke first, which was probably for the best; his eyes were a shade of bronze that looked gold in comparison to the eyes of the other two. Or Tiamaris, for that matter; his were orange.

"Lord Sanabalis."

"The fief is yours?"

"It is mine." The edge in the last word could slice skin. It did not, however, make a dent in Dragons. Sanabalis seemed entirely unruffled by Tiamaris's response.

"And do you disavow our castelord?"

A brief pause. "No," Tiamaris said at last. "But he does not rule here."

"Hoard Law applies," Sanabalis said carefully. "Within the boundaries of the fief. He understands the necessity of a stable, strong Lord at this time, and if you accept the rules of the Caste, he will not be forced to declare you…Outcaste." When Tiamaris said nothing, Sanabalis's brows drew together in a familiar expression of mild irritation. "There *is* precedence, Tiamaris," he said, dispensing with the formality of title. "The Arkon's hoard is the Library, and it exists entirely within the Emperor's domain."

"The Arkon has always been an exception."

"There has never been a Dragon fieflord, to our knowledge. You can make, of yourself, a second exception. Or you can fly to war. It will be a brief flight, and it is a fight that we cannot afford." He paused again, and then—to Kaylin's surprise, given the gravity of the situation, lifted his fingers and pinched the very human bridge of his nose. "You considered this, of course, before you challenged the Tower Lord."

"It wasn't like that," Kaylin said quickly.

"He did not challenge the Tower Lord." Sanabalis did not stop pinching the bridge of his nose.

"There sort of wasn't one. And sort of was. It's complicated."

"Of that I have no doubt." It was his classroom voice. She didn't bridle, because Tiamaris didn't, and because Emmerian and Diarmat had that seconds-away-from-killing posture. But she noted that the tone of his voice had brought their eyes from near red to an unpleasant shade of orange.

"Illien is still in the Tower."

Sanabalis's brows rose. "Alive?"

"In as much as he can be. He's not entirely undead. He's not what the Barrani would call alive."

"I would hear more of this, but not at this present time. Tiamaris, your decision?"

"I will attend the Emperor," Tiamaris replied carefully. "But I will not surrender the fief to anyone living while I draw breath. Not to shadow, not to the Outcaste, and not to our Lord."

Emmerian and Diarmat exchanged a brief glance, and the color of their eyes dimmed to a safe bronze. They didn't speak.

"You have found your hoard," Sanabalis said, almost gently. "Many older than you have yet to do so. Tread carefully, Tiamaris. Wisdom can only be gained if you are alive to benefit from experience." It wasn't a threat. It was a statement. "I will return to the Emperor with your decision. He will convene Court, and he will summon you. Do not fail to accept the summons, or we will meet again under less-fortunate circumstances." He surprised Kaylin, then: he bowed.

Tiamaris bowed in return, and then he turned to where Tara and Morse were standing. He nodded in their direction, and Tara very timidly began to walk toward the four Dragons who stood in the open street.

Sanabalis raised a brow, his eyes narrowing slightly as he looked at Tara; Diarmat and Emmerian failed to notice her presence at all.

"This," Tiamaris said, taking her hand and pulling her gently toward Sanabalis, "is Tara."

"Tara. I am called Sanabalis, or Lord Sanabalis when at Court. You are?"

"Tara," she replied. "I am—"

"The avatar," Tiamaris told the Dragons, "of the fief's Tower."

"It is a pity," Sanabalis said at last, "that the Arkon chooses not to travel. I think he would very much like to meet you."

"We will meet," Tara said quietly—and with utter certainty. "When it is darker, and the times are less stable, we will meet." She bowed to Sanabalis.

Tiamaris nodded instead. "And now, if you will forgive us,

Lord Sanabalis, we have much to do to make the fief a more appropriate home for both the Tower and the fieflord. I will send Private Neya and Corporal Handred to their respective homes." But he looked, for a moment, at his teacher, and his eyes were now golden. "I have chosen a hoard," he said, his voice so soft it was almost hard to catch the words.

Sanabalis's smile was not without sadness, but it was genuine. "I know. I know, Tiamaris." He turned to Kaylin. "For your sake, Private Neya, I sincerely hope you remembered to activate the Arkon's memory crystal. If not for your sake, then for the sake of every Tha'alani serving the Emperor at this crucial time."

EPILOGUE

Two weeks later, when Kaylin entered the office, Caitlin met her by the guards. They were used to this, and tried not to look resentful at being treated like the more traditional architecture they were, in theory, watching. "Dear," she said quietly, lowering her voice without quite tailing off into a suspicious whisper, "there's someone waiting for you in the office."

This was not, admittedly, as unusual as it would have been a couple of years back, but still. "Who?"

"I'm not sure."

Which meant not Sanabalis. He had put all lessons in abeyance for two weeks, and advised her to enjoy the partial freedom while it lasted; the Dragon Court would be in session for most of those weeks, and he was likely to exit it—when he did—in a "less than charitable humor." She had been counting days with a certain amount of dread.

She had also taken a route home that was about fifteen minutes longer than her normal route, and she had lingered by the bridge—the Barren bridge—near the Ablayne, watching the skies for some sight of the Dragon that now lived in the fief. Rumor, of course, had spread—probably the minute Tiamaris's wings had—and as usual, it drew neighbors of all stripes, some literal, together in their need to share opinions, dread, and fascination.

Kaylin felt no need to share, and no dread. But if Tiamaris flew the skies of his fief, he flew them when she wasn't there to see him. She shook herself, smiled at Caitlin, and followed her into the office.

Morse was seated—for a value of seat which meant sprawled—in a chair directly in front of Marcus's desk. His paperwork, which was growing again, was the only thing between them, and Morse looked about as comfortable in the Hawks' office as a scrawny, bedraggled cat might look when surrounded by feral dogs.

"Morse?"

Morse shed the chair, grimaced, and said, "When they told me you kept unpredictable hours, I should have gone home."

"Been here long?"

"Long enough." She cast a side-glance at Marcus, who looked up.

"Good to see you could join us today," he said, in a flat voice. "I have a message for you." It had been set to one side of his desk, and was in no danger of being lost in the rest of the paperwork, which was too damn bad.

"Looks official."

"It is. Apparently, on my time, you're required to run an errand."

"What kind of errand?"

"Message delivery."

Kaylin looked at Morse. "Is your visit related to this message?"

"How the hell should I know? He told me to wait. I waited. I waited," she added, "a long damn time."

"Why are you here, anyway?" Kaylin asked, hoping to avoid a discussion about the hours she kept, at least while Marcus was pretending not to listen.

"You're not the only overpaid messenger-boy on the streets today."

"You have a message for me?"

"Yeah. An invitation to visit."

Kaylin almost laughed. Morse could deliver hideous death threats with perfect precision; apparently invitations were harder on her dignity. "Tiamaris sent you?"

"Lord Tiamaris sent me, yes. There's some occasion today. He'd like your company."

"What occasion?" Kaylin asked her.

"If you'd care to read your other message," Marcus put in, "you'd know. No, *don't* read it here. Your mouth moves over the words and I am trying to pin down this week's rounds." He paused, and then added, "Good work, Private. If you fail to embarrass us today, I'll consider your—" he stretched and picked up a small sheaf of papers "—hundred and eighth request for consideration for promotion. Visit the quartermaster on the way out."

"Why?"

"Read the damn message first. At your own desk."

"It's not a dress," Kaylin told the quartermaster, when she turned in her chit. "It's just dress uniform. I've never destroyed those."

His expression hovered between glare and cringe, without choosing. "You've had almost no reason to wear one."

She shrugged. It was true. "If there's a dust up at the Imperial Palace, they're going to be looking at something more than our books. Look, I've already got good reasons to behave *perfectly*. I won't destroy anything this time." Not that any other time had been her fault. She didn't bother to point this out, since the quartermaster didn't care. She took the pile he handed her, hit the change rooms, changed, and met a very tense Morse.

"It's this place," she said. "I don't like it. Too damn open, for one. Too much Law, for another. You ready? I gotta get out before I start something."

Kaylin was ready. Severn met her when they exited the front doors.

"Don't tell me," she said, as he fell into step beside her. "You've been requested as escort, as well."

"What gave me away?"

"You're shiny."

He laughed. "So are you, more or less."

"I'm not," Morse snapped. "And if I am, it's sweat."

Kaylin laughed. As they walked, she said, "How's Tiamaris?"

"Fief or Lord?"

"Lord, I guess. I can't quite think of a fief as Tiamaris, yet."

"It'll come. I have no trouble with it. Staring into Dragon's jaws generally has that effect on me." She chuckled slightly as she said it. "He's crazy."

"Good crazy?"

Morse shrugged. "Crazy crazy. We run the fiefs at night. Hit the ferals. He goes Dragon half the time. Sometimes he likes to rip them in two with his bare hands. I'm not kidding about that," she added. "It's pretty damn impressive, even in the dark."

"He doesn't like things eating his people," Kaylin said.

"Unless it's him."

"He's been eating people?"

"One or two stupid ones. Trust me, it was no damn loss." Morse, characteristically, spit to the side.

"Where?"

"You'll like this part. He shut down the brothel district."

"Shut it down?"

"Yeah. Left the buildings standing. Said they'd be useful."

"The people?"

"The people he cared to, he 'relocated.' There were some he didn't care for."

Kaylin was silent for a couple of blocks. "What's he going to do for money?"

"Beats me. And he's going to need a crapload of it soon. He's decided," she added, eyes rolling, "that we need a 'proper' market. Whatever the hell that means. We lost a lot of people," she added, voice dropping, "by the borders, but also in the center of the fief. We're still finding corpses. Some of them even resemble humans. He's pulled some of the live ones in to help with his 'reconstruction.'"

"What…else does he think he needs?"

"Apparently, more guards. You know what he has *me* doing?" Kaylin was curious.

"Babysitting *carpenters.*"

"He what?"

"No shit. I meet 'em at the bridge with four or five of my own people, and we form up around them, take them to the new market—which is a big damn circle in the ground right now— and then we set up posts and we make sure they're safe. We've got another group that watches their supplies. He's with that group," she added.

"Tiamaris?"

"Yeah. Him and the Lady." The way she said the last word made Kaylin raise a brow. "She's scary, that one."

"What—the avatar?"

"Whatever you call her. She's just damn scary. We call her the Lady."

"What's so scary about her?"

"She has eyes fuckin' everywhere. She hears every damn word we say."

"Does she act on it?"

"She asks us what it means," Morse said with a grimace. "She's not the brightest star in the sky. But she goes where he goes most days. He's demolished some of the structures on the borders," she added. "They were infested—that's the word she used. We're rebuilding those next."

"He's not going to get carpenters down that far."

"Yeah, that's what I said. Not from across the river. He says we've got some. Or the Lady did. Doesn't matter." She paused as they reached the bridge across the Ablayne. "He doesn't much care for the bridge, either. It's too flimsy."

"This is flimsy?"

"Ask him. I just work here." She started to walk, and stopped at the midpoint, looking down into the waters. "It's different. It's not what I know."

"Better?"

"Who knows." She shoved hands into pockets that Kaylin hadn't seen until that moment. "I spent years making sure people were afraid of me. I'm supposed to spend years making sure they're not."

"But—"

"He wants respect, not fear."

"People are going to fear him."

"Yeah. But he's okay with that—he figures it's part of the territory, being a Dragon and all. Come on. We're already late."

When Kaylin caught sight of the Tower for the first time since she'd left it, she stopped walking. Morse made half a block before she noticed she'd lost her, and turned and came back. "You haven't seen it yet."

"It's…certainly different."

Morse shrugged. "Yeah. I don't like it."

Which made Kaylin laugh. It was still a Tower, or rather, a Tower still rose— but nothing about that Tower and the one she had first encountered were the same. Not the stone, which seemed so white it was almost blinding; not the shape, not the height. There was something that looked like gold across both its roof and its midsection, and a flag was flapping at the height of a pole on top of that roof.

"Does it take up more space on the ground?" she asked Morse, when she at last looked away.

"Not much. But the inside is a lot bigger."

"The gates?"

"He took them down."

"He what?"

"He took them down. Or the Lady did. They're gone."

"What about the weeds?"

"Those are gone, too. Look, trust me—only the drunk, the young, or the very, very stupid are going to touch or damage anything on the Tower grounds."

"So...no gates. Guards?"

Morse snorted. "We're better put to use watching carpenters and their supplies, apparently." She added, "Not that he needs us. We're there to stop people from doing something so stupid he has to kill them, as far as I can tell."

Kaylin shook her head. "But it's good work?"

"It's boring work. Except for the feral runs. But...I can live with the boring. I thought—" She shook her head. "Doesn't matter. You asking me if I'm happy?"

Kaylin shrugged. "Not really."

"Good. You may have forgotten, but happy is not one of my strong suits." She walked ahead for half a block, and then slowed enough that Kaylin and Severn could catch up without running. Turning the corner, they came to the Tower.

Morse was right. There was no gate. No fences. No guard-house. There was a garden—if you could call it that—but it was an odd tangle of plants that did not look to Kaylin's admittedly ignorant eye like flowers or the usual things you found on the lawns of the powerful and the mighty.

"Don't ask," Morse told her.

"Those are—are those carrots? Please tell me I'm not seeing carrots."

"Fine."

"What are they *doing* here?"

"Apparently an 'open experiment'. I don't think the Lord was fond of the idea, but the Lady was really taken by it. She wants to see what will grow here, if she puts her mind to it. If it's useful, she wants to see how far across the fief she can encourage things to grow. Those were her words. Swear to gods, he doesn't say no to her if she asks for anything.

"I'm just grateful all she's asking for is a patch of dirt and few seeds. That building there, the one that looks like it's made of glass? It's hers."

"It's not glass?"

"You try breaking it. Once. After you ask permission first." Morse grinned. She was right: she wasn't *good* at being happy. But if this new life disagreed with her, it was hard to see how.

"This is where you found me," Kaylin said softly.

"Yeah. That was a day. Feral runs then, too—but those were more risky." A brief smile twisted her lips and faded. "Come on. Door's over here."

"It has a door?"

"Well, two. The usual."

"And it's just a door?"

"You have a problem with doors?"

"Not normal ones, no." Kaylin walked up the path between rows of orderly plants; they fell away, revealing flat, pale stone that eventually became stairs. The stairs were long, the rise low; she climbed them, pausing to glance at the building that now seemed to rise, in a more regular form, around the base of the Tower. The doors led to that.

She glanced at Morse, who looked at her as if she were insane, and then looked for a knocker or something; the doors were over ten feet in height, and they weren't exactly narrow. She didn't need one, though; before she could actually touch the doors, they began to roll inward.

Standing between them, were Tiamaris and Tara. Lord and Lady. Tara was wearing what looked like gardening clothing, however. She smiled at Kaylin, and there was nothing shy or hesitant in her smile; she was quietly, peacefully, happy. "There are no wards," she told Kaylin, before Kaylin could speak.

"She did not believe you liked them. I can't imagine why," Tiamaris added, with the hint of a smile. "However, she insisted that they not be part of the functioning visitor's door. She likewise rejected a portal, although I believe that *is* traditional."

Kaylin hesitated for just a minute, and then she walked quickly to Tara and wrapped her arms around her in a brief, tight hug. Tara returned it; there was nothing insubstantial or ghostly about her arms, now. "Take care of him," Tara whispered, before they parted.

Of course. Tara couldn't leave the fief. Tiamaris had to do so.

But there was no fear of abandonment on the avatar's face.

Tiamaris reached up and gently brushed strands of hair from her forehead.

"Morse," he said, without looking at Morse. "Remain with her until I return."

"Oh, good!" Tara said. "Morse, you can help me! And you can tell me the rest of the story."

Morse froze. Kaylin kept her face as expressionless as possible, mostly because Morse with wounded dignity wouldn't generally think twice about causing damage.

"It's not that kind of story," Morse muttered to Kaylin out of the corner of her mouth. "It's a real one, about some stupid kid who gets lost in the fiefs, and stays. But…she seems to like it."

"She would," Kaylin replied. "It could be about her, in a way. If she's happy, it will be good for the fief."

"Like I care about the fief." But Morse went where Tara led.

And when they were out of sight, Tiamaris said, "Thank you."

Kaylin started to ask him for what, and stopped herself; they would have been just words. "Ready to face the Emperor?"

"Are you?"

"No."

"Good. You are there to escort me. You are not actually expected to attend the Court session. You are, however, expected to wait until it's done. Corporal Handred, on the other hand, is expected to attend." He laughed at the expression that flitted across Kaylin's face as she tried to choose between relief and irritation.

"We have plans for the fief," he said, as they began to walk. "But we hope, in the end, it will be a place that you would have been happy to grow up in."

She felt some tiny part of her unclench and relax, and she began to ask him what, and why, and how, as they walked, and she didn't even mind when he got all technical and half his words went straight over her head.

★ ★ ★ ★ ★

Nightshade's response to this adventure? Find out in

CAST IN CHAOS

when portals bring more trouble to Kaylin—and Elantra.

Coming in 2010 from Michelle Sagara and LUNA Books.

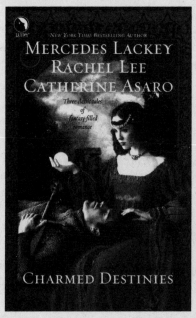